Catherine Dunne

The Things We Know Now

PAN BOOKS

First published 2013 by Macmillan

This edition published 2013 by Pan Books
an imprint of Pan Macmillan, a division of Macmillan Publishers Limited
Pan Macmillan, 20 New Wharf Road, London N1 9RR
Basingstoke and Oxford
Associated companies throughout the world
www.panmacmillan.com

ISBN 978-1-4472-0931-7

1 3 5 7 9 8 6 4 2

A CIP catalogue record for this book is available from the British Library.

Typeset by SetSystems Ltd, Saffron Walden, Essex
Printed and bound by CPI Group (UK) Ltd, Croydon, CR0 4YY

Visit **www.panmacmillan.com** to read more about all our books
and to buy them. You will also find features, author interviews and
news of any author events, and you can sign up for e-newsletters
so that you're always first to hear about all our new releases.

For Fergus:
for so many things – and for
the day that was in it . . .

Sunday 20th September, 2009

'TAKE ME HOME,' Ella said. 'I need to go home.'

At first, I thought that I might not have heard her properly. The wind was whipping at her words, tossing them over the side of the *Aurora*. 'What is it?' I called. 'Are you not feeling well?'

We had just heeled over, at a good forty-five-degree angle. The spray soaked the two of us and small pools of water blistered across the deck. They glinted up at us, filled with late afternoon sunshine. We were in our element.

Always at such times, we'd grin at each other, winch in the sails, get ready to come about. Ella had been a fast learner: she took to the sea and the wind and my small sailing boat as though she'd been born to it. I felt proud of her, proud to be her teacher. And it delighted me, the way the salty exhilaration of it all never failed to thrill her. Until now.

She half-turned from me, pulling strands of wet hair away from her mouth. Suddenly, I saw that her fingers were shaking, her face pale despite the wind and our exertions on deck. Her cheekbones seemed even more prominent than usual, the spattering of freckles across her nose like dark exclamation points, startled question marks.

I couldn't hide my alarm. 'Darling, have you hurt yourself?'

She shook her head. 'No. No, I'm okay. But – I keep thinking something's wrong. I don't know what it is – but I can feel it.'

3

'Wrong? Wrong how?' I didn't know what else to ask.

I kept us on course as steadily as I could while I waited for her to say something – anything at all. But she held up both hands, as though pushing back the force of my unasked questions. 'I don't know, Patrick. I can't explain. Just take me home.'

My wife is a very considered person. Competent, calming: the sort of person who is good in a crisis. The sort of person I have always been glad to have by my side. I had never seen her like this. Never seen her *distraught* – it was a word that came to me, unbidden, unexpected, like a freak wave over the side. It startled me because it didn't *fit* her. I saw her press her fingers to her lips, trying to hide their down-turning. I saw her eyes fill. And I saw her turn away from me once more; all in an instant. I did not hesitate, not then.

I pulled the cord on the outboard, and the engine roared into life. 'Take the tiller,' I said. 'Head for home, I'll do the rest.'

She nodded, already far away. At that moment, I could feel her slipping out of my reach – as though she were falling and I couldn't catch her. I busied myself taking down the sails, tying them securely into place, making sure everything was stowed and safe and locked down. I even packed the rucksack that we had earlier abandoned in the cabin. It contained what was to have been our lunch. A baguette, some Camembert and fruit, a couple of bottles of beer.

Weeks later – at least, I think it was weeks later – I came across that rucksack in the boot of the car, along with our oilskins. The smell had begun to puzzle me. The fruit and cheese had somehow melded together, rotting slowly, eating away at the fabric of the backpack. I didn't even open it, just tossed it into the bin, my chest a tight fist of grief.

We arrived back at our familiar harbour in under thirty minutes. Michael was on the jetty, waiting to take the ropes. His ready smile faded towards uncertainty when he saw us. He looked from one to the other, but he didn't speak. It was clear that something was amiss. By then, an electrical tension had ignited between the two of us – a force potent enough to be sensed by others. I felt that the least I could do was acknowledge it.

'Something's wrong, Mike. Tie her up for me, will you? Talk to you later.'

Ella was already running towards the car, yards in front of me, pulling impatiently at her oilskin, shrugging her way out of it as she ran. From that distance, she looked even smaller, her vulnerability emphasized by the oversized glare of the yellow jacket. Michael nodded, asked no questions, and I fled.

'I'm cold,' she said, as soon as I turned the key in the ignition. She tugged at the seat belt, clicked it home. I didn't bother with mine. She stared at me, her eyes glassy, bright blue and far away. I wondered if she even saw me. I turned on the heater.

'Can you tell me what you're thinking?' I asked. I kept my voice quiet, calm. I felt that I now needed to be the one who was good in a crisis.

'Thinking?' she turned to me, her whole face expressionless, as though it had suddenly frozen. 'No, no: not thinking. Feeling.' She stopped. Her hands were pressed together tightly. To stop them from shaking? This was my *wife*. I no longer recognized her.

'Feeling what?' I was tentative: part of me feared that she would snap if I pushed her. She seemed brittle, her eyes had darkened like seawater.

Then she looked at me, her expression no longer vacant. She was present again, and I felt a sigh of relief take grateful flight, somewhere deep inside me.

'Fearful,' she said. 'Cold and fearful. *That's* what I'm feeling.'

I pressed my foot harder on the accelerator. Sunday lunchtime, the dog days of September. The city was mercifully free of traffic. For once, I ignored the speed limits, broke all the rules. I felt that events were unravelling somewhere in a parallel universe, spooling ahead of me at the speed of light. I felt the growth of a momentum that would take my life beyond my control. The only thing I could do was try to outrun it, whatever it was.

For the next forty-five minutes, neither of us spoke.

Ella jumps from the passenger seat before I've even cut the engine. She stumbles on the porch step, but I don't call out to her to be careful. She moves with the speed of one possessed. As I follow her, hurrying to keep up, I have the strangest sensation that I have been waiting for this moment, this day. It seemed to me then that sixteen – almost seventeen – years of the best kind of happiness, the uneventful kind, had finally started to slip away from me. It had begun to dissolve even earlier: in the grey, turbulent arms of the wide-sweeping bay. I don't know how I knew that back then, but I did, at some visceral, animal level that does not possess the language to articulate it.

She flings open the kitchen door. 'Anyone home?' she calls – her standard greeting, one that always brings us to wherever she is, drawn by the cheer, the affection in her voice. But now she keeps moving, keeps calling, no longer waiting for us to come to her.

'Sweetheart, are you home?' The emptiness of the living room, the dining room, the TV room is her only answer. They all have that still, uninterrupted, slightly quizzical air that settles around everything when no one has been there for some time.

She runs towards the back of the house and takes the stairs two at a time. I notice, again, her surprising agility for a woman of fifty. She has always been slender, fine-boned, always light on her feet. As I try to keep up, I become more keenly aware than ever of my twenty years' head start on her. Some knowledge, some intuition tells me to recall all the details of this day, that I will need them later to help me untangle what is about to happen. That I will need memories in order to make sense of whatever it is I still don't know.

I notice, for example, that the wallpaper at the top of the stairs is newly scuffed; that the umbrella-plant on the landing needs water; that the towels are folded neatly over the banisters. I notice all of these things. I want to crowd my mind as much as I can. I want to cram it full of irrelevancies as quickly as possible, to stop it from being gripped by the chill tentacles of dread that reach back to me from my wife's hurrying form.

She opens a bedroom door: Daniel's bedroom. At first, I cannot see what I am seeing. The door swings to the left and reveals a dimly lit interior. The curtains are still closed, which is odd. It's lunchtime, and our son is an early riser. Besides, he left before we did this morning, rucksack swinging as he mounted his bike for the short journey to Edward's. A wide grin, a backward glance, a wave. Then the crunch of gravel, and he was gone.

But now, as we watch, shapes begin to form themselves out of the shadows. At first, they have no familiar contours: I try to grasp at their meaning. We stand there, in that timeless space until pictures begin to emerge, one after the other. My mind becomes a camera, the shutter speeding and clicking as it captures the images before me.

I grapple at the switch on the wall to my left and light floods the room. We stand there: a mother, a father, blinking in the sudden glare.

Uncomprehending.

The boy is somehow suspended in mid-air. He sways slightly as our stumbling entrance disturbs the eerie stillness. And then

I see it: the open trapdoor in the ceiling, staring down at us. The rope, creaking slightly under the boy's weight. The expertly constructed noose. That is what I remember: that is what is burned forever onto the retina of my mind's eye.

And the chair. The blue chair, now on its side, like a rebuke. My boy always loved blue.

And then Ella screams and screams and I wake. The stillness shatters around us, tossing shards of sound, slivers of light everywhere. My body is catapulted forwards, astonished into action by the force of her anguish. I rush for the boy's legs, lift him up, try to release the murderous grip of the rope. My rope. The rope from the *Aurora*. But I know by the weight of him that he has already gone. My son, my Daniel, was weightless, gentle. He left no footprints; this boy is heavy, cold. A stranger.

I struggle with the noose, all the time lifting, lifting, trying to free the boy's neck, to breathe life again into those blue lips. But he falls against me. I stagger under his sudden weight: I can feel my knees begin to buckle.

I cannot fall. The thought is made of ice: cold, clear, unforgiving. I must not fall. I finally gain control and pull my son into my embrace. His arms sigh by his sides, his head nestles onto my shoulder.

And now Ella has fallen, too. She kneels, rocking back and forth, keening a high-pitched cry. It is a sight I have seen often in the Middle East, in Asia, women tearing at their hair like that, their grief heedless, unearthly. But never here, never in an ordinary bedroom, not in my life. Not like this.

I hold my son close, whisper to him, soothe him from his mother's cries. But there is another voice that I don't recognize. A hoarse, choking sound that for a moment, I think comes from him. I stroke the hair back from his forehead – that unruly cow's lick that he has inherited from me. I close his blue eyes. And then I know it is not his voice but mine. My grief, my sobs.

Even at that moment, I know that the best part of my life is over. One instant, and the present becomes the past. That is all it takes: one instant, and the future is born. We hurtle headlong into a life that is not ours, one that does not belong to us. And we cannot find a foothold, no matter how hard we try.

On that afternoon, the only question – an inchoate, insistent one – is *why?* What has made our lovely boy abandon us? What has made him leave all the joy, all the bright promise that was his?

I can still see the three of us. The suddenly stooped and elderly man; the lifeless boy; the keening woman. A pietà, of sorts.

But here there is no resurrection possible.

Part One: Stories

Patrick

TODAY, THURSDAY 21ST MARCH, 2013, is my seventy-fourth birthday. Three and a half years have passed since Daniel left us. Three years and six months, almost to the day.

Later on this evening, my wife and my daughters and my grandchildren will all gather together again in the living room and I shall pretend to be surprised by the cake, the candles, the champagne. The children enjoy that sort of thing. My wife enjoys the children. My role, I believe, is to stay out of the way until then.

This evening, however, is a significant one. It marks a kind of twin celebration – although I am not entirely comfortable with the notion of unrestrained joy that the word seems to imply. Acknowledging the passage of years is one thing; coming to grips with the past is another. And celebrating this . . . this new *future* that has suddenly presented itself to us: that is something else again. However, I have promised myself not to let my story run away with me.

I make no claim to be a writer. I am – or have been, at various times in my life – an engineer, a photographer, a sailor. But those active days are gone, and not just for reasons of physical limitation. Perversely, the less active I become physically, the more of my attention my mind demands. Memories have become particularly troublesome of late. It was Ella who suggested I write them down, untangling their threads with pen and paper. I agreed, partly because I believe that, recently, I have become too curmudgeonly even for my ever-patient wife, testing her endurance to the limit. And so I have taken myself away to the attic, to that place designated as mine many years ago.

This large space once housed my darkroom. I find that ironic now. It is, once again, a dark room; but for different reasons. Every morning, I sit in my old swivel chair – one of the few things I brought with me from my other life – and I write at the gleaming mahogany desk that once belonged to my father-in-law, Dan: a man who, sadly, I never met. As part of my new start-the-day ritual, I run my hand over the tooled green leather of the desk's surface, and the more I sit here, the more I feel as though the old man and I are connected at some bizarre molecular level. To me, it feels that a connection exists between us apart from my wife, or from Daniel – my son, his grandson. Ella has always spoken of the likenesses shared by Daniel and her father. A likeness that depended not so much on their appearance, but on certain *active* similarities. The way they buttered bread, for example, or held a glass, or swifted a paintbrush over paper.

Around me are all my old cameras, lenses, framed photos and drawings – some of them by Daniel – and nautical bits and pieces: all the paraphernalia of a different, more emphatic life. A more youthful, less resigned life.

Lately, though, my memory draws me inexorably back to one particular day, more than twenty years ago. It seems to me now that so much had already been decided by then. My trajectory had already been mapped, the pathways signalled, just like the navigation lights around a harbour. Here, I imagine, is the light that illuminates the end of my old life: that horrific morning when Cecilia died, shattering my universe, scattering shrapnel across all the years of my future. My first wife; my wife for a full quarter of a century. My friend, my lover, my companion. I still mourn her.

And here, here is the brightly coloured beginning of that new and unexpected life: that strange, hopeful evening when I met Ella for the first time. I have always regarded myself as particularly fortunate in that regard. I am one of the lucky few who are gifted a second chance. Spread out before me, I see so many bright moments of significance: this day, that night, this meeting, that coincidence.

The afternoon of which I now wish to write – that glorious August day in 1993 when my grown-up daughters met Ella for the first time – is perhaps the most significant moment of them all. I was nervous that afternoon, and had been for weeks beforehand. Sometimes, my eldest daughter, Rebecca, made me feel that I was the recalcitrant child, she the disapproving parent. She'd always been Cecilia's daughter, first and foremost. I was just the also-ran. My daughter would see it differently now, I am sure; but then, let her tell her own story. As I've already said, this is mine.

About two years after I met Ella – or rather, two years after we began seeing each other outside her role as therapist – I felt it was time for my daughters to meet her. Ella was somewhat reluctant. She was acutely aware of the competing dynamics within a family when a parent has died, particularly the mother. Children, she said, can often feel abandoned – no matter what their age.

'We need to take things slowly, Patrick,' she said. 'You don't want to alienate them. Your daughters have a perfect right to feel ambivalent about me.'

We were standing in my kitchen, the buffet lunch spread out all around us. Chicken, poached salmon, salads – we had been working hard all morning. In just under an hour, Frances and Sophie and Rebecca and their respective menfolk would all be on my doorstep. Ella and I had had this conversation before: about my daughters, about their ambivalence, about their rights. Too many conversations; too many times.

'It's more than three years since Cecilia died,' I said quietly. 'Don't I have the right, also, to pick up my life again? Don't forget: my daughters were the ones who arranged counselling for me.' I smiled at her. 'None of us expected this happy result, but there you are.' I kissed her on the forehead, lightly. But she would not be distracted. Instead, she sighed.

'Just don't make too big a deal out of today. Let them get to know me gradually. And remember – I won't take any hostility personally,' and she smiled. 'It's the idea of me that must be hard for them. They *will* feel resentful – they'll see me as someone who's trying to take their mother's place.'

I made to protest and she took my hand and held it against her cheek. 'Just promise to introduce me as Ella. No talk of anything else – no wedding, no future, no plans. Not yet: let all that emerge over time. Promise me, Patrick. Please. We are not in any hurry.'

Ah, but I was. I wanted to put our relationship on a proper footing. I was twenty years older than Ella – perhaps my sense of mortality was a little more finely honed than hers, even then. And, if I'm honest – which is, after all, the whole point of telling my story – a bit of me was afraid that unless I captured her then and there, someone younger, more vital, less encumbered, would claim her as his own. I was almost fifty-four at that time, a newish widower with three grown-up daughters, at least one of whom was likely to spell trouble. I didn't feel as though I was the best prospect in the world.

'Okay, okay, I'll do as you ask.' I held her, surprised all over again at the depth of the affection, the tenderness I felt for her. I hadn't expected ever to feel like that again.

I had not always been a model husband to Cecilia – a fact that Rebecca made sure to mention from time to time. As the eldest child by a good five years, she had become privy to some – shall we say – difficulties between her mother and myself that had been resolved long before the twins were born. Rebecca had always been an observant child, although Cecilia used to insist that *all* children see and understand way more than we give them credit for. Listening at doors, creeping around late at night, sitting at the top of the stairs overhearing their parents' heedless conversations: oh, yes, children hear far more than they are intended to. And Rebecca had probably had more opportunity than most. Always precocious, she'd ruled the roost for all that time before the arrival of her sisters. Mothers tended not to work outside the home in those days, and so Rebecca had had Cecilia's undivided attention for, arguably, the most formative years of her life. As a result, she had become her mother's champion very early on and remained so until Cecilia's sudden and untimely death.

I remember, and I suspect that Rebecca does too, that one seminal moment in our father–daughter relationship. As I write this, I realize that it must be all of forty-three years ago. It was certainly Christmas Eve and Rebecca was still only four, although within a few months of her fifth birthday.

I am ashamed to say that at that time, I had been captivated by a willowy young woman, a secretary – or personal assistant, as political correctness would have it now – who had come to work for me, for my business partner Matt and me, to be precise, about six months earlier. I know now, of course, that Cecilia suspected our affair, and that my absence from the bosom of my family on such a special day must have confirmed it.

When I finally arrived home, at around eight in the evening, I had a store of excuses ready. Last-minute drinks with colleagues; the difficulty, as the boss, of extricating myself from the raucous seasonal celebration; the impossibility of getting a taxi anywhere in the run-up to Christmas: you know the kind of thing. As it happened, I had spent the afternoon in Janet's flat, specifically in Janet's cramped and uncomfortable bed, and left when her tears had become tiresome.

My affair with Janet, I have to confess, had followed a pattern that by then had become all too predictable. The initial, delicious shock of mutual discovery; the heady potency of secret trysts; and finally tears and clinging and the inevitable plea for commitment. I should have known better; indeed, perhaps I did. That day, it seemed to me that I was merely playing a role, but one that had finally taken on a life of its own. And so, as I extricated myself later on that evening, it was with a feeling composed almost entirely of relief. A small amount of regret, perhaps, but nothing that could dampen my sense of having *escaped*.

In fact, I did have considerable difficulty getting a taxi; I even had difficulty making my way along the crowded footpaths, pulsing with shoppers and gawkers and drunken youths. I arrived home some two hours after I had planned to, dishevelled and irritated.

Rebecca met me in the hallway. And she was angry. She glared at me, both fists clenched by her side. Before I had time to say 'hello', she marched towards me and unfurled one small hand. I bent down to lift her, to hug her, to swing her in the way that she liked, but she moved faster. She smacked me, hard, right across the cheek. For a moment, I was speechless. All I could see was her furious face, her brown eyes already beginning to fill.

'You made my Mummy cry,' she said. 'I *hate* you.' And she fled upstairs, slamming the door of her bedroom behind her.

I stood in the hall, helpless, looking after her small figure, still seeing her white socks as she disappeared around the turn in the stairs. All my irritation leached away. In its place, a searing sense of my daughter's vulnerability began to flood me, making the light dance in front of my eyes. Those small white socks, the determined hands, the tears trembling on her lower lashes. And, for the first time in many years, I felt ashamed. It was as though that slap had loosened all that was decent in me, all that had lain dormant for far too long. I made up my mind there and then. *Now* I understood St Paul on the road to Damascus. But mine was no thunderbolt: rather a calm, single moment of clarity, a moment that unpicked all the seams of my life, tearing the fabric in two. There was before, and there was after: it was as blunt, as simple, as clearly illuminative as that. On that evening, I became transformed into a man with a new and urgent sense of purpose.

I walked into the kitchen where Cecilia was sitting at the table, a cup of tea in front of her. Her eyes were reddened, her face lined with unhappiness. I pulled her gently to her feet, took her in my arms. She resisted and I held her more tightly. I needed to speak and I needed to speak *now*. I could not let this moment pass.

'It's over,' I said. 'I promise you, it's over. She meant nothing to me, nothing at all.'

How many clichés can one man utter? The fact that it was true, that it was all true, what I had said and what I was about to say, didn't make it any better. As I stood there, holding Cecilia as she battled a fresh storm of weeping, I did indeed discard Janet – if I had not already done so earlier that afternoon. 'Forgive me, Cecilia, please,' I said. 'It won't happen again. You're the one I love. I'll make it up to you, I promise.'

She stepped back from my embrace. I could feel her slowing down her breathing. Her hands, just like Rebecca's, were now clenched at her sides. 'I can't do this any longer, Patrick,' she spoke over my shoulder, her gaze averted. 'You have to decide.' Her voice was choked. Her pain was an almost physical presence between us as she struggled to form the words. 'It's us or the others – you can't have both.'

I was startled. She saw me flinch. Her eyes filled with

challenge, widened in disbelief. 'You think I didn't know? You think you were so clever, that you hid your tawdry little affairs? You think you fooled *me*?' She was suddenly alight with all the pain of my betrayals.

I had no reply other than the one that still makes me cringe, even all these years later. 'I never meant to hurt you.' I made to move closer to her, both arms already open in supplication.

But she stepped away from me, her hands on my chest, pushing me back. I could feel the white heat of her contempt through my shirt. 'Choose, Patrick,' she said. Despite her distress, her tear-stained face, she stood up straighter, lifted her defiant chin. 'Choose now. Either you pack your bags and leave or you decide to be a proper husband and father. I am *not* living like this, nor will I have my daughter live like this.'

She moved even further away from me. I was frightened then. I felt that if she left the room, I would have lost her, that she would have made the decision for me. But she stayed. Her face was now closed; I already knew the anger that lived there. When she spoke again, her voice was quiet, but it was impossible to ignore the steel in her tone. 'You've always wanted a son, or so you say.' She paused, looked directly at me, her expression almost puzzled, as though she was trying to figure out something particularly stupid that I had said, or done. 'Has it never occurred to you why we have no more children? Don't you even *ask* yourself why there hasn't been another baby?'

I opened my mouth to reply and closed it again. Clearly, she was going to tell me and I wanted the full force of her rage. I welcomed it. I felt it might cleanse me.

'Because I will *not* bring another child into . . .' she spread her hands to indicate the kitchen, as though everything around us was further, sullied, proof of all my treacherous impulses, my lack of faithfulness to her. 'Into . . . this.' She wiped tears away angrily. 'Decide and decide now.'

I did. I stayed, of course. I may be many things, but a fool is not one of them. It was a very strange time in my life. I see it now through the prism of all my lived years as a discrete episode, bookended by Cecilia's and my wedding day – some five years earlier, in the summer of 1964 – and by the Christmas Eve to which I now refer.

It seemed to me – even at the time and certainly in retrospect – that no sooner had I committed myself to one woman for life than all the old shackles of fidelity and buttoned-down, stifling suburban lives began to fall away all around me. The world was in turmoil: it was changing beyond all recognition. Certainties were being felled like ninepins, beliefs were being stripped bare, traditions shorn of their falseness. I loved Cecilia, never doubted that I loved her, and she me. But it seemed to me then, as a man in my early thirties, that my marriage had been the result of the worst possible timing on my part. Just when all the world was breaking free, I had made myself a prisoner. A square. A victim of . . . well, whatever the prevailing rhetoric was at the time around governments, the patriarchy, the stifling noose of conformity.

Even though Cecilia and I had enough money, more than most young couples because her father had seen to that, and even though we enjoyed the same things – books, theatre, music: Cecilia was a superb pianist – I became instantly restless. That whole decade had been a restless one. The blossoming of free love, flower power, the exuberant loosening of all those burdens that had defined our parents' small and meagre existences. I wanted a slice of that freedom for myself.

Overnight, I felt trapped by the *husbandliness* of my life, and soon by the demands of fatherhood. And so I strayed. 'Tawdry little affairs,' Cecilia had said. She had no idea how close to the mark her description was. I seemed to seek out in that parallel life things that I would neither tolerate, nor even contemplate, in my real one.

Later that evening, Cecilia went up to Rebecca's bedroom, and brought the unwilling child downstairs with her. We did a reasonable job, I believe, of placating her – or at least, Cecilia did. I kept a physical distance from my daughter that night. I thought it right to respect her anger. We said all the usual things parents tell children in situations like this – that sometimes mummies and daddies fight, even when they care for each other. That we both loved her very much. That Daddy had promised not to make Mummy cry ever again. I repeated that promise to my small daughter, carefully, slowly, until I judged that she was ready to believe me. It was a solemn moment that eventually ended in a hug – albeit a wary one on Rebecca's part – and several bedtime stories.

I kept my promise. From those very rocky shores, Cecilia and I forged a long and loving relationship. I never cheated again.

A psychologist might make much of this, I suppose. That I had kept on and on doing what I was doing until I was found out, that at some level I *wanted* to be found out. That it gave me permission to return to my life: a life that had been waiting patiently in the wings, waiting for me to grow up. That my parallel life had become tired and meaningless, as much of a burden as the one I believed I'd been trying to cast off.

All I'd wanted, in the end, was to come home.

I told Ella most of this, of course, during our early therapy sessions. Not everything: some observations about my perfidy I kept to myself. But the truth is, that in the immediate aftermath of Cecilia's sudden death, and before I met Ella, I could not forgive myself for what my wife had so generously forgiven me, all those years before. The world darkened around me. Even the four walls of my home were nothing other than constant, crowding reminders of all the ways in which I had failed Cecilia – and of all the ways in which I was now condemned to be alone.

And it was this psychic aloneness that terrified me: that sense of alienation from the world that descended upon me in the wake of Cecilia's death. Part guilt, part terror, part self-loathing: I felt that I would never again create a meaningful connection with another human being.

My twin daughters were terrified by the storms of weeping and creeping lethargy that they saw in their normally active and purposeful father. They took charge of me. Six months after Cecilia's death, Frances sought out Ella. She had been recommended to her as one of the best counsellors in the country – and one who happened to have a consulting room in the city centre, a mere twenty-minute drive away.

Initially, I resisted. I was determined that I would endure my punishment like a man, that Cecilia deserved nothing less than a long, protracted period of self-flagellating mourning. I see now how close to some precarious edge I had travelled. It would not have taken much to push me over into an abyss from which I might never have returned. I felt useless, worthless. I felt that I belonged nowhere in any real, authentic way.

Finally, my three daughters enlisted the help of my GP, Eugene, in order to overcome my resistance. Eugene was a serious and thoughtful man, one who had seen me – seen all of us, Cecilia and the girls – through the myriad health worries that befall the normal family. I trusted him.

'Your daughters are perfectly correct, Patrick. Enough is enough.' He spoke firmly, if not sternly. I had no wish to meet his gaze. 'I have a duty of care to you, and I insist that you seek help. We can work on this together: I'll prescribe antidepressants if necessary, but only in tandem with bereavement counselling.'

Eugene then leaned closer, forcing me to look at him. He must have been conscious, as I was, of my daughters' silent presence behind the closed door of the kitchen. He lowered his voice. 'You are causing Rebecca, Frances and Sophie to suffer even more than they already are. They have just lost their *mother.*' He paused and looked at me closely. He seemed to be judging the effect of his words. 'Do you want them to lose their father as well? They're still young, and you're placing a huge burden on their shoulders. Do you really want that?'

Somehow, it was Eugene's use of the girls' names that startled me into awareness. In my own wallowing, I was barely conscious of them as individuals; they were simply my daughters, out there somewhere on the periphery of my life. Frances and Sophie, in particular, now looked after me, taking up where their mother had left off. Sometimes they arrived home together, sometimes separately. They took charge of the domestic things: washing, ironing and so forth. They also made sure I was fed, on at least four nights a week. Those are the things that I *do* remember.

At that time, the two girls shared a flat, close to the university. I don't think I gave too much thought in those days as to how I had suddenly colonized their lives. I was aware on one level, of course, of their studies, their part-time jobs, the social whirl that most young students inhabited. But my needs were greater. I was the one suffering, after all – I had lost my *wife*. They still had their partners: Rebecca had her brand-new husband, Adam, the other two their boyfriends. They were mere onlookers. I was the main event. That was how I saw things back then.

As it transpired, Eugene's words were enough of a catalyst. I suddenly saw myself through my daughters' eyes. I understood that this state of affairs could not continue. And so I agreed, reluctantly at first, that I would accept help. Almost at once, and to my surprise, I began to feel a lightness settle around me. I now had something to do, something to come to grips with. I had a purpose at last. I called my three girls to my side and apologized to each, one by one, for hurting them, however unintentionally. Rebecca's forgiveness was perhaps a little less emphatic than her sisters', and I was reminded all over again of how far short of her expectations I always seemed to fall. Nevertheless, I embraced the three of them, and in that embrace I felt that a tightly pulled knot had somehow begun to loosen inside me, that somewhere out there, hope might lie in wait.

It did. It resided with Ella and her therapy, in that sense of safety I encountered at last, right from the first moment we met. A sense of safety that blossomed serenely inside me as I sat, surrounded by the walls of her office. It grew alongside the quiet intensity that inhabited our weekly meetings and it deepened with the relief I felt each time I arrived and each time I left. Eventually, I grew to accept that my wife had forgiven me, and that my daughters no longer saw me as a burden.

All this took time, of course, and perhaps I did project my own wishes somewhat onto my daughters' attitudes. And now, on that bright August afternoon, these same daughters were about to arrive, back to their family home, back to where their father awaited them, transformed at last. Daughters who had been born and brought up in the safety of that home: the one Cecilia and I had created together after the events of that long-ago but always momentous Christmas Eve.

'I think it's time to open the wine,' I now said to Ella, glancing at the clock on the kitchen wall. 'Rebecca is always early; we can depend on that.' We folded some more napkins, polished some more cutlery, set out more serving spoons. Anything to displace the nervousness that we both were feeling. And then the doorbell rang. I looked at Ella and smiled with a reassurance I didn't really feel. 'Ready?'

She nodded, her elfin face paler than usual. I loved how she looked: slender, her bones finely wrought, her hair glossy and dark. Even in my mid-fifties, I was still a big man: tall, robust, with no suspicion of the stoop that would later develop – but there are reasons for that, reasons other than the natural processes of ageing.

I answered the door. Rebecca and Adam stood there, he holding a bottle of something or other, she with a large dish covered in tinfoil. I had always felt a little sorry for Adam – although, as events later transpired, I should have tempered my sympathy somewhat. It turned out to be misplaced.

'Come in, come in,' I said. I could hear my too-hearty tone, but there was no time to wince.

'Hello, Dad,' Rebecca said, giving me her usual perfunctory kiss. 'We've brought a salad with us. Will I leave it in the kitchen?' Rebecca took after her mother: tall, vigorous, competent, with a mane of russet curls and those startling brown eyes.

I felt a small itch of annoyance. I had told all three of them not to bring anything at all, that Ella and I were happy to prepare everything ourselves, delighted to treat them to lunch. But I think I hid it well. 'Fire ahead,' I said, cheerfully. And then, as a deflection, 'This looks wonderful, Adam – I'll put it in the fridge straight away.' I hurried after Rebecca.

When I reached the door, I saw Ella make her way towards her, one hand outstretched. 'Hi,' she said, with one of her shy smiles. 'You must be Rebecca. I'm Ella.'

Rebecca shook hands. 'It's nice to meet you,' she said.

'And you. I've heard so much about all of you.'

'Really?' This time, I could hear the slight edge to Rebecca's voice. Time to intervene. I crossed the room and stood beside Ella, facing my daughter. I rested one hand lightly on Ella's shoulder.

'Ella was very interested to hear about your PhD,' I began. 'Your fields are quite closely related.' It was awkward, and it didn't come out as I meant it to. There was only the most tenuous of connections between psychotherapy and conflict resolution, but I was grasping at straws here.

'Oh, it's kind of been on hold for the last while,' Rebecca said, looking at both of us. She allowed a long silence to develop, one that seemed to stop all of us in our tracks. Particularly Adam, who stood in the doorway to the kitchen, one foot across the threshold, the other not. He looked uncomfortable, as if he was holding his breath, apprehensive of whatever grenade his wife might toss in our direction next. Having secured everyone's undivided attention, Rebecca spoke again, this time holding my gaze. 'I haven't really had the heart for it since Mum died.'

So there it was, out in the open already. Another unfurled hand, another slap across the face.

'It takes time,' Ella said, gently. 'Concentration returns slowly after such a profound loss. And sudden death is always devastating.'

For a moment, I could see that Rebecca was taken aback. Before any of us could respond, the doorbell rang again, and there stood Frances and Sophie. I could make out their shapes through the glass. I felt giddy with relief at their timely arrival. Frances is open and kind and full of good humour. Sophie is more reserved, but friendly and thoughtful. I had never been so glad to see them.

'Excuse me, please,' I said, and hurried to let them in. I was aware that I was leaving Ella and Rebecca alone together, but I had no choice. I glimpsed Adam as I passed, slinking his way back into the living room again.

I threw open the front door. 'Come in, come in, come in,' I said, hoping that in some absurd way the warmth of my greeting would make up for what had just transpired in the kitchen. 'Where are your men?' I asked, responding to my daughters' hugs and kisses in the hallway.

'They'll be along shortly,' said Frances, throwing her eyes up to heaven. 'Someone, somewhere in the world is playing cricket, so they're glued to the telly. We've given them half-an-hour's grace.'

I didn't believe it. Martin, Frances's partner, wouldn't know sport if it came up and bit him. Peter, Sophie's boyfriend, was a bit of a fan, but I had never known him to be stuck on cricket. I thought that this was a kindness on Frances's part, and I was moved by her gesture. It meant that Ella would not be overwhelmed. Even at twenty-two, Frances displayed all the emotional intelligence that her elder sister seemed to lack.

'Hi, Dad,' Sophie said. She took my hand. 'Great to see you. You are looking *really* well.'

I found that I couldn't speak. I squeezed her hand in reply, my eyes suddenly moist. That's two in my corner, I thought. And I felt a surge of gratitude, a great welling of love for both of them.

'Come and meet Ella,' I said, leading the way into the living room. As I crossed the threshold, Ella was standing with her back to the window. August sunlight streamed all around her, making her hair shine, her face glow. Rebecca was off to one side, but it was obvious to me that she had just spoken. For a moment, the scene looked frozen, with something suspended in the air above them, and then it was over. Our arrival seemed to release energy into the room. Everyone moved towards everyone else, there were handshakes, hugs, words of welcome, glasses of wine were poured.

And then the afternoon proceeded pretty much as such afternoons will do. Ella was bright and friendly, and I could see that both Sophie and Frances were taken with her. I was glad to see that Martin, in particular, was attentive to Ella from the moment he arrived, and I felt grateful to Frances all over again. I could see her hand once more in this: that talent she had for making people comfortable, putting everyone at their ease, something she had inherited from her mother.

Even Sophie, whose reaction had also concerned me – but

for different reasons – seemed calm, responding with warmth and humour to Ella's lively conversation. She was my youngest by twenty minutes: a fact that used to incense her when she was a child. She hated being 'the baby'. She and Frances had been barely nineteen when the cataclysmic events of that awful day shattered all of us.

Sophie had come to visit her mother and me during her reading week in January, taking a rare day off from her studies. It was she who had discovered Cecilia, slumped forward in the conservatory over the morning newspaper. I'd gone out to pick up the dry-cleaning. It haunted me afterwards – and still does from time to time – what if I had been there, at Cecilia's side? What if I had been the one to discover her? Might there have been a different outcome?

'Absolutely not, Patrick,' Eugene had been very firm. 'It was a massive heart attack. Even if she'd been sitting in my surgery, there's nothing I could have done for Cecilia. Death was instantaneous.'

Nevertheless.

I'd returned home, several plastic-covered garments swaying against me as I struggled with the front-door key. At first, I thought that the wailing I heard was something on the television, or the radio. Then Sophie appeared in the hallway, her face streaked with tears. What then flashed across my mind was that she and Cecilia had had another set-to. They had been known to go at it head-to-head from time to time.

'She's gone, Dad! Mum's gone!'

'Gone?' My initial response was an inappropriate irritation. 'What do you mean – gone? Gone where?'

The rest is a blur. Disbelief. Shock. The police calling. The burly ambulance men, whose kindness eventually made me break down. Sophie's strength on that day had impressed me, and it impressed me all over again on the August afternoon of which

I write. She looked over at me, catching my eye on several occasions, and smiled. She could not have been more articulate had she spoken. I was glad – proud and glad.

But Rebecca angered me. Perhaps nobody else noticed, but I did. I saw the monosyllabic replies to Ella's questions, the polite rebuff of all attempts at conversation. Ella handled her well – didn't pay her too much attention, chatted easily to the others, laughed at all the usual sisterly lore that is spread out like the family silver on occasions such as this.

Rebecca and Adam were the first to leave, at around six. I wasn't sorry to see them go, could read the future plainly in my daughter's cool goodbye to both of us. Adam looked vaguely embarrassed, and as he turned to go – instead of my usual sympathy – I felt a flash of anger. Be a man, I wanted to shout at him. Stand up to her. Stop doing your passable imitation of a doormat. I simmered for the next hour or so, mulling over all the things I was now determined to say to her. Frances and Martin were the next to leave, and finally Sophie and Peter. It was almost eight o'clock and, frankly, I was anxious to be alone with Ella. Nevertheless, I would not have wished Sophie to catch my furtive glance at my watch. She deserved better.

She stood up at once, nudging her boyfriend. 'Come on, Pete – it's time we were off. Another Monday morning looms. The ironing awaits!'

Peter groaned and grumbled good-naturedly. 'Dunno which is worse. Monday mornin' or the bloody ironin'.'

I liked Peter. He was solid and unimaginative and devoted to Sophie. He was just what she needed. He was a good five years older, too – closer to Rebecca's age, in fact. I felt that he was a steadying hand; I knew that he would look after her well: my youngest, gentlest girl. As she was leaving, Sophie hugged me close, whispering into my ear. 'She's a sweetheart, Dad. Don't let her go. And never mind the Wicked Witch.'

I grinned. 'I've no intention of letting her go. And I've no idea to whom you're referring.'

She laughed. 'Wicked Witch' was Sophie's childhood nickname for her older sister. It was years since I'd last heard it. 'Okaaaaaaaaaaaay,' she said, waving back at me over her shoulder as she and Peter walked down the driveway, hand in hand.

I stood in the porch, looking after them, watching until they disappeared from sight. Her words about Ella had touched me deeply. I waited until the wave of emotion had subsided, and then made my way back to where Ella awaited me on the sofa, her feet curled under her in the way that I loved. Without a word, she handed me a snifter of brandy, and we clinked glasses.

'That went well,' she said. 'The twins are very like you, in all sorts of ways.' She leaned towards me, kissed me on the cheek. 'And thank you for keeping the afternoon so low key. Today was not the day to spring surprises on your family.'

I had to ask her. 'Something happened earlier with Rebecca, didn't it? When I was answering the door to the others?'

'Yes,' she said, without hesitation. I loved this directness of hers: this belief that, no matter how painful something is, it is better to look it in the eye, to articulate it, give it a shape. She often reminded me of a jeweller, intent on examining all the facets of a stone, careful in judging its authenticity.

'What did she say to you?'

Ella smiled. 'Pretty much what I had expected, given your excellent preparation.'

I could feel something inside me begin to fall, as though from a great distance. It was hope, I realized. I had wanted desperately that Rebecca would give Ella a chance; give both of us a chance. I should have realized, should have known. I waited for Ella to continue.

'Rebecca was quite straight with me. She said, "I will never accept this, you know. My mother was an exceptional woman

and my father does not know what he is doing. He never has." '
Ella took my hand. 'We knew that this was likely to happen.
Now it has – so we know what we're dealing with. She's angry,
and she's grieving. We have to give her time.'

'And if time doesn't work?' I felt furious, being held to
ransom like this.

'Then we accept it.' Ella's voice was quiet. 'We can't make
her like our relationship, but maybe she'll come to terms with it
in her own way. Eventually.'

I thought about my daughter's words. Yes, her mother had
been an exceptional woman: I have cause to know it and I would
never dispute it. And while I accept that there have been times
in my life when I clearly did not know what I was doing – other
than, in Rebecca's words, making 'my Mummy cry' – I resented
her summary dismissal of me, the contempt that fuelled her
words.

Loving Ella was my second chance, at a time in my life when
I thought that love and sex and intimacy were all over for me,
that I would live out my days a sad and lonely and bereft old
man, enduring dutiful visits from my daughters, being shopped
around from one to the other at Christmas and Easter, like some
latter-day King Lear. Ella had saved me from that. And I loved
her for herself, too, of course: for her quiet presence, her
sensitivity, the exquisite emotional articulacy that she displayed,
first as a professional, and afterwards as a lover. I was a fortunate
man, and I knew it.

But Rebecca's words stung, and I know that Ella, too, had
hoped it would be otherwise. But it was beyond us, in all senses.

The only thing we could do was wait, and continue to hope.

But I am not very good at waiting.

Rebecca

FRANCES AND SOPHIE must both be idiots. Either that, or they are cowards. Personally, I tend towards the latter view.

Our father – or in this case, *my* father, given that the other two do not share my opinion – has finally lost the plot. And last week's sham little happy family get-together has only reinforced my long-held view of him. He is a selfish man, both shallow and spoilt.

I have never understood what a woman like my mother saw in him – never. All I can remember throughout my early childhood is her tears, her suffering; his bad behaviour. He made me furious, even then. Frances and Sophie's memories are different, of course. Well, they would be. I think that by the time they came along, our father had at least learned to be circumspect. They still try to persuade me that our parents doted on each other, that our father had been a model husband and dad. That, as their childhood had been idyllic, my memories have to be suspect. We've had far too many conversations on the topic.

And my sisters still refuse to accept that each child, notwithstanding the fact that they belong to the same family, has different parents. But in this case, in this firmly held belief, I am in a minority of one.

I have never fully trusted my father. I still retain a shadowy memory of a promise he made when I was a small child: an undertaking of good behaviour given after I had slapped him when he arrived home late one Christmas Eve. I remember my mother sobbing by the Christmas tree, on her knees as she tried to find the one faulty light that was preventing all the others from working.

At first I was frightened: mummies don't cry. I know better now. But the sight of her tear-stained, swollen face told me everything I needed to know. My father had promised to fix the lights, to be with us on that special day, to make everything right for 'his best girls' as he called us. But he hadn't. The lights still weren't working and he still wasn't home. It wasn't hard to put two and two together – even as a small child. Children have, I believe, inbuilt antennae. They track down lies and broken promises faster than you can change a light bulb.

I'm sure my mother tried to say something, to give some explanation; if she did, I wasn't listening. Or I have forgotten that part. What I have not forgotten is the rage I felt. Had I been older, I might have articulated it thus: there goes *my* Christmas. At almost five years of age, however, all I knew was that things were not as I wished them to be: and I knew who was to blame. And so, the giving of that slap is a recollection that is not at all shadowy. I can still feel the intense, sharp satisfaction of my small hand on the smooth, always-smiling plane of his face. And his reaction, too, of course. That is not to be forgotten. I can still see the astonishment. For once, someone else had, quite literally, got the upper hand.

I have remained watchful ever since. My teenage years in particular were suspicious, and not without good reason. I am still convinced of that. My father was away a lot – Africa, India, South America: long absences that I welcomed. The house was always calmer without him. There were no sudden flurries of tidying up, no elaborate dinner rituals to endure, when he wasn't around. We were all somehow less on high alert when he wasn't home. My mother missed him, I know, as did my sisters. I did not.

He has always been a charming man, my father, smooth, articulate . . . seductive. He had the kind of clichéd good looks that made women fall for him: the tall, dark, broad-shouldered kind. I recognized seductiveness in him even then, although I might not consciously have understood it, or known the word with which to name it. As I grew older and got to know the world a little more, I did not believe that my father denied himself female company during all those times he was away from home. And I *still* believe to this day that he was not what he claimed to be, despite his tearful assertions to the contrary shortly after my mother's death.

'You know that I was faithful to Cecilia for all these years,' he said. 'I need you to know that. You above everyone.' We were standing in the kitchen of my old home – that same kitchen since colonized by another woman – and it was shortly after Mum's funeral. My father had followed me from the front room, where we had all gathered after the brief, almost brutal ceremony at the crematorium. When he stood beside me in the kitchen, I felt for just a moment that he was going to reach out and take my hand. He didn't, but the room around us filled with silence: it was one of those strange lulls in an otherwise crowded, intensely emotional day. Although he and I were alone for just a moment or two together, I remember feeling the oppressive presence of so many unsaid things between us. The whole kitchen felt inhabited by ghosts, swirling around us, offering tempting little morsels that might now be spoken. I felt panic gather, like millions of atoms clustering at the base of my throat. I tried to make my getaway, laden with yet another tray of sandwiches. I had almost made it to the door when he chose that moment to speak.

'You know that, don't you? I loved your mother. I kept my word,' he said.

Even I could not bear to see his ravaged face. I was filled with a mixture of fury and compassion, and could hear Mum's voice inside my head, urging me towards gentleness. 'Of course I know that, Dad,' I said. 'But we don't need to talk about it today.'

Keep moving, keep moving, I told myself, as I angled the tray in order to push past him, out the door, back to where other people waited, surrounded by their meaningless words of comfort.

His response surprised me. 'Then when?' he said. His tone had a sharpness to it that took me aback. I think it startled him, too. I stopped, the tray of sandwiches between us, and our eyes met – really met. I was surprised by what I could read there. There was a perceptiveness in his watery gaze: he knew that something unresolved still lingered between us, more than two decades later. But I couldn't go there, not that day. In the event, Sophie came into the kitchen and the moment passed. We daughters spent the rest of the afternoon and evening making tea, pouring drinks and moving around one another, each in a separate orbit of grief.

We did not speak of it again, my father and I. Not that day, not since. Sometimes, I regret the missed opportunity, if only for my mother's sake. She'd spent her life trying to keep him happy.

Adam and I stayed over that night, occupying my old room.

'Are you sure you're okay to stay?' Frances had asked me earlier, as we loaded the dishwasher together.

'Of course,' I said.

'I don't think he should be on his own, not tonight.' She glanced towards the conservatory, towards the table where Mum had been sitting when it happened.

'It's fine,' I said. 'It's too late to drive home, anyway.'

Frances gave me a strange look. In fairness, once the words

were out, they had a quality that I had not intended. A harshness. I had merely meant that Frances should not worry about my being inconvenienced; Frances always worried about others. But, once spoken, the words fell into that pit of misunderstanding that so often yawned between us. Why should you not be inconvenienced? I could almost hear her ask, he's your father, too. Or: I wasn't worrying about you; I'm worrying about him.

As usual, we let it slide.

Earlier, both my sisters had disappeared up the stairs together. I caught sight of them just as they went into the master bedroom. Sophie took me aside afterwards.

'We've changed the bed,' she said. 'We thought it might be better.'

I felt an unaccustomed shock of sorrow for my father. Now even Mum's imprint was gone: he would retire to sterile, cold, detergent-smelling sheets. He wouldn't even have her scent to comfort him. But Sophie looked so earnest, so miserable, that I didn't have the heart to say anything. The girl still had the glazed eyes of someone not yet fully conscious of her new and terrible surroundings. 'I'm sure you're right,' I said, and squeezed her hand. It is never difficult to be gentle with Sophie.

My father, Adam and I sat up together until four in the morning, long after Frances and Sophie had gone home. From about midnight, once the house had settled into its new and uncomfortable silence, I wanted to be alone. I needed the solace of an empty room where I could start to unravel this pain that had not relinquished its grip since Sophie had phoned me three days earlier, giving me the news that I still could not comprehend. But I could see that my father was reluctant to go to bed. And so we stayed, sipping whiskey, watching the fire burn down, sharing memories of my mother.

When we finally retired, I couldn't sleep. I lay awake until dawn, weeping silent, cleansing tears, while Adam snored softly in the single bed beside mine. In those lonely early-morning hours, I felt sorry for my sisters. They lived so much closer to my father than I did – geographically and in every other way – and I knew that trouble was in store.

As my sisters so rightly pointed out – both at that time and so often since – our father was a man of his generation. He neither cooked nor shopped nor in any way took part in the normal domestic chaos that is the warp and weft of other people's daily lives. His gesture towards equality had always consisted of cutting the grass, putting out the bins and collecting the dry-cleaning. My mother had seemed to think it enough, although it had made me furious on several family occasions. He'd sit at the head of the table, carve the joint, rhapsodize over the wine, tell all those stories that showed him in a good light.

'Rebecca, your dad and I have worked out our arrangements; you and Adam have yours. Just accept that men your father's age are different. That's all.' I can still see my mother's expression: that mix of defensiveness and affection that used to set my younger self alight. 'I've forgiven him – why won't you?' she'd asked me once, out of the blue, years ago. She spoke very quietly, after he and I had had yet another row and I'd slammed upstairs to my sixteen-year-old's bedroom, full of rage and hormones.

It was the only time she'd ever directly alluded to that long-ago, long-significant Christmas Eve, and I'd been surprised at her question. But I realized even then that she was right. The truth of it was, that in my eyes, my father did not deserve to be forgiven.

Watching him the afternoon of my mother's funeral, I wondered how my sisters would be able to deal with all of his learned helplessness.

I hadn't long to wait.

Patrick

A FEW MONTHS into my relationship with Ella, she gave up her consulting room in the city. The drive was too much, the cost was too much, the time spent in coming and going was too much: everything conspired against her. 'I have plenty of room at my house,' she told me, 'and more clients than I can cope with. It's time for me to make a choice.' And so she began working from home, a good two hours' drive from where I was living, in my old family home. We no longer had the occasional stolen hour or two for a leisurely lunch in the city, or a visit to the gallery, or a walk on the beach. All of that stopped overnight.

When it did, I missed her dreadfully.

Thrust back upon my own devices, I could feel myself begin to descend once again into that slough of despond from which I had so recently emerged. The rooms of my house – no longer my 'home', without Cecilia – felt suddenly vast and barren. Visits from Frances and Sophie notwithstanding, I felt very much alone there. My footsteps seemed to echo, their empty sound feeling like a reproach. In my mind's eye, I saw Cecilia everywhere, preparing dinner, filling cupboards, moving easily around the confined space. She loved her quirky, old-fashioned kitchen. She refused to update things, saying she liked them just as they were.

'What would you like me to do?' she used to say, in response to our daughters' urgings to modernize. 'Rattle around a huge empty kitchen during my declining years, bumping now and again into your father?' And she'd grin over at me. 'I don't think so.'

How prescient those words seem to me now. Except that, by then, I was the one 'rattling around' the empty house on my own. I was the one, on more than one occasion, who felt as though I was bumping into my own past. Too many memories, too many.

However, I do believe that I eventually learned to come to terms with what I had lost. No: that is not quite true. I don't believe that such a tidy reconciliation is ever possible. But I had managed to reach some sort of shore, some littoral place that felt firmer underfoot. Pain no longer ambushed me. My sadnesses became quieter than before. And, as the pain dimmed somewhat, I knew with certainty that I did not wish to live alone.

Cecilia's death had made me fully conscious of my own mortality. It was only the second time in my life that I had had such heightened awareness around death and dying. The first time was when I lost my friend and business partner, Matt.

Matt and I had set up our company together as soon as we had been awarded our degrees in structural engineering. 'No one else will have us,' he'd said, cheerfully, 'so we might as well look out for ourselves.' It felt like an adventure. Our partnership was sealed on one heady evening – fuelled by equal amounts of optimism and alcohol. Matt and I had met on our first day at university and that was it: an instant, enduring friendship was forged. One that saw us share flats, resources, youthful triumphs and disappointments – and even, on one memorable occasion, a girlfriend.

Matt had just the right amount of recklessness. I was more cautious by nature. His energy and his work ethic were extraordinary. Very early on in our partnership, his 'can-do' spirit netted us an initial contract in Kuwait, followed by another in

South Africa, and yet another in Bogota. All on a wing and a prayer.

Our thirties were frantic times. For the first few years, though, I'd held the fort at home – after all, I was, at that time the 'family man'. I don't know if Matt ever learned of the irony. If he had, I think he'd have appreciated it. The 'family man' pursuing his 'tawdry little affairs' while the singleton – is that really a word these days? – looked after the business of getting his hands dirty thousands of miles away. And then the singleton met Olivia. A whirlwind romance, a wedding, a baby – all in the space of a scant nine months – changed our working landscape for good.

I still remember the day Matt told me. 'We'll have to regroup,' he said, from behind his famous wreath of smoke. 'We'll have to share the away time. I'm a family man now, too.' He stubbed out his cigarette and immediately lit another.

I can also remember my response. Inside, I had a sick feeling: part apprehension, part shock, part resentment. I had a comfortable niche: I ran the home front efficiently, made sure the books balanced, kept the clients happy. Now I feared that I might be found wanting. I wasn't sure whether I had the panache to deliver the goods when forced to operate so far away from the familiar. Matt's stories of managing disputes or making sure workers 'stayed in line', as he put it, or manoeuvring his way around local bureaucracies: these were all his strengths, not mine. As it turned out, I loved being in the field. However, I digress again. That is yet another story, for another time. In Matt's late forties, just when he had accumulated enough to retire – we both had – he was stricken with lung cancer.

I bought him out of the business, of course. His treatment was lengthy and expensive. I was not ungenerous during our negotiations. Soon afterwards, I sold the business. I'd had enough. Over the years, work had expanded to the point that the weeks ran into one another without any discernible definition. Holidays together with Cecilia were an aspiration, rarely a reality. Weekends no longer existed and travel consumed much of my life. We had money, certainly – more than enough. But I'd become aware of a new restlessness, a growing discontent. And that restlessness had little to do with my wife's more frequent, more plangent, complaints.

Instead, it had to do with the nagging question that kept on repeating itself, often at the most inappropriate times. A small, internal voice that whispered 'Is this it? Is this all there is?'

I found that when Matt finally died, I didn't want to work any more. Everything, everyone I knew, suddenly became more precious to me. Cecilia gave up her job as a music teacher, we bought a bigger sailing boat, spent months at a time away from home and had some intensely happy days.

'This was such a good decision, Patrick,' Cecilia said to me, on several occasions. The one I remember best is when we'd arrived at a tiny fishing village on the south coast of Greece. The sailing that day had been exhilarating and challenging. We'd worked as a team – fluidly, fluently, with hardly any words exchanged at all. We both knew what we were doing. After we'd berthed and were sitting in the sunshine, Cecilia turned to me, her face glowing. 'We're so lucky to have this time together, Patrick. Thank you so much for making it happen.' And she kissed me.

I have wondered since whether Cecilia had any inkling of the future that lay in wait for her – for both of us. I'll never know, but I am content that we shared those rich, memorable days between us, for – what? Two years, three years at most? That was what we had together at the end. It was not enough, not nearly enough. But I am grateful for it nonetheless.

Remembering all of this in the now silent kitchen of my empty home, I knew at once what I needed to do.

Whatever time I had left, I wanted to spend it with Ella.

The first night I spent with Ella in the sanctuary of her home was a very special time for both of us. That is how I felt about her home back then: it charmed me. I loved the location, the way the garden sloped away from the house, down towards the bright water below. A curved wooden bridge drew the eye with it into the woodland beyond the stream. Japanese maples dotted the lawn, and that same week, some magnolia stellata had exploded into flower just outside the conservatory window. It seemed to me then to be a serene and peaceful refuge and I felt instantly at home there.

That occasion, and all that went with it, is a memory that has become even more luminous with time. It was a warm and tender evening, although not without its apprehensions beforehand. I need not have worried: Ella's and my developing intimacy was such that no physical awkwardness could disturb it.

I have never been able to understand the modern compulsion for vulgar frankness about sex; all I will say is that I know Ella and I did not disappoint each other. In the welcoming glow of her bedroom, we were easy and relaxed and loving. It was an emotional time for both of us. We spoke of Cecilia that night, too, and of the future and of my daughters. I was content. I felt that all the waiting was at last beginning to come to an end. The past had had its due, and we were able to look forward. It felt good to be, once again, making plans. Later, as we sat in the conservatory, sipping wine and looking out at the falling light, Ella said that she had something to tell me.

She looked so grave, so intent, that I became immediately

consumed by the need to hear her, in the way that she had so often heard me: unravelling the unspoken, acknowledging the painful. She spoke softly, music playing in the background.

Rachmaninov. Second Piano Concerto. My chest had constricted for a moment when Ella chose the CD. Cecilia had played this on our piano, often, for just the two of us. I now put that memory quietly aside and directed all my attention to listening to Ella's words.

'Four years ago,' she began, 'my father was taken ill. Overnight, he changed from an active eighty-five-year-old, fiercely independent, a good cook and a great gardener, into someone who could no longer tie his own shoelaces.'

'A stroke?' I hazarded.

She nodded. 'Yes. He was almost completely paralysed, apart from his right hand. But he was grateful that his mind stayed alert and that his speech wasn't as badly affected as it might have been. A miracle, I think. Caring for him taught me to appreciate the smallest of mercies.'

I wondered, for a moment, how I would have fared had I been called upon in that way to look after someone I loved – someone who demanded all of my selfless devotion. I was honest enough to feel that I might not have come up to the mark. 'That must have been a difficult job,' I said.

She nodded. 'It was physical, yes, and demanding – but not tough in any real way. In fact, I think it probably saved me.'

I looked at her. 'What do you mean?' I began to sense that we were about to traverse some old and precious territory: including, no doubt, some painful places.

'Before Dad got ill, I had been in a relationship for three years with a man called Fintan MacManus. I met him when I was twenty-seven, he was a few years older. We were both students on the same psychotherapy diploma course.'

I had to quell an irrational stab of jealousy. I hated the

thought of her having been with anyone else. I hated the younger man whom I had never met.

Ella looked suddenly thoughtful: that careful, considered expression that I knew so well. 'I know now – and I think I knew even then – that I was ready to meet someone, ready for marriage and children.'

She stopped. 'I think, because of that, I believed that Fintan and I were right for each other. I believed that I could have what I wanted with him.' She reached for the wine bottle and refilled both our glasses. Even I understood that this was a displacement activity; her face had become shaded with emotion. 'After about a year, we moved in together. We were spending all of our time with each other as it was, and it made sense on every level.' She paused. 'I moved into Fintan's place as it was much bigger than my small flat. Not as convenient, but there was a study we could share and—' she shook her head, dislodging some memory.

'What?' I asked, as gently as I could.

'Nothing really. I remember having a kind of shadowy feeling that giving up my own place and my independence might not have been such a good idea. It was a warning bell: a distant one. But I didn't listen: I didn't *want* to listen. I truly believed that Fintan and I had a solid future together.' She smiled at me. 'You have to remember that I am telling you this now that the relationship is over. Hindsight, and all that. Twenty-twenty vision.'

I nodded. I understood.

'I was very happy,' she continued. 'I believed we both were.'

'What happened?' Watching Ella's expression, I felt guilty all over again. I did not know then – nor was I even able to imagine – that her past had contained anything remotely as painful as mine.

'A year or so later, I became pregnant. It wasn't planned, but Fintan and I had discussed having children, and it was something we both wanted. When I found out, I was thrilled. I was so excited that nothing felt like an issue. Not the fact that we weren't married, or that we hadn't planned this baby, or that we were still working on our professional qualifications: nothing. I believed we could overcome all obstacles.

'At first, Fintan seemed to be as happy as I was. Then, after the first few heady weeks, I began to notice a difference in his behaviour. He became withdrawn and he refused to talk.' Ella shook her head. 'He'd turn away from me in bed, leave the apartment each morning without a word. It was very painful – I was bewildered by what seemed to be a complete change of heart. It just wasn't like him.' She stopped for a moment. When she spoke again, she sounded different: almost brisk. 'I'm going to give you the short version here.'

'I'm not going anywhere, Ella.' I sat forward on the sofa, leaning towards her. 'Make the story as long as you like.'

She smiled, but I could see the strain across her eyes. 'As it happened, the pregnancy turned out to be ectopic. I was rushed to hospital one Monday evening – I collapsed during a lecture and the college called an ambulance. I've never felt agony like it. Never, before or since.'

Ella's delicate face was paler than usual, and I could recognize all too clearly the grief that stalked her. I sat very still and waited.

'Fintan was kind, came to visit, held my hand. But even on that first day, I sensed a relief in him – as though he had had a lucky escape.' She shrugged. 'As it turns out, I think I was the one with the lucky escape.'

I looked at her, more puzzled than shocked.

'I don't mean losing the baby, Patrick. I mean losing Fintan.' Her eyes were very blue just then. I could see the corners of her mouth tremble.

'Ah. Go on.'

She took a deep breath. 'I couldn't contact him the following day and so I discharged myself early from hospital. The doctors were very reluctant to let me go, but I couldn't bear being surrounded by other women's babies.' She paused for a moment. 'I insisted. Said I had plenty of help at home. When I got back to the apartment – devastated, grieving, beside myself with unhappiness – Fintan was there. I was surprised: he hadn't answered either his mobile or the phone in the apartment.'

'What was wrong?'

'What was wrong was he'd been having an affair. It had coincided almost exactly with the news of my pregnancy.' Ella looked at me. 'And, yes, I can see by your expression that you don't need a diploma in psychotherapy to work that one out.'

I nodded. It never ceases to surprise me how those who are supposed to know themselves the best often know themselves the least. The chaos that it causes.

'And Fintan then told me that he'd decided he didn't want to be a father after all – at least not with me, and not at that time. He claimed I'd shut him out once I got pregnant, that I had damaged our relationship.' Ella took a sip of wine. I noticed how the beads of condensation had gathered on the curve of her glass. 'Then he started to cry. He insisted that I had got pregnant deliberately in order to compel him to marry me when he wasn't ready. He said it was my behaviour that had forced him into the arms of another woman.' Ella's voice finally came to rest on the last two words: 'another . . . woman'.

I wanted to punch this man, whoever he was. 'He blamed you?' I was stunned by the violence of this sudden bolt of anger. I wanted to go and find this Fintan person right away. Instead, I asked: 'What did you do?'

'I packed my bags. I called him all the names under the sun: coward, liar, traitor – that's only some of what I can remember. It was not a pretty sight. And then I left. I called a taxi and went to stay with a colleague – a friend from university days.' She paused. 'Karen was wonderful. She was a nurse as well as a therapist, and she looked after me. I stayed with her for three months. She came with me to every hospital appointment and every therapy appointment. She used to drive me over to see my father, as well. With Dad, I'd pretend that everything was fine, that nothing had changed. He wasn't fooled though, not for a moment.' Ella smiled at the memory. 'He told me afterwards that he hadn't liked Fintan at all. He told me I needed to set my sights higher.'

'I will never do anything to hurt you, Ella,' I said quickly, remembering the last time I had made such a promise to a woman. I was profoundly grateful that I had always kept that vow to Cecilia, as I now would to Ella. She reached across and squeezed my hand.

'They say things happen in threes,' Ella went on. 'I'd lost the chance of a baby, I lost my relationship and, three months later, my father had a stroke. I moved home at once.'

'How long did your father live?'

'Six months,' she said. 'I employed carers as well, because there were some things I couldn't do for him: some intimate, personal things he didn't *want* me to do. He said he needed to maintain his dignity.'

My eyes fell on the old man's photograph on the table in the conservatory. His face is pressed close to Ella's, his expression proud, his gaze direct.

She followed my glance. 'That was on his eighty-fifth birthday. We had a small party here – some old neighbours and Karen and Christopher and Donna. He had such a good time.'

I had not yet met, at that time, these friends and acquaintances of Ella's. She had been cautious around her friendships, too, guarding them until she was ready. Even without knowing her, I felt enormously grateful to Karen and thanked her privately the first time we met, for the way she'd looked after Ella during that crucial time. I found her warm and engaging, and we took to each other at once.

'It's your job now,' she'd said, smiling at me. 'I'm so glad she's with you, Patrick. She deserves to be happy.'

I was more circumspect with Christopher. He'd been Ella's supervisor and I was nervous that he might discover a fatal flaw in my character. I worried that he might dissuade Ella from being with me. But he and I got on better than I might have hoped.

'Your father must have been very happy to have you back with him,' I said.

She nodded. 'We had a wonderful six months. We spent every day together, in this room and outside in the garden if it was fine.' She looked around her, as though seeing this lovely house all over again, through her father's eyes. 'It gave him so much pleasure. Those last months with him healed me a lot more than I was able to heal him. I'm glad we had the time.' She looked at me. 'It's so much easier to let go that way than with a sudden death. One morning, Dad simply didn't wake up. He just slipped away – and on the previous night he'd told me that he hadn't liked Fintan one bit. That was his phrase: "Not one bit," he said. He told me that I needed someone kind, someone who would look after me and appreciate what he'd got.'

She was smiling at me, almost mischievous now.

'I do,' I said, unable to keep the earnestness from my voice. 'More than you know.'

She took my hand. 'There is something else you need to know.'

I waited.

'Because of the damage done by the pregnancy, it's unlikely I'll ever be able to have children.' She paused. 'It's just one of those things. One tube was completely destroyed at the time, and I found out that the other one had never worked properly anyway – something which I hadn't known. It was a complete fluke. So,' and she looked at me, her eyes bright with sadness, 'I need you to know that about me before you and I go any further.'

I stood up and pulled her to her feet, wrapping my arms around her, feeling her warmth against my chest. I felt a rush of pure elation. She had handed me my opportunity. It was time.

'I want to be with you, Ella,' I said. 'I want to make you happy. A child is not my priority, but I understand you may feel differently. What do you want us to do?'

She shook her head, looking up at me. 'Nothing,' she said. 'I've had time to get used to the idea. I'm resigned to it. I wish it could have been different, of course, but it's not. I'm just glad I have you in my life.'

I was aware that it was not right to want to rush this gentle, lovely woman, but I could not contain myself. I was filled with longing to be with her, to protect her, to make her laugh. I held her closer. 'Marry me,' I said. 'God knows, I'm old enough to know what I want. And I don't want to wait. Let me make you happy.'

She counselled patience again, of course, and taking things slowly, gradually, getting to know each other better. All of which I heard, even though I did not wish to listen. The only thing I was conscious of was this astonishing realization of having been gifted a second chance, a second life.

I believe that our being together was sealed on that night – that Ella knew, as I did, that it was the right, the inevitable thing for both of us. But I had to wait another year before she finally gave me the answer I had been waiting for.

I have returned to that occasion many times in my memory. It stands out from dozens of others because so much that was important passed between us. I am sure that my recollection of the words we spoke is accurate.

Knowing what I know now, I have often wondered since that night what makes God play such tricks on us. The God in whom I had started to believe again, once Ella had come into my life; the God whose existence Ella still doubted. At that time, all our chances to become parents together seemed to be outside our reach. Ella's difficulties, my – to be frank – initial, secret reluctance to embark upon fatherhood again in my fifties: it seemed that the odds were stacked against us.

Daniel's arrival, his brief stay with us, altered everything: my life, my view of the world, my view of myself.

However, it has always felt perversely cruel to me that the odds of which I speak altered so dramatically, and then altered back again – taking from us the very thing we believed that we were never destined to have.

Rebecca

THE PHONE CALLS began almost at once. Certainly by the middle of February 1990, just a couple of weeks after my mother's death. Once the usual fuss had abated. I don't mean that unkindly. I just mean that neighbours, acquaintances, even friends had all gone back to their own lives after the funeral – as people must. I certainly had: I'd no choice. But I don't think my father realized he'd be thrown back onto the scant resources of his own company quite so quickly.

Frances and Sophie soon started calling me, one after the other. At that time, during the first six months or so of 1990, I was travelling a lot, particularly to and from the States. The private college I worked for back then had a sister organization in Boston. Their senior lecturer had absconded with one of the secretaries and the whole business had been thrown into chaos.

And so I got roped in; although my PhD was on hold, I was more than qualified to lecture to the junior students. Much against my will, I got shunted back and forth for months. I felt like the stopgap that I was, and I was all too aware that I was being treated like this because I was the youngest – and a woman.

I hated all the travelling: the endless airports and the hotel rooms and the time differences. But in a way, such busyness distracted me from my grief, and from what was going on at home. It was also, in a way, a relief not to be always available, not to be physically present back home, but the twins' calls certainly took their toll in other ways. I don't much like being a distant participant in a situation over which I have no control.

Dad, my sisters said, wasn't eating. He wasn't leaving the house. He was drinking way too much whiskey. I listened. And listened. And listened. And then I was furious with him. We three had all had to get on with our own lives, despite the yawning, grief-filled gap that each slow day did nothing to lessen. Why didn't he at least make an effort?

My mother's absence was still a physical ache, a weight that pressed down upon me, waking and sleeping. I knew, no matter what, that my father had to be suffering similarly. I tried to make allowances. Each time my sisters phoned I was, I believe, both sympathetic and sensible in my suggestions as to how to handle him. But nothing worked. It felt like a very long few weeks to me – and, in fairness, even longer for my sisters. I returned home from the States, hoping to fly back, as it were, below my sisters' radars. I'd been deliberately vague with each of them about the date of my return.

I know now that it was Adam who told them, not only the date, but the time and the number of my flight. I've often wondered about that. Was it an early attempt by my husband to punish me for abandoning him every couple of weeks? I'll never be sure: but I do know that he never had any problem spending all that I earned. No problem at all.

And so I'd barely landed when they called again: Frances early on the morning of my arrival, just as I was getting into my car at the airport. Sophie called late that same afternoon, waking me from that awful, sluggish, post-time-difference sleep. And then Frances phoned again in the evening. Both of my sisters sounded distraught.

It was a Friday, I remember. I'd had the week from hell – and that's apart from the developing jet lag. I was longing for an evening without interruptions. Before my sisters' outbursts, an empty weekend had stretched out languidly in front of me. I couldn't wait to kick off my shoes and curl up in front of the television. I wanted to doze my way through Saturday morning, then go for a walk, maybe have lunch by the sea somewhere with Adam, whom I'd hardly seen in nine weeks. The last thing I wanted was to drive right into the epicentre of an emotional ice storm.

'It's not just about looking after himself, Rebecca; it's not just the practical stuff that's causing problems. All that can be taken care of.' I heard Frances take a deep breath. 'Dad has imploded – I can't think of any other word for it. It's not just sadness: it's as though he has given up living. I'm actually frightened he might do something to harm himself.'

Frances is not an alarmist. I decided I'd better go and support her and Sophie as soon as I could manage it. 'I'll drive up early on Sunday,' I suggested. I tried to sound both firm and tired.

There was a pause. 'You don't understand,' Frances said. 'I wouldn't have rung you again if I didn't think it was an emergency. Sophie and I haven't slept in two nights. You have to come now.'

'What about Doctor Eugene?' I stalled. My father had always had great time for stolid, unimaginative Eugene. Personally, I thought he was old fashioned, out of touch with current medical practice and limited in his diagnoses. But then, who was I to be choosy at a time like this?

Frances's reply was chilly. I knew the tone well, from all those other occasions in the past on which she and I had crossed swords.

'Eugene is away. He has a locum – a woman I've never even met. Do you really think it's wise to bring a stranger into the middle of this crisis, given the state Dad is in?'

And that is how, at eight o'clock on a Friday evening, I found myself driving through freezing early March rain to meet my sisters at my father's house.

I'll admit that his condition shocked me. He looked gaunt, old. He'd always taken great pride in his appearance – I think he has always had a wide streak of vanity in his nature – but now he was unshaven, his corduroy trousers stained and baggy, his shirt reeking of perspiration.

'Come with me, Dad.' I dumped my overnight bag in the corner of the living room. I hadn't even taken off my coat. He looked at me, finally registering my presence. Almost without thinking, I'd used my mother's tone. I think it was my voice that sparked that instant of recognition, that flash of something in his eyes that looked like hope. I know, too, that I look like Cecilia did when she was young, much more so than either Frances or Sophie do, and I played on that, shaking my hair free of the combs I'd used to restrain it.

My father stood up, followed me like a lamb. I think my sisters were relieved to have me take charge. To them, his disintegration had been gradual; he became just a little more unkempt every day, a little more cranky, a little more solitary. To me, the change was astonishing – like a slap in the face. We took the stairs slowly and I became aware of his laboured breathing.

What on earth? I thought. And: Why didn't they call me sooner? But wisely, on that occasion, I said nothing. Nothing at all.

When we reached his room, he sat heavily on the bed and I left him. 'I'll be back in a minute.' I turned on the shower and led him, by the hand, into the bathroom. 'You need to wash, Dad.' My tone was stern. 'Take your time and I'll have clean clothes ready when you are.'

He showered and dressed; we made tea and sandwiches and

all of us sat around the kitchen table. On that occasion, my father wept and shuddered and drew long, shaky breaths. Other than that, he was uncommunicative. He shook his head every time one of us spoke, and eventually, we helped him up the stairs to bed.

I sent both my sisters home. Their exhausted faces were too much for me.

I told them to sleep, to take time out, to stay away from our father's house until Sunday. Then I called Adam to say I'd be away until Sunday night at the earliest. And then I began a silent rehearsal of what I was going to say to my father over breakfast.

The following morning, Dad came into the kitchen just as I was making coffee. He looked defeated, his face grey and hollow. He seemed to sag, as though the effort of projecting himself to others was too much for him. I began to understand the depth of my sisters' alarm.

We talked. Or, at least, I talked and he listened, or seemed to listen. He looked up at me from time to time, his eyes empty.

'Dad,' I said, as gently as I could manage, 'Mum would hate to see you like this. We all miss her. I miss her too, desperately, but she was always someone who believed in getting on with things.'

He nodded. 'I know, I know.' He suddenly blurted, 'Sometimes I'm ashamed of myself. But I just can't seem to make myself care about anything any more.'

It was the first coherent sentence he had spoken since I'd arrived. I felt we were getting somewhere. 'This can't go on, Dad. Sophie and Frances are beside themselves with worry. And I live so far away—'

'I know, I know,' he said again, interrupting. 'I know you all have busy lives. I'm sorry. I'm sorry.' And he began shaking his head, his distress growing all over again. 'I just don't know what to do.'

My cue. I jumped in, at once, before he forgot what he'd just admitted to. 'I've called someone – a man recommended by Doctor Eugene,' I said. A lie, but we'll let that pass. I'd phoned a doctor friend of mine, living close by. At least he'd be able to prescribe medication, if that was where we were headed. I thought of it as a holding mechanism until Eugene returned.

'We're all very worried about you. This man, Doctor Morris, has agreed to see us – or to see you on your own, if you prefer – at eleven.' I paused, waiting for an indignant response. My father has always hated being told what to do.

To my astonishment, he nodded. 'That's probably a good idea,' he said. He never even asked why Eugene wouldn't, or couldn't see him.

I took the ball and ran with it. 'After that, I'm taking you to lunch at the harbour.' I could see he was about to protest, so I deliberately used my mother's tone again. 'Please don't fight me on this. You're spending far too much time in the house. We'll come home immediately afterwards, if you want, and I'll stay with you again tonight. You won't be on your own. We can talk and try to figure out what we need to do next.'

I saw him look at me as though he didn't know me. And, frankly, this was not my normal role. My father and I have had something of a tempestuous relationship over the years. However, I was disturbed at what I was seeing before me; I felt an obligation to do whatever I could, even if only to honour my mother's memory.

I don't know what Jack Morris said to my father, but he looked a little less grey when he emerged from the surgery. Over lunch, he asked about Adam, about my job. I could see that he was struggling – but at least he was making an effort.

By Sunday afternoon, when Frances and Sophie called over, he'd even had a moment or two of animated conversation. I could see the relief on my sisters' faces.

'Don't know what you did, Becky, but that's certainly an improvement.' Frances hugged me as she left. Sophie kissed me warmly.

That must have been the first time in over ten years that Frances had called me 'Becky'.

I have to admit that I felt rather pleased with myself. However, I thought it best not to offer any advice to either Frances or Sophie. Apart from anything else, they had both been dealing with this emotional minefield on a daily basis for months. I had not.

'Just let Doctor Eugene know that Dad's been to see someone. I don't think anything was prescribed, but I can't be sure. He got a bit prickly when I asked.' I ushered both of my sisters out the door, keeping an eye over one shoulder in case my father should suddenly appear and overhear our conversation. 'Anyway, give me a ring if you need me,' I said. I made sure that my tone was back to normal, that Dad could eavesdrop on this generous invitation if he wished. The moment the words were out, I wished that I could recall them. But it was too late: the look on both my sisters' faces made their relief all too plain.

The next time they called me in a panic, a month or so later, things were worse than ever. Our father had stopped getting out of bed. Frances and Sophie had tried some tough love in an effort to force Dad to do things for himself, but all that happened was that the house descended into chaos. Our father descended into chaos. And so I jumped in the car yet again – a Wednesday evening this time in late April, the days just edging into May – and drove once more to my old family home.

This time, Doctor Eugene was there to greet us. I could see the look of shock on his face as he took in all the signs of my father's deterioration. I think he also feared our collective anger at what I still believe was his lack of adequate care. However, this time, he stepped up to the plate, and the rest, as they say, is history. Except that it isn't: the rest is a trajectory that has brought us from my mother's funeral to my father's tentative recovery and now to this, a short three years later – to someone called Ella.

I had no wish to meet this Ella. When the invitation came, I had no wish, either, to make the journey of an hour and a half – two if the traffic was bad – when the Sunday papers, my own garden and a glass of good wine were way more appealing. But my sisters were adamant. I may have once been the cavalry, arriving at the eleventh hour when they needed me, but my sisters had fought a more lengthy fight – the good fight, as they would see it – on our father's behalf. I had to accept that, however unwillingly. And Frances and Sophie never lost an opportunity to remind me, lest I forget.

'What is all of this about?' I demanded. 'I mean, how ridiculous, how inappropriate is this . . . infatuation? It's embarrassing, that's what it is.'

We were sitting in Frances's kitchen, the three of us. Our men had made themselves scarce, drifting away out to the morning sunshine on the deck, cans of beer in hand. We'd agreed to meet here at midday, an hour or so before we all obeyed the royal summons to our old family home for lunch. Frances, Martin, Sophie and Peter were already here when Adam and I arrived. I couldn't help the feeling that the four of them had planned this as a pre-emptive strike.

'You're overreacting, Rebecca.' Frances's mouth had become a thin, disapproving line as I spoke. 'Give her a chance. She makes Dad happy.'

Sophie nodded, watching me warily as she poured the coffee.

I, however, was determined to be heard.

'A chance?' I said. 'A chance for what? She's a gold-digger – plain and simple.' I hadn't meant to be so blunt, not at first, but my sense of indignation had got a firmer grip than I'd thought.

'Why do you insist on thinking the worst?'

I could see that Frances was beginning to get upset, and I was glad. Now we'll come to the nub of it, I thought. At last we can confront it: what we have each been pussy-footing around for months. She sat down beside me, her face a little closer to mine than I would have wished. In the background, Sophie, silent Sophie, stood by the patio door and exhaled nervous blue smoke out into the Sunday morning air. She hadn't smoked since our mother's funeral – or at least, that was the last time I had seen her do so.

'Let me tell you a couple of home truths.'

I was startled at Frances's tone. It was harsher than I would have expected.

'When Mum died, you know that Sophie and I picked up the pieces for months.'

I made to protest, but Frances wouldn't let me.

'Wait. Just listen to me. You live over a hundred kilometres away. Nobody expected you to be here on a daily basis. What I'm saying is not an accusation: it is a fact.'

I waited.

'We did his washing, his ironing, his cleaning; we fed him and minded him. We dropped in several times a week. We rang you only when we felt we didn't know what we were dealing with. *We* had on an everyday basis what you saw both times you arrived here. Eugene was horrified: it was he who insisted that Dad be persuaded to go for counselling. We'd run out of options at that stage.'

I didn't need to be reminded. I remembered all too well both of those appalling visits home.

'And don't think it stopped there,' Frances went on. 'Just

because the crises were further and further apart doesn't mean he was all sweetness and light to deal with in between.' She paused. 'He lived a roller coaster of emotions for months. And, by definition, so did we.' She glanced over at Sophie. 'We didn't call you, because we were able to handle most of it between us. But don't think it was easy.'

Sophie turned at that point towards where we were sitting. She didn't speak, but I saw her watch Frances closely.

'I think,' Frances said, 'that we can all count ourselves lucky he has found someone. To be very blunt about it – and I'll only speak for myself – it has taken an intolerable burden off me.' She paused. 'I'm sorry, Rebecca, but I'm pretty damned determined to like what I see this afternoon.'

Then Sophie spoke. She'd always spent more time observing than speaking, even as a child. 'What's the real problem, here, Rebecca? I don't think you're being honest with us.'

To my dismay, I felt my eyes fill. 'It's way too soon,' I blurted. I couldn't stop myself. 'How can he discard Mum so easily?'

Frances stiffened. 'How can you say that?'

Sophie stubbed out her cigarette. 'You have no idea,' she said, looking directly at me. 'You have no idea how that man grieved.'

I said nothing.

'And how do you know,' Frances's voice was even, controlled, but I could sense the effort, 'that he is not still grieving now? Just because he has found someone else does not diminish what he had with Mum. He's entitled to grieve and recover at the same time.' She stopped. 'What gives you the right to judge?'

It was my turn to get angry. 'That doesn't change the fact that it all happened so quickly. It's just not – appropriate. For Christ's sake, she's twenty years younger than him.' I paused. 'She could be his daughter.'

The silence in the kitchen was a shocked one. Out of the corner of my eye, I saw Martin begin to make his way back in from the garden, crushed and empty beer cans in hand. He took one look at Frances's face and retreated.

'Is that what this is about?' Sophie's voice was soft. 'Your feelings, your sense of moral outrage, rather than Dad's happiness?'

I stood up, dusted down my skirt. 'Don't be so melodramatic,' I said. Even I could hear the coldness in my tone. I tried to soften it. 'It's about everything,' I said. 'I think she's taking advantage of him and, yes, I still feel that it's an insult to Mum.' I looked from one to the other. 'And it's way too soon.'

'How long would you like him to wait, then?' asked Frances. 'And what would you like him to do in the meantime?' She glanced over at Sophie. 'What would you like *us* to do in the meantime?' I could hear something dangerous growing in my sister's words. 'Would you like to come here and look after him?'

I could see Adam's shadow at the door. I knew that he was standing on the deck, listening. 'He's only fifty-four,' I protested. 'For Christ's sake, he's well capable of looking after himself.'

'Says who?' Sophie walked towards me, her eyes alight. 'He should be –but the truth is, he's never had to. It's one hell of a learning curve. Would you like to come and teach him?'

I held up both my hands, a gesture of faux-surrender. 'Have it your way,' I said. 'But this will end badly.'

'It may well do,' Frances said, quietly. 'It may also end well and give Dad another shot at happiness. Either way, it's his choice.' She stopped there, but I had the sense that she wanted to go further.

I looked from her to Sophie. 'I suppose you feel the same way?'

'Yeah,' said Sophie, nodding. I watched as Peter crossed the room, put one arm around Sophie's shoulder. 'I'd like to get my life back, too. It's been a long three years.' The bright flash of bitterness in those words brought me up short. Peter took her hand and squeezed it. The gesture made something inside me shift, as though it was making room for something else.

'Okay,' I could hear myself sigh. 'I'll go and meet her – but I'll reserve judgement.'

'You can reserve whatever you like,' Frances's tone was sharp. 'Just don't upset Dad today. If we have anything to say, let's keep it until tomorrow.' She turned away from me. 'You and Adam go first, then we'll follow. Best if we don't all crowd in together.'

Why? I wanted to say. Is this Ella such a delicate flower that we might overwhelm her? But I kept my powder dry. I was flooded with an almost overpowering instinct to get in the car and drive home. I wanted to have nothing to do with this spurious celebration. It took all of my self-control to walk the half-kilometre to my father's. Even Adam knew when to remain silent.

I should have stuck to my guns. The afternoon was hardly bearable, right from the get-go. My father was ungracious about the food we'd brought with us, barely looked at the wine that Adam handed him – a bottle that he had bought against my wishes. It had cost a fortune. And she – well, she pretended interest in my PhD. I cut that conversation short, I can tell you. I had no intention of discussing with her the reasons I'd had to put it on hold. My mother's death was only one of them.

And I was both furious and offended when she tried to issue advice about how to grieve for Cecilia. About how 'sudden death' was always devastating. What would she know about my feelings?

We left, Adam and I, as soon as it was reasonably polite to

do so. My father was like a puppy, all big eyes and lolling tongue, dancing attendance on this . . . this *interloper* is the only polite word that comes to mind.

Frances and Sophie were all over her, of course, as I had known in advance they would be. They have never had the courage to confront our father. Frankly, I found the whole set-up appalling. I don't believe my sisters have thought through any of the ramifications of this. Sophie is, and has always been, naive. But I thought Frances might have been somewhat more practical.

What if the relationship failed and this Ella person took Dad to the cleaners? What if they married and there were children? What then?

It didn't bear thinking about. And I determined that I would tell him that, too. I knew I would get the opportunity. He has always sought my approval.

All I had to do was bide my time.

Patrick

THAT FIRST YEAR PASSED, and gradually my daughters became more accustomed to Ella's presence, to her place in my life. Or to be more accurate, two of them did; Rebecca continued to live down to my expectations of her.

My eldest daughter's disregard for my happiness caused me pain, I admit it. We exchanged words on that topic, on more than one occasion; words that became heated. There are only some of them that I regret.

I hadn't told Ella, but I'd made two separate attempts to reach out to my eldest child, to invoke her blessing. I admit that I was a man accustomed to getting what I wanted. I didn't take kindly to impediments being placed in my path. Once I made up my mind, I was impatient to get where I wanted to go. At least, that was how I characterized myself then.

Now, of course, things are very different.

That first meeting with Rebecca was a mistake. We met in my home – our old family home – late in 1993. Coming up to Christmas, I believe. I'd hoped to disarm her with the familiar, with happy memories, with pleasure at seeing her father back to his old, energetic self again. I'd cleaned and shopped for tea and biscuits, had flowers everywhere in the vases Cecilia and I had bought together in Venice. The house had become warm again, inhabited again. I was proud of my brand-new home-making skills – basic though they might be – happy that my surroundings were sunny and bright, redolent of a future.

Sometimes, I can be very obtuse.

When Rebecca arrived, I greeted her cheerily, just as I had done on that day when she'd first come to meet Ella. This time, of course, I had hopes of a different outcome. Those hopes dissolved the moment I led my daughter into the living room. She looked around and, in a flash, I saw the room as she saw it. Everything of Cecilia's was now arranged to proclaim the arrival of another woman. Vases, pictures, the newly reopened and gleaming piano. I could have kicked myself. Better to have left it shabby: perhaps that way I might have elicited some reluctant sympathy as an impractical and incompetent male.

Without a word, Rebecca turned on her heel and left.

For our second meeting, I enlisted Frances's help.

'Somewhere neutral, Dad,' Frances said. 'Somewhere that doesn't have so many memories.' Frances herself was upset; tight-lipped in a way that wasn't natural to her. The strain had begun to tell on all of us. Even Sophie. I felt that her initial support of me was beginning to wane. She no longer called Rebecca 'Wicked Witch', for example. Instead, she had murmured something about Rebecca's needing 'more time', about 'transition' and 'turmoil'. I could only imagine the sisterly conversations that were taking place in private, the alliances that were forming and re-forming, the history that was being written and rewritten.

For our second attempt a couple of months later, we met in a coffee shop in the city, Rebecca and I. It was January 1994, almost four years after Cecilia died. Rebecca and I met by arrangement through Frances, and in an establishment so far away from any familiar haunts as to be perfectly anonymous. Our meeting was tense, brittle, right from the very beginning. It was just a couple of months before Ella and I planned to marry. It was my last chance to secure my eldest daughter's blessing.

'I wanted to meet you, Rebecca, just the two of us, to ask you to please consider how your behaviour is hurting me.'

It was not the most delicate of openings, and even as I spoke, I realized my mistake. Stick with how *you* feel, Ella would always advise. Focus on *your* feelings, not the other person's behaviour. But of course, in the heat and anxiety of the moment, all that advice fled as far from me as though I had never heard it before.

Rebecca immediately went on the attack. '*My* behaviour is hurting *you*? Are you for real?'

I winced. Both at the ferocity of the assault, and the use of Americanisms that Rebecca knows I cannot abide. I decided to ignore both.

'Let's talk about real,' I said, leaning across the table. 'My feelings for Ella are real. Our relationship is real. And the fact that I have asked her to be my *wife* is real. Is that enough reality for you?' By now, I was incandescent. I wanted to slap Rebecca's face, the way she had slapped mine all those years ago. I felt that if I had deserved an unfurled hand on that occasion, she certainly deserved one now. Just in case, I kept both of my hands flat on the table, one firmly on either side of my cup.

She sat back in her chair and looked at me, aghast. 'You've what?'

'You heard me,' I said coldly. 'And what is more, Ella has said "Yes".'

Rebecca nodded. She gave a short laugh. 'I'll bet she has,' she said. 'She knows which side her bread is buttered on.'

At that, I stood up. I needed to do something to displace the anger that was suddenly white hot, making the top of my head tingle and my fingertips itch. 'Your mother would be ashamed of you,' I said, quietly. 'Cecilia above all would have wanted me to be happy. We used to talk about such things. We realized that no matter what happened, one of us was likely to end up on our own.' I stopped, tried to calm myself. 'We always said we'd have hated the other to be lonely. But I suppose that is too inconvenient a truth for you to hear.'

'Don't speak to me about my mother.' Rebecca's tone had turned to ice. Her face was a mask of pallor. 'It's obscene. The whole thing. A complete breach of ethics. Taking advantage of a widower like that. She deserves to be reported.'

I sat down again, faced her directly. For an instant, I was confused. I didn't know who she was talking about. Then the very absurdity of her accusation almost made me laugh. 'Is that what you think?' I could hear the astonishment in my voice.

'Anyone can see it,' she almost hissed. 'Twenty years between you, all that "little girl lost" stuff she goes on with – she's reeled you in good and proper.' Rebecca had wrapped her hands around her cup. I could see that the knuckles had turned white, peppered with the startled darkness of freckles. I leaned forward, so that my face was now close to hers. She didn't flinch: I wouldn't have expected her to.

'Now you listen to me,' I said. 'I had the best part of a year's counselling with Ella. After it finished, I didn't see her, didn't speak to her, for more than six months, because she sent me away.' I waited.

'What do you mean – sent you away?' The disbelief in my daughter's tone was palpable.

'I wanted to ask her out – just a dinner to say "thank you".' I raised both my hands in the air, pushing back the force of the attack Rebecca was just about to launch. For a moment, my own hand gesture reminded me, blindingly, of Cecilia in our kitchen on Christmas Eve, all those years ago. But I would not let it deflect me. 'Let me finish,' I said. 'Ella's sessions made a huge difference to my life. I could function again, smile again, feel a sense of purpose again.' I stopped, looked Rebecca in the eye. 'Isn't that what you wanted for me? You and Frances and Sophie?'

I was aware that I was not telling the whole truth. Admitting to Rebecca that, even then, I'd felt drawn to Ella – that would have been a disastrous mistake, most particularly on that occasion.

Rebecca sat up straighter. 'We're not talking about us,' she said, stiffly. 'We're talking about *her*. And you.'

'Her name,' I said, softly, 'is Ella. And Ella refused my invitation, said it would not be ethical.' I paused, watched to see this sink in. 'She insisted that we have no contact for at least six months. I agreed. I felt she was worth the wait.'

My daughter looked at me with disgust. 'And you fell for it.'

I drew one deep, steady breath. 'For six months after *that*, I met her once a week, for coffee.' I stopped. Part of me was indignant at having to justify myself to my daughter. The other part was just plain angry.

'She *played* you.' Rebecca tucked a strand of hair behind her ear: a gesture that was a startling reminder of her mother. Cecilia used to do that, too, whenever she felt upset or nervous. But Rebecca's face was implacable.

I sighed. 'What do you think Ella's motivation was, then? Money? Security?' I deliberately used her name. I thought it might help Rebecca to see Ella as an individual – a *person* – rather than as some anonymous woman whose eye was only to the main chance. Then exasperation overcame me. 'What is *wrong* with you?' I heard my voice begin to rise. I lowered it at once, glancing around the café in case I had been overheard. But it was empty, apart from a young woman in a far corner feeding a toddler. 'I may not be the greatest catch in the world,' I continued, softly, 'but is it that difficult to believe that someone might love me for myself?'

Rebecca stood up, pushing her cup away from her. Its greying contents spilled over into the saucer. She was shaking her head at me. 'It's obscene,' she said.

The reappearance of that one word was what made me finally lose my temper. 'There is nothing obscene about it,' I said, keeping my voice low with some difficulty now. 'If anyone's behaviour is obscene, it's yours.'

She bent down, her mouth close to my ear. I could feel the heat of her breath, smell her perfume – the same one Cecilia had always used. She yanked her bag onto her shoulder and began to speak. 'You are about to be a grandfather,' she said. 'Do you realize that if *she* has a baby, your grandchild will be older than your own *child*?'

She'd blindsided me again. I never saw it coming. Suddenly, I had to grapple with a welter of conflicting emotions: joy, anger, sorrow that Cecilia would never see this grandchild, anguish that I was being asked to choose, that I would lose no matter what I did. Because that was what this meeting was about. Make no mistake. My own daughter was forcing me to choose between my grandchild and the woman I had asked to be my wife.

'You're . . .' I began, but she would not let me finish.

'Yes,' she said. And she waited.

I stood up, reached out for her hands. 'Such wonderful news,' I said. My voice was choked. Grief was now taking me by surprise, just as Rebecca had. That old, familiar ambush of pain and loss and yearning. I thought I had done with it all, at least for now. But it had not gone away; merely lain in wait for another opportunity. 'Please,' I begged her, 'don't ask me to choose between you and Ella.'

I felt torn in too many different directions. Now was not the time to tell Rebecca that it was unlikely Ella and I would ever have children. How could I even begin? 'Please,' I repeated, urging my daughter to look at me, to engage with me.

But she was immovable. She snatched her hands back from mine, as if she had just been burned. She settled her bag on her shoulder, more firmly this time. 'You just have,' she said. 'You've just made your choice.' She left the café, the glass door swinging shut behind her. I watched her march away, remembered her small white feet on the stairs all those years ago. I could hardly breathe. My eyes filled, over and over.

'More coffee?' asked a voice at my elbow. I looked down into the sympathetic eyes of a young waitress.

'No, thanks,' I struggled to pull my wallet out of my jacket pocket. My hands were shaking. I took out a ten-euro note and handed it to the youngster. She couldn't have been more than seventeen.

'Your change!' she cried, as I walked towards the door that led to the street. I didn't turn back.

'Keep it,' I said. And the door swung closed behind me. I was aware, even then, of the metaphor. That glass door seemed to cut off any communication, any understanding between me and my eldest child. I felt angry, bitter. Cecilia had always warned about a 'house divided against itself' whenever the girls had had a serious quarrel. She always made sure that they made up with each other before bedtime.

I apologized now to my dead wife. It seemed to me that our house, always so carefully nurtured, had finally turned in on, and resolutely against, itself.

Frances

I WAS AFRAID THAT Dad and Rebecca's meeting would end badly. I said as much to Sophie.

When Dad called at the house on my day off, I knew that something must be afoot. He'd got so much better about things like that: Sophie and I put it down to Ella's good influence. He'd learned that time off work was precious and he no longer intruded in the way that he used to. It was such a relief, this new sensitivity of his. Particularly given what our lives were like, Sophie's and mine, in the immediate aftermath of Mum's death. Back then, he'd trail after me even if I went to use the bathroom. His hovering used to set my teeth on edge. I'd feel sorry, angry, guilty: all at one and the same time. He *did* change after those dreadful years, but Rebecca would never hear of it. She refused to see it, to give him any quarter at all. She insisted that the only things that had changed in the previous four years were his allegiances. And that his primary loyalty was still to himself. Heigh-ho.

Anyway, on that afternoon, Dad asked me if I would set up another meeting between himself and Rebecca. I had my misgivings. The first one had been a complete disaster – his fault, and he admitted it – and I was afraid of a repeat performance.

'Can't it wait?' I'd asked. I think I already knew the answer, but I put the question anyway. It gave me a bit of breathing space.

'No,' he said. And I knew that tone. There was a pause. I decided I would not be the one to fill it. I filled the kettle instead, and put it on to boil.

'The thing is,' he said, and cleared his throat. 'The thing is, I've asked Ella to be my wife, and she's said "Yes". We plan to marry in the next couple of months, probably sometime in March.'

I'd already known it was coming. I'd felt its texture in the air for several months – don't ask me to explain. But I knew it for sure, right in my gut, the moment I'd seen my father's shadow in the porch on that grey January afternoon.

'That's wonderful news,' I said. I put one hand on his shoulder. He reached up and patted it. 'Really wonderful. Dad, I am so happy for you.' And I meant it. My sudden, private stab of sorrow for my mother was my own business.

He looked like a boy, then: proud, bashful. He fiddled with his cup, smiled, cleared his throat all over again. 'Thank you. I knew you'd be happy.' There was just enough emphasis on the 'you' to let me know what he was thinking.

I said nothing. Instead, I waited.

His face was suddenly serious again. I know that look, too: it meant he was ready now to get down to 'brass tacks', to use his own phrase. With Dad, that usually meant that he was hell-bent on getting whatever it was he wanted.

'I want all of you to be happy,' he said. 'I knew that you and Sophie would give me your blessing. I don't want this estrangement between Rebecca and me to fester. I want to make things right.'

I believed him. The problem was that the issue with Rebecca wasn't the real issue here, if you know what I mean. The decades of strife between her and Dad were the issue – this marriage to Ella was just icing on the top of that old and precarious and particularly explosive cake.

To make a long story short, I agreed to help. I suggested a coffee shop close to the centre where I did my training days back then: that gloomy and echoing youth centre where I used to spend glorious hours teaching all those little darlings. Preparing them for rewarding and fulfilling careers in the catering industry. Not. Anyway, the local neighbourhood café, Roy's Place, was just fine, clean and good and wholesome: a bit like Roy himself. It was also a whole world away from those city-centre places which would either evoke a whole raft of family memories or run the risk of Dad and Rebecca bumping into acquaintances.

I made the call and Rebecca agreed to meet him – but reluctantly. I'd expected that. I latched onto the recent news about her baby as the perfect reason to effect a reconciliation between them before things went too far. We three sisters had already celebrated this pregnancy together, already shared our joy and our plans and our delight at becoming both mother and aunts at last.

What Dad didn't know back then, of course, and Rebecca had insisted that neither Sophie nor I ever tell him – we had to swear on Cecilia's life – was that Rebecca had already suffered a long series of miscarriages.

The first – an unplanned and accidental pregnancy – happened early in 1992. It coincided almost exactly with Mum's second anniversary. Then there were two more losses in rapid succession – the last one about six weeks before we all went to meet Ella for the first time.

I didn't know it then, but in retrospect it helps explain how incredibly difficult Rebecca was that day. I wasn't yet a mother at that time, neither was Sophie, and I know now all those precious things that I didn't know then. How poor Rebecca must have suffered. I regret that I didn't understand.

But how could I? All I know is, I would have been kinder to her if I had. That's hindsight for you.

Rebecca had just told Sophie and me, quietly, over Christmas, that she was pregnant again. Everything *seemed* fine, she said. But I could see how nervous she was. Above all, Dad was not to know. She warned us not to share her news without her permission – particularly with him. Sophie glanced over at me, and I felt, rather than saw, her shrug.

Between the two of us, Sophie and I had also discussed at length the coming baby's power to do good for our family – to heal the breach, to be the buffer between the past and the present – but naturally, Rebecca had not been part of *that* conversation.

On the afternoon I phoned her, I was really anxious that she gave Dad another chance: particularly with his and Ella's wedding taking place in a couple of months' time. However, I certainly wasn't going to deliver *that* piece of good news either. There were times when I felt very fed up – always having to be the piggy-in-the-middle.

'Come on, Rebecca. Give him a break. He really wants to put things right between you. And he's made all the running.'

'You didn't tell him, did you?'

I sighed. Spiky as ever. 'No, of course I didn't. The baby is your news – I wouldn't dream of saying anything. You should know that by now.'

Silence.

I tried again. 'It feels cruel to cut him off from his grandchild – whatever your feelings are about Ella.'

I could hear her sharp intake of breath and I began to get annoyed. So we couldn't even mention her name now, was that it?

'Rebecca—' I could feel the frost in my voice.

'All right, all right. I'll do it. Where did you say?'

The thing is, Rebecca is just *so* like Dad that their titanic clash of wills was pretty much inevitable. She, Rebecca, came here straight after they met and I don't think I've ever seen her so angry.

'How dare he!' she fumed. 'He went on the attack straight away. Told me *my* behaviour was hurting *him*!'

I let her rant and rave for a bit. I held back and I didn't remind her that she had pretty much gone on the attack herself, the first time the three of us had met Ella. I handed her a cup of herbal tea. Rebecca had given up tea, coffee, salt, sugar, alcohol, cheese, seafood and red meat once she discovered she was pregnant. My sister is nothing if not extreme.

'I was ready to meet him halfway, I really was,' Rebecca said. There was a small catch in her voice, a suspicion of tears. I was surprised at that. My big sister has never been a weeper. She once said she despised crying: it showed weakness, lack of moral fibre. Most of all, it allowed someone to see how much they'd hurt you. It was all that, she declared, or else it was used as a tool of manipulation. Even at Mum's funeral she didn't weep. I remember that. She turned to stone, certainly – but she did not weep.

'Did you tell him about the baby?' I asked. I kept my tone neutral, my voice soft. I needed to bring the temperature in my kitchen down a notch or two.

'I wanted to tell him the minute we met, but all he'd talk about was that bloody woman, and how he's going to marry her! I never got a chance. And by the time I did, he'd made me so mad it just pushed us further apart. So much for reconciliation.'

I could hear the exasperation in her tone. Mind you, I have my own views about how Rebecca might have presented the news about her impending motherhood. After that famous Sunday when we all met Ella for the first time, Rebecca declared that if she never saw 'that woman' again it would be too soon. So she stayed away, always managing to be busy or out of the country on the three or four occasions afterwards when the rest of us got together with Dad and Ella at our old family home.

And right then it looked as though we were facing a permanent falling-out between them. Once they'd locked horns, Dad and Rebecca were repeating all the old patterns. One of them is more stubborn than the other. The only person who could ever pull them apart and then draw them back a little closer together again, was my mother.

I admit that Dad's new relationship had felt strange at first, but Ella was incredibly sensitive to Mum's memory on each of the occasions when Dad gathered us all together. She never once tried to take her place. I remember noticing that it was always Dad who went into the kitchen, who opened those familiar cupboards, who served everyone at the table. Ella always deferred to us, to Sophie and to me. I really don't think she could have done any more than she did to make us all comfortable.

My view was – and I shared this with Sophie on numerous occasions – that my big sister was indulging in some emotional blackmail.

It went something like this.

I, Rebecca, am pregnant. This child is your and Cecilia's first grandchild. Choose me – choose us – and we can all share in this joy together. Choose her – Ella – and you are on your own.

That was it, in a nutshell, as far as I was concerned.

Another thing was that Rebecca was petrified that Dad and Ella might have a child together. I was mystified by this particular fear. So what? I asked her. But she just looked through me as though I did not deserve an explanation, given that I was stupid enough to ask the question.

We never saw eye to eye on that, Rebecca and I. How could we? All I saw was that her antipathy towards Ella was extreme, and while some of it may have been natural in the circumstances, there were parts of it that I really did not understand.

My view was – and Sophie agreed – that it was time we all got on with our lives. Including our father.

And if Dad were to have another child – would that be such a bad thing, such an impossible thing to get our heads around?

I am glad that I never asked Rebecca that again. Somewhere deep inside, I think I must have already known the answer.

Patrick

With Frances and Sophie's blessing, Ella and I married quietly in the Seychelles – on the island of Mahé, to be precise – on 1st March, 1994. We completed all the paperwork the day after we arrived; we were effectively married as we left the registrar's office. But Ella had wanted a ceremony, a blessing – some sort of traditional ritual that was more fitting to the occasion. I agreed, of course, and we had our ceremony on the following afternoon.

It was a day of astonishing blueness – sky, sea – all glowing around us. We stood in a secluded corner of our hotel grounds, with the flimsiest of coconut roofs over our heads, and looked out over the ocean. Our minister was a wise and witty old man who made us laugh; our witnesses were shy young Islanders; and our wedding breakfast – late in the evening – was eaten under the stars. Ella wore a simple sheath of ivory silk. I wore a navy linen suit that she liked, complete with bow tie – something I had sworn never to wear again once I had sold the business. I'd always hated ties: no matter how loosely knotted, they always made me feel that my breathing was restricted.

I reached for her hand across the table. 'Happy?' I asked. I stroked her fingers, admiring the way the gleaming wedding band nestled into the old simplicity of her mother's engagement ring.

'Completely.' Her eyes shone. 'And you?'

'Yes.' I looked around me at the low bungalows, the profusion of red and orange and purple flowers everywhere. All I could see was the vibrancy of their tropical colours, even after night had fallen. I didn't know the names of any of them, not then. And I could just make out the roll of the sea in the distance. I felt content. 'It's another world, isn't it? We were right to come here.'

She smiled. 'A welcome break from reality,' she said. 'We'll have to face it soon enough when we go home.' She paused, not letting go of my hand. 'I'm sorry about your falling-out with Rebecca, particularly with the baby on the way.'

I looked at her in astonishment. For a moment, I couldn't speak. I'd decided not to divulge that piece of information until after our honeymoon. 'How did you know?'

'Frances let it slip, about a month ago. She thought I must have known.' Ella smiled. 'She was most embarrassed that I didn't. I promised I wouldn't discuss it with you until we were here, but she was very upset.'

I cursed myself. It seemed I couldn't do right for doing wrong, as Cecilia used to say.

Ella watched me. She has always been able to read my face. 'I'm telling you now, Patrick, on our wedding day, for a reason. I don't want us to have any secrets. Secrets are toxic. Please don't shut me out.'

I felt the familiar pain of loss all over again, mixed with a potent sense of relief. At least Ella now knew. She knew about the row and she knew about the baby. And it was all okay. I could see by the way she looked at me, the way she didn't let go of my hand. 'My own daughter forced me to choose,' I said. 'I had to choose you, choose our future. And I don't regret it. But I'm sorry I kept it from you.' I spoke quickly and then stopped, wondering if I was going to be able to continue. 'What I regret, most deeply of all, is that I may never get to see my own grandchild.' I shook my head, willing away the gathering storm of emotion.

Ella pressed my hand to her cheek. 'Babies have a way of healing people, of bringing them back together again,' she said. 'We'll have another chance to make things right when we go home. Either way,' she made me look at her, 'you *will* see your grandchild. Frances and Sophie are determined – let them work away in the background for now. If Rebecca continues to shut me out, I'll deal with that. But you *must* make things right between you and her, independently of me. Don't harden your heart.'

I could not speak for gratitude. 'I won't,' I promised, eventually. 'Thank you. Thank you for understanding.'

'We'll get there,' she said, 'we'll get there. Keep believing that.'

We didn't need to say any more, not that night. We returned to the topic, of course, more than once. But I grew in confidence that Ella and I would make our way through this minefield together, that Rebecca could not shut me out forever.

Those three weeks of our honeymoon seemed to me to compose the music of our relationship for all the years that followed. *Piano, pianissimo.* We rarely argued, never disagreed on fundamentals. We were serene together, peaceful. I almost believed in God again, almost thanked him for my undeserved good fortune.

Ella laughed at me when I told her this. 'Go right ahead and pray,' she said. 'Let me know if you do, whether anyone is out there listening.'

In mid-June of that same year, we held a party to celebrate our wedding, in Ella's beautiful garden. It thrilled me that this was now my beautiful garden, too: our own private Eden. Again, the gods of weather smiled down upon us. The magnolias and maples were in full, extravagant bloom, the river sparkling, the great sweep of green inviting and restful. Ella had no family left to speak of. Instead, her colleagues turned up in droves, her friends from university, neighbours for miles around. I recall Karen in particular, of course, and Christopher and Donna, and a woman called Maryam and her husband, whose name I always have difficulty remembering. They were an immigrant couple that Ella had recently got to know.

I saw Ella and Maryam embracing for a moment, set apart a little from the crowd. They looked so joyful that I remarked upon it afterwards to Ella.

'Maryam is pregnant,' she said. 'She has just found out. It's her first. Isn't it wonderful?'

Wonderful, indeed. I watched my new wife closely for some time afterwards. I was concerned that Rebecca's absence and Maryam's pregnant presence might reopen old wounds for her. But her serenity that day was complete. She caught me looking at her more than once. Each time she smiled and blew a kiss in my direction. I relaxed into the blurring of goodwill that the afternoon became, surrounded by laughter, happy faces, animated conversation. I don't remember the names of any more of Ella's guests right now, but I know that she wrote them on the backs of all the photographs that I afterwards developed in my own new darkroom, tucked under the eaves of this rambling house.

Frances and Sophie were at the party, too, of course, and Martin and Peter. Frances had pulled out my old address book and contacted everyone she could. I was touched – no, moved, deeply moved – by people's genuine delight at my marriage to Ella. It was a joyous occasion, one that made me grateful all over again for the depth of my happiness.

Cecilia's sister, Lynn, was there, with Steve and their grown-up children. At first, she and I had an awkward moment. 'Congratulations, Patrick,' she said, but her eyes filled at once.

I drew her towards me and we hugged. 'Thank you for being here,' I said. 'It means a lot.'

She dabbed at her eyes with a tissue, tried to smile. 'I'm sorry, Patrick,' she shook her head, 'we weren't much use to you after Cecilia died. I was too wrapped up in my own grief at first, and then Mo's illness just felled all of us.' She paused.

I had learned shortly after Cecilia's death that Lynn had her own troubles. Her teenage daughter – our niece, Mo – was stricken with some unknown disease that had taken months to diagnose, further months to treat. But I hadn't absorbed that fact until it was too late. I left the burden of family communications to my girls – that is, if I thought about anyone at all beyond myself. I let things drift and then the chasm between me and everyone else had become too wide to fill. Or that was how it seemed.

'Frances told us what a desperately difficult time you had,' Lynn continued. 'I feel we abandoned you.'

I was touched by her honesty. And, yes, I had felt abandoned, truth to tell. It seemed to me that a tinfoil army appeared at my door every day for a month after Cecilia's funeral; I amassed enough casseroles to feed a regiment. Afterwards, Frances and Sophie had to trawl the neighbourhood, returning dishes and bowls and oven trays.

But that wasn't the sort of sustenance I craved. I know, because my daughters told me, that people did continue to call for a while, that they tried to converse, that they issued invitations to their homes – none of which I accepted – but I remember very little of it. And Lynn, in particular, who had been a constant presence in our home whilst Cecilia was alive, seemed to disappear, magicked away almost at one and the same time. It felt that I had lost both of them: that Cecilia's death had claimed not one, but both sisters.

'You didn't have your own sorrows to seek,' I said, gently. Cecilia's phrase: Lynn recognized it at once, and she smiled. 'And I need to be forgiven for not doing something for Mo.' I looked over to where she was standing with her father. Steve had a protective arm around his youngest daughter's shoulders. 'She looks wonderful.'

Lynn nodded, her face flushed with happiness. 'She is. We were very lucky. There's not a day goes by that I don't count my blessings.' She took my hands. 'I want us to be friends, Patrick, as well as family. That's why we're here.' She looked around her. 'I've just spoken to Frances and to Sophie. They look wonderful. And I understand you are about to become a grandfather?'

I nodded. 'Yes, it's very exciting news. All of us are looking forward to the new arrival.' I hated the false cheer in my voice. I could hear what sounded like a rasp of insincerity in everything I said when Rebecca was mentioned. The truth was that I had not discovered a formula of words that would embrace both my longing to see my grandson (I'd believed from the beginning that it would be a boy – this preponderance of females had to end sometime) and my sadness at the breach with my eldest child. Even to my own ears, as I spoke to Lynn, it sounded as though I was way too wrapped up in my own happiness to bother about my absent daughter's. I regretted that, but I had no way of putting it right.

Lynn just smiled and looked over at where Ella was pouring champagne. 'We'd love to get to know Ella, too, as well as the new baby. Let's just forgive each other: life is too short.'

Of course, Rebecca and Adam did not appear. I had not expected them. Sophie had prepared me for their – to me –

pointed absence from our wedding celebrations. Rebecca had used the excuse of her advancing pregnancy: a reasonable excuse. I must accept that. The heat, she said, the car journey. The fact that the baby was due at the end of July. But she sent a card, with her best wishes. I was grateful for that, at least. I wasn't sure whether it indicated a softening of her attitude, or whether her two sisters had insisted on that small measure of appropriate behaviour around this happy occasion.

We stayed in the garden until well into the night, only moving inside when the air began to chill. By that time, there were some fifty or so guests left, all of whom seemed reluctant to leave. It was after midnight when Ella finally kicked off her shoes after we'd waved goodbye to Frances and Sophie. I watched as my daughters left with their partners and felt an almost overwhelming tenderness for the absent Rebecca. It was a feeling that was as sudden as it was unexpected: but it was so clear on that day how Frances and Sophie were almost two halves of the same whole. They were not identical twins, but they were indivisible, inseparable nonetheless. Now, along with Martin and Pete, they seemed to complete a contented universe of four. I suspected – indeed, I had seen with my own eyes – that there was no love lost between Adam and these two men. I felt sad just then to think of Rebecca on her own – I mean, without the company of her sisters, on a day like this. I decided to try again to reach out to her. I would not abandon her; nor would I let her abandon me. I followed my wife into the conservatory.

'My kingdom for a cup of tea,' Ella groaned, tucking her feet under her on the sofa. I made her a pot, just as she liked it. 'Builders' tea,' she exclaimed, sipping in delight. 'You are a little treasure.'

My abiding memory of that day is the brightness of all the

women's dresses against the vibrant green of the lawn. And something else, too: it truly felt like the beginning of a new life. New connections were forged on that day, old ones renewed, forgiveness had been given and taken. I felt a contentment that threatened to spill over into tears, and perhaps would have done, had Ella not taken the final glass of champagne away from me.

I was conscious, too, of a growing sense of anxiety and excitement as the date of Rebecca's due date approached. I wanted above all to see her, to welcome the baby on behalf of Cecilia and myself. And I wanted, somehow, to give my eldest daughter a share of my own new happiness: a gift for the coming child.

But I had to resign myself to waiting.

I know now, of course, that in the meantime other events were already beginning to unfold. But back then I was completely unaware of them.

They were about to change my life – both of our lives – in ways I could not possibly have imagined.

Rebecca

WE DIDN'T GO, of course. Wild horses could not have dragged me there. I sent a card with Adam's and my best wishes, and I'm sure I'll get around to buying some sort of a wedding gift after the baby is born. Besides, I'm tired. Frances and Sophie were not impressed when I told them to count me out. I knew that just by looking at them, but at least I have a visible, swelling, lumbering list of excuses for not travelling. They can't deny that.

My back, my feet, my neck. My inability to stand for long stretches of time. My inability to sit for long stretches of time. The heat, the car-sickness, the fact that the seat belt is torture. I marshalled all of these soldiers to my cause and, eventually, my sisters retreated and left me alone.

It was a strange day, I'll admit that, the day of Dad's party. Adam had to work, even though it was a Saturday. I wasn't pleased – it has been happening a little too often lately for my liking. Now that I was on maternity leave, we needed to start getting things together for the baby's arrival. But Adam has been infuriatingly vague recently. 'Soon', he keeps saying. Or 'plenty of time', or 'maybe next weekend'.

At any other time, I'd have fought him. But I am more laid back these days than I have ever been, and I decided to let it slide. A small, superstitious part of me was strangely relieved, if I'm honest: better to wait, maybe, until the baby is safely here. Let's not tempt fate. Let's not even think about tempting fate.

And so I spent the afternoon in the garden, lying in the gauzy shade of the willow tree. I dozed and read and remembered. Perhaps it's because all my hormones are wandering where they will these days, but I found it a very emotional day. I revisited so many places, so many happenings from my early life, so much childhood stuff; the clarity of all those memories was startling.

What Frances and Sophie do not realize is that Cecilia was my friend. They have always had each other: they have never needed to look beyond that complete, tightly contained, exclusive universe of two. I don't think they even realize how indivisible they are. By the time they were born, I was very much the older sister – already separate, maybe even unreachable in their eyes. When they were seven, I was thirteen: already a bolshie teenager. I was at university while they were just starting secondary school. And now I was about to become a mother while they were merely girlfriends.

We inhabited different generations; we always had done.

I have never found it easy to make friends. And with Cecilia, I never had to. Occasionally, girls came and went throughout the years, but Mum was always there, always in my corner. She was barely twenty-four when she'd had me and, besides, her outlook was always younger than her age. I didn't feel the need for friends: I already had all the closeness I could handle. And that is not to say that we didn't argue, she and I: we did, but our disagreements never lasted.

Up to the morning she died, we phoned each other at least twice a day. It used to exasperate Dad: the fact that we'd have just left each other a couple of hours earlier and then we'd be on the phone again, chatting, planning, sharing.

On my wedding day, Sophie and Frances were my bridesmaids, naturally. It would never have occurred to me to ask anyone else. And even if it had, there was no one close to me that I'd have been happy with. Our cousins were scattered everywhere – Australia, New Zealand, Wisconsin. All of Dad's older brothers and sisters – he was the youngest of a big family – had upped sticks and left Ireland in the fifties. And Aunt Lynn was so much younger than Mum that her children – the 'baby cousins', as we called them – hardly counted. And so we grew up without an extended family network. My sisters have always missed that, or so they say. I have not.

But while Frances and Sophie were my bridesmaids, it was my mother who arranged the day with me – down to every last detail. It was Cecilia who came to help me choose my dress; Cecilia who tried out make-up with me before the big day; Cecilia who helped arrange the posies for the guests' tables. She even held my hand and soothed me through my pre-wedding jitters.

'You'll be fine,' she kept saying. 'It's just nerves. Everybody feels like that.'

'Did you?' I asked. I could have bitten my lip. I didn't want to rake up the past again, not when I was just about to get married myself.

She smiled. 'Yes. Yes, I did.'

And look how that worked out for you, I shot back – but silently. I didn't give voice to the words. Even I knew better. But it was as though she understood, anyway. That was another thing: Mum never needed to have things like that spelled out. She already knew what I was thinking.

'Your father and I worked things out a long time ago, Rebecca. We've been happy.' She tucked a strand of hair behind my ear. 'And you girls have made me happiest of all. I wouldn't change anything.'

And then there was the time we spoke about my having

children. We were squeezed into a changing room together, reflected into infinity by the long mirrors on every wall. 'I want to wait,' I'd said. 'I want to give it five years at least. I need to get my career sorted, and then we'll think about it.' I remember I was struggling into a choice of going-away outfits – one of those dresses with the ridiculous way-too-short zips that barely reach your shoulder-blades. I pulled it off again and tossed it to one side. I hadn't the patience for that. Mum was looking at me. 'What?' I said.

She didn't answer at once. When she did, all she said was: 'Don't leave it too long.'

I remember teasing her. 'You just want a gaggle of grand-children.' I pulled off another dress, placed it in the 'maybe' pile. I faced her, my hands on my hips, pretending challenge.

Her eyes lit up. 'Yes,' she said. 'Yes. I can't think of any-thing more delightful at this stage of my life. I'm really looking forward to it.'

'What about Dad?' I asked. After my earlier question, I felt the need to include him here, if only for her sake.

'Oh, yes,' she said, smiling. 'Your Dad adores the three of you. But for him, a grandchild would be the icing on the cake.'

'You mean a boy,' I couldn't resist.

She laughed. 'You two are so alike,' she said. 'Always owning the last word.' She reached over and handed me the next outfit: a silk dress, stunning in its simplicity. 'Your father will take what he gets, but, yes, he's been drowning in females all his life. You can't blame him for wanting a bit of male company.' She smoothed down the dress I'd just stepped into. 'Now this is *nice*.' Then she looked at me. 'I'm happy either way. I'm just glad I'm still young enough to enjoy any grandchildren I might be lucky enough to have.'

After she died, her words haunted me. She'd been cheated out of that, as well as out of so many other things.

I missed her. I missed her voice, her advice, her . . . solidity. I still miss her. Dad has always felt much more insubstantial to me, despite his huge physical presence. I was trying to explain that to Adam a few weeks back, when the whole wedding-party issue came up, but he just looked at me. His eyes had acquired that glaze of indifference that greeted me too often recently.

'I think you need to start getting over that, Rebecca,' he said. 'It's time to move on.'

I hate that phrase. It's so neat and clean, all swept up and dusted away. It makes me feel as though emotions are supposed to be bookends, or doors that open and close at will. All you have to do is straighten up, tidy up whatever happens in between. *I* am not a door, I wanted to shout. Things in *my* life don't open and close that easily.

Get a life. Move on. Get over it.

But nobody tells you how. Nobody tells you how to fill the well that opens up inside you when each day dawns and makes you feel no closer to the people in your life than you were the day before.

I can hardly wait for this baby. Secretly, I hope for a girl.

I'll call her Cecilia. That is, if I can get Adam to agree. He doesn't like the name.

It won't be long now.

Patrick

WHEN ELLA AND I returned home after those weeks in the Seychelles, I realized something quite profound in the days that followed. The thought articulated itself suddenly one morning, taking me by surprise. This quiet time after our honeymoon was, in fact, the first truly *reflective* time I'd ever had, in all of my then fifty-five years. I felt as though I had finally stepped down from a speeding vehicle. I felt calm, cherished, cocooned. The world seemed to sit still all around me. Contentment engulfed me: I felt undeservedly fortunate. It is the only way I can explain it.

One morning, I was sitting outside on the deck, a couple of weeks after the wedding celebration in our bright, light-filled garden. Now, though, I was surrounded by tidy mounds of hedge clippings, grass cuttings, all the bits and pieces of my midsummer clean-up. It was the first chance I'd had in some time: it had rained relentlessly for the previous couple of weeks.

On that morning, at least, the rain held off and I was well satisfied with my work. I'd been hard at it since nine, taking ridiculous pride in how physical effort still energized rather than tired me. And it pleased me, too, to keep the garden as Ella's father, Dan, might have done. I felt I owed him that much. Although in my previous life I hadn't ever been much of an enthusiast, with Ella I'd learned. She taught me and together we'd cleared and weeded and planted. We'd even painted the little wooden bridge over the stream, and renewed the varnish on the bird tables. We'd been careful not to tame things too much, though. Ella said her father had always liked a little bit of wildness.

Suddenly, she was there beside me. I was startled: I hadn't heard the front door. 'Hi, there,' I said, standing up. 'I was just about to make coffee. Can I get you some?'

But she didn't answer. Instead, she sat at the patio table, her attention seemingly fixed on the bird table to her right. I was puzzled. This was a complete change from earlier that morning, when she'd left to meet Maryam in the village. Then, she'd been animated, her usual chatty self, full of plans.

'Sweetheart? What is it? Is something wrong?'

She brought her gaze back to me. 'I think you'd better sit down.'

There was an intensity to the way she looked at me, almost a sense of something vibrating beneath the surface of her skin. Mystified, I sat. 'What is it?' I asked again, part of me fearful of her answer.

She sat up straighter, looked directly at me. 'I'm pregnant.'

'What?' A stupid reply – but the one that had sprung all by itself into the suddenness of speech. I thought of all the times Ella and I had discussed children, of the impossibility of our having any, of our acceptance of the inevitable. Then I thought of the years before I knew Ella, of her time with Fintan, and of the loss she had endured.

I say 'thought' but really what happened was a series of vibrant impressions that were not articulated: more a kaleido-scope of awarenessess, one laid down on top of the other. All of it took no more than an instant. And then I was filled with a shock of delight that left me breathless. 'Are you sure?' I was on my feet again.

Her eyes widened, as though she still hadn't absorbed the

surprise herself. 'It seems so. Gillian is convinced – and she's convinced that everything is as it should be. She called to see Maryam this morning and she – Maryam, that is – told her what she suspected. The next thing I knew, Gillian had bundled me into her car and we were on the way to the surgery.' She grinned. 'I don't know which of us was the more excited.'

Something wasn't clear. 'But – had you any idea?'

She shook her head. 'None!' She lifted her hands off the table, palms outstretched, uncomprehending. 'Things have been erratic over the past few months – but that's always been the case whenever I'm nervous or excited – or even when I'm travelling. I paid no heed. It was Maryam who got suspicious. And now this!'

She'd begun to smile, I think in response to the delight I could feel spreading, almost despite myself, across my face.

'But that's wonderful!' I was overjoyed. I knew how much this meant to her. My own private reservations dissolved as I watched the brightness of her glance, the glow of her face. I'd get used to broken nights again, to late feeds and baby-dominated days.

I pulled her to her feet and hugged her hard. I found that I couldn't speak. Ella was laughing. 'I need to breathe!'

I looked down at her, smoothed the hair back off her forehead. She looked happier than I had ever seen her. 'Do we know when this baby is due?'

She shook her head. 'I'll have to have a scan. Gillian thinks probably late January to mid-February.' Her eyes filled. 'I can't believe it, Patrick. I just can't believe it.'

We held each other for a long time, neither of us caring that the rain had started once more, soaking us both as we stood there.

That is what I remember above all: the two of us, standing in the garden, overcome.

To be honest, as well as the delight I felt, I experienced an undertow of relief. I was being given yet another chance: the chance of being a better, more unselfish father this time around. I vowed to be the best I could be.

The only shadow that tempered my happiness on that day was something to which Ella alluded later that evening, as we sat over dinner. 'It will be difficult, you know,' she said, looking across at me. For a moment, I was lost. On that day, for once, the whole world seemed to me to have resolved its difficulties. 'Rebecca's baby is due at the end of this month. We'll need to keep this under wraps as long as we can. It will probably seem like deliberately hurtful timing on our part.'

I hadn't thought of that. Right then, Rebecca seemed a million miles away from us. But I nodded. 'Yes, you're probably right. But let's enjoy today. We can worry about Rebecca tomorrow.'

Already, I was seeing the future. A future filled with opportunity.

It is probably a good thing that we can't see around time's corners.

In the days following Ella's announcement, I kept waiting. It felt as though someone was standing behind me, just out of sight. I often glanced quickly over one shoulder, sure that I had caught something out of the corner of my eye. I kept waiting for the call, the sign, the news that would bring Rebecca into view again.

And then, at six o'clock one Thursday morning, Frances phoned. 'No detail, Dad. You'll have to find that out for yourself. All I'm telling you is that you are now a grandfather. Everyone is just fine.'

My hand had trembled when I heard her voice. My relief that my eldest daughter was safe, that my grandchild was safe, was enormous. I put down the phone and turned to my wife. 'Rebecca's baby's here,' I said to Ella.

She kissed me. 'Call her and go to them.'

I phoned Adam at once. I got a cool reception, which is more or less what I'd been expecting. But Ella and I had discussed this thoroughly beforehand, so I was prepared. Forewarned is forearmed. Right now, she didn't speak. She just held my hand tightly and lay even closer.

I kept my voice steady, controlled. My tone was warm, jubilant – and the latter was no effort. 'Adam, I am absolutely delighted to hear your news. Congratulations on becoming a father. Are mother and baby doing well?'

There was a pause. I could almost see him: taken aback, flustered, needing to defer to his wife.

'Um . . . yes, thanks . . . Patrick. They're both very well indeed. It's a boy.'

I heard a muffled sound in the background. I knew that he'd used my name deliberately – he never called me 'Patrick', in fact, he never called me anything at all. He'd just address me directly as though our relationship was something of an embarrassment to him. I could imagine him now, gesticulating furiously at Rebecca, asking what to do about this unwelcome, uninvited caller.

Suddenly, I heard my daughter's voice. My guess is that Adam just handed the responsibility over to her, along with the phone. Fair enough, I suppose: I *am* her father. Nevertheless, this was one of those countless times that I wished my son-in-law had more spine.

'Dad?'

'Rebecca.' And then I couldn't say any more.

'Everything went well. A healthy little boy. We're calling him Ian.' She paused. 'Ian William, after Adam's father.'

That hurt, I don't deny it. I swallowed, hard. Even my name

was tainted in my daughter's unforgiving eyes. But I rallied, remembering Ella's encouragement.

'It's just such wonderful news, Rebecca, and I am very happy to be Ian's grandfather. Happy and proud.' I paused, willing myself towards my final salvo. 'I should very much like to come and visit you all. I really want to make my grandson's acquaintance. Would tomorrow afternoon suit? Or Saturday? You decide.'

I was pleased with my performance, I must say. I could feel Rebecca hesitate, imagined her mulling over my words. My tone was such that it was clear I would keep on asking until I forced her to answer, one way or the other. And I suspected that even she would not be able to harden her heart against me completely at such a thrilling time.

Ella squeezed my hand.

'Saturday would be better,' Rebecca said. She spoke slowly, as though trying to find a last, late, loophole. I didn't give her the chance.

'Great. I'll see you around four, then. I'll only stay an hour: I know that these are very busy days.'

'Okay.'

I heard wailing in the background and blessed Ian William for his timely intervention. My next trick was now to tell my daughter that my mobile was giving trouble: I had no intention of answering it, should she try to call to cancel. But in the event, I didn't have time. She dashed off to attend to her son, and our conversation ended every bit as abruptly as I would have wished.

Ella waited until I hung up. I turned around to face her.

'Well?' she said.

I wrapped both arms around her and kissed her soundly. 'A treat,' I said. 'It worked a treat.'

*

Adam opened the door to me. 'Come in,' he said. He smiled briefly. 'Let me take your coat.'

I heard voices in the living room. I recognized Frances and Sophie's at once and smiled to myself. I could do with some support.

'Come this way.' Adam was stiff, formal, as though I had never visited him and his wife before, as though I did not know my own way into my daughter's living room. I felt a flash of anger. Although I had never warmed to this man, I had often felt sympathy for him. Rebecca was a much stronger character, often a fiery one, and sometimes, I felt she got her own way too much. Today, though, I suddenly realized how much I disliked Adam. In a strange way, it made this visit a whole lot easier. I gathered my flowers and my card and my gift and made my way resolutely towards my grandson.

I remember everything about that first time I saw Ian. Memories of all the other visits that followed have melded together over time and I cannot tease them apart. Indeed, the years that followed seemed to be filled with nothing but babies. First and foremost, there was Daniel, of course. Then Frances's twins, Tom and Jack, arrived in 1998, just a year after she and Martin married. Sophie and Peter tied the knot, quietly, that same year, so that life felt like a whirl of weddings and christenings.

But that first time I saw Ian stands out, for so many reasons. For himself, of course, and the relief of his safe arrival; for the memory of Cecilia; for my own unborn child and all that promise of a bright new future. However, that first visit was not an easy one to make. On that afternoon in Rebecca's house, Sophie and Frances's presence made all the difference. Their joy, their unbridled delight at their brand-new status of Auntie, and their warmth towards me eased us all past what could have been a very awkward hour.

Rebecca was gracious, at least, on that occasion, 'Thank you, Dad,' she said as she accepted the flowers and the gift – some soft, blue and yellow garments that Ella and I had chosen together. I remember the day we went shopping: Ella's joy at choosing baby clothes, our shared knowledge that soon we would be doing this for ourselves.

I intimated none of this on that first afternoon, of course: I am not so foolish as that. But when Rebecca handed me my grandson for the first time, I was overwhelmed with emotion. I wept copiously, embarrassingly, and I think she was taken aback. I could not explain to her the source of at least some of that emotion. That would have to wait.

On that first afternoon, Cecilia's presence was palpable. She was there with us, in the same room: I imagined her standing guard over the Moses basket in the corner. I could not pretend otherwise. And I would not wait for Rebecca – or even Frances or Sophie – to mention her name. I wanted to be the first to acknowledge her. 'Cecilia would have doted on this little guy,' I said, gently. 'She always wanted grandchildren.'

Rebecca stiffened. Frances intervened at once. She must have seen her sister's face. She stroked the baby's cheek, moved closer to me on the sofa. 'Yes, it's a real shame Mum never got to see him. She'd have spoiled him rotten.'

Adam came back into the room just then. 'Anyone want tea?' he said. 'Or coffee?' He was oblivious to what had just transpired and I suppose that saved us. Frances shook her head at me when Rebecca wasn't looking. Leave it, her look said. Leave it for now.

On one of my subsequent visits shortly thereafter, there was talk of the christening party. I'd dreaded its mention, had worried about it ever since Ian was born. I hoped that Ella would not be excluded – could, in fact, see no possible way for Rebecca to manage it, without a complete breach with me.

I had fallen in love with my grandson at once, of that there is no question. But if I am truthful, some, at least, of my visits to see him had an underlying ulterior motive. I had formed the intention of making it impossible for my eldest daughter to behave anything other but appropriately towards Ella on the occasion of Ian's christening. In the event, it was easily settled – more easily than I might have dared to hope.

'Will Ella be with you at the party?' Rebecca asked me. Her casual tone didn't fool me for a moment. I'd driven the hour and a half once more to see her and Ian, a couple of weeks after he was born. Ella and I had purchased a beautiful Victorian cradle and we wanted to deliver it as soon as possible. But my wife had not come with me.

'Let Rebecca be the first to remark on my absence,' she said. 'Then at least the conversation will be opened. You'll be able to take it from there.'

I was well able to read my daughter's expression as she asked the question. I suspect that there was a touch of embarrassment there, too, along with an undertow of defiance. I had hoped – I admit it – that Ella's and my generous gift would at least give her pause, that she might re-examine her attitude towards me, towards us. I suppose above all I hoped that the arrival of her baby might have softened her a little.

I sat back in the chair, my grandson in my arms. The room had gone very quiet. There were just the two of us here, facing each other; and the baby. I looked straight at my daughter. 'Will she be welcome?'

Rebecca looked away. She didn't quite shrug, but her words did. 'She's your wife, Dad. You know how I feel about that. But I'm not going to exclude her.'

I wanted to say: 'No, I no longer know how you feel about that. Lots of water has flowed under the bridge by now. Tell me how you feel about that.' But I thought the better of it. Acceptance of Ella's presence – however grudging – would have to do for now: perhaps welcome would be extended at some other time in the future. 'Well, then,' I said. 'We'd both be very happy to be here.'

And that was it. It was not mentioned again.

Ella's pregnancy was not yet visible. Our afternoon at Ian's christening passed off without incident. Rebecca was polite, if distant. But she was not disagreeable. I was grateful for that. Announcing Ella's pregnancy was another hurdle that would have to be overcome on some other occasion. For now, I was satisfied at the outcome. Little by little.

Holding Ian on that celebratory afternoon, though, filled me with a most extraordinary sense of completion. It was as though my life had come full circle. And now, with my own child also on the way, my new life was beginning that circle all over again.

I felt exhilarated, fortunate, full of anticipation.

Rebecca

THEY WERE HERE YESTERDAY, both of them. My father was his usual public, charming self. Ella was polite and understated and took care, I think, to stay out of my way. I saw little of her, which is just as well. Cecilia's absence at Ian's christening party was enormous enough all by itself. I did not need any additional reminders of my loss. My first child, after so many painful false starts. Her first grandchild. I would have given anything for her to be there.

My father and Ella left, along with all the older guests, at around seven o'clock, once the cake and the champagne were done. I didn't try to stop any of them.

I stood at the door and waved and smiled as they all drove away. By then, I was gritting my teeth, and not for the first time that day, at yet another one of Adam's recurring absences. He seemed to have developed the ability to vanish at crucial moments. When he reappeared, just as I'd closed the front door, I said nothing. I felt we'd had enough spats for one day. And I particularly didn't want one in front of my sisters. But I was tempted.

'All the old farts gone?' he said, as he walked back into the living room. I followed, irritated at his false cheerfulness.

'Yeah, it's safe to go back in the water,' Sophie said and we all laughed. I sank into the sofa, glad to kick off my shoes and relax with her and Frances. Suddenly, I wanted Adam not to be there with us: I couldn't guarantee not to lose my temper.

'Why don't you guys head off for a pint, if you'd like? I'm sure you've had enough of babies for one day.' I kept my tone casual. Adam's face brightened at once. He looked enquiringly at the other two.

Martin stood up at once. 'Sounds good to me,' he said, glancing over at Frances. 'Okay with you?'

'Sure, but I'd like to be on the road by nine. Early start tomorrow.'

Martin nodded. 'Not a problem.'

'Have fun,' Sophie said, and Pete stooped to kiss her.

Right then, the easy affection between them made me ache.

The three of us sisters settled in and talked about the day. We avoided anything contentious – we'd got good at that. When Ian woke, I fed him and then we passed him around among us like a parcel. My sisters are going to be great aunties. They almost fought each other to wind the baby, to change him, to bath him.

And we are all agreed: my son is a delight. The only pity is that my sisters and I live too far away from each other. I'm beginning to see the advantages of being within walking distance.

I am besotted with Ian – we both are, Adam and I. I am relieved at my husband's reaction. During the last few weeks of my pregnancy, I felt that an increasing distance had opened up between us. I can always read his moods; I usually know what he is thinking. I felt that he was not excited enough by our baby's arrival. I said nothing about it, though, not then. I had enough to contend with. But I did afterwards, as soon as I felt I could, certainly within the first week.

Adam looked at me in surprise when I brought it up. 'I was just *nervous* coming up to the birth. What did you expect?' Then he smiled. 'Sorry – that didn't come out right.' He patted my hand and immediately, I felt myself ignite. I have always hated that gesture. It is patronizing in the extreme. I opened my mouth to reply and Ian began to wail. I decided not to pursue the conversation. The baby's cry was just one more interruption. What's one more among so many? Besides, I was probably just over-sensitive since the birth. I'd been warned by the midwife – but gently – about feeling hormonal, and I must have been. I was crying at the drop of a hat: me – who hated seeing tears of any kind, either mine or those of others.

I walked away from Adam and went to pick up my son. We'd kept his cradle on show downstairs, ever since my father had delivered it. I'd decided to leave it there until after the christening. I wanted people to see it: it was beautiful, and I have to admit it was a generous gift – that, and the significant cheque that came with it.

But its presence made me feel . . . I don't know. Perhaps resentful is too strong a word. But part of me felt that I was being bought off. I could sense my father's expectations of me on the afternoon that he delivered it; I could see the hope in his eyes. It seemed to flutter there, every time he looked at me.

After my father left that day, I spoke to Adam about my ambivalence. It was not the first time we'd had such a conversation. In fact, we had had it more and more often as the date of the baby's arrival approached. I think I was trying to find a way to absorb all my new realities – Ella among them – and talking was the only way I knew how to do it. Recently, Adam had not been all that receptive; I'd seen his vagueness, noted it for later. But this time, his reply stunned me.

'Get over it,' he said, cracking open a beer. He had his back to me, but I could see that he began to drink from the can. He had to know how much I hated that. The curtness of his tone, however, made me forget all about the beer. I was furious. He had dismissed me like this once before – on the day of the wedding party. 'Move on,' he'd said. Time to let go. But at least on that occasion, he had looked at me, engaged with me. This time, he didn't even face me. It was as though I was no longer there.

We had quite the row, I can tell you.

Afterwards, I did not feel that the issue – and perhaps there was more than one – had been resolved. There was an uneasy truce between us for several days. Then lack of sleep and soreness and just plain bone-weariness made any further connection between us impossible.

But I have not forgotten. Nor have I forgotten his behaviour yesterday at the christening party, when he thought I wasn't watching.

In the six weeks since Ian's birth, I have never known such chaos. The physical chaos is only part of it. I can turn a blind eye for days on end to the mountains of washing and ironing, the baby paraphernalia strewn everywhere, the hasty plates and mugs that litter the living room. Anna will come twice a week, as usual, and magic everything back into its proper place. That is not what concerns me.

What does concern me is my own lack of internal equilibrium. I feel as though something fundamental has ceased to be calibrated properly. I feel off-balance, no longer sure of foot – metaphorically, of course – even when surrounded by the familiar. It disturbs me. And I have no one to ask. No one I know has a baby.

Adam's cold injunction to 'Get over it' – whatever 'it' was – was the first time since Ian's birth that that lack of equilibrium had finally found a focus. There was relief in the anger that followed, a sort of cleansing fury. One thing became clear when the rage-fuelled fog lifted: Adam may be attentive to his son – during his own waking hours, anyway – but he is certainly not attentive to me.

There were perhaps fifty or so people here yesterday at the party – not all at once, but drifting in and out all day. The doorbell rang constantly. Plates needed to be replenished, drinks refreshed, seating arranged and rearranged. But more often than not, whenever I looked for Adam, he wasn't there.

He reappeared for the cake and champagne. I made sure we were in the kitchen together for a moment, gathering together the champagne flutes. 'Where have you *been*?' I spoke as quietly as I could. I was aware that there were too many ears about.

'Hmmm?' he said, reaching up to the highest shelf of the cupboard. 'Sorry, what did you say?'

That's a tactic of his: that faux-absent-minded 'Sorry, what did you say?' I know it well. He does it to infuriate me.

'Adam – I'm run off my feet. Where have you been?'

He looked at me, his face a mask of innocence. 'Looking after our guests, of course. As you say, we're run off our feet.' He turned on his heel and walked off into the living room, carrying maybe three or four glasses.

I bit back my reply. It would have to wait until later.

But I watched him closely. He seemed to skulk in the empty corners of the room. Or he'd disappear to answer the door and not reappear for ages. I had to go looking for him when some of our guests wanted to take photographs.

And I spotted him, at least twice, leaving the room with his mobile phone in his hand.

My blood ran cold. There is no other way to describe it. Everyone that was important to us, for one reason or another, was in this room, here, now. Who else could be calling, or texting, on a day like this?

I kept moving about the room, filling glasses, making sure

everyone was looked after. It was a relief, finally, to take Ian up to the bedroom again for his four o'clock feed.

As I sat with him, his small body tucked close to mine, I suddenly thought of that awful Christmas Eve, all those years ago. I could feel tears gather and I forced them back. I could see the tree, the failed lights, my mother on her knees, sobbing.

And I wondered, for the first time, whether I had married a man just like my father.

Patrick

THE 3RD OF FEBRUARY, 1995 is another day I will never forget. Ella's calmness. Me, like a headless chicken – her words. The anxious journey to the hospital.

The routine busyness at first. And then, activity all around my wife late that morning; activity that suddenly became urgent. People began to move swiftly, purposefully. They bundled me out of the delivery room.

'What's wrong?' I said, immediately panicked. The young nurse ushered me towards the door. 'What is it? What's happening?' She saw the alarm on my face and she took pity on me.

'The cord is wrapped around the baby's neck,' she said, glancing back over her shoulder. 'It'll be fine, don't worry, but the doctor has to intervene quickly. Now go – I'll call you just as soon as you can see Mrs Grant.'

I prayed. Please, God, I said, not this. Anything but this. Take me if you must, but leave her the child. I have never prayed so compulsively, so fervently, so sincerely, either before or since. I paced. I sat. I clenched my fists to calm my hands, to control their sweaty trembling. I swung around each time I heard the door behind me opening.

Finally, after a lifetime, the young nurse who had ushered me to the door now emerged from behind it, smiling.

'Everything is fine,' she said. 'Congratulations, Mr Grant. You can go to your . . .'

I didn't wait to hear any more. I ran. Ella was safe. The child was safe. I no longer cared if the baby was a boy or a girl. Up until that morning, I'd nursed a small, secret, selfish longing for a son – although I had never confessed as much to Ella. We'd discussed preferences, many times during those long, expectant months, a kind of meandering, languorous conversation that always looped us back to the same starting place: we didn't mind, either way. 'As long as the baby is well,' Ella would say. That was as close as either of us could come to confronting the unthinkable. We hadn't wanted to know the sex of our child in advance; we'd resisted others' urgings to find out. To me, it felt like tempting fate. I was glad Ella felt the same way.

'I want it to be a surprise,' she'd said. 'I want everything to wait until the baby is here.' The only decisions we had made were the names: Daniel for a boy, after Ella's father; Deirdre for a girl, after her mother. I was perfectly content with that. Indeed, I had encouraged it. When I finally exploded into the room where my wife and child lay, I thanked God that he had listened to me, that he had allowed me to keep both of them.

It is not easy to describe that moment, the moment in which I first met Daniel. When I burst through the door, Ella was already sitting up, the tiny bundle nestled against her in the bed. Her face was streaked, tired, radiant. She held out one hand to me. I bent and kissed her. We held onto each other for a long time.

'Thank God you're safe,' I said. I was trembling, and I was also conscious that I'd been perspiring profusely. 'I've been out of my mind with worry.' But it was as though Ella hadn't heard. Her focus was on me, on my face, my eyes. She never averted her gaze from mine.

'It's a boy,' she said, softly. 'Come here and meet your son.' She pulled back the fine wool blanket and for a moment all I saw was a small pink face. Squashed, unremarkable in its babyness. And then it hit me: this baby was mine. I had a son at last. Tears came and I could do nothing to stop them. I was embarrassed at this show of emotion in front of my wife, this time, but I couldn't help myself. In that small and overheated room, there were too many of us. Cecilia. Rebecca. Frances. Sophie. Ian. And now, us.

Above all, us: Ella, Daniel, me.

'Hold him.' Ella handed me the white bundle and I sat, overcome, into the plastic armchair beside the bed. She smiled at me. I could see how exhausted she was. Tiny red veins had exploded in the whites of her eyes: starbursts of remembered pain. I was about to speak, to say how awful it must have been for her, but she stroked the baby's forehead and said: 'It was touch and go for a while, but he made it.' Then, very softly: 'I think you're right, you know. There must be someone out there listening, after all. Someone who looked after us.'

The baby's lips made small, searching movements. The restless, snuckling noises brought me back some thirty years – to Cecilia, to Rebecca: just like this. As I had done with each of the girls when they were born, I sought one of my son's hands and held it in mine. Babies' fingernails have never ceased to delight me.

When I could speak, I said: 'Are you sure you're all right?'

Ella was smiling at both of us now. Her face was a mix of pride and utter devotion. I could do nothing but look at her, filled with equal parts fear and gratitude. She waved one hand in the air, dismissing my unspoken questions for now. 'I'm fine. I'm fine. We'll talk about all that another time.' She gestured towards the baby. 'Just enjoy him, Patrick. He's perfect.'

The wave of feeling as I held my new son was like an assault. I felt proud, humbled, sorrowful – choked with a sense of all the love and loss that can inhabit one man's life. 'He's beautiful,' I said. 'Just like his mother.' I stroked his soft cheek.

Ella sighed, leaning back into her pillows. 'I can't believe we've been so lucky.' She closed her eyes.

I sat for an hour or so as Ella dozed and Daniel slept. I watched both of them: how alike they seemed to me, how vulnerable their faces in the dimming afternoon light. I allowed myself to become sentimental. I vowed tearfully, silently, that I'd always look after them both, that I'd do whatever it took to protect them.

On that day, in that small hospital room, I knew that I had arrived at the centre of my own universe. I remembered some lines by John Donne from the poem 'The Good Morrow'. Donne was the only poet whose words had ever resonated with me. It was as though I'd learned them off by heart all those years ago in preparation for this day.

> *And now good morrow to our waking soules,*
> *Which watch not one another out of feare;*
> *For love, all love of other sights controules,*
> *And makes one little roome, an every where.*

Ella and Daniel were able to come home with me the following day.

For the next few weeks, the house was a blur of people coming and going. I have never seen such a variety of soft toys: birds, teddies, monkeys. And cards, full of love and good wishes. Frances and Sophie were constant visitors. They came, not to sit, but to make themselves useful to Ella. Rebecca came just the once. She came armed with her sisters, one on each side. At that time, I think I no longer cared about her hostility. Ella and I had a new universe and Rebecca scarcely orbited it. On the afternoon in question, my eldest daughter was polite and appropriate and the visit passed off tolerably well. Frances and Sophie saw to that.

I think that both my younger daughters were surprised to find how house-trained I now was. Surprised and pleased. I caught them a couple of times, looking at each other, when I called them into the conservatory for lunch: a simple soup that I'd made from scratch, sprinkled with herbs from the garden. Or poached fish with some of the spectacular salads that Ella had taught me to make – with rocket and nettle and chard and things I'd never heard of in my other life.

I minded everybody. I took delight in everybody's company. I lived in a benign, forgiving world. And I could feel the edges of myself softening. It was as though a whole fund of wisdom, of tolerance, of understanding had been unleashed within me, a serenity to accompany the gift of late fatherhood.

Daniel slept well, fed well, thrived well: everything was in accordance with the textbooks that Ella had stacked all around her. During those early months, our lives acquired new and unexpected dimensions. A sense of wonder, of pride, of – and this was a strange thing for a man in his mid-fifties to feel at last – belonging.

Those are now the days and weeks I look back on most: the time against which the rest of my life is measured. It is only now that I have felt able to do so. Until recently, the all-pervasive loss of Daniel had clouded all those earlier, happier times. At least now I begin to feel that I may be able to inhabit those times again. I have also begun to wonder whether there is a compensatory scale in the universe, after all. Perhaps we have to pay back, in full, for such happinesses as we receive, no matter how ordinary or extraordinary they feel at the time.

And it is also from the memory of those days that my most persistent question to myself now arises. It is from that point that I keep on asking the same things, over and over again, to the extent that I almost drive myself mad. What, starting from then, would I, should I, could I have done differently? Would

I – would we – have been able to ensure a different outcome, had we behaved otherwise?

At what point did we become blind? Did we perhaps cease to see our son?

I still have no answers, but there continues to be a clear, painful comfort in asking the questions.

Rebecca

ELLA, PREGNANT.

At least my father told me himself. He didn't wait for me to find out through Frances or Sophie. I suppose I should be grateful for that. Grateful that I didn't have to discover it as a result of someone else's careless comment, someone else's casually malicious observation.

This is a very small country. Six degrees of separation are not possible here. With any luck, you get maybe two, perhaps three, at a push. But news always travels – particularly news such as this.

Couldn't they – couldn't she – have waited?

I always suspected that this might happen, despite my father's original protestations to the contrary. This new child was to be only four or five months younger than Ian. Its impending arrival seemed to me to unpick whatever little remained of our family tapestry. It felt to me that, strand by strand, our shared past was becoming unravelled and a new, ill-fitting, uncomfortable future was being woven from all that forgetting.

My mother, brushed aside by Ella. And now her grandson, brushed aside by this new arrival. I'm sure all of this showed on my face the day my father told me.

'I'm sorry if you feel hurt by this, Rebecca.' He was uncharacteristically gentle – something that infuriated me even more.

Once again, he had what he wanted: now he wanted me to like it. Same old, same old.

'It's been a huge surprise – completely unexpected. A delightful one, of course, but . . .' and then he trailed off.

At first, I could say nothing. I had a lump in my throat that made speech impossible. Eventually, I managed to congratulate him. The following day, Frances could not understand why I was so upset.

'Is it to do with money, Rebecca?' She sounded tentative, genuinely puzzled. She had Ian on her knee. She'd been looking intently at him, and now she raised her eyes to me. I thought she seemed embarrassed. 'I mean, I'm sorry, I don't understand why you are so distressed. Are you worried about your inheritance, or what?'

I shook my head. 'I doesn't matter,' I said. 'Forget it. I'll get over it.' And I tried to smile. How could I explain? The truth is, back then, I did not understand it fully myself. I have spent a lot of time trying to figure out the warp and weft of all that emotional entanglement. I know now, and I think I also knew then, that it wasn't simple. Hindsight has not illuminated everything.

Leaving my mother aside for the moment, what *was* simple was that I did not like Ella – had never liked her. And not just because she became my father's new wife. I didn't like her professional faux-empathy. All that eye contact, that kind attentiveness to your words, the goddam reasonableness of the way she looked at the world.

Am I a bitch? Quite possibly. My sisters certainly think so.

But, apart from all the feelings that had to do with Ella, it seemed to me more and more that my real life had been lived in my old family home. Since Cecilia's death, I'd felt cut off from that life; abandoned. It was like being set adrift. My anchor had slipped and I'd been carried along on the rolling tide towards another life that wasn't mine.

And being married to Adam had not changed that. Our life together had a quality of waiting attached to it. As though I was killing time, as though all that was significant was taking place somewhere else. I kept waiting for my real life to catch up with me – the one that had slipped from my grasp around the same time as my mother did.

The years that followed her death were awful ones. All that loss, all those cruel pregnancies filled with hope and desolation. Looking back, I am surprised that I did not go out of my mind. Perhaps I did.

And then Ian arrived. My son grounded me: he, at last, made me feel that beside him at least, I had a place. There is no doubt about that. Our bond was clear and strong. Being with him made me happy. Once I was with him, I felt that I belonged to something bigger than myself. But outside that charmed circle of two, everything else felt in disarray.

And so the news of Daniel's arrival came wrapped up in a grief and a sense of loss that I found myself quite unable to explain. I felt surrounded by it: as though past and future were both defined by it. I knew, too, that I had never forgiven my father for the way he treated my mother – something else that my sisters did not understand. And so we never discussed it.

Over the years, I learned to let it all slide.

After the day that my father announced Ella's pregnancy, he never mentioned it again to me, not in that way. It was now a fact, an accepted future for him and his new family, something that need not be spoken of, other than in terms of universal delight.

But, by that time, there wasn't a lot of contact between us anyway. Oh, I went along to the christening: pretty much frogmarched there by my sisters. The baby was a boy, of course. Somehow, I had known it would be. To me, it felt inevitable that, once again, my father would get whatever it was that he wanted.

I went along to some of the subsequent family gatherings, too. But only when I had to. My sisters were tireless in their efforts to create and maintain a nurturing family network.

'It's what Cecilia would have wanted, too,' Sophie snapped at me one day. 'Get over yourself.'

I was shocked. First Adam. Now silent Sophie.

I decided there and then that I would keep my feelings to myself. My sisters' views were different; my husband was clearly not interested. And so I did my best: I remembered birthdays, exchanged gifts at Christmas, turned up on family Sundays when my punishing schedule permitted, and just got on with things.

Patrick

I SAVOURED EVERY MOMENT of Daniel's young life: from his first faltering steps across the wooden bridge at the end of our garden, to his fascination with the birds that visited us, to his endless tree-climbing and bicycle-riding summer days. But to tell the truth, of the two of us, it was Ella who was the more occupied with him while he was still a small child. I see now that I was more an observer of, rather than a participant in, all the more robust activities of my son's earliest years.

I have always found it easier to relate to my children once they become older – not necessarily more sensible, just more sentient. I did, of course, my share of bathtimes and bedtime stories. I took part in both of these activities with alacrity. I loved tucking in my son's small, sleep-furled body at night, smelling of soap and warmth and vulnerability.

However, when he was about eight years old, Daniel seemed to become quieter, more self-contained, almost overnight. And although a dizzying array of children came and went during those early years, including his growing brood of cousins – even Ian, from time to time – for birthday parties, sleepovers, day trips to the lake, athletic contests in the garden, I began to notice that, more and more, Edward became Daniel's chosen companion.

Maryam and Rahul's eldest son – also born just a few months before Daniel – Edward was a sweet, gentle boy, a little in awe of us, I always felt. And Daniel felt it, too – he even spoke to me about it on that memorable day when we went fishing together – but that part of my story comes later.

Edward was the eldest of four boys – the energy they unleashed together could have powered the national grid. Home for Edward was noisy, busy and, truth to tell, somewhat cramped. Maryam and Rahul's rented farmhouse was a short drive from us. It was one of those old sixties monstrosities – drab and poorly insulated and lacking in any coherent living space. Our house was an oasis for Edward; we loved having him. The other side of that particularly satisfactory coin was that Daniel loved the chaos and the jostling and the perpetual motion of Edward's family – or he had done for all of his first eight years.

What I remember best, that autumn when Daniel became very precise about his age – eight and a *half* – is his developing passion for colouring, painting, collage work. He and Edward used to spend every evening after school with their heads bowed over their sketchbooks or their scrapbooks. I was curious. It surprised me that such a relatively quiet activity had sustained two energetic young boys for so long. It seemed to be a focus that had come out of the wide blue yonder.

One afternoon, I glanced over their shoulders as I placed a glass of milk before each of them. I took a furtive look at Edward's page first – he was closest to me – and I pushed the plate of biscuits and fruit towards the middle of the table. His painting was as I would have expected it to be: some smiling stick figures in the foreground, a two-storey, double-fronted house in the background with smoke curling towards the sky from a squat and ill-proportioned chimney. It seems that this is the sort of house all children love to draw. Perhaps it is the symmetry that they like. Perhaps the regularity of its features is what pleases them, no matter how far this ideal is from their own home-place. The colours of Edward's picture were vivid, some leaching into others, the paper rising and bubbling under the watery application of poster paint.

'Very nice, Edward,' I said. 'I love all the happy faces.'

He smiled, shyly, and reached for a biscuit.

I felt that I could now look over Daniel's shoulder – politeness had been adequately served. I can still remember the sense of shock I felt as I looked. The page shimmered. The painting was, unmistakably, of our garden: but a garden transformed into a kind of pastoral transfiguration scene. The colours were astonishing: I could see where Daniel had mixed his own shades in the old, chipped saucers that Ella had given him for the purpose. Two figures – not stick figures – but well fleshed-out human children – flew kites high into the cloudless sky. I could have sworn that the kites fluttered, that the two boys moved, across the garden, down the slope to the river. The scene had energy, life – a vibrancy that was wholly out of keeping with the tender age of the artist. And I know that I can be accused of seeing something with a highly indulgent parent's eye: perhaps. Nevertheless, I also know that another, more critical part of my photographer's eye was equally arrested by the power of my son's painting.

'Very nice, too, Daniel,' I said. 'I like the kites. Well done, you guys.'

I spoke to Ella about it in the kitchen afterwards. 'Is it me?' I asked. 'Or is he just very good?' I was unable to hide my amazement.

She smiled as she handed me the plates for the dishwasher. 'No, it's not just you. The teacher spoke to me this afternoon, actually, when I collected the boys. She said he has real talent.'

I was pleased. What father wouldn't be? I began to watch Daniel more carefully, encouraging him whenever I could. I suppose our relationship shifted somewhat as a result of this burgeoning talent. It might sound callous to say that my son suddenly interested me more, but that is the truth. I loved him completely and unreservedly, of course, and I always had done; but now there was a different conversation beginning between us. I felt that there was a whole other level on which we could engage.

Years later – in fact, during those heady, optimistic months of his first year at secondary school – I had cause to recall that earlier fully formed picture of the kite-flyers. I rejoiced in his transfer to secondary school: he was fired up about everything. It was wonderful to watch his interests expand, to hear of how teachers encouraged him – particularly in art and English – and to watch how he blossomed under the new regime. One after-noon, sometime in late October of that first year, I think, we were in the conservatory, Daniel and I. I was wrestling with the remains of that day's cryptic crossword, he was sitting at the table, his paints and sketchpad and some sheets of A2 spread out in front of him. He often painted there: the light was better and there was more space at the round table than at the desk in his bedroom. His head was bent in concentration, the cow's lick falling, as usual, over his freckled forehead. I knew better than to interrupt. Besides, he often showed me his work during those early months, once he felt he was finished. I think he trusted my eye: his questions would always revolve around perspective, or proportion, or form – never around the subjective. He never asked me whether I 'liked' what he had done. And so I felt free to be critical; constructively so, but critical nonetheless.

I had told him once that the Chinese believed that painting was the outcome of the harmonious relationship between the hand, the eye and the heart. None of these three should be missing. He never forgot.

That evening, he stood up from the table and carried his work over to where I was sitting. As ever, his expression was a mix of excited apprehension and earnest awareness. Daniel knew well that he had talent; he carried that knowledge lightly.

'Miss O'Connor told us to paint "Farewell". That's all – just one word. We were only to use black and white, and one colour of our choice. What do you think?'

I put down my newspaper. 'Stand back a bit into the light, and hold it up so that I can see it properly.'

It was our lake – of that there was no doubt. Waves were painted here and there with suggestive, undulating flashes of black: the expanse of water was implied rather than explicit. Casey's boatyard – which we had visited together, during that summer – was a smudge in the distance, the pier a ghostly finger reaching out into the dark water. The scene brought a delicious shock of recognition with it.

Two figures sat in a lake boat – George Casey's lake boat – and they were painted in silhouette. The boat pretty much filled the entire page. As I looked more closely, I could see Edward's long nose, the unmistakable shape of his gangly body, leaning forward, intent on something between his fingers. There was just the glimpse of a grin – a mere flash of white teeth. Across from him sat a boy with a cow's lick falling across his forehead. One of his hands was raised – whether in greeting or farewell it was hard to say: a nice piece of ambiguity. And above the boat was a psychedelic starburst of blue – a sun, a moon, a planet: it didn't matter. The scene was imbued with an extraordinary stillness, the intimacy of friendship. It struck me then, and not for the first time, how fortunate Daniel was to have such a close friend, something that had eluded me all my young life.

I found his painting moving, and I told him so.

'Hand, eye and heart?' he asked, grinning.

'Absolutely. I think you've got it just right. The proportions are excellent. There's a sense of mystery to it, too. I like that. And there's something extra for me, of course.'

He looked at me, questioningly.

I pointed to the smudge in the distance. 'Casey's boatyard. It's always good to see familiar places.'

He frowned, quickly, as though he had missed something. 'And if they're not familiar?'

'There's more than enough to intrigue. People bring their own experiences with them when they look at a painting. Don't forget that. There's a real story here – the background is just an extra.'

He nodded, satisfied. 'Okay. It's for next week, so I'll just leave it and see what we think in a few days. Something might need to be changed.'

That 'we' thrilled me. My son always made it easy for me to be a good father.

Some three years earlier, when Daniel was nine, I took him sailing with me on his own. I'd hoped that this would be a regular activity for just the two of us. We had six Saturdays in a row to spend together, while Ella pursued some training course or other in the city. He had grown somewhat sturdier during the previous winter. For his birthday that February, he had asked for nothing other than a pair of binoculars.

That pleased me, too. I felt that, soon, I could teach him the rudiments of photography. I already knew that he had a keen eye.

The first Saturday, we went to the lake very early. The mist was just rising. There was an eerie stillness: water, sky, air – nothing moved. Great swathes of steel-blue mist ribboned across the countryside.

'Can we go to the bird sanctuary?' Daniel asked suddenly.

'Sure we can,' I said. 'When this mist clears, it's going to be a really fine day. You'll have a great view.' I smiled at him. He seemed so serious, standing there on the quay wall, watching carefully as I untied the *Aurora*. He looked suddenly small and fragile, and something tugged at my heart. 'Hop on board,' I said. 'We'll have to use the engine. But there should be a bit of a blow later on this afternoon, if we can trust the weather forecast.'

He jumped lightly onto the deck. His landing barely made a ripple. I started the engine and Daniel fended us off the quay wall. Then he sat and opened up his rucksack. I had made us sandwiches and flasks of soup. I wondered how he could be hungry already – barely an hour after breakfast. But he wasn't interested in the food. Instead, he pulled out a brand-new sketchbook, some pencils, a box of charcoal. He placed the binoculars around his neck.

'I want to try drawing the birds,' he said. 'I've never tried before. Do you think we'll be able to get close enough?' His eagerness was touching.

'We'll do our best,' I said. 'We'll need to sit still and be very patient, though.'

He nodded. 'I know that. I'm ready.'

'Do you know what you're looking for yet?'

'Oh, yeah. I've looked up loads of stuff.'

I smiled. His and Edward's familiarity with technology never ceased to amaze me. It was as though they'd been born with an extra gene – one that is capable of absorbing new things effortlessly, rather than having to learn them. His ease with a keyboard, a mouse, even a mobile phone, astonished me. I felt slow and fumbling and awkward in comparison.

And old. Let us not forget old.

'I'll read the names to you.' Daniel looked over at me. 'The site says they're all here – you just have to look for them carefully.' He flipped back the cover of his sketchpad. Immediately, he began to recite.

'Blackcapfieldfareperegrineskylarksparrowhawkmerlinshort-
earedowl, stonechat. The stonechat is very rare, but . . .' He
paused finally and drew breath.

The engine fired and sputtered. 'Right, then,' I said, let's get
underway.'

We didn't see the stonechat, but we did see a sparrowhawk,
some fieldfare and several skylarks. We crouched in the grasses
until I could no longer feel my legs. But Daniel's enthusiasm
was infectious.

Eventually, I persuaded him to come back to the boat for
lunch. We sat in the sunshine, a breeze blowing that would soon
become stronger, brisker. 'I think we might be able to sail back,'
I said. 'Would you like that?'

He nodded, his head already bent over his sketchbook, his
sandwich beside him on the seat, uneaten. I watched, silenced
by what I was seeing. The birds took flight under his fingers. As
he sketched, he moved from pencil to charcoal, to occasional
vivid whispers of colour. The sketches were not just faithful
representations of what we had seen that morning, sharing the
binoculars silently between us. Instead, these birds had real
personality – their heads cocked cheekily this way or that, their
beady eyes gleaming with some ancient knowledge. They took
my breath away.

I didn't want to disturb him. The focus, the concentration
across his eyes was extraordinary. Suddenly, my son looked
older, much older. I felt that I was seeing the face he would
grow into. I could see what he would look like as a young man.
And then, just as quickly as the vision had appeared, it disappeared. He was a nine-year-old child again.

'Those are very good, Daniel. Very good indeed. We should
frame some for your bedroom.'

'You think?' his face lit up.

'Absolutely.' I smiled at him, ruffled his hair. 'And now, I also think it's time to eat that lunch. Get stuck in there, buddy, eat up. Or your mum will have my guts for garters.'

We had an exciting journey back. The wind gathered in strength and the placid waters of the lake began to make themselves felt in small surges under the bow. The sail flapped and strained, the noise it made suddenly violent and unearthly in that silent place. Daniel responded well to learning the ropes: he was quick, light on his feet, he could anticipate what needed to be done next. We reached the shore just before the late April downpour unleashed itself upon us. Laughing, shouting, trying impossibly to dodge the shower, we tied up the *Aurora* and raced each other to the car.

'That was cool!' he exclaimed, launching himself into the passenger seat.

I laughed. 'Not only cool – I'm freezing! We're soaked through.' I rubbed my hands together, feeling the sticky chill of the rain that trickled down the back of my neck.

'Can Edward come with us next time?' he asked. He wiped his sleeve across his face. His hair stood up in dark, slick spikes.

'Of course. Any Saturday you wish.' I tried to ignore the small sigh of disappointment that ruffled my contentment with the day. It was unworthy, and I knew it. 'Edward is welcome anytime.'

And so, for the next five Saturdays, Edward kept us company. He proved to be a useful little sailor, too. Some of that usefulness, I think, came from his eagerness to please me. No matter – both he and Daniel learned some new skills, and I learned a little more about both of them and their lives. Edward was talkative, more expansive, once he was on the water; he became easily absorbed in doing things, the sort of physical activity that seemed to make him forget his shyness. Daniel was content to let him chatter.

I observed that, for Edward, the joy of those days came from the process of learning – reading the wind, filling the sails, getting to know about ropes and knots – whereas for Daniel, it was something different.

Sailing was simply something that brought Daniel to wherever he wished to be: to the bird sanctuary, to the swans, to the autumn woodlands that were ablaze with colour after a particularly icy winter. The journey was simply a means to an end. He filled several sketchbooks that year.

I still have them. I look at them from time to time, their contents reminding me of those light-filled Saturdays. When I turn the pages, I can see Daniel again. I can read his happiness in the soaring flight of the sparrowhawk, or the curve of the mute swan's elegant neck.

At least I have that sure and certain knowledge of my son's happiness. It is the only certainty that I *do* have. Ella and I will never know the exact nature of the process that drove our sweet boy to despair. That drove him to step bluntly out of his life, out of ours, leaving behind a crushing void that can never be filled.

On those earlier days at least, aboard the *Aurora*, in my company and with his best friend beside him, my son was happy.

There is some comfort in that.

Rebecca

IT WAS, IRONY OF IRONIES, sometime during the Christmas holidays of 1999. I can't remember the exact day or date: just that the whole world seemed to be convulsed with *fin-de-siècle* angst as the turn of the millennium approached.

Except that it wasn't the turn of the millennium at all: call me pedantic, but that had yet to happen. We were all a year ahead of ourselves that December, egged on by the harbingers of doom and the end-of-the-world-is-nighers and the new-agers and the certain predictors of the Second Coming. The 1st of January, 2001, on the other hand – the real beginning of the third millennium – slipped by us, passing under our collective radar while we had all turned the other way.

Ah yes: the momentous event that happens when we are too busy looking at something else. I know the feeling well.

That Christmas of 1999 in our household had been rather a tense one. Nothing new there; it was merely the continuation of a long year that had also been rather a tense one. Adam and I had been wrestling with some 'issues', as he called them. To wit: my frequent, disruptive absences from our home. The pressure he felt under at work. The weight of all that domestic and child-rearing responsibility that fell squarely upon his shoulders.

Except that it didn't. We – that is, I – had put structures in place: people and things that stopped all the mother-shaped gaps when I wasn't around. My international trips had dwindled to just the occasional few days away, much to my relief. But I still had to travel around Ireland, delivering modules in our sister colleges the length and breadth of the country. Dull overnights in overpriced and dingy hotels; under-resourced lecture theatres; uncooperative colleagues. Not the stuff that career dreams are made of.

For my absences, national or international, I'd hired a daily housekeeper. A rota of childminders. And still the guilt came home with me in every suitcase, every time: those solid blocks of the family edifice that travelled everywhere with me, that saw me pick up the slack on all those other days when I *was* there. Days that outnumbered my absences by a factor of three to one.

Anyway, it was one of those lull days, sometime between Christmas and New Year's Eve. The previous week had been the usual whirl of activity, visits to and from the children's friends and cousins, family expeditions to indoor playgrounds and cinemas. I was exhausted. I wanted a day at home, to call a halt to all the *doing*. Ian was a sturdy five-year-old, a child happy in his own company. I can't remember which computer game was all the rage that Christmas, but he had it. As long as he varied it with books and physical activity, I didn't mind. Ian has always been an easy child.

Aisling was three, as clingy as a vine, constantly wailing about the unfairness of life. She'd wangled her way onto my knee again, just after lunch, and I felt a sharp stab of sorrow for her. She didn't lack attention, or affection, or love – but nothing was ever enough. Right now, she was in search of another story. I held her close, kissed the top of her head, inhaling the scent of soap and shampoo and my perfume, which I'd earlier dabbed on her wrists and behind her ears.

'Which one, sweetheart?' I asked. 'What story do you want?' Her books littered the sofa, where Adam was sitting, half-asleep, something mindless flickering across the TV screen.

She pointed. 'That one,' she said. 'I'll get it.' She wriggled off my knee, and clutched *The Gruffalo* to her chest, tripping over Adam's feet in her anxiety to get back to me.

He jumped, startled awake by the sudden movement. His face filled with annoyance and I reached down and scooped my daughter into my arms, hoping to drown out whatever sharp reprimand was coming her way.

'C'mere, sweetie,' I said, settling her on my knee. I turned to face Adam, about to shake my head, to ask him to stop, not to say whatever it was he was about to say.

And right at that moment, his phone rang. He pulled it out of his trouser pocket and frowned at the screen before he answered. I can still picture him: it was one of those moments in which we see something with an extraordinary clarity. The force of the illumination stunned me, made me sit back in the armchair as though I had been slapped.

My husband's face suddenly lit up as he answered the call – a brightness that had nothing at all to do with the reflected light from the screen of his mobile phone. Right then, I knew. I said nothing. I watched as he struggled into standing. I watched as he left the room. I listened to his claim of 'bad signal' in the living room when he returned. Smiling. Cheerful. And still I said nothing. Nor did I say anything later when he mentioned, casually, that he had to go out to see some colleagues from the UK who had just arrived in town for New Year's Eve.

Down through the years, I have puzzled over that reticence of mine. It is not one of my most defining characteristics – as anyone who knows me will agree. Perhaps the fact that my husband was having an affair felt like my fault. Perhaps I felt it was what I deserved for being absent from home, for demanding that I had a supportive partner, one who believed in equality and justice and a fair shake for working mothers. Perhaps. Whatever the reason, I stayed silent.

Except for one occasion. Maybe six months after that Christmas, when Adam's behaviour had grown increasingly furtive – there is no other word for it – I decided to confront him.

'Is there something we need to talk about?' I asked. The children were in bed and we were alone in the kitchen. That in itself was unusual. I seized my moment.

'Hmmm?' he said, barely lifting his eyes from the newspaper. 'Sorry, what did you say?'

'Adam. Do we need to talk?' I tried to be calm, but even I could hear the urgency in my own voice.

He looked at me then. 'What is it?' He still held onto the raised newspaper. An air of impatience surrounded him, like an aura. I could almost see its colour shimmering.

'You seem very preoccupied. Is everything okay?'

He kept his gaze level. He took a moment before he replied. I had the impression that he was weighing his words, carefully. 'What an extraordinary question,' he said. 'What on earth could be wrong?'

I didn't answer. I waited instead.

'You don't need to worry,' he said. 'Everything is just fine.' Then he put the newspaper down and left the kitchen.

I thought I understood that conversation. It told me that nothing was fine, that everything was wrong, but that, neverthe-less, he would not rock the family boat. I sat at the table, long after he'd left, fear alternating with numbness. For the first time in my life, I didn't know what to do. I was consumed by a terror of abandonment.

I had two children. I had a life entangled with Adam's – no matter what thread I pulled, the whole fabric came apart, leaving holes and gaps and weaknesses that could never be filled or mended.

And so, I did nothing.

Daniel

Dad took me to the open evening. Mum came along later on because she had to work. But she didn't miss much, just the principal, Mr Murray, waffling on about stuff. I wanted to get going to see the classrooms, but Dad said we had to wait until all the boring bits were over. The bits about being welcome and a whole new chapter and the different routines of secondary school. Things like that.

Pretty much everybody from sixth class was there. Mikey and Cliodhna and Maggie and Brendan. I saw them with their parents. Edward too, with his mum. His dad was working as well. I spotted James and Jeremy, but they were way back, at the end of the hall. Anyway, we don't bother saying hello any more, not since the time they used to pick on the smaller kids in the playground. I never told on them back then, but they think I did. Them and Jason, but he's in America with his mum and dad now.

When the speeches were over, we were allowed to see the classrooms. In the Woodwork Room they had all kinds of stuff on display. Mug racks, bedroom lockers, even small tables with tiny coloured bits of mosaic on the top. When Mum came, she really liked them, especially the tables. She and Dad both said I could do any subjects – options they called them in the school – that I wanted. So that night, I picked woodwork. The teacher, Mr Byrne, was cool. He chatted to me for ages and I told him about all the stuff in Granddad's garage.

On one of the other corridors, there was the Art Room. Miss O'Connor was there. I thought she must have run real fast from the hall to get there, because she was the deputy principal as well and had to say some of the speeches. She talked to me for a good while about what they do in art, to me and about three others. Mum and Dad stood at the back but she talked to us instead and I liked that. I told her about drawing the birds and she asked to see them. I said I'd bring my sketchbooks in on the first day. Mum and Dad said it was fine if I wanted to do art, so that was two subjects.

Then we could hear piano coming from the Music Room, just down the corridor. Mr Kelly teaches English and music and he's in charge of the school band as well. When Mum told him I play the violin he got real excited. So I joined the band there and then and said I wanted to do music. He told me about the syllabus and it sounded good so that was three subjects. I'm not sure about the last one but Dad says there's no hurry. It can wait until September.

But I can't wait. The school is great. There's loads of room and you move around to each teacher after every class: you're not stuck sitting in the same place every day. And you get lots of teachers, not just the same one. I always liked Mrs MacCarthy though, our sixth-class teacher. She was like another mum. She told us loads of times that we were a group with 'exceptional talents', that's what she said. And she said we had a duty to go out into the world and develop all our talents to their 'fullest potential'. She said as well that we must never forget to be kind, both to ourselves and to others. Mum said that it sounded like a pretty good philosophy to her.

Miss O'Connor's Art Room was deadly, though. For the open evening she showed us all kinds of things like lino-cutting and a kiln for pottery and the option of doing photography on a Wednesday afternoon – a kind of club that met because of the half day. I can't wait to get started. And Mr Kelly says I can learn another instrument if I want as well, not just stick to the violin.

We met up with Edward on the way out. He's really excited too except he doesn't like the navy uniform. I don't care. There was a notice on the door on the Green Corridor – they call it that because the doors are painted green and all the different colours make it easier to find your way around the corridors – about drama workshops after school, and that they needed people to paint scenery for the end-of-year show. How cool would that be for next year?

Graduation from sixth class is at the end of May. Then there's the summer, and Dad has promised loads of trips for me and Edward on the *Aurora*, maybe even an overnight.

And then it'll be September. I don't really want to show it but I am so excited I wish it was the end of August already.

Patrick

THE FIRST TIME that I took Daniel fishing belonged to a very special time in our brief life as a family. It was during that wonderful, long summer that marked one of the first major transitions of my son's life. He'd just finished primary school, had graduated along with his classmates on an evening so full of talent and ceremony and youthful exuberance that Ella and I had been charmed.

As we left for the school that evening – the evening of his 'graduation' ceremony – Daniel said he had a surprise for us. We could both sense his mounting excitement. But no amount of teasing or guessing or bribery could get him to divulge his secret. 'Wait and see,' he kept saying. 'You'll just have to be patient.' And he grinned at me. He'd just used one of my own favourite phrases against me.

The school hall was thronged when we entered. We were welcomed by the staff, by a delegation from fifth and sixth classes, by members of the board and the parents' committee. Such warmth and inclusivity took me aback. I looked around me, saw how every space in the hall was now filled from floor to ceiling with the children's paintings. Daniel's covered almost one full wall. I knew without being told which ones were his. He loved blue: every conceivable shade of it.

'Is this the surprise?' I whispered to Ella, motioning towards the wall of blue as we were shown to our seats.

'I have no idea,' she said. 'We're going to have to wait until he tells us. We'll just have to be patient.' And she winked.

As we waited, I was suddenly overwhelmed at the contrast between my own schooldays and those of my son. Memories – all too vivid ones – transported me back to the early fifties and my own days at primary school. In sixth class we were 'the big boys' – almost ready to be unleashed upon the world. The world of work and apprenticeships for most, and of secondary school for those few – and I was among them – who were more economically fortunate.

We all, however, had the privilege at the start of that final year of childhood of moving 'upstairs' – via a ramshackle wooden stairway that led to the biggest, coldest, bleakest class-room in the school. No pictures hanging there: no plants, nothing to lighten the all-pervasive shadow of Mr Gradgrind. We were warned to keep our lunches in our desks: rats had been known to climb into the schoolbags of the unwary. I could still see the rows of hard wooden benches; feel the freezing winter air that the turf fire in the corner did nothing to soften. And I could never forget the frequent sting of the leather across my palms, or the pain of a slapped ear.

Once, Tommy Lalor, who sat beside me, got the worst beating I had ever witnessed. He had had the temerity to complain at home about the toilet block in the schoolyard outside. The floor ran with water and waste: the pans leaked constantly, blocked up on a daily basis, overflowed. The stench made us gag. Tommy's mother, a feisty woman, brought her complaint to the Brothers. In class the following day, Tommy was hauled up to the top of the room and beaten across the head, the legs, the hands by the vicious Brother Michael, with a savagery I had never witnessed before. He wielded the leather with uncanny accuracy. He knew just which of its angles hurt the most. 'Sticky', we knew him as – although the derivation of that nickname had long been lost.

The rest of us boys were cowed into a terrified silence. We sat, with our arms folded, and watched the drama unfold instead. Terrified we may have been, but our fear also contained the hard, grateful kernel of our relief. Once the day's victim had been chosen, the Brother's rage would have been purged. The rest of us were safe – at least until the next day.

'If your home was as clean as the toilets here ye'd have nothing to complain about,' Sticky hissed. Tommy's cries eventually brought Brother O'Malley in from next door. We all stood, immediately. '*Dia is Muire dhuit, a Bhráthair,*' we chorused. I think I remember, even at the time, that our Pavlovian response struck me as somewhat absurd. I believe we'd have demonstrated this unquestioning obedience even if the classroom had suddenly burst into flames.

'I'll deal with this,' Brother O'Malley said, sharply, to Sticky. 'Sit down, boys.'

A howling Tommy was removed from the classroom. He didn't appear on the following day. When he finally did turn up, the rest of us never mentioned the beating. All I know is, nobody ever complained again.

Ella nudged me. Confused for a moment, I looked up. A group of boys and girls from Daniel's class had begun to sing, under the direction of their teacher. I watched the way they owned the stage; the whole space bathed in streaming evening sunshine. These youngsters looked joyful, confident, full of innocent optimism. I found the whole performance almost unbearably moving. To my horror, I welled up on several occasions. I think such extremes of feeling were composed partly of a sense of loss on my own behalf – even all those years later – and a sense of profound hope on Daniel's.

I turned to tell him this, but he was no longer in the chair beside me. I hadn't noticed him leave. It occurred to me that my obvious emotion might have embarrassed him in front of his friends and I began to look around for him anxiously.

Then Ella nudged me again. 'Look,' she whispered.

I just caught the principal's last words. 'Very proud,' she was saying. 'All their own idea, very little input from us: please welcome the "Sixtus String Sextet".'

And then Daniel stood before us, his bow raised, his violin resting on his shoulder. The five other young musicians stood to his right and to his left: solemn, expectant. 'Ladies and gentlemen,' Daniel said, his voice clear and unwavering, 'this evening, the Sixtus String Sextet have pleasure in playing *Palladio* by Karl Jenkins for you, as part of our end-of-year celebration.'

The audience fell silent. Ella's hand searched out mine. I looked at her, my eyes asking the question: did you know about this? She shook her head. I was glad. I wanted to feel that both of us ranked equal in our son's affections, particularly this evening.

Daniel nodded to his companions. We watched him count out the beats: one, two, three. And then they began to play, all their young faces filled with concentration. The exquisite notes of Jenkins's music swelled and filled the room.

When the last notes faded, the reaction was uproarious. Stamping of feet, whistling, cheering. This was not the occasion for audience restraint. What astonished all of us was the sheer quality of the playing: there were some scratchy moments, without doubt, but there was also sureness, passion and technique.

'Told you,' Daniel said, suddenly appearing beside us again. 'Told you I'd surprise you.'

What I remember above all from that evening – and Ella concurs – is the uplifting wave of promise that all of us parents felt. We left, fuelled with hope, with pride, and with no small sense of confidence in the future.

In the days and weeks that followed, Daniel and Edward were a constant presence around the house, the garden, the garage. They had both been haunting me for some time, begging me to take them fishing. Daniel in particular was filled with his typical eagerness, and wanted to get going just as soon as he'd spotted his granddad's old fishing rod in the garage.

'What's that?' he said, pointing to the ceiling. I'd been putting back the gardening tools late one Monday morning and he'd followed me in. He was at a bit of a loose end that day, as I recall. Normally, Daniel made himself scarce when he saw the mower and the shears and the trowel appear. Gardening was emphatically not among the activities that he enjoyed.

I looked up. 'That belonged to Granddad. He bought a lake boat with some friends when he was a young man and he used to go off fishing with them whenever the mayfly was up.' I didn't tell Daniel that these brief trips away had all suddenly stopped once Ella's mother died. I saw no reason to cast a shadow over his young day.

'Where is it?' he asked, his voice beginning to fill with excitement.

'Where's what?' I was puzzled. Daniel's eyes were glued to the fishing rod as he spoke.

He looked at me then, that blue, direct gaze full of curiosity. I was struck that day, I remember, by the complete lack of guile in his expression. I don't know why I was so aware of its absence on that particular day, rather than any other, but it made an impression upon me then.

'The boat,' he said patiently, as though explaining something to a rather slow parent, which is, I suppose, how he must often have seen me. 'Granddad's boat?'

I laughed. 'I have no idea. Resting at the bottom of the lake, perhaps. It was all a very long time ago.'

'Was it at our lake?' he persisted. 'What I mean is, where did he go fishing?'

I was surprised that he didn't know this. But then, *I* knew only through Ella's occasional references to how her father's life had been curtailed by his sudden status as a widower, and by all the duties that befell a single parent, struggling to make some sense of his life. This is not something she would have discussed with Daniel – at least, not with that emphasis.

'Yes,' I said. 'It was at our lake. But around the other side, where Casey's boatyard is.'

His eyes were immediately alight. 'What are we waiting for?' he asked.

'Hang on,' I laughed. 'I can't drop everything, just like that, you know.'

He grinned. His expression said: why not? Why can't you drop everything? What is so important about today that it can't be postponed? And he was right.

'When can we go?' He was already on the move. I could see him poised for flight, eager for anything new.

'Aren't you waiting for Edward to come over?'

He shook his head. 'Not today.' He avoided my eyes as he spoke.

I made no comment. This was the other side of my youngest child, one that I was beginning to see from time to time: a private, secret side. When it happened, he would offer no explanations, and I had to try hard not to be too curious. I wondered, though, whether there had been some sort of a falling-out between him and his closest friend. Looking at him, as he stood in the middle of the orderly garage, his gaze fixed on the fishing rod, I had a strong sense of how darker moods might be lurking just below the surface.

On an impulse, I said: 'Okay, you win. Why don't *we* go, then, just the two of us?' To tell the truth, I was delighted at the increasingly rare opportunity to have my son to myself. I was aware, too, of how much I wanted to please him, to see him happy.

Ella used to make the motion of tying some string around her little finger and wiggling it at me whenever she observed exchanges such as this. 'I know, I know,' I used to protest. 'But what the hell? What else am I doing? And next year, once he is at secondary school, he won't want to bother with me at all. I'm making the most of whatever time we have left.'

Those words haunt me now.

Then Daniel had smiled the slow half-smile that made him look so much younger. 'Yeah?' he said, his voice rising. 'Really? We can go to the lake right now?'

'Why not?' I said.

He pointed at the fishing rod. 'Will we take it with us?'

'I think not,' I said. 'That one will need a lot of TLC before it'll be of any use to us. Besides, it's much heavier than the modern carbon ones – too difficult to handle. We'll just borrow one, along with a lake boat from Casey's. Now come on, before I change my mind. Let's grab some lunch from the fridge.'

Daniel tumbled into the car in his eagerness to get going. He dragged his rucksack after him, stuffed it between his knees. I already knew what it would contain: a variety of sketchbooks, all of different sizes, some pencils, and now, just recently, a palette of watercolours. 'Will I text Mum?' he asked.

'Yeah. Do that. Let her know we'll be back sometime around six.'

I often felt guilty when Ella had to work and I didn't. I sometimes felt a sense of embarrassment that I had an inordinate amount of free time. Not to mention a fixed and generous income every month: I was aware of how privileged I was. I had more than enough for both of us – for all three of us. But Ella always waved away my concerns. 'I don't want to retire just yet, Patrick,' she'd say. 'I love my work, and I'm vain enough to think I can make a difference. Besides, it's only twenty hours a week: that hardly counts as a coal mine.'

I used to wince at her idealism. I was more than cynical enough by then. In my late sixties, I no longer believed that anyone could ever make any significant difference to anything. But perhaps I used advancing age as an excuse. Truth to tell, I had always been a sceptic, a non-believer, a cynic – whatever the appropriate word is. Sometimes, I've even been honest enough to admit that such a suspicious view of the world became an admirable excuse over the several decades of my life for never doing anything at all that was either altruistic or unselfish. But I digress.

We drove to the lake together, Daniel and I – a matter of some ten or fifteen minutes. Old George Casey was sitting in the sun, reading a newspaper. His ever-present pipe was clenched between his gums. I'd never seen that man without his pipe. I'd even learned to understand the guttural tones that emanated from somewhere between the stem and the stumps of what remained of his teeth.

'Morning, George,' I said.

He looked at us, his eye lighting on Daniel. He didn't bother to conceal the frankness of his curiosity. Nobody in this part of the world ever does. It was something I'd had to get used to, once I moved here to live with Ella after we married.

'Is this the *gasúr*,' he said, more statement than question.

'It is, indeed. This is Daniel. Long time since you've seen him.'

Daniel stretched out his right hand, as I had taught him. He and George shook hands, gravely.

'Lord, but you've grown in the past couple of years. I believe you're a grand young sailor,' George said. I felt relieved that these words, at least, were clear enough to be understood. I could see Daniel's face already beginning to colour with embarrassment.

'I like to sail,' he said. 'Dad and I go whenever we can.'

'But ye prefer the sea to the lakes, I hear.' George scrutinized him, his air of amusement growing all the time.

'We like the lakes too. Dad and I go to the bird sanctuary a lot.' I could see that Daniel was at a bit of a loss. I could see that he felt he had failed in some way, that he had been unable to fulfil George's expectations of him. I stepped in. 'It's time to introduce him to the glories of fishing, George,' I said, full of cheer. I clapped one hand on Daniel's shoulder. I knew that George would understand this masculine language. 'And I couldn't think of a better man to do it.'

He nodded, accepting the compliment. I could see that he was pleased: we had now covered all the required politenesses. 'Not too many youngsters doin' it nowadays,' he observed.

'I'd like to learn,' Daniel said suddenly. 'My mum told me that my granddad Dan was a great fisherman.'

George's face lit up. 'He was indeed, and a thorough gentleman at that. All my family had great time for him.' He folded his newspaper with something like enthusiasm. He placed it on his wooden chair and anchored it with a mug that hadn't seen clean water in some time. Clouds of brownish scum clung to its insides. 'Come with me now and we'll get you started.'

Less than an hour later, Daniel and I stood on the pier on the southerly tip of the lake, right behind the island. George had been insistent. 'Try there first,' he said. 'More fish bitin' over yonder these days.' He'd snapped Daniel's life jacket closed, giving it a good tug downwards to make sure it was the correct fit. 'Away with ye, now. Make the best of the day. Clouds comin' in from the east later.' He grinned. 'Had some fellas here from Connecticut last week, day like this.' He squinted up at the clear sky, bare of cloud. 'I warned 'em, but they wouldn't listen. Came back like drowned rats, the three of 'em.'

I laughed. George always loved to tell stories that dwelt upon the foolishness of strangers – in his eyes, an amusing counterpoint to his own native wisdom. In fairness, though, about all things meteorological, George was rarely wrong. 'We'll see you around five, then,' I said.

He nodded. 'No later.' He handed Daniel a fishing rod and a small bucket of bait. He'd shown him how to tie on the spinners and I'd watched my son's delight as he stroked the brightly coloured feathers with his finger. 'Now, young man,' George said. 'Learn to be patient and quiet. And remember, when you feel the tug, yank the rod upwards. Otherwise the fish will get away.' He glinted at Daniel. 'Clever little bastards around here,' he said, with a wicked, toothless grin.

We stepped into the lake boat, its varnish glistening everywhere. I watched with pleasure as Daniel pulled the cord on the outboard and nosed the boat gently and accurately through the jetties. I could see George nod approval, and I was filled with a ridiculous pride.

'You've just passed George Casey's test,' I whispered. I am always conscious of how voices travel over water. 'Well done.'

Daniel nodded, his eyes on the island ahead. But I could tell he was pleased.

*

Just as I had been on so many occasions at the bird sanctuary, I was surprised all over again at Daniel's patience. I sat beside him on an upturned bottle crate that some other fisherman had abandoned. There were empty beer cans strewn everywhere in the bushes behind us. Otherwise, the place was deserted. I had learned over the last couple of years that Daniel and I communicated better shoulder to shoulder, as it were, rather than face to face. I was content to sit and watch and wait. I hoped that there was something, anything, that he might want to ask me. Whenever he did, I felt humbled at the trust he seemed to place in me.

It was, perhaps, one of the most perfect afternoons of my life. More and more, I had begun to hold close to moments like it, always aware, sometimes painfully conscious of mortality. It was, of course, my own mortality that exercised its grip on my imagination. Not my son's. Never my son's.

Finally, he spoke.

'Can we bring Edward next time we come?'

'Of course,' I said, easily. 'He's part of the family. You don't even need to ask.'

Daniel kept his eye fixed on the surface of the water. He moved the rod slowly from time to time, up and down, up and down, just as George had shown him. He'd had a couple of startled nibbles, but nothing substantial. We'd baited the hook at least three or four times already. I remembered George's words about the fish around here being 'clever little bastards'. At the time, I'd taken it as something of a slight. I thought I'd felt a sting in its tail: I didn't think it was the fish he'd been talking about. People around here often speak, as they say, out of both sides of their mouths. Particularly to runners, or blow-ins or whatever other names they give to people who have not been born and bred within the same few square miles. Now I wondered whether I had done poor George an injustice.

'Why are Edward's parents so poor?' Daniel asked suddenly.

I was surprised. I hadn't expected this. I felt the need to tread cautiously. I was sure, too, that this was a question of some significance – something Daniel had been mulling over. He rarely asked questions to which he hadn't already struggled to find the answers himself.

I stopped what I was doing. I left the sandwiches and fruit and cheese in my rucksack and gave him my undivided attention. 'Why do you think they're poor?' I hated myself for kicking to touch, but I needed to find out where this conversation was headed.

He shrugged. 'Dunno. I see where they live. And Maryam makes all their clothes. Edward says she has to – it's not 'cos she wants to. And his dad works really hard.' I could hear the rising indignation in his voice.

'Well, four children is quite a big family,' I said. 'And perhaps they are helping other people at home in India.' I paused. 'You know, sending money back. People often do that. People used to do it in this country, too.'

'Why?'

'Because family members where you come from might not be as well-off as you are. Maybe Edward's grandmother needs help, for example.' I remembered that Edward's paternal grandfather had died about a year ago. He and Rahul had returned to India for the funeral. 'Or perhaps some of his aunts and uncles. Family responsibilities can be very important, particularly when people live so far away.'

Daniel moved the fishing rod up and down, up and down.

'But they've been here forever; they came even before Edward was born.' He sounded astonished: eternity was measured by the span of his own lifetime. Twelve years seemed to him to be the sum total of the known universe.

'Yes. But sometimes people need ongoing help. The world is

badly divided, Daniel. Some people have too much, some have too little. I don't like it, but that's how it is.'

And Ireland is booming, I thought. Wealthy beyond what I'd ever dreamed as a child growing up in the grim forties, reaching adulthood in the even grimmer fifties. Some of the new prosperity had also filtered down to our remote haven. Super-markets springing up around holiday homes; unsightly blocks of apartments all around us; bigger boats on the lake. I never thought I'd see the day. I was glad to be at that stage of my life where I needed to have nothing to do with it all.

'So we're some of the people who have too much, then,' he shot back. 'We have a big house and two cars and lots of money.'

I sensed that we had reached the nub of the matter.

'Yes, we're very lucky. And in the scheme of things, you're probably right. Dan left your mother the house, so we don't have a mortgage like other people. And I have a pension from all the years I worked. We've had a lot of good fortune.'

'It isn't fair, though. Is it?' I heard his voice catch.

'No,' I said. I paused. 'It isn't. Life isn't fair. At least, not always,' I added. I thought I should try and temper a little some of the pessimism of this conversation.

'Edward has to work with his dad today. He said he needed someone to hand him the tools and to fetch and carry stuff from the van.'

I nodded. 'Does Edward mind?'

Daniel shrugged again. 'Don't think so.'

I continued to press a little. 'Do you mind that he's not here with us?'

'A bit.' He turned away.

I suspected that that was the end of our conversation for now. He would come back to it again if he needed to. I've always believed that Daniel had a strong sense of social justice.

I remember him stepping in to stop a child being bullied in the playground when he was about seven or eight years of age. I caught only the tail-end of the incident, and that by chance, when I arrived to pick him up after school. At that time, he favoured long, colourful T-shirts with birds and animals emblazoned across the front. They were certainly distinctive. We'd bought him several from a wildlife site on the internet that he liked to visit. As a result, he earned himself the moniker among his school mates of 'T-shirt Boy'.

That afternoon, just as I arrived, a small child was howling in the doorway of a classroom. His mother was crouched down in the corridor, trying to console him. 'T-shirt Boy', I heard among the sobs, and I froze. Had Daniel done this? Had he made this small child cry?

Just then, my son came bounding up to me, his face flushed, his sweater tied around his waist, his schoolbag flung over one shoulder. 'Hi, Dad!'

At that moment, the mother stood up. I gripped Daniel's hand firmly. But she didn't look angry. Her approach was a friendly one. And so I waited, curious to see what would happen next. 'Hello, there,' she said to Daniel, smiling at both of us. 'What's your name?'

'Daniel Grant.'

'They call you "T-shirt Boy", don't they?'

He nodded.

'I love the eagle!' She reached out one hand and touched Daniel's chest lightly. 'We just want to say thank you very much. I understand that you helped Anthony when some older boys picked on him.'

Little Anthony was hiccupping, the wire rims of his glasses askew on his elfin face. His cheeks were smeared with snot and tears. I felt sorry for the poor little chap.

Daniel shrugged. 'I said he was my friend, that's all.' He tugged at my sleeve, ready to go.

'Well, thank you. That was a kind thing to do.'

Anthony's mother and I smiled at each other and that was that.

When we were in the car on the way home, I told Daniel I was proud of him. 'That was a really good thing you did, son, standing up for the little guy that way.' I could see him shrug back at me.

'It wasn't fair. Jason an' James were pickin' on him. Called him specky four-eyes.'

Jesus, I thought. Does it never change? The casual playground cruelty brought back so many uncomfortable memories from my own schooldays that I was taken aback. 'There are bullies everywhere,' I said, catching his eye in the rear-view mirror. 'You did the right thing.'

And now, some years later, standing on the quay wall waiting for the fish to bite, Daniel's personal mantra had not changed. First Anthony, now Edward – and God alone knows how many others in between – things weren't fair.

Right now was not the time to suggest to Daniel that he cultivate other friendships. Ella and I had already spoken of this, but only to each other. We both loved Edward – he was a very lovable child – but we worried that Daniel would isolate himself by such an exclusive relationship. He needed others – if only to play second fiddle when Edward wasn't available.

My own memories of school returned yet again to niggle at me. After one particular incident on the rugby pitch – of which more anon – when I broke Pete Mackey's jaw, the other boys pretty much left me alone. For almost three years, I endured an isolation that I can still remember: an acute loneliness that accompanied me for the grim remainder of my days at school. I watched my son as he concentrated on the fishing rod in his hands, barely moving, his attention focused on the water below.

'Well,' I said, 'let's make sure we invite Edward for next week, and maybe another boy or two, if you'd like?'

But he never answered. At that moment, there was an almighty tug on the rod, and it bent forward in a wide, graceful arc, sweeping downwards towards the surface of the water. I leaped to my feet. 'Hold on tight! Pull the rod upwards, Daniel, and keep pulling backwards!' I rushed to his side. He was shrieking with excitement.

'Help me, Dad! Help me!'

I put one hand over his and together we landed the trout, gasping and wriggling, onto the flat surface of the pier. The fish flailed wildly, arching its back. 'Watch out!' I called, 'Or it'll throw itself back into the lake!'

I got hold at last of the gleaming, silvery body. I could feel the small heart beating wildly under the shiny surface. I watched the gills expand and contract. As gently as I could, I removed the hook from the fish's mouth.

'Well done,' I said to Daniel, and he grinned. 'Now, it's your call. We can throw it back, after we take a photo of course, or we can have it for supper. It's up to you.'

'Back,' he said, without hesitation. 'Let's do it quick, or it mightn't survive.'

He pulled his mobile phone out of his pocket. I held the fish as he took the picture.

'Put it back, Dad,' he said. 'Do it now.'

We got down on our hands and knees and I slipped the heaving body back into the waters of the lake. Daniel and I both watched as the fish seemed stunned for an instant, testing its new environment, as though it couldn't believe its luck.

Then, with one twist, one flash of its undulating body, it was gone.

'You're a fisherman,' I said. 'Your granddad would be proud of you!' I was glad to see that Daniel's face had cleared. None of the former anguish remained. Instead, his cheeks were flushed, his eyes bright.

'That was cool!' he said. 'Wait till I tell Edward!'

We sat together, each of us perched precariously on a corner of the upturned beer crate. We ate our lunch and talked of fishing and sailing and spinners and feathers. When we didn't speak, we sat in companionable silence. Afterwards, we baited the hook again and Daniel had another go, but I sensed his heart wasn't in it. He'd been troubled by the removal of the hook from the fleshy inside of the trout's mouth.

'Does it hurt them?' he asked.

'I guess so,' I said, 'although some people say not as much as you would imagine. They're supposed to have different nerve endings. But I don't know.'

He nodded. 'I'm glad we put him back. I'll be able to draw him from the photo. It's not fair to kill him.'

It wasn't long before clouds began to gather in the east, just as George had said they would. 'Let's go,' I said. 'I think we should make tracks before the weather changes. You'll have time if you want to cycle over to Edward's and show him the photo before dinner.'

We made it back to Casey's yard just before the first fat drops of rain began to fall. There was an ominous rumble to the east.

I have searched, over and over again, for some significance in all the conversations that I can recall with Daniel over the last two years of his life. I drive myself mad, looking for the answers, and all the questions that I might have missed. Once he went to secondary school, he changed. Not immediately, and not even all at once. But he changed.

Gradually, the child I knew became transformed into someone else. And not just into an adolescent: that would have been natural. As a father of three daughters, I was already inured to the slamming door, the mutinous silence, the outburst of temper. It was something else with Daniel, something I then did not know. But that is no excuse: I should have known, should have seen what was already so familiar to me from my own boyhood. I didn't. And now I have to live with that.

Would I have spotted earlier that things were gravely wrong, had Daniel been a girl? This, like so many other questions, is impossible to answer. And after Daniel died, I could not ever ask them of Ella. Of the two of us, I believe her burden of perceived guilt to be the heavier. She will never forgive herself. 'How could I not have known? How could I not have seen it? My own child.' She said this, or something like it, over and over again.

Nor will I forgive *my*self. But then, there is so much more that I have to feel guilty about, responsible for.

Things I may never be able to tell my wife.

Rebecca

'ADAM?'

I kicked the front door shut, not caring about the way it slammed. It sounded just about as angry as I felt.

'Adam, are you home?' A stupid question: his car was in the driveway; the front door of the house was closed but unlocked; the alarm was off. And the kids' schoolbags and gym gear were strewn across the hall. I could feel my irritation grow. I made an effort to contain it, although I was aware even then that I was fighting a losing battle. Clear, cold rage was lurking just below the surface, and once that ice-cap began to melt – look out, world.

Lately, Adam had been absent far too much from the bosom of his family. I'd been caught out several times, just like this. When he'd promised to do something or other with the kids, he'd turn up late or not at all. Or he'd plead busyness. It made me furious: that silent, unspoken *male* assertion that his time was more valuable than mine. I should have recognized the signs, should have known better. Do we learn nothing from our previous experiences?

He'd had a vacant look about him recently, even when he *was* home and, in a completely uncharacteristic development, he'd suddenly begun listening to music while wearing head-phones. Not the small, white dinky ones that the kids wear with their iPods – but huge, padded capsules that completely covered his ears and made him, in Ian's words, 'look like a dork'. I'd chided my son on a number of occasions for remarks like this. Secretly, though, I agreed with him.

Aisling came downstairs, already dressed for ballet. 'Where's Dad?' she said. 'He's taking me today, isn't he?'

'Yes, he's taking you and Susie. Did you remind her at school today that it was our turn to collect her?'

Aisling nodded. 'Yeah.'

I hoped Susie would be ready this time. I think she liked to keep us waiting. Good training for her future career as a real drama queen.

'What time will Dad be home?'

'Isn't he here? Maybe he's listening to music somewhere.' I began to make my way towards the kitchen, to dump the three bags of groceries I was carrying.

Aisling walked quickly beside me. She started tugging at my sleeve, her upturned face a mask of thwarted desire.

'Aisling, don't *do* that, please.' I lifted my arm, shaking her off. I eventually managed to get the bags onto the counter before one of them split.

'Dad was here earlier. But he said he had to go out.'

I stopped what I was doing. 'He what? Are you here on your own?' I was shocked. Adam had never done that before.

But she didn't answer. In a way, it was just as well; at least she hadn't been frightened to be alone. But I would certainly tackle Adam later.

'*Muuuum*, I'm going to be late.' Aisling fussed with the skirt of her tutu as I started putting stuff in the fridge. I deliberately turned away from her. I knew it would only be a moment before she put her hands on her hips and became disapproving. Ah. There it was now; right on time. I reached for the bags of lettuce.

'It's our *rehearsal*.' I didn't need to see the glare: I could hear it. 'Can't *you* take me? We're supposed to be collecting Susie at *five*.'

I could hear the whine I knew so well. Could hear it grow in scale and pitch. It set my teeth on edge, made my already packed evening look a whole lot bleaker. I had a conference call in half an hour here, at home. Nothing too taxing, but it would be a real nit-picking, way-too-lengthy discussion about new admission requirements for incoming students.

It was easier, given the five-hour time difference, to do that sort of work from my own study at home. At least I could take my shoes off and put my feet up; sip on a mug of coffee. I could even, from time to time, climb into a well-chilled, long-earned glass of Sauvignon blanc. I could do all of that, since the Americans couldn't see me. It was a relief, sometimes, to escape the disapproval – no, the tyranny – of their relentless political correctness. I'd wondered many times whether it was the nationality of the persons I was dealing with, or simply the nature of the work I did. I could never be sure. I just knew that my whole lymph system felt as though it was fuelled by irony in the blood: there had been many times when I felt like slamming the phone down on conversations to do with teaching conflict resolution.

The one thing I *was* sure of that afternoon was that I couldn't really leave the house, not at that point – I'd never be back in time. Besides, this was Adam's job. I pulled my mobile out of my jacket pocket, not even attempting to hide my anger from my daughter. I'd already tried him, several times, but his phone went straight to message minder.

'Adam? Can you please call when you pick this up? It's almost five o'clock. We're waiting. Aisling is going to be late.' I snapped the phone shut, tried to smile brightly as my daughter sulked. I hate to admit it, but she looked – still looks – a lot like me whenever she does that. 'Where's Ian?'

By then, Aisling had already started to hop from foot to foot. I remembered how I used to do that, too, particularly when I didn't get my own way with Dad.

'He went over to Philip's,' she said, her whole face creased into an expression of enraged pleading. 'Please, Mum, why can't we go now?'

I had one more tack to try, one last shot in my locker. 'How about I call Susie's mum? She's—'

'*Nooooooooooooooo!* We need to go now!'

I did a quick calculation. With a bit of luck, and a little less traffic, I might just make it. It didn't look as though I had any choice.

'Right, come on.' I hustled my daughter out the door.

By seven, I was anxious. Still no sign of Adam, no word, no call, no message. In the past, we'd often left notes for each other behind the boxes of detergent in the utility room. We figured it was the one place the kids wouldn't go poking around. But that was a long time ago: a different life and a different house. And although I searched with mounting unease, I didn't really expect to find anything. As I rummaged, I had the strangest sense of something closing in around me. Anxiety began to gnaw, somewhere underneath my ribcage.

I had made the conference call, put a hurried dinner together, collected Ian and swung by to get Aisling from Susie's. Not for the first time, I longed for all this transitional coming and going to be over and done with. Adam and I and the kids had been living in Dad's house – my old home – for almost six months now, waiting for our new place to be finished. My father had been generous, I admit it. Rather than sell our old family home – which he had been intending to do for several years now – he put his plans on hold. Mind you, I don't think that his heart was ever really in it: why else would he have delayed so long? But that's another story. Anyway, he offered Adam and me the house instead, somewhere to settle into while we were waiting for the builders to complete our dream home.

At first, I'd hesitated. I could see all the potential baggage that might come with such an offer. There is no such thing as a free lunch. And my father's anxiety to please was palpable – at least to me. But then, I have always been able to read him better than anyone else.

'It's yours, Rebecca,' he said. 'For as long as you need it. Plenty of time to put it on the market when you guys are finished with it.'

I thanked him, of course I did. Profusely. The house had all the blessings of familiarity at a modest rent. My sisters had no objection to this arrangement: I think they were both pleased at what they may have seen as a rapprochement between me and our father. And I could see that Dad hoped that this generosity on his part might, by some process of osmosis, ignite some more warmth into my relationship with his wife. I still thought of her as his 'new' wife. But of course she wasn't. Not any more. Ian was ten, so that's how long she and Dad had been married. It didn't feel that long – I don't really know what it felt.

Anyway, as things turned out, moving into my old family home didn't really change much: I mean between me and Ella. I just didn't like the woman. Her calmness, her supportiveness, her bloody-well understandingness really pissed me off. Besides, my life was busy. I didn't get to swan my way through it, working a mere twenty hours a week, surrounded by the gardens of Paradise.

Once we moved in, I made sure to abide strictly by the terms of my agreement with my father. I paid my rent like clockwork; maintained what needed to be maintained around the house; kept the gardens in apple-pie order. I was determined not to muddy the family waters any further.

By eight o'clock that night, when Adam still hadn't returned, still hadn't called, I was frightened. I couldn't wait to put the kids to bed. Something bad had happened, and I needed to find out what it was.

'Daddy's at a meeting,' I said, as we cleared the table after dinner. 'Silly me, I forgot.' At ten and eight years of age, my children weren't really interested in the movements of their parents: as long as we were around to fetch and carry, to feed and water, to dole out comfort and 'dosh', as they called it, they continued to inhabit their own self-contained universes, each one circling us, and the other. I tried to remember if my sisters and I had been quite so detached. I don't think so – but I can't be sure, at least not about Sophie and Frances.

At nine, the house was finally quiet. But my restlessness was growing. I phoned a few people, could hear the false brightness of my tone. Nobody had seen my husband. It struck me then – it had struck me before, I'll be honest, but not with the force that it made itself evident on that particular evening – that Adam and I had very few friends left in common. Very few acquaintances, even. Three calls later, and I had exhausted all the possible avenues of overlapping friendships.

I climbed the stairs to our bedroom. There was something different in the air here, something I could not yet put my finger on. I closed the door to the landing and opened Adam's wardrobe, aware that my heart had developed an uncomfortable rhythm. Even as I did so, I knew what I was about to find, what had been lying in wait for me to discover. His suitcase was gone. His new suits were gone, new shirts, sweaters. The only things that remained were those jackets and trousers that had seen better days.

All the worn-out stuff, I thought. It was a sudden almost blinding realization, accompanied by a bitterness that was unsurprised, even then. Even before I knew the detail of what had happened to me, I knew. And the feeling grew and swamped me, making me angrier than I had ever been in my life.

I found his mobile phone, stuffed under his pillow. I ransacked the bedside table, the chest of drawers, the filing cabinet in what had been his office. Empty. All of it. As though he had never been, as though *we* had never been. The only evidence of our fifteen years together was what he had discarded: a phone, some unpaid bills, his children. A life. Me.

I know it struck me that night with some force: the bitter irony of my situation. Here I was, an expert in conflict resolution, an accredited mediator. Here I was, skilful in guiding couples towards reconciling their differences, or in parting with dignity and structure. Here I was in my father's house: and my own husband had just walked out on me.

I fled downstairs and headed straight for the wine rack. I poured myself a large glass of red, even then warning myself that this was not a good idea.

Then I sat down at the kitchen table and rang my sister Frances.

Patrick

THAT DAY WHEN we went fishing at the lake is the last vivid impression I have of being on my own with my son. Perhaps there were other times – in fact, I am sure there must have been – but in my memory, so many of those were family occasions, rather than his and my shared ones.

One such time was when we went to France, to the Camargue, in 2005 when Daniel was ten. We brought Edward with us that year, much to both boys' delight. We had to be sensitive, of course, to Maryam and Rahul's other children: we were concerned that they might resent the opportunity that Edward had been offered. But it seems that Edward's position as the eldest in the family held some sway, and the matter was settled almost at once, and with no visible ill-feeling.

I admit that I embarked upon the holiday with some trepidation. Pushing seventy, I remained to be convinced that camping was an appropriate way for a soon-to-be elderly gentleman to spend a holiday. In the end, it was Daniel's excitement that persuaded me. I was, to be sure, relieved to find that Ella and I would be staying in a mobile home, with a proper bed. She had teased me beforehand. 'Oh, but Patrick, a tent will be so much *fun*! It'll bring you back to all your boyhood adventures.' My boyhood adventures were the last place to which I should wish to be transported, but no matter. The joke was on me.

The boys, however, did have a tent, pitched just outside our doorway. I remember that the evening of our arrival was punctuated by cries of 'Deadly!' and 'Cool!' and 'Wicked!' At around ten that night, I had to speak sharply to both of them, insisting that they temper their shouts and their enthusiasms: there were others around who deserved not to be disturbed. Nevertheless, Ella and I could hear muffled giggling and mimicry going on until well after midnight. It must be said that Edward was an excellent mimic: his version of my tone, and my mode of expression when I am irritated, was uncannily accurate. I enjoyed hearing it, and the lack of reverence of which it spoke. I did not like to feel that the boy was in awe of me.

'Be careful what you wish for, then,' Ella had said that night, laughing at me. 'I think that Edward has your number.'

We rarely saw the boys during that holiday, Ella and I. They swam, practised archery, played boules. They looked like a pair of urchins throughout: in cut-off shorts, grubby T-shirts, knees skinned and bruised. We went on day trips from time to time – the most memorable being to see the wild horses that are native to that part of the world. And we – Daniel and I – mastered the art of barbecuing at last, after several days of burned offerings.

I know that I wondered on at least one occasion, with a wry smile, what Cecilia might think, should she be able to see me, long fork in hand, turning sausages and steaks. A modern, twenty-first-century man.

I see those weeks as bathed in blue, shimmering light. I can still feel the heat of the midday sun, the intensity of well-being as Ella and I sat in the shade, reading our books, sipping a pastis or a white wine, smiling at one another as we heard the hoots of delight coming from the pool or the cycle track or the adventure playground.

On the wall behind me now, here in the attic, are some of Daniel's drawings from that time. The horses of the Camargue gallop across the pages, their shapes ghostly with the pastel shades that Daniel had chosen for them, their manes flying in the wind. Ella had four of the drawings framed for my birthday the following year.

Then there was the time we went camping in Italy, just the three of us, when Daniel was twelve – the year he finished primary school. It was his choice: he wanted to visit Florence. We took him there for a day. He seemed indifferent to the heat and the crowds and the discomfort of long queues at the Uffizi. He was captivated by the gallery. He seemed to glow on the journey back to the campsite. I'd never known him so quiet. To be honest, I was relieved. Florence had exhausted me. I dozed on the train for much of the journey back.

Daniel spent hours drawing in the days that followed, but most of what he produced there he tore up, despite our cries of dismay.

'Not good enough,' he kept saying. 'They're just not good enough.'

'Fine – but at least let me keep three or four of the sketches,' I pleaded. 'The human body is notoriously difficult to draw.' He looked at me then, paused in the midst of his act of destruction. At least I had his attention. 'If I keep even a few of your attempts, then we'll be able to see how much you've improved by the time you go to college.'

Daniel had already decided that the College of Art was what he wanted. We encouraged him, Ella and I. We were secure enough financially to help him make his dreams come true. We did not need to entertain the misgivings of others that something 'more sensible' or 'more practical' or even, God forbid, 'more marketable' might have been a better choice. We supported all of his aspirations in every way we could. Daniel finally did hand over some of those charcoal sketches to me, signed and dated with a flourish. *Daniel Patrick Grant. July 2007. Campsite at*

Siena. They are here beside me now, resting in the wide middle drawer of my desk. I am acutely conscious of their presence.

And then there was our last holiday together in 2009, an InterRail adventure in Europe, just before he went back to school that September, to begin his second year. Daniel and I had four weeks together; Ella joined us for two. But that was when everything changed.

That's not quite true: things had already changed. I sensed something of it even then, but I was unaware of how much, how crucially, how irrevocably my son's universe had turned. I should have listened, should have had a parental ear attuned to what I now know he was trying to tell me, on all those long journeys we shared. They were truths I had to confront later: I was not equipped to do so then.

The afternoon we spent in that hotel room in Madrid haunts me. It is no excuse to say that I hardly knew what I was looking at, that I hardly had the words to explain it to myself. My son, wrapped in a bath sheet: the scars that were suddenly visible as the towel fell away for an instant. The opportunity that I lost at that moment: an opportunity that never came again.

The opportunity that I never *created* again.

I regret that bitterly.

There were other things, of course, that occurred during those years too: wider family things that I have not dealt with here. I have not dealt with them because, as I have said, this is my story and they did not seem to form part of it.

However, I have discovered whilst writing this that 'my' story is extraordinarily difficult to separate from the myriad stories of others. Our lives are so intertwined that sometimes I am no longer certain what is 'mine' and what is 'theirs'.

Two years after Ian's birth, Rebecca and Adam had a little

girl, Aisling. She was born in August 1996. I was startled at how like her mother she was. Not just physically, although that too: but she later resembled Rebecca so much in the force of her character, the strength of her will, that I had the strangest sensation of having been catapulted back the best part of forty years. We did not see all that much of each other, Rebecca and I. Perhaps some of the heat had gone out of our estrangement, but it had been replaced by a calm indifference on my part. To be honest, once I had Ella and Daniel, I wasn't too bothered about seeking out the company of others, particularly Rebecca. Frances and Sophie and their husbands and children, along with Lynn and Steve with theirs, were regular visitors to us, and we to them. It was enough.

However, when Ian was ten and Aisling eight, something terrible occurred.

It was Sophie who told me. When she phoned, she sounded hesitant at first. I remember the call well. It was the week of my sixty-fifth birthday – March 2004. We'd been joking with Daniel about his dad being officially an old-age pensioner. 'I'm telling you this, Dad,' Sophie said, breathless, 'because I think you should know. Rebecca will probably be mad at me, but I don't care.'

My fatherly antennae were already on high alert. 'What is it? Is anybody hurt?' I could hear Sophie draw a deep breath.

'No. Everyone is safe. But Adam has walked out on Rebecca and the kids. He's cleaned out their joint bank account and all their savings. He came home from work yesterday afternoon and just disappeared. There is no note, nothing. She has no idea where he's gone.'

I swore silently. A phrase leaped to mind, unbidden. Even the worm turns.

'Where is she now?'

'At home – you know, our old home.'

'Have you seen her?'

'Yes, this afternoon. She asked me to collect Ian and Aisling. She doesn't know what to tell them yet. They'll stay here with us for a few days; it'll give Rebecca a bit of breathing space. And their cousins will be a distraction.'

I sighed. 'Right. Thanks for letting me know, Sophie. Say nothing. I'll go over straight away.' I hung up, pressing the heel of my hand against my eyes. Ella was at my side at once.

'Patrick – what is it?'

'Adam has done a runner. Left Rebecca and the kids high and dry. That was Sophie on the phone.'

'What *happened*?'

'I have no idea. Just that he's left, cleaned out the bank accounts. That's all I know.'

'Are you going to her, to Rebecca?'

'Yes. I said I'd go right away.'

'Let me take you,' Ella said. 'I'll drop you and collect you. You're as white as a ghost. I don't want you driving all that way alone. We can talk on the way.'

I was grateful that she didn't ask for explanations. 'What about Daniel?' I asked.

'He's on a sleepover at Edward's, remember?'

I did – once Ella reminded me. Lately, my forgetfulness had started to bother me. I was letting ordinary arrangements slip from my grasp, catching them only when someone or something jogged my memory. 'Of course. A lift would be great, if you don't mind.'

Ella smiled. 'There's a great bookshop not far from your old house. It even has a coffee bar. What's to mind? I'll enjoy a couple of quiet hours there. You can take your time.'

'Okay, then. Let's go.' I kissed her quickly.

She picked up her bag and the keys and we locked up and left.

Your house. Our old home. Ella and Sophie's words brought to the surface a whole sea of complications. Six months earlier, Adam and Rebecca had sold their substantial home in the midst of a rising property market. They had made, in Adam's jubilant opinion, 'a killing'.

I was happy for them to move into our old family home. Happy to put my plans for sale on the back burner. I had very little heart for it and Rebecca had been grateful. I have no difficulty remembering that. I do believe it meant a great deal to her to be back in her mother's space once more.

And I knew that I would never live there again – even if something unthinkable were to happen between Ella and me. And so I planned, eventually, to sell up and put something aside, to keep something back, just in case. I have always regarded *King Lear* as a particularly cautionary tale for a man with children.

When Ella dropped me outside, I walked quickly to the porch door and inserted my key in the lock. As I did so, I rang the bell with my signature three blasts. I wanted to give my daughter some warning of my arrival, but at the same time, I did not want to allow her time to shut me out.

Story of my life, I thought grimly as I stepped into the hallway. 'Rebecca?'

The door to the kitchen opened and she stood there, her face streaked with tears. 'Dad?' she said. 'What are you doing here?'

I was shocked. I have never seen Rebecca cry. Not even when her mother died. The last time I remember her in tears was when she was about four years of age.

I walked towards her, pulling her into a hug. 'I know what's happened. I'm here to see that you are all right.'

She resisted a little, but I pulled her back firmly. Ever since Ian's birth, I thought that Rebecca had softened just a little towards me. Not towards Ella, nor indeed towards Daniel. But at least the hostilities were no longer so open.

'What happened?' I asked. I could feel her fight for control and I let her go.

'Coffee?' she asked.

I nodded. 'Sure.'

She stood at the sink and I could see the effort it took not to break down. At that moment, I was reminded strongly of her mother. Despite Rebecca's American fridge and freezer, this was the same kitchen in which the events of that momentous Christmas Eve had taken place. When Rebecca sat, she sat in almost exactly the same place her mother had sat more than thirty years earlier. None of these ironies was lost on me.

'He's run off,' she said. 'My husband has done a runner with a blonde bimbo half his age. Not only that, he's cleaned me out. Current account, savings account, the lot.' She poured coffee for both of us.

I didn't want to ask, but I felt compelled to. 'Do you know the woman concerned?'

She shook her head: not denial, just dismissal of my question. 'I don't want to talk about it, not now.'

I could see the rage in her eyes. 'When you say he has taken everything – not all the profit from the sale of your house, surely?'

She nodded vigorously. 'Yes. Every euro of it. I haven't got a red cent. I'll never be able to complete the contract on the new house.'

I was filled with dismay. 'But that was—'

'Three hundred and fifty thousand in cash,' she finished for me. Her voice was flat. Without emphasis. As though such betrayal was to be expected. 'We lodged it in a savings account, waiting until our new mortgage came through.'

Alarm bells were ringing. I began, hesitant: 'Do you think, I mean – was any of this planned in advance? The sudden sale of your own house, the move back to the city – the whole thing?'

She nodded. Her hands gripped her cup, the same way they had on that morning when we'd met in a coffee shop and she'd told me I was about to be a grandfather. I saw the same dark freckles litter the whiteness of her knuckles all over again. 'I believe so. I think the whole thing was premeditated.' She shook her head, angrily. 'I trusted him. He'd been behaving oddly for a while, kept saying he was fed up living where we did. If we sold up and moved closer to the city, we'd make a better pension investment, and have a fresh start somewhere new. I thought it was a midlife crisis. Little did I know.'

My thoughts were speeding. I found it hard to comprehend such duplicity. I had once felt sympathy for Adam, because I believed Rebecca had worn the trousers, to use an old-fashioned expression. And perhaps she had. But all that was irrelevant now.

'Have you called the police?'

'For what?' Rebecca looked at me, astonished.

'He's cleaned you out. He has children he must support. You can't just let him walk away from his responsibilities.' I tried to keep the indignation from my voice. It was her decision, after all. I could support whatever she decided; but I could not insist.

'They were joint accounts. There is no comeback. And if he ever tries to come near his children again, I will kill him.'

I was shocked. But I believed her. I thought it best not to pursue that subject any further for now.

And so Adam disappeared without trace. To this day, we have heard nothing of him, nothing from him. He discarded his life and his children like a worn-out overcoat.

That evening, I felt a deep rush of sympathy for my daughter. Ever since, I have admired the drive and determination she has shown in providing for her two children. And she is still in our old family home – with her sisters' generous acquiescence.

Quite simply, she has nowhere else to go.

Frances and Sophie have had less dramatic lives. As I've already related, Frances married Martin in 1997 and within a year, had twin boys: Tom and shy, gentle Jack. And the year after that, Sophie and Pete tied the knot quietly: neither had wanted the fuss that had attended Rebecca's and Frances's nuptial extravaganzas.

Their three children, Pete Junior, Cecilia and Barry brought the grand total of my grandchildren to seven: steps of stairs, as they say, today ranging from Ian – now almost nineteen, to Barry, just turned eight.

And those are the children who will gather this evening in order to celebrate the completion of my seventy-fourth year on this earth. They are all, as yet, unaware of the nature of the twin 'celebration' that will be taking place in their grandfather's home. But that is not for now: that is for later in my story.

For it concerns that new and uncertain future, that whole sea of possibilities that I am not sure I have the ability to navigate, not yet. It is difficult enough attempting to deal, however imperfectly, with what has already passed; the problems posed by the unknown are even more daunting.

But back to this evening: I love all of my grandchildren, as does Ella. Nevertheless, there are times when I cannot bear to be in their company. They are all, each of them in their separate ways, a living reminder of what I have lost. Jack, with his violin. Cecilia with her piano, Barry with his precocious talent for art.

Each of them, in his or her own way, makes live again that September afternoon when Daniel stepped out of our lives and the world ceased turning.

Part Two: One Week in September

Sunday 20th to

Sunday 27th September, 2009

Maryam

MARYAM HEARS DANIEL's light, rapid footsteps on the stairs. He must have left something at home. She looks out of the kitchen window and sees where he'd propped his bike up earlier, its bright blue pannier a coloured shout against the brownish hedge. It had never grown properly, that hedge, never thrived. When she and Rahul had first come here, she'd had great hopes for it, despite its sullenness. But now, her husband doesn't even bother to trim it.

Maryam jumps, startled as the outer door crashes back against the wall. She sees the boy hurtle towards his bike. His white trainers flash against the dull grey of the flagstones. For a moment, she stands by the sink, transfixed. She tries to decode what she is seeing. Navy tracksuit; bright blue sky; silver-flashing bike. She has the sense, a familiar one, that there is some nuance here, some thrust of language that she does not understand. It is all too quick: like someone speaking too fast, careless of their listener, not waiting for her understanding to catch up.

Something must be wrong. In the time it takes her to wrench open the kitchen door, to step outside into the sunshine, the boy has already leaped onto his bike and even now is reaching the gate to the roadway.

'Daniel!' she calls, waving at his retreating back. And 'Daniel!' again. But he doesn't stop. He doesn't even turn to look at her over one shoulder, the way he always does as he says goodbye. He doesn't wave. Instead, he turns left, towards home. Slowly, Maryam lowers her arm. Daniel is a nice boy, a good boy. He respects his parents and the parents of others. She stands, watching the space where he has just been. It seems to shimmer in the sunlight, filled with his absence, redolent of his presence. Maryam turns back towards the house and goes up the stairs to her son's bedroom.

She'll have to be a little bit careful. Edward is changing. She has spoken of this to Rahul, but he has brushed her words away. 'He's becoming a man,' is all he will say. He becomes impatient at her probing, tells her to leave the boy alone. But she can't. Edward is her eldest, her firstborn; her son. How can she *not* want to know? How can she *not* want to understand the things that are happening to him? Particularly here, where everything remains so different, so puzzling, even now.

She knocks on Edward's door.

'Yeah?'

She hears the word, still hates it. 'Edward? May I come in?'

There is the faint sound of shuffling. She wonders what he is hiding from her this time. The door opens. Edward stands before her and there is an air of defiance around him, a gauzy light that she can almost taste. A kitbag, still unzipped, sits on top of his unmade bed. 'Is everything all right?' When he doesn't answer, she gestures towards the stairs. Perhaps more explanation is necessary. She says, in a tone as light as she can manage, 'It's just that Daniel left in a hurry, and I thought he looked upset.'

Edward shrugs. 'He got somethin' wrong, that's all.'

Maryam waits. She has discovered that waiting is often a good tactic.

But Edward turns his back to her and goes towards the bed. He zips his bag closed. The sound is brisk, final, like a full stop. Then he seems to change his mind, to offer her something after all. 'Daniel forgot that I have football practice this morning. He wanted us to do other stuff. But I couldn't.' He hefts the bag off the bed, slings its strap over one shoulder.

'I see.' But what she sees is her son's troubled face. His expression is shadowed with something that she cannot read. 'Will you call him later?'

'Yeah. I said I'd text him, but—'

She looks at him. She can't help it that her whole face is now a question.

'I can't be with him all the time.' Now Edward is impatient, on the verge of another explosion. Instead, he grabs his bag tightly and pushes past her. 'I have to go.'

Maryam stands back, leaving space for her son's anger to follow him down the stairs. He slams the back door shut behind him. She hears the metallic rattle of the bolt on the bike shed, the shriek as it slides back, then forward again. By the time she reaches the kitchen, her son has gone. Nonetheless, she watches anxiously to make sure that he has safely made the right-hand turn onto the road that leads to the school, and the football pitch. She still feels that he is way too careless of speeding cars. Just because there is so little traffic around here doesn't mean that you don't need to look out for the unexpected. She tells him this, over and over.

But she knows that he doesn't listen.

Patrick

MONDAY DAWNED AT LAST.

I watched as the dirty orange light finally crept over the horizon. The whole world was tainted, it seemed to me; everything had changed, changed utterly since the day before. My mind, my memory, my whole self was enmeshed in the endless replaying of the previous afternoon. The salty tang of sea air; the quick, racing terror of the drive home; the moment in my son's room when our future – Ella's and mine and Daniel's – fell away from us. It seemed to me then that I had never felt, never truly experienced loss in all its rawness, until that moment. Not even after the death of my beloved Cecilia. *This* was grief of a different order. I was unable to tear myself away from that single instant of discovery. I kept seeing it over and over again in my own private cinema. Each familiar scene brought with it the most exquisite pain: a new and refined form of torture that left me at times both doubled over and breathless.

On that awful afternoon – which, as I write, three and a half years later, still feels as though it was only yesterday – we laid Daniel on his bed together, his mother and I. We covered him gently with a blanket. He might have been asleep, but for the ghastly blue-tinged pallor of his face. Ella wouldn't leave him, kept one of his hands pressed between both of hers as though she could warm him back to life. 'I'm going to call Gillian,' I said. 'She'll know what to do. I've got to go downstairs to get her number, but I'll be right back. I'll make the call from here.'

But Ella shook her head. 'Outside,' she whispered, her voice already hoarse from weeping. 'Outside the door, on the landing. But stay where I can see you.'

I stroked the hair back from around her face. She leaned her cheek into my hand, and we stayed like that for several moments, looking down at Daniel. I needed to feel her touch. I was afraid that this loss would have the power to drive us apart. I wanted, above everything, to prevent that from happening.

'He looks more peaceful now, doesn't he?' she asked. I could hear the appeal in her voice. My beautiful boy, she'd said, over and over, as we carried him together to his bed, wrapping him with agonized tenderness in a blanket – as though he were a baby again.

'Yes,' I said. 'He does.' For one wild moment after we had taken him down, I believed – hoped – that the boy in my arms was not my son. I did not want to remember his expression. I was comforted now to see him begin to inhabit his own features again.

I called our family doctor, Gillian, who took over, as I knew she would. Trusting her with all that was practical meant that I could go back and be with my family and sit with them. We had perhaps an hour together, Daniel, Ella and I, or maybe a lifetime – I no longer know, time was a substance that lost its contours that day – before the ambulance arrived, and the police. I knew what was happening and what would happen next. I had seen it before. I was swathed in some merciful armour of numbness, otherwise I doubt that I would have been able to watch my ravaged wife.

Grief-stricken. Never was a phrase more apt. Stricken, felled, undone by loss. When the ambulance men removed Daniel's body – and they did so as gently as they could – I brought Ella into our bedroom and wrapped her in the duvet. She rocked back and forth, rhythmically, her occasional shivering cries like the whimpering of a wounded animal. I was afraid that pieces of her were breaking away, that her whole self had shattered. I put both my arms around her and gathered her to me. I remember being filled with an overwhelming need to put her back together again.

But she wasn't with me; not in any real sense. Afterwards, she had no memory of those hours – she still hasn't. We have often spoken of them since, at her request. I fill in all the details, over and over again. But those hours remain, in my view, mercifully blank: they are white, she says, and flat, just like paper.

The only thing she remembers with any clarity from those first two days is the moment when we had to discuss Daniel's funeral. I think I brought it up, as gently as I could, sometime on the Monday night when we were finally alone.

'No church,' she'd said at once. 'Absolutely no church: I'm far too angry at God.'

I didn't pursue it.

Gillian arrived on that Sunday afternoon within twenty minutes of my call. She embraced both of us, and left us alone with Daniel until the ambulance arrived. 'Sweetheart,' she said to Ella as my wife howled, her eyes unseeing. 'I'm going to give you something to help you rest, just for a couple of hours.' Then she turned to me.

'Patrick—?'

'I'm fine, Gillian. I'm fine. You just look after Ella. I need to call my daughters.'

She nodded. 'We'll speak later. Don't worry. I won't leave her. I'll take care of her for you.'

I went downstairs and made one more phone call, to Frances.

Within the hour, it seemed, she was on our doorstep, with Sophie in tow. Both of my daughters' faces were ashen. We held each other without a word. We waited until Ella woke, and they sat with her, holding her hands, letting her wail, or fall silent. From time to time, they wept with her, with me, the two of them embracing us and each other. I could see on both their faces the shocked realization of what had happened. Their eyes reflected back to her Ella's own horror.

'Why?' she kept saying. 'Why? What was wrong that we didn't see?' She looked dazed, her small face like the faces of the refugees I had once seen in South Africa: grey, bewildered, out of time. But she was desperate to be present, substantial again. I could see it in the way she spoke to my daughters, the way she struggled towards coherence. And I was grateful for that.

'What was it that we didn't know? When we left, he had already gone over to Edward's. We watched him cycle away. He even waved and smiled back at us. He was happy. What happened to make him do this?'

She asked these same questions over and over again, as though some meaning, some answer, would reveal itself to her by dint of repetition. Later, she would do the same with physical activity: walking around and around in circles, searching, always searching for the answers that neither of us could find.

Neighbours started to call, as is customary in this place. The unusual activity of the ambulance and the police car had alerted people for miles around, all going about their normal Sunday evening business. And so they came, offering comfort, whispered words of condolence, promises of help at any time.

I felt sorry for the elderly priest and the even more elderly minister when they came to pay their respects. They arrived together, shortly after Daniel's death had become public knowledge. Ella raged suddenly at both of them, and Frances and

Sophie tried to calm her. I had to ask both men to leave, but I was deeply moved by their distress and by the kindliness of their intentions.

'Forgive us,' I said, 'this is a most difficult time for me and my family.'

'No, Mr Grant,' one of them said – I can't remember which one. 'It is we who are sorry, not to be able to bring you and your wife any solace.'

In the end, Ella relented, and Daniel was brought to the local church: mostly because we had no resources to organize an alternative service of our own. I regret that. I feel it might have offered us greater comfort.

The school principal, Frank Murray, called, along with the school chaplain. Ella refused to see them. Once Frances and Sophie had left, she said that she would see nobody else that night. I continued to answer the door, the phone, the mobile. I did so until half-past ten that evening. Then I locked my front door and shut down all methods of communication.

I still feel badly, however, even at this remove, that I did not answer the door to Maryam. I caught a sideways glimpse of her as I came back down to the conservatory at one point, having lowered all the blinds upstairs at Ella's request. I know that she cannot have seen me: I stood well back from the window. It is always possible to see far more clearly when looking out than looking in. I was suddenly saddened by Maryam's arrival, I have to admit that. It cannot have been easy for her to come here. Watching her, all I could think of was how Daniel and Edward had been joined at the hip since they were babies. Nursery school, summer holidays, primary school: they were always together. Edward was the brother that Daniel would never have.

It was precisely for that reason that I did not wish to see Maryam; precisely for that reason that I ignored her ring at the doorbell. Part of me was filled with an abrupt, incandescent rage. Her son was still alive; probably watching TV at this very moment, his long body slung all over the sofa. I had a sudden, shocking memory of Friday – barely three days earlier – as he and Daniel battled each other in some computer game. They sat together on the floor of the TV room, their eyes riveted to the leaping figures on the screen. They didn't even hear me come in.

'Just one of the neighbours,' I said to Ella. 'We'll deal with them tomorrow.' She nodded, hardly hearing me, I think.

Rebecca did not call. At first, I focused all my rage on her. Look what has happened, I wanted to say; now are you proud of your coldness towards me, my wife, my son – your brother – for all these years? Now do you see what you have done?

But it was Sophie who reminded me, gently, that Rebecca was in the United States, on a plane home even as we spoke. For an instant, I felt sorry for her: hurtling through the glowering skies, unknowing. Then I gathered numbness around me again. It was easier than feeling.

'We've left a message on her mobile,' Sophie said. 'And on the answering machine at home. Don't worry, Dad: we'll phone whoever needs to be phoned. Just take care of yourself and Ella.'

I reflected bitterly that I hadn't been able to take care of us in the only way that mattered. After Frances and Sophie left, Ella and I sat together until well after midnight. We talked, wept, agonized. Any movement was painful: walking to the bathroom, switching on a lamp, entering the kitchen. Every activity was overshadowed by the loss of Daniel: he will never do this again; we will never see him smile again; he will never be here with us in this house again. The light has gone out of our lives.

And now a whole new day had to be faced: one that already felt menacing in its approach. It was just after six on that first Monday morning when I came down to the kitchen. Ella had finally slept at around four – a Seconal-induced slumber that would probably last only a short time. Gillian had insisted. Ella had refused at first, and I didn't push her.

'I'm afraid,' she'd whispered. 'If I sleep I'll dream about Daniel. And then I'll have to wake and find that he's not here.'

I couldn't argue with the logic of that. I'd had to stop myself several times from thinking about the terrifying emptiness of the next day, and the day after that. I focused instead on getting us through all the minutes of that first evening, one after the other. I became utterly intent on the present, albeit a present that was shadowed by the unspeakable vision of my fourteen-year-old son stepping bluntly to his death. What stalked me too was the agony of not having been there to protect him, to stop him. To understand him.

On that first morning after the world had changed, I came down to the kitchen, alone. I'd been afraid that I might disturb Ella, that my restlessness might penetrate her fragile sleep. Oblivion was impossible for me, besides which I felt the need to be awake, to guard my wife, to be alert to any further threat.

I had become aware – also sometime around four in the morning – that I had something urgent to do, something that I needed to finish before my wife woke. That knowledge had come to me as a shock, like an extra-loud heartbeat, out of the silent darkness of the bedroom. But once it had gripped me, I was unable to close my eyes again. I waited until Ella's breathing had steadied, and I judged that she was safely asleep.

I made my way, as soundlessly as I could, out of the bedroom and down the stairs. I opened the door that led from the kitchen to the back garden and made my way across the decking – some of the worn boards now treacherous with dew – to the lawn. Ignoring the crazy-paved pathway, I took the short cut and hurried across the grass to the gravel driveway. I could feel the morning moisture soaking its way through my inadequate slippers, but I didn't care. I didn't stop. The double garage loomed up at me, as though only now taking shape: emerging out of the darkness into the creeping dawn light, fully formed.

I hurried around to the side door – the one that cannot be seen from the house. Just in front of it, Daniel's blue bike lay on the grass. Its air of abandonment was intense, resonant. I felt it might speak to me. I lifted it to standing, wanting above all to get it out of sight before Ella saw it.

As I suspected, the old-fashioned iron key was already in the lock, the wooden garage door swinging open. We rarely parked the cars there, Ella and I; this place was for storage, for gardening bits and pieces, for, above all, Dan's personal belongings. Ella could not bear to throw out any of her father's things, and so we just added to them over the years. There was always the satisfying sense of the old man's presence: a growing one, as we put more and more into the safe keeping of his personal space.

New tools took their place among the old guard; the outboard from the *Aurora* took up residence there during the winter; boxes of old halyards and mooring lines populated the shelves, along with buoys, bits of sailcloth, fenders past their prime.

And then I saw it. The box in which I kept the ropes from the *Aurora* had been dragged from the lower shelf on which it lived and upended in the middle of the garage floor. The sight broke me. I stood, one hand on the saddle of Daniel's bike, unable to move either forward or back. From the tumble of knotted old coir and cotton and nylon, Daniel had chosen what was strongest. The blue polypropylene weave: the one with the most murderous grip of all.

A sob escaped me: a harsh sound, more bark than lament. I could see my son, see him kneeling on the floor right there in front of me, his hair falling across his forehead, his whole body curved over the box like a question mark, steeped in the urgency, the intensity of his quest. For this had to have been the decision of a single, singular moment. Something had propelled my son off his bike and into this garage, his mind already consumed with a sense of deadly purpose.

Edward. I had to speak to Edward. That was where my boy had been yesterday, before it happened. He had gone there, with his bright smile and his wave and his cheerful young face. What had happened there? Who had hurt him? Why had he chosen to do this thing to us, to his mother, to me? Had we not loved him enough?

Angrily, I kicked the box. Then I propped the bike up against the garage wall and plunged my hands into the tangle of ropes, rummaging fiercely to see if they concealed some clue, some hint, some secret of which I was unaware.

Nothing. I piled them back into their plastic fish-box and placed the lot back on the shelf. I glanced around to see if anything else should be concealed, anything removed before Ella came here, as eventually I knew she would. The concrete silence all around mocked me.

I locked up, put the key in my trouser pocket and made my way quickly back to the house. Ella must not be alone.

I put on some coffee and took a moment to still my trembling hands. A first, I told myself. Making this pot of coffee is your first normal activity since it happened. Daniel's death is already yesterday: you only have to focus on one thing at a time. Little by little. You will survive this because you have to.

Then I sat at the kitchen table, weeping silently into my hands. Another ordinary Monday was beginning to stir all around me. I could hear the occasional car drive past, imagined the breakfast scenes in the kitchens of our nearest neighbours, saw the daily domestic routines unfold – all those insignificant beginnings to each new morning that had forever been taken away from us.

And then I heard Ella's cry. I moved swiftly to the stairs, calling out all the time. 'It's all right sweetheart, I'm here. I'm here.'

But of course, it was not all right. Nothing was right. And it felt as though nothing would ever be right again.

Maryam

IT WAS AFTER EIGHT O'CLOCK on that terrible Sunday night when Rahul came home. I was worried: he had gone only to the local shop for milk and bread and should have returned almost immediately. I knew at once by his face that something had happened. We have lived together for so long that there are many times when we do not need to speak. Many times when we have found it best *not* to speak – something that Edward finds it hard to learn. 'What is it?' I ask. Rahul has closed the door to the hall. We are on our own in the living room.

'You must prepare yourself,' he says.

Immediately, quickly, inside my head, I locate my sons. Edward is in his bedroom – I saw him moments ago. Joseph and Stephen are together in their room. They are reading. David is asleep in our bed. Later, we will carry him to his own bed in Edward's room, just before we ourselves retire for the night. It is working, this distribution of space. Edward craves time to be alone. We respect it, Rahul and I, although we confess to each other that we do not understand it. But that does not matter now. What matters is that we are all here, together. There is no immediate threat. Whatever has happened has happened outside the tight web of our family.

'I spoke to Mrs O'Keeffe,' Rahul says, slowly.

I nod, impatient. Rahul cannot tell a story quickly. I must wait. Mrs O'Keeffe is the source of so much talk. Ella called it 'idle gossip' when I came here first: she wanted me not to worry about the things that people were saying. I was grateful for that, for the friendship more than anything. There *had* been some murmurings, expressions of discontent in this place when we arrived first. People found it difficult to adjust to the sudden foreignness that was growing in their midst.

We kept ourselves to ourselves very much in the early years. We moved quietly, cautiously among people. And although Mrs O'Keeffe is always anxious for news, I have discovered over all that time that she is not a woman who lies. And so I wait, because whatever she has told my husband has affected him greatly. His face has that drawn, grey look that I have seen too often in the past.

'Your friends, Patrick and Ella,' he says. I do not reply. They are *our* friends, I want to say, but even as I wish to, I know that it is not true. Rahul does not desire new friends. I do, and I am grateful that Ella came to me, welcomed me, us, and later our children, into this small community. 'There is trouble,' he says, and now he is not able to meet my eye.

'Daniel?' I ask. I don't know why. Perhaps because trouble for so many mothers has to do with our sons. 'Has something happened to Daniel?'

He looks as though I have somehow seen through him, that I have somehow divined his secret. 'Yes,' he says, 'there has been a terrible accident.'

My hand flies to my mouth. I sit. 'Tell me.'

Rahul sits down on the sofa beside me and takes my hand. This gesture of tenderness on his part prepares me for the worst, for something I could never even begin to imagine.

'The boy has died,' he says and I cry out. He leans towards me. 'You have to be calm. We will need to tell Edward.'

I stare at him. 'He has died? But he was here this morning, *with* Edward.' I struggle into standing again, unable to absorb what my husband is saying. I cling to that fact: that the boy was here, in our home, today. I want to feel that Daniel's presence in this house, under our roof, means that nothing so terrible could have happened to him – to anyone's child – in less than twelve short hours. I want to prove my husband wrong.

Rahul's grip tightens. 'The boy is dead. It seems that he killed himself.'

For several moments, I am unable to speak. 'What happened?' I ask at last. I can feel the dread build until my hands and legs lose all of their strength. I sit down again and lean back against the cushions. 'Tell me. Tell me, please. I will be calm.'

'There is no mistake,' my husband says. His eyes do not leave mine. 'The poor boy has hanged himself.' He shakes his head. There is sorrow in every line of his face.

'Oh, my God, my God, my God,' is all I can say, although I have long stopped believing. 'Why?' Even though I know that it is a stupid question, an unanswerable question.

'Who knows,' he sighs. 'Who knows.'

I think of Edward, upstairs on his bed, unknowing. I see Daniel's face – his smile as he waved at me this morning as he arrived. 'Hello, Mrs Maryam,' he said, his bike skidding to a sudden halt on the gravel. Rahul and I had agreed on this form of address. Mr Rahul, Mrs Maryam. People here find our surname unpronounceable. When Edward was born, I insisted on a given name that would not emphasize, above all, our difference. I wanted my children to belong. I had to fight Rahul on that, too, and I won. Edward *did* belong – does belong – his friendship with Daniel was proof of that. It gladdened my heart, always, to see them together.

I'd seen the boy's arrival through the kitchen window this very morning, and waved back at him, smiling. It was always easy to smile at Daniel. 'Good morning, Daniel. Welcome.' I watched as he propped his bike against the hedge, as usual. Then

I heard the back door open, and his footsteps on the stairs as he made his way up to Edward's room. Later, I would call them downstairs for some sandwiches, just like every other Sunday. Edward is always hungry.

But there were no sandwiches today. Nor was there any smile on the boy's departure. I remember that clearly. Something else is scratching at the door of my memory, too – not just that he left much earlier than usual, but that he pedalled away much more quickly than usual. That he didn't wave; that he didn't speak.

I was not easy with this. Something was not right. But afterwards, Edward, he would only tell me: 'I've got football practice. Daniel forgot, that's all.' I did not believe him, not fully. Edward's face was closed to me, but I knew he was not happy. Now I wonder if they fought, if my son said something unkind, something unpleasant that upset Daniel. He is a sensitive boy, a gentle one, and sometimes Edward's tongue can be sharp. But how can I ask him, now? How can I make him feel responsible for what has happened to his friend? I do not tell Rahul any of this. I will let these things develop in their own time, as they must.

And then I think again of Ella. Of those first days, when I knew little, understood less, about how things were done here. Smiles at the shops, yes, even some friendly hellos from many people, but no one to take us by the hand and show us what we must do. No one to welcome us into their homes. Until Ella. She stopped her car one day, as I was walking back from Mrs O'Keefe's with some shopping.

'Hello,' she said, through the open window. She was smiling. 'I'm Ella. My husband-to-be, Patrick, and I are your neighbours. Please, let me drive you home. I'm going your way.'

I wasn't sure, but Rahul wasn't there, so I took a chance. We shook hands.

'It's lovely to meet you,' she said. 'I understand that you and your husband have moved into the old Kerrigan place?'

'Yes, that is right.' I said. I was embarrassed – I believed that I sounded too eager. And yet some part of me also held back. I was not sure what was merely friendly, what might prove intrusive. Rahul was always warning me. 'Forgive me,' I said, 'my name is Maryam.'

'Well, Maryam, I'd love it if you could join me for a cup of tea,' was what she said next. 'If you can spare the time.'

I felt a great jolt of delight. Until then, I had not realized how much I longed for another woman's conversation. 'That would be wonderful!' I did not even try to keep the joy from my voice. I liked this woman, I wanted us to be friends. I decided I would not allow Rahul's words to influence me, not today.

We went to her house, where she made me tea. Such a beautiful house. I don't think I have ever seen such beautiful things. And everywhere was so calm. The garden, the little river, the house itself: it felt like a real home, warm, welcoming. It made me a little sad to think of the grey, damp walls of what was now our home, Rahul's and mine.

In the weeks that followed our meeting, Ella introduced me to people – but quietly, without any clamour. I met Mr O'Keeffe, who delivered people's shopping to their houses. I met Michael, the postman, who still delivered the post on his bike in those days. I met the Nugent brothers: each of them shook my hand with that slow, measured courtesy that reminded me, suddenly, of my father's elderly friends at home.

'Peter Nugent is the baby,' Ella said afterwards, smiling. 'He must be sixty if he's a day, and Robert and Peter are at least fifteen or twenty years older: but nobody knows for sure.'

After Ella's introductions, all these men and women spoke kindly to me; the men raised their hats, some of the women even sent me Christmas cards. I was very grateful – a gratitude I could not fully share with Rahul: he has different views about how friendship works in this country.

And so I had to fight with my husband also to make him come to Ella's wedding. It was the first time that I had ever felt brave enough to insist on anything so important. But it felt right, and I would not let it go.

Then, our babies came, Daniel and Edward. Fifteen years of friendship, of our children knitting together closer and closer. I cannot believe what I have just heard. I look at my husband, but his face tells me. I do not need to ask again, but I must. 'Are you sure?'

He nods. 'I met some people. Everyone is talking about it. It is true, Maryam. The boy is dead. And we must tell Edward.'

'I must go to her,' I say. I begin to cry. 'We must tell Edward together and then I must go to her. You must stay here and comfort our son.'

He nods.

We wait for a while. We talk some more. I dry my tears and try to rearrange my face. Then Rahul stands up and goes to the bottom of the stairs.

'Edward?' he calls. 'Edward, come downstairs, please.' Although he has raised his voice, his tone is gentle.

Edward appears at his door. He looks guarded, as though he has something to feel guilty about.

'Your mother and I need to speak to you,' he says.

Slowly, our son begins to descend the stairs.

Edward

I GO BACK UP TO MY ROOM and open the door. When I go inside I lock it and the key scrapes like it always does. I know that Mum hears me do it because she is standing in the hall looking up at me but she doesn't try to stop me not tonight. I know what they have just told me but still it feels like I don't know. Daniel was here this morning and he's not here tonight. He's not anywhere. But I saw him arrive on his bike. We sat just like this on my bed until I told him I had to go to football practice. I know I told him about it on Friday but he'd forgotten. Daniel's been forgetting a lot of things lately ever since we went back to school. This was just one more but we didn't have an argument not really. His face kinda fell in on itself and I knew he didn't like what he was hearing and that made me feel a bit bad. But I couldn't spend all my time with him could I.

First year was different because all of us from the old school pretty much stuck together but in second year that sort of stuff changes everyone says so. Football? he said. Around his mouth was pale, like it had got a fright. Yeah I said. I told you. He just looked at me and I felt like I do when Fathersir is about to give me a tellin off but then he looked away. Daniel did I mean. He said Oh. I started puttin my kit into my bag. Is it the Jays? he said. Will they be there? I felt hot but it wasn't the hot of the room. It was the kind of hot that made my hands prickle and it itched at the back of my neck. I didn't want him to ask could he come with me. They're on the team yeah. Daniel stood up then and took his rucksack off my bed. See ya. I didn't want him to go not really and I didn't want him to stay it all made me feel heavy inside. Yeah. See ya later – I'll throw you a text when practice is over. But he didn't wait for me to finish he just ran down the stairs and out the door. I heard the angry sound that his wheels made goin down the path.

I'll never see him again. The word never makes a sinking feeling in my stomach like the time when I was a kid and I tried to understand what eternity meant. I looked out over the roofs and the fields that went on forever trying to imagine what the end of the world might look like if you could get to it once you reached the end of all those fields. It felt scary and that's how it feels again now that he died and he's dead and he's never comin back.

I would have gone over to his this afternoon once practice was over but Mum had me stay and babysit. I texted him but he didn't text back he couldn't have come with me to football but Jason and James and Jeremy would've ripped the piss out of him like they always do. I was just happy to get a tryout for the subs that's all. I mean I like all the other stuff that Daniel likes but I like football too. It didn't mean that I'd end up calling him faggot and steamer and queer like the Jays did. It didn't mean that I was the same as them. I wanted to tell him that but the words wouldn't have come out right.

Mum says she doesn't know how he did it but I don't believe her pills maybe. I don't want to go to school tomorrow but she says that I have to. The school will know she says and they'll talk to us like that'll make a difference. I want to lie down on the bed and sleep and maybe not wake up for the longest time. I feel as if I've broken something and there are splinters everywhere. I saw my grandfather after he died in India and it didn't feel like this. I keep imagining what Daniel did and what he must look like now that he's not really there but I can't see any proper picture it's all blurry.

Even though I only saw him this morning I can't remember what his face looks like he was my friend. And I think I did something to let him down or he thinks I did something to let him down I suppose it's pretty much the same thing. He was my friend and now he isn't here any more. I don't want to go to school tomorrow. I don't want to go to school ever again.

Frances and Sophie

'HEY, FRAN, WHAT'S UP?'

I could hear the surprise in Sophie's voice. We'd only just spoken, maybe five minutes earlier, making an arrangement to meet up for a quiet lunch together, just the two of us.

I tried to steady my voice. I could feel it trembling away from me, just as my fingers had shaken above the keypad of my mobile phone, unable to land safely. 'Something terrible has happened.'

'What?' All at once, the air stilled between us.

'There's been . . . there's been . . . an accident. Daniel.' That was all I could manage.

'Jesus. How bad?'

I couldn't say it. My throat seemed to have closed over. I couldn't breathe. It felt as though I was choking. For a moment, I lived the full horror of what it must have been like for my little brother.

'Is he dead?'

The word, spoken aloud at last, seemed to unleash all the anguish that had built up inside me. 'Yes,' I could hear myself wail. 'Yes.'

'I'll be with you in ten. Don't move. I'm on my way.' A pause. 'Is there anybody with you?'

I shook my head, as though my sister could see me. 'No. Martin's gone to collect the kids.'

'Don't move,' she repeated. 'I'm in the car. I'm on my way to you.'

Ten minutes later, I heard her key in the lock. We've always shared our space like this: our houses, flats, rooms, going back to when we were small children together. The comfort of it is inexpressible.

And now, that other part of my self – the better part, I often believe – walks into the kitchen. I don't know what I would do without Sophie.

She takes my hand, wraps her other arm around my shoulder, pulls me to her firmly. She makes me feel the ground beneath my feet again. But I cannot speak and my eyes fill, over and over.

'What are you not telling me?' she asks.

I look at her. Shake my head.

'Say it,' she urges, gently.

And then, I am unable to stop. I tell her what Dad has told me, word for word. It is his voice that comes out of my mouth, not my own. I tell her about the dash from the harbour, the silent house, the boy in his bedroom. About the attic and the rope. The rope from the *Aurora*.

Dad's sailing boat: the one where all of our children, Sophie's and mine, had learned to master the wind and the waves. The boat that Daniel had learned to sail as though it were an extension of his own slight, strong body. I could still see my father's proud smile, hear his jokes about the next generation of sailors – a particular delight, as none of his three daughters had been the slightest bit keen on the sea.

Rebecca had always declined to be interested on principle – I think Dad accepted that. But he'd had hopes for us, for Sophie and me. As in so many areas of my life, I was too terrified to try, too scared to risk. Sophie had always been too busy doing other things: running marathons, training teams, that sort of stuff. It was either that, or she had her head stuck in some computer code book. Dad understood none of it – neither my physical fear nor Sophie's constant, sporty busyness. He particularly couldn't get his head around her technological obsessions. I felt suddenly, startlingly sorry for my father and all his unmet expectations.

I don't know why all of that seemed so important again on this awful evening. I don't know why I was so filled with regret as I sat across the table from my twin. It was as though my brain had lost its ability to filter thoughts. It gave access to every painful, jagged fragment of childhood guilt: as though, somehow, if I had been a better daughter – perhaps if we *both* had been better daughters – then Dad would not have been made to suffer like this.

'Oh, dear God,' Sophie says, slumping down at the kitchen table opposite me. Her face is paper white. It seems as though the skin has thinned suddenly. I can see the fine tracery of blue veins below its surface. 'Do they have any idea why? Oh, Christ, is that a hugely insensitive question?' She drags her hands through her hair, at that moment looking so much like our mother that she shocks me. 'I'm sorry, I just can't take this in.'

'I have no idea what happened.' I can feel my voice about to break again. 'I can't even begin to imagine what was wrong, nor can they. Dad says he – Daniel – had cycled over to Edward's before himself and Ella left this morning. He smiled to them, waved; all was well.'

Sophie shivers. 'We must go to them. Straight away. Come on. I'll drive.'

I stand, shakily. 'I need to tell Martin.'

'Call him from the car.'

'Does Pete know?'

Sophie nods. 'Just what you told me, about an accident. I've asked him to say nothing to the kids just yet, not until we get back.'

'I'll do the same,' I say. 'We can tell them together.'

Sophie drives. As I watch the road spool out in front of us, I have the strangest sensation that my brain has begun to unfreeze. Images of my father, of Ella and Daniel, begin to break over me in waves.

Daniel's thirteenth birthday party, some twenty months ago. He hadn't wanted one this February, according to Dad. In fact, he was so adamant about *not* wanting a party that I think my father was hurt. 'Come on, Dad,' I'd said. 'He's fourteen now. Way too cool for family birthday parties. He's growing up. Maybe he wants to do something with his mates.'

'I suppose you're right,' Dad had looked brighter, suddenly happier with that explanation, but I'd no idea whether I *was* right. Anyway, last year, we'd all gone, all made the trip to be with Daniel, with the three of them. Dad loved our visits, and I know Ella did, too. She and I have become very close. I suppose our friendship really started when my twins were born, and Daniel was just three. It's amazing how having children bonds you to other parents. I have great respect for Ella: she has her finger on the pulse of most things involving young people. Her insight, her empathy – and her patience – are all quite extraordinary.

Anyway, on that occasion, the occasion of Daniel's birthday party, Rebecca's children, Ian and Aisling, were there too, along with our two, Tom and Jack, and Sophie and Pete's three, Pete Junior, Cecilia and Barry. All of us arrived at Dad's house – Dad and Ella's house – within minutes of each other. And Rebecca had been gracious about attending on that occasion: there is, after all, something about reaching the teenage years that marks a rite of passage. I think we all understood that.

My father couldn't hide his delight. He has always been a wonderful grandfather, scrupulous in his generosity towards all of his grandchildren – he showed no favouritism.

He couldn't have: Daniel was quite simply the sight of his eye. No one else came near; no one else could come near. I felt sorry for Dad sometimes, that Daniel was so often taken for his grandchild rather than his son. It was a natural mistake: people never intended to be cruel. But still. It must have hurt.

Seven adults and eight children make a great deal of noise – or at least, they do in my family. We held the early afternoon bit of the birthday party in Ella's garden, on the patio; I often think of the garden as hers, even still, but Dad has really made it his own, too, over the years. He'd never been a gardener in his other life; his domestic duties had always been rather on the light side. But with Ella, all of that changed. He learned to cook; he learned to love planting and painting and just plain pottering. I thought it was great: a poke in the eye for all those people who believe that you can't ever change the habits of a lifetime.

That February day was a bright, sunny Saturday, all the chill banished by the patio heaters going at full blast. It was wonderful to sit outside even for an hour at midday: a sort of welcome-back party for the brighter days, the lengthening evenings that break the spell of winter. Even the garden obliged; we were greeted by a riot of crocuses and snowdrops. I found their colours cheering.

We sat at long tables which were set with the beautiful white embroidered cloths that had once belonged to Ella's mother. Years before, nervous about lemonade and chocolate stains when the children were younger, I'd suggested to Ella that she might want to remove them, to put them away safely. But she just smiled.

'I want to use beautiful things every chance I get,' she said. 'My mother would not have approved of these being stuck in a drawer. Dad always said so. I want to get as much pleasure as I can out of using them.' I was very struck by that at the time. It was as though Ella was guarding against a day when beautiful things would no longer bring solace, as though at some level she was aware that out there somewhere, in the not too distant future, tragedy might loom.

I hope that doesn't sound too fanciful, but I really felt something wistful in her words that day. I thought immediately of my father, naturally. I had often wondered how much Ella worried about losing him, given that he was so much older than she was. Twenty years' difference is a lot. Who wouldn't worry about it? That was what I thought then.

Little did I know. Who could? Who could even articulate such a nightmare?

At the end of the evening, just before we got ready to go home, Dad did his usual thing of hosting the kids' party pieces. We'd all gone inside again after the long lunch, a bit reluctantly, on my part. But although it was still bright, we needed to move indoors to escape the increasing afternoon chill. 'It's freezing,' Sophie murmured, nudging me, just before we left the garden. 'Aren't you cold?' She had begun to shiver. I rarely feel the cold, though: perhaps because my bones are way more upholstered than those of my slender sister.

Dad brought Aisling to the piano first and she played her party piece – Chopin's Prélude in E Minor, op. 28 no 4 – and very well, too. Ian was next. He was obsessed with Bob Dylan that year and played 'Don't Think Twice, It's All Right' on his brand-new guitar. He played it extremely well; he even managed to mimic Dylan's aloofness from his audience. A tall, strapping thirteen since the previous July, he was already well on his way to becoming a man. His physical resemblance to Dad on that day was very evident. When he finished the song, his face was flushed with pride. Daniel whistled and stamped his feet and I caught a sudden glimpse of the hero-worship that I'd never seen before. I was suddenly sad that these two had never had the opportunity to be close.

I glanced over at Rebecca then and saw that her eyes had filled. I felt an ache of sorrow for my sister. She had lost so much. I'd never really warmed to Adam – but then, he wasn't mine to like. No matter what way you cut it, Rebecca was lonely, although she was far too prickly to let anyone know that, even her sisters. Perhaps particularly her sisters.

My two, Tom and Jack, played the duet they had been practising. Trepak, from Tchaikovsky's *Nutcracker*. They acquitted themselves well, particularly Jack. I think we all knew that, while my mother's musical talent seemed to have bypassed her daughters, at least her grandchildren had it in spades. I was proud of all of them.

And then it was Daniel's turn.

Perhaps my memory of this party has acquired its particular luminosity because of hindsight: that because it was the last time all of us were together – Dad used to take Ella and Daniel away skiing every Christmas – it has acquired a clarity, a kind of brittle significance that other gatherings have not.

Do I remember it like this just because Daniel is no longer with us? I don't think so. I know that I was already aware on the day that it was, in some way, remarkable. That it would be memorable in ways that other gatherings were not. I don't know how best to express it. All I do know is that Daniel's playing on that day moved me in a way I cannot explain.

I watched as he tucked the violin under his chin, expecting some of the scraping and grinding that I used to hear from my neighbour's daughter, until she abandoned music completely – to my considerable relief. I'd heard Daniel play a few times before, of course, at other family gatherings. Children's pieces mostly, whose names I have forgotten. I didn't pay all that much attention: there was no need to. His was just one more party piece among so many others.

But there was a different quality to him, and to his playing, on that day. He looked comfortable, confident, and I have to say that I wondered whether this was the self-possession of an only, treasured, doted-upon son, accustomed to praise, rarely criticized, unaware of the cut and thrust of sibling rivalries.

Within moments, though, I had the grace to feel ashamed of myself. Daniel played with a sureness – an authority – way beyond his years. His tone was clear and true, his fingering faultless, his stance that of a true musician. He played Scarlatti's Arioso in D Minor – not a particularly challenging piece – but he played it with an access to vulnerability, to loss, that moved me deeply.

This was not just the technical perfection of the well-schooled; this was the nuanced playing of a mature, emotionally articulate, *experienced* musician. I had difficulty reconciling the slight, animated boyish figure that stood in front of me, with that unruly lock of hair – so like my father's, falling across his freckled forehead – with the emotional depth and range of the music that I was hearing. I may not play an instrument with anything other than passing competence, but my mother taught me well. I know how to recognize the real deal when I hear it.

When he had finished, we clapped, we hooted, we whistled, we cat-called. Daniel took a bow, his mischievous grin lighting up his face.

'Aw, Aunt Frankie,' he said, when he saw my tears. He walked into my embrace and we hugged for quite a time. I liked the fact of how unselfconscious he was – he didn't shy away from my emotion, nor from my arms. He called each of us 'Aunt' – Rebecca, Sophie, me. I'm not sure why. I think it might have been his way of being respectful – or perhaps our first names embarrassed him: their use might have forced him to remember our slightly unconventional relationships. I know from my own two sons, that young boys – in particular, I think – are terrified of being seen as different from their peers. All they want is to be the same as everyone else.

That is, until they are older. Then all they want is to be maddeningly different from everyone else.

'Daniel, that was truly wonderful. Your grandma Cecilia would be so proud of you.' The moment I said it, I embarrassed myself into silence. I'd got the relationships horribly wrong. But Dad was smiling hugely, as was Ella. I realized at once that the last place Daniel would have got his musical talent was from my mother – there was not even the most tenuous of blood relationships between them. But, right at that moment, I'd forgotten that. I think that on that day, more than at any other time in the previous thirteen years, Daniel felt, truly, like my brother. Perhaps that is why I remember it all so well.

'Thanks, Aunt Frankie. Glad you liked it.' He was a boy again, shy, bashful.

Ella joined us. 'Well done, young man,' she said. 'That was the best I've heard it.'

He looked at her, impish, his head to one side. He'd had that cheeky expression even as a baby. 'Worth all the times you said it made your teeth shriek?'

Ella laughed. 'Every last one of them.'

'Golden Boy', Martin said that night as we drove home. My husband is not a malicious man – quite the contrary. There isn't a nasty bone in his body. No, he said it with admiration, with a kind of reverence that has also stayed with me.

I think everybody saw on that night – with varying degrees of resentment and affection – a boy who had it all. Love, security, financial certainties, talents to burn. Daniel had been persuaded by Dad to show us his black-and-white photographs: the ones of birds and wildlife that had just won him first prize in the local photographic club competition. That led the conversation back to the camera, which in turn led us back to the photo essay, which led back to the school prize. And yet all of it was without bluster, without even a hint of youthful arrogance. If anything, Daniel was a bit embarrassed, his face flushed an unaccustomed pink. 'Come on, Dad,' he said. 'Leave it.'

I have my own photograph of that instant: the one that went 'click' and filed itself away in that part of my brain called memory. Dad, beaming. Ella, surrounded by every single one of the kids – she'd always drawn them to her. Aisling and Jack in particular used to stick to her like glue – had done so ever since they were small children. She was a real child-magnet: and she always had time for each of them.

Martin and Pete, I remember, were leaning against the wall, their hands in their pockets. And Sophie stood, watching it all. I know because I caught her eye. At exactly the same moment, we looked over at Rebecca. She was stiff, unyielding in the over-sized armchair, refusing to sink into its embrace. For a moment, her face was suffused with loss and longing, and something else; I don't think it was bitterness, not any longer. But something was there, just for a moment, that same moment that Sophie and I caught each other watching her. If I didn't know my older sister as well as I do, I'd have sworn that what I saw was guilt.

Then Ian, Rebecca's lad, broke the brief silence – a silence that had not yet become uncomfortable, but was probably about to.

Ian said loudly: 'Jaysus, Daniel. You've just made it impossible for the rest of us. Thanks a lot, man.'

All of us, adults and children alike, dissolved into raucous laughter. Even Rebecca, who looked both surprised and amused. It was perfect, I thought. Ian's response was both a rueful acknowledgement of Daniel's many talents, and at the same time a celebration of them. But above all, there was a palpable sense of 'us', shared by all the kids – Daniel, the uncle who was pretty much the same age as his nieces and nephews – was also one of them: equal, independent, and part of the necessary conspiracy against their parents' expectations.

And that birthday celebration is the last time all of us were together.

I've quizzed Tom and Jack as gently as possible over the past few years about what might have gone wrong for Daniel, but they have been unforthcoming.

I know one thing, though: it was something outside the embrace of that home that Dad and Ella had created. It had to be. Nothing else made any sense at all.

Rebecca

I LISTENED TO FRANCES'S voicemail for the third time. I had the oddest feeling that this was a language that was unfamiliar to me: a grammar that was foreign and unforgiving. I could understand each disparate word, knew each individual meaning, but the message made no sense. I was tired, jetlagged, but that couldn't be the whole reason. Some part of my brain was refusing to process what it was receiving. And underneath that refusal was the simmering of something I'd been feeling for some time, but had chosen to ignore.

It was the onset of an obscure and irrational feeling of culpability. I don't know when it started. All I know is that that morning, I immediately felt as though I was responsible for whatever ill had just befallen my father. And this *was* bad news regarding my father and Ella, there was no doubt about that. The urgency of Frances's tone left me in no doubt about that.

I listened to the message again. I was torn between rushing to my car and switching off my phone. But I could do neither. I was paralysed. I stood in the middle of the crowded arrivals terminal, bodies pushing their irritable way past, mothers and fathers managing cases and children and lack of sleep. I called Frances.

'Rebecca, thank God.' My sister's voice was harsh with relief. 'What on earth has happened?'

And she told me, her voice choked, her words disconnected, fractured, but their meaning all too clear.

'Jesus Christ,' I said. 'When?'

As if the timing made any difference. But it was one of those details I needed, something solid to anchor me to what I was hearing. To help me construct some sort of a reality that I might begin to comprehend.

'God almighty,' I said. I wanted to see my own two children, to hug them with all my strength, to feel their hard young bodies close by my side, where I could keep them safe. Protecting them felt more and more urgent in the face of what I was hearing. I did not want them to end up like Daniel.

'What should I do?' I could hear my words, somewhere outside my head; I barely realized that I had spoken them.

'You must go to Dad and Ella at once, Rebecca. That's all that matters. Everything else is irrelevant.'

I was grateful for the simplicity of her response. My ever-reliable sister: she always knew the right thing to do. In fact, she and Sophie always seemed to know the right thing to do. Sometimes they appeared to me as two halves of the same whole. I'd always envied them their closeness.

'And don't worry about Ian and Aisling,' Frances said now, answering my next question before I'd asked it. 'They're here with us. Martin went to collect them as soon as we heard. We felt they should be here with their cousins, with all of us.'

I almost wept. I was filled with horror that my children had been with a childminder when Daniel died. A perfectly nice and responsible and competent Polish girl, but nonetheless. At fifteen and thirteen, my children lived very independent lives. Magda was there when I couldn't be. She filled in all the practical spaces that I left in my wake. But right now, none of that mattered. The only thing that mattered was that I hadn't been there for them, there with them.

At a time like this, family was what counted above everything. It was probably the first time I had articulated that thought to myself quite so clearly. I know that for many years I'd lived on the defensive. Who needed Adam? I could do very nicely without him. My alternative arrangements were impeccable. Who needed extended family? I could manage quite well on my own, thank you all the same. I had no need of a suffocating network of support.

But right now, I had never been so grateful to have sisters. 'Thank you, thank you. I am so glad you did that, so glad. Can I speak to them?'

'It's not even seven o'clock, Becky. They're fast asleep.' Frances's tone was kind, reasonable. But I could hear the question in it. 'I'll wake them if you like, but—'

'No, no,' the words came out as a sob. My sister's use of my name – my childhood, affectionate name – had touched a nerve. 'Leave them be. Tell them I'll call them later.'

'Of course. You drive carefully – do you hear me? And come here afterwards. Don't be on your own. I mean it. We're here, anytime.'

I nodded. I could no longer speak. But it was as though Frances could see me.

'Okay, then,' she said. 'See you later.'

In a dream, I started to make my way towards the bus that would take me to the car park. But I couldn't remember where I had left the car: not the bay, not the number, not even the colour code. I rummaged for the ticket in my purse, hoping that I'd written down the information I needed to retrieve a car I wasn't even sure I'd recognize.

And suddenly, I was weeping. I stood right there in the concourse, made no attempt to hide the tears, no attempt to brush them away. I didn't want anybody to stop and speak to me – wouldn't have known what to say if they had.

But no one did.

I found the ticket at last, folded and placed into the compartment of my purse where I always kept it. But it was as though I had never seen it before; as though I had never seen anything like it before. The world looked different to me, and everything in it. Everything now had a sharper edge, a more defined outline. Things stood out against each other, as though each object was discrete, separate unto itself; as though the world had suddenly lost all coherence.

It felt like hours later when I finally made my way out of the car park and into the tangle of Monday morning traffic.

It seemed to me, as I pulled into the driveway, that Ella's house was shrouded in silence – or something that felt like silence. The air was extraordinarily still, as if everything here had stopped suddenly and was holding its breath. I had always thought of this house as Ella's – my father merely a temporary resident there. Frances and I had spoken about this once, as I recall. But our views on that, as on most things, diverged significantly over the years.

After Daniel arrived, it became his house, too. But never my father's. Not in my eyes. He had always looked out of place there, on the occasions when I'd felt forced to attend those family get-togethers arranged by my sisters.

'The children should know each other, should grow up together.' Frances had been firm. 'Just don't stand in their way.'

I hadn't. But my job meant absences over which I had no control – particularly once Adam had fled the coop, and I had two young children to look after and a financial meltdown to repair. Frances and Sophie held frequent gatherings of their own, and Ian and Aisling slotted into their family routines easily, happily. Both my sisters had offered second homes to my children, homes where they felt loved and welcomed. It was some kind of solace for their father's abandonment of them.

But I found it hard to be surrounded by all that happy family stuff. Each gathering was a reminder of what I no longer had – perhaps had never had. Not in my own parental home, nor in the home I later made with Adam. And once Adam left, I knew with some certainty that I would never have the chance of it again, would never trust a man again.

My husband left a huge absence on his departure. Not just the lack of his presence; hindsight has perhaps taught me that things were never as I believed them to be between us. The biggest, most hurtful chasm is the one he left in his children's lives – even if they don't fully understand that yet. They are, and always have been, fatherless.

I have begun to believe that even a father to fight with is better than no father at all.

I'll never forgive Adam. For myself, I don't care any more. Don't care that he replaced me with a younger model: a colleague of his, the exotic María Isabel, who had visited our home on several occasions, as we had visited hers. I don't care that he became a walking, talking cliché in his fortieth year. I don't even care that he wiped me out financially. I've recovered from all that.

But not to be a father to your children: that is unforgivable.

I parked in Ella's driveway, trying to still the uncomfortable rhythm of my heart. It had begun to pound just as soon as the house came into view. I noted that all of the blinds were up, the windows open. So my father and his wife were at home, then. And awake. I took several deep breaths before I opened the car door and stepped out onto the gravel.

Whatever I might accuse my father of in this new family of his, I could not for a moment doubt his devotion to his son. Standing there on the threshold of my father's other home, I regretted above all the bitterness I had allowed to grow and fester between us. I felt the width and depth of the breach that had existed between us for so many years. And I knew that it was of my own making.

Nothing but sheer willpower enabled me to take the dozen or so steps to his door. My legs felt weak, rubbery, as though they might give up on me at any moment. Apart from the physical sensation, I was not at all sure of my welcome.

I rang the bell.

It was he who answered. We stood looking at each other for a moment, he blinking in the morning sunlight, I trying to make out his face, stark against the shadows of the hallway.

'Rebecca,' he said.

'Dad, oh, Dad,' I stepped towards him, my arms out, my courage wavering. For an instant, I thought he was going to turn away from me. Everything seemed to fall away from me in that moment. I saw a stooped and elderly man, a face grey with grief, unruly white hair: I realized with a shock that my father was no longer as I had envisaged him. The strong, handsome, robust fifty-something-year-old that had for so long been embedded in my memory, my imagination – call it what you will – had somehow been transformed into this frail and vulnerable old man. The realization made me falter. It was as though my feet were planted in something unyielding, something that stopped me from moving forward. I could no longer walk towards him, no longer pull him into my embrace.

'Rebecca,' he said again, and this time, he moved towards me. 'I am so glad you are here.'

The simple generosity of his welcome scooped out my insides. I felt shame, sorrow, horror – there seemed to be no end to the emotions that choked my words, blinded my eyes.

'Come inside.' He drew me in after him. I stepped into the cool hallway, and there, at the end, stood Ella.

It is here that things get a little blurred. I am no longer sure of the sequence of events – I just know that they all happened. One moment, I am standing there, aware of Ella dressed in something long and white; another moment finds me on the floor; another feels my body rained with blows. And all the while a high, chill keening fills the space around me – a keening that is suddenly accompanied by a deeper note, a bass note that sounds with increasing frequency: my father's voice. And then I can make out Ella's words.

'Are you happy now? You don't need to hate us any more! Daniel's gone, gone! He's dead! Have you got what you wanted at last?'

With each word, Ella's small hands flail against my chest, my head, my face, while my father kneels, trying to grapple her into quietness. But I don't resist: not even the instinctual raising of hands to shield my face. Her words meet something inside me – that growing sense of culpability – and I welcome the violence of her attack.

'SShhh, sshhh, darling, darling,' my father soothes, his hands finally around his wife's shoulders. 'It's all right, it's all right. I have you.'

I watch as she collapses into him, how her grief howls through her, through both of them, shattering the shroud of silence all around us.

It is much later, and the three of us are sitting in the conservatory. The beauty of sunlight on the green garden outside is obscene. There is no other word for it. Its brilliance makes me ache. I don't even want to imagine what these two people before me must be feeling.

My father pours coffee.

I hold Ella's hand. I haven't let her go since she sobbed herself into exhaustion on the floor of the hall. I can't remember what I said after she had collapsed into my father's arms – I know I begged her to forgive me, my words tumbling over the years like balm. She clutched at me, and the three of us stayed like that for some time, holding onto each other, letting old hurts make way for new.

It was my father who first extricated himself, finally, gently, giving us all space to get to our feet. 'Come, let's have a seat in the conservatory and we can talk. Can you stand, sweetheart?'

Ella nodded. The tenderness between them made my eyes fill. 'Yes,' she said. But she stumbled and I gave her my hand, quickly, without thinking. She hesitated, only for a second, and took it. I cannot describe the welling of gratitude that accompanied her simple, forgiving gesture. It was not blind instinct that made her hold onto me. She had considered it, and made her choice, bringing me back into the circle of family. At that moment, I hated myself.

We made our way slowly towards the back of the house.

And now, I stroke her small, pale hand. I feel the smoothness of the skin, see the glint of gold on her finger, the bright arc of her nails. 'Tell me what happened,' I say. 'I want to know – if you can bear it.'

And together, they tell me. Of an ordinary Sunday – aren't they always? – a premonition, a journey. Of the unthinkable sight of their son, swaying forever out of their reach. And of why.

Ella shakes her head. 'I don't know – neither of us knows.' She looks towards my father as she says this. He nods assent, although there is something in his eyes that makes me remember to speak to him afterwards, alone. There is something he is not saying. I know him well enough to know that much.

And so we sit, until well into the afternoon. There are phone calls and visitors and things to be attended to. All the paraphernalia of loss.

In the afternoon, at my father's insistence, I sleep. 'You're not driving home having been up all night,' he says. 'I've called Frances and she and Martin will come and collect you. Martin will drive your car home. Frances will take you. I'll have no argument.'

I nod. I hope that my sister will know not to bring our children. I feel guilty, glad and relieved and horribly guilty all over again that all my sisters' children – and mine – are safe.

I walk out to the car to take some things from my suitcase. Then I make my way to the spare room.

'Let me know if you need anything,' Ella says.

I simply don't know what to say.

Despite myself, I sleep. And I dream – of strange and surreal things. Of car parks and trees crying and white dresses and Daniel's bright smile.

Before I drift off, I remind myself again to speak to my father about whatever it is he is hiding behind the tired dullness of his eyes.

Patrick

WE FINALLY GOT ELLA to lie down, Rebecca and I, sometime around five that evening. Almost immediately, Frances and Martin arrived. They'd parked on the roadway outside and made their nearly silent way across the gravel on foot to the front door.

'We thought Ella might be asleep,' Frances said. 'Rebecca texted us to say that she was resting.'

'Yes,' I said. 'Just in the last twenty minutes or so.' I could no longer stifle the deep sigh that now escaped me. I felt suddenly drained of energy, hardly able to keep myself upright. I began to tremble all over again and shoved my hands into my trouser pockets.

I didn't think I could absorb any more sympathy. I felt that I would overflow, emptying myself out, if I had to suffer any more kindness.

'Dad?' Frances said. She stood by my side and placed one hand on my arm. 'I know all you want to do is to look after Ella. But you're exhausted. Please, let us take care of you.'

I know that I grimaced. 'I'm okay,' I said. 'I'm going to lie down myself now for a while.' I tried to smile at her. 'But thank you.'

'We'll be back tonight, Sophie and I,' she said. 'Call if you need us to bring anything.'

I nodded. What could I possibly want that anyone could give me now?

Rebecca came over and put her arms around me. 'I'll be back again tomorrow.' She kissed me on the cheek. I could hear the break in her voice. 'Just as soon as I've spent time with the kids.'

At her words, a silence fell. A brief, appalled silence.

I nodded again. Speech had temporarily deserted me.

They left together, quietly. I welcomed the now-blossoming quietness in the house, a poignant stillness that grew once the door had been closed. I wanted, needed, to be on my own, just for a while.

I had been taken aback at Rebecca's arrival earlier. I had not expected that. In fairness, she had been in the air when the blow struck: she knew nothing of her brother's – or half-brother's, as she used to insist – death, until she'd picked up her phone messages. But at least she lost no time in getting to us; she simply turned the car round at the airport and drove in our direction instead.

When I saw her at the door, I hesitated. I admit that. I was angry. Angry at her treatment of my son, my wife. Angry at all the wasted years between us. And then I was sad. Sad that it had taken a tragedy of unspeakable proportions to effect even the shakiest of reconciliations between us.

I stepped towards her and we embraced. I think I told her I was glad that she was here. I hope I did.

I know that Rebecca has suffered greatly. I know that her own life has not been as she would have wished it to be. And I know that, by the time she arrived back into my newly bereft existence, I had learned almost not to care any more.

Ella flew at her at once, unable to contain her rage. I did not try to stop her. But my daughter summoned kindness from somewhere and, with astounding generosity, Ella responded. We spent a gentle afternoon together. And I was glad for that, at least.

But, I have to confess, that by the time Rebecca arrived on that Monday morning, my life was over. Or the life that I had known for so many years, was over. For the first time, I felt old. I became stooped and hollow overnight – as though all my physical robustness had been scooped out of me as I lifted my son in the half-light of his September bedroom.

It would take anger to motivate me again. Rage, such as I had never known, was waiting for me. I was ready for it. I welcomed it.

Even now, I can feel how it thrilled my veins, sharpened my memory, fuelled my determination to know, to find out. It draws me ahead of my story, but right now I cannot help that. I cannot help it because there is nothing more powerful than knowledge.

After Rebecca left with Frances and Martin, I made my way towards the conservatory. The evening sun was still shining. I knew that if I sat in one of the armchairs, there was a good chance I might sleep. Sitting up, I felt that I could doze better and still keep one eye, one ear, open for Ella.

Just as I eased myself into the cushions, I felt the mobile vibrate in my shirt pocket. I glanced at the screen and answered at once. 'Gillian?'

'Patrick. Can you talk?'

'Yes. Ella is upstairs, resting. This is a good time.'

'Can we meet, do you think? I'd prefer to speak to you face to face.'

'No.' My tone was more aggressive than I'd intended. 'Sorry, Gillian. I mean, no, I can't. I can't leave Ella. I gave her half of one of your sleeping tablets earlier, and she's just dozed off. But I don't know how long she'll sleep for.'

I could feel Gillian's uncertainty.

'I'm fine, Gillian, really. I can do this. Tell me, please.'

'I'm concerned about you, too, Patrick, it's—'

I cut her short. 'I know you are, Gillian, and I appreciate that. Truly. But right now, this is my job, my work, my only focus. Tell me what you've found out.' I waited, feeling the tension grow like a steel band tightening across my forehead. For a moment, it felt as though the air in the room tightened, too, in sympathy. Time hovered and I waited.

'I spoke to Colm Tracey just now, once he'd completed the post-mortem. He was reluctant to give me any details, but I persuaded him.'

I tried to calm myself. I could hear Gillian draw a deep breath. 'There is evidence that Daniel has been self-harming, and probably for some time.'

I closed my eyes. It was what I had been waiting for. That July day – a mere seven or eight weeks ago – the hotel room in Madrid, my young son: all swam into view again. Daniel, the bath sheet suddenly falling away to reveal scars that criss-crossed his white, vulnerable flesh. The crowding memories of the swift red marks were all too vivid. I didn't need to ask *how* he'd harmed himself. But I asked her anyway.

'Patrick?'

'I'm here. What sort of evidence?'

'Significant scarring across both thighs, his abdomen and several on both inner forearms. Some on his shoulders. Probably done with either a blade or a sharp knife.'

I was grateful for her clinical precision. 'Old or new?'

'Both,' she replied, without hesitation. 'Most of the scars on the thighs and the abdomen are maybe seven or eight months old. Others, particularly those on the forearms, are very recent, possibly even within the last week or two.'

I opened my eyes again. Gillian's words seemed to hang

between us. I could almost see them before me in the air, suspended on wings of accusation.

'It's very difficult to spot, Patrick. When kids cut, they tend to be very clever about hiding what they've done. None of these would have been visible, unless you'd seen Daniel naked.'

I couldn't reply.

'Would you like me to come over?'

'No. Thank you, Gillian, but no. I will tell Ella in a couple of days, once the funeral is over. I cannot ask her to endure any of this right now.'

'And what about you? You are enduring this right now. How are you coping?'

I gave a short laugh. 'I'll tell you when I know.'

'Have you someone with you?'

'Yes,' I lied. 'My daughters. They are a fantastic support to both of us.' At least that much was true.

'Okay. Talk to them, Patrick. Confide in someone, it's important. Call me anytime if you have questions. Day or night.' She paused for a moment. 'Do you need anything to help you through the next few days?'

'No, thanks, I'm fine. I'll manage.'

'All right, then. We'll talk about this again. Don't forget I'm here if you need me. Take care of yourself.'

Why? I thought. Why should I bother taking care of myself? I leaned my head back, filled with the same extraordinary urgency I had felt on the previous day when we'd found Daniel. I needed to know. I needed to understand *why*. And for that, I needed to remember.

What was I going to tell Ella? And how could I tell her without all the Furies being unleashed upon me? I'd seen the marks on my son's young flesh, and had done nothing about it. I'd chosen to believe that all was well, that whatever had caused

Daniel grief in the past was just that: in the past. The couple of months that had now elapsed since our last holiday had all seen my boy revert to his usual, happy self. Once Ella arrived in Madrid, the mood of that tense afternoon in the hotel dissipated at once. Daniel had been bright, funny, interested in everything again.

So much so, that I'd begun to question what I'd seen. I'd keep a close eye on him, certainly: I promised myself that much. And I'd involve Ella the moment I saw any further cause for concern. But I hadn't. I didn't. There was nothing else that caused me to worry.

I forced myself now to remember. The InterRail trip, that afternoon in Madrid, what exactly I'd seen and felt. In a strange way, I also needed to remember so that I might, someday, be able to . . . not forget, no, not ever that. But to absorb, to accept, to understand what had suddenly come crashing into our safe, secluded family. It was difficult to form any coherent train of thought just then. I felt suddenly ill, weak with exhaustion. Pinpoints of light danced before my eyes, mocking me.

I allowed my head to drift, rested it slowly against the chair's broad back. And then, there was nothing. Nothing but deep, welcoming darkness.

Rebecca

As soon as we got back to Frances's on that first dreadful Monday night, I collected Ian and Aisling. I went straight home with them and locked the front door. We talked for hours. The white stunnedness of their young faces made me want to weep. And I had no answers. But they were old enough to understand that. Old enough to know that sometimes there are no answers.

After they went to bed, I shut up shop. I left messages with my clients that normal service would not resume for at least two weeks, due to the sudden, tragic death of my young brother.

Nobody asked questions. Nobody complained about my lack of availability. So much for thinking yourself indispensable.

The following afternoon, Tuesday, I drove back once again to see my father. Magda came over to stay with the kids. Ian and Aisling had refused to go to school, and I didn't push them. Time enough after the funeral. There was constant toing and froing between my sisters' houses and mine during those awful early days. I think that Frances and Sophie were as unwilling to let any of our children out of their sight as I was. My house – ironically, our old family home – became the 'centre of operations' as Magda called it. She looked after everyone's kids while my sisters and I looked after Dad and Ella, as best we could.

And she was brilliant, always available, never intrusive. Aisling really opened up to her, for which I was extremely grateful. Even Ian, to my surprise, spoke to Magda about Daniel in a way that he hadn't spoken to me.

Sometimes, I suppose, families are just too close: sensitivities are too raw, too close to the surface. And ours was a particularly tangled extended family, perhaps, for all sorts of reasons. But Magda was an objective, affectionate ear. She dutifully reported back to me the substance of whatever she and the kids had talked about. Without them knowing, of course. It made it easier for me to judge when to intervene, when to step back. I looked on her with greatly increased respect after that.

I had the grace to feel ashamed of myself for my earlier reaction – about a 'childminder' being with the kids when Daniel died. I guess it said a lot more about me than I would like: about my feelings around myself and my own frequent absences from home.

When I got back to Dad's house at about four on Tuesday afternoon, Ella was in bed. I was relieved. Now at least I could seize the opportunity to speak to my father on his own.

'She's exhausted,' he said. 'I got Gillian to give her something stronger. Even for the next three or four days. She can't go on without sleep. She hardly closed her eyes last night.' He shook his head. 'She just can't go on like this.' He led the way through to the conservatory.

Nor can you, I thought. Nor can you. I followed him down the hallway, noticing all over again the pronounced stoop of my father's shoulders. He appeared to shuffle as he walked. He looked at least ten years older. And he was unshaven and slightly unkempt: an all-too vivid reminder of how he had given up on life, on himself, after my mother's death all those years ago. We sat, facing each other in the conservatory, surrounded on all sides by the glory of Ella's autumn garden.

'How are *you* doing?' I asked. 'You're trying to keep it all together for both of you. You must be exhausted as well.'

He nodded. 'I suppose I am – although I'm not sure if exhaustion is the right word for it. I can't go on, but I must. I don't know if we'll ever get through this.' He shook his head again, his eyes lingering for a moment on the expanse of green outside the window. It had been another cruelly perfect September day. Abruptly, my father stood up and walked across the room. He closed the curtains roughly, almost savagely. I said nothing. I just stood up and switched on a couple of the lamps.

'I can't bear all that beauty,' he said. 'It's like a physical hurt. My son is dead and the trees and shrubs keep on blooming.' He gave a harsh laugh. 'What sort of justice is that?'

I knew he didn't need an answer. 'Sit down, Dad,' I said. 'I'll get you a brandy.'

'Whiskey,' he said, curtly.

I didn't argue.

When we'd settled again, I braved it. 'Dad,' I began, 'I have no right to ask you this, but I'm going to ask it anyway.'

He looked over at me, frowning. His face clouded with suspicion.

'Is there something that happened to Daniel that you're reluctant to talk about?' I saw him stiffen, but he didn't speak, so I took my courage in both hands. 'I just feel that you have some kind of inkling as to what might have made him unhappy. I can understand that you don't want to distress Ella any further.' I leaned forward, bringing my face closer to his. 'There is a lot of turbulent water under our personal bridge,' I said. 'But if you would like to trust me with this, I swear I will never divulge a word to another soul, if that is what you ask.'

He didn't answer at once. I remembered the tired dullness

behind his eyes yesterday morning. I knew then that he was concealing something. His silence now confirmed it.

'I can't be sure of what it was,' he said, finally. 'But that's because I didn't listen.' He looked at me then, his eyes filling. 'I didn't listen, because I was so intent on having the perfect son that I didn't want to hear.' He put down his glass and laced his fingers together, as though he was trying to hold on.

I reached across and took his hands in mine. The knuckles were shiny, prominent. His hands felt almost papery, insubstantial. When I looked at him, up close like this, I was shocked at how much thinner he suddenly seemed.

'You and Ella were wonderful parents,' I said. 'Nobody could doubt that. Whatever happened to Daniel, happened outside of these four walls. Teenagers are very secretive creatures.' I stopped. I could see the anguish grow across his eyes.

'That's the point,' he whispered. 'He tried to tell me about some of the things that were happening at school. And, God forgive me, I didn't take him seriously enough. Me, of all people.' He bent his head.

I knew something of my father's own experiences of school. He had told all of us when we were teenagers about his years as a boarder. How he loathed it. He used to say how lucky we were to be girls, to be in an atmosphere where the bully did not reign supreme. Little did he know – and we never told him anything different. There is more than one way to inflict pain. And girls don't need a rugby pitch to do it on.

We protected him, I suppose. I know I did. I believe that children do – they instinctively hide things from their parents, the things that might make us angry on their behalf.

'Dad, don't torture yourself like this. Tell me what happened.'

He took his hands away from mine and reached into his trouser pocket for a handkerchief. He wiped at his eyes, sighed, blew his nose. 'I've been trying to put the pieces of the jigsaw together,' he said, finally. 'I can think of nothing else.'

'Start anywhere,' I said. 'You don't need to recall things in order.' I remembered from my childhood how insistent my father had always been that a story be told logically, sequentially. It was as though he needed to *own* the information. Asides frustrated him: looping back and forth in the plot left him helplessly lost. With films, he hated flashbacks and interconnecting tales. It wasn't that he couldn't follow them: it was that he didn't want to. He prized logic and scientific rigour over imagination. I am an engineer, he used to say, indignantly, not a bloody poet.

'You remember Daniel's thirteenth birthday?'

I nodded. 'Of course.'

'When all the kids played their party pieces?'

I nodded again. 'I remember it clearly. It was a very special day.'

'It started after that,' he said. 'Or at least, I really became aware of it after that.'

'Go on.'

'Something happened to Daniel's violin a couple of weeks later. He wouldn't say what. But it got damaged. Ella tried to talk to him about it, but he shrugged it off. Said he hadn't tied it properly onto the bike.'

'And you didn't believe him?'

He shook his head. 'No. I got the violin repaired, and when I gave it back to him, I tried to probe a little bit. But he just said, "Leave it, Dad." Ella and I discussed it. We decided to file it away in the memory bank, for later.' He finished his whiskey in one gulp. 'We watched him over the next few weeks, but he seemed fine. So we never brought it up again. We had no evidence of anything, but both of us were uneasy.' He frowned, remembering. 'Then he seemed to settle again. And he was so happy during the summer that, I suppose, we just regarded the incident as a one-off.'

I thought that was reasonable, and I said so.

'Yes,' he said, standing up. 'So did we.' He reached for the bottle of whiskey.

I let the silence linger for a moment. 'Did something else happen afterwards?'

'Nothing that I was aware of. I've been desperately trying to remember anything from the past year, and I can't. But when we were in France and Spain this summer, before Ella joined us, he tried to say something to me then. We were on the train to Toulouse, just the two of us. And out of the blue, Daniel said he wasn't looking forward to going back to school.'

'That's normal, surely?' My two moaned constantly, come every August. I'd learned to ignore it.

'It was the way he said it. He looked . . . haunted. Then we were interrupted by other people coming into the compartment. The train was really crowded that day. And, God forgive me, I never went back to it again. I never asked him why.'

He filled his glass almost to the brim. I said nothing, but I wondered how much my father was stitching into his recollections. Had these moments been really significant, or did they just seem so in hindsight? It was so hard to tell: too much guilt. I could feel it hover in the air between us. And I didn't know how to say that.

'And there was one other time,' he said, sitting back down and facing me. 'We were in Madrid, just about to go into the Prado. He'd been really excited about it.' His lip began to tremble. I reached forward, squeezed his hand.

'He'd been texting all morning, or surfing, or whatever kids do on their phones.' He looked at me. 'And suddenly, he just went white. All the blood drained from his face.'

I began to feel sick.

'I asked him what was wrong. He wouldn't tell me. He kept saying "Nothing, there's nothing wrong." And then suddenly, he said he didn't want to go into the Prado after all. He'd had enough of galleries.'

This was delicate territory. How could I say that no fourteen-year-old I knew would want to set foot across the threshold of a gallery? That perhaps the visit was of my father's making, and not Daniel's?

'I know what you are thinking,' he said. He half-smiled. 'Believe me, the Prado was all Daniel's idea. I'd have much preferred to sit in the shade somewhere and have a beer.' He shrugged at me. 'I'm an old man, Rebecca. I was tired out by that stage – I was just holding on until Ella joined us.'

'I'm sorry, Dad. I didn't mean—'

He waved my words away. 'Daniel wanted to go to the College of Art,' he said. 'He talked about it a lot. After that day in Madrid, he never mentioned it again.'

'So what happened?'

'I quizzed him. But he wouldn't give. He said he was too hot, too tired, the museum would be too crowded. So we went into a café and he had an ice cream and a Coke. He hardly spoke to me for the rest of the day. When we went back to the hotel, he asked if he could use my laptop.'

'And?'

'I lay down on the bed, but I watched him. He had his back to me, but I could feel the intensity of whatever it was that he was doing. Later, when we had dinner together, I tried to talk to him. But he just clammed up.'

My father was still holding something back. I could feel it. 'What was going on, Dad?' My voice was barely above a whisper. Something in the air was about to break. I could feel it straining between us. He put his head in his hands.

His voice had dropped so much that I had trouble hearing

him. 'Daniel and I were sharing a room, just until Ella arrived.' He ran one hand across his mouth as though trying to stop the words. But he couldn't. 'He had a shower before we went out that evening and he wrapped himself in one of those enormous hotel bath sheets.

'When he came back into the bedroom, he went straight over to the laptop again, but he was clutching the towel to him as though his life depended on it.' He sighed. 'I had this amused, random thought about how modest youngsters are, how embarrassed by their bodies. But I said nothing.'

He seemed lost in this particular memory; his face had softened, his eyes filled. I could see that he was reliving whatever it was that had happened next. I sat and waited, afraid to interrupt.

'I was lying on my bed, dozing. I let Daniel think that I was asleep. I thought it might make him less self-conscious. He spent a few minutes at the laptop and then went to go back into the bathroom, I suppose to get dressed. But the towel got snagged on something – I don't know what, maybe the door handle – it doesn't matter. The towel fell away from him and I saw his thigh, his left thigh, completely uncovered.'

He looked over at me. I have never seen my father so distraught, so beyond himself. 'His thigh was cut, again and again, just here,' he motioned to the top of his own thigh, 'and I swear I saw more scars higher up, onto his abdomen. I don't think I even properly knew what I was looking at.'

And then he cried. My father wept, his body crouched forward, broken.

I went to him and held him. After a few moments, when he was quieter, I asked him: 'Did you speak to Daniel about this?'

He shook his head. 'No,' he said. 'God forgive me, but I didn't. I was so shocked I didn't know what to do. I knew that the marks had to have been made by his own hand. I decided to wait until Ella arrived. I thought she'd know how to handle it.'

'And?'

He shrugged. 'I couldn't. I couldn't bring myself to say anything. They were so happy to see each other, and he seemed to be fine for the rest of the holiday. I promised myself I'd tackle it when we got home. And then – I began to question myself. Had I imagined it? Had I been asleep and dreamed it? But I know I didn't.'

'Have you told Ella any of this?'

He shook his head. I moved back a little. I needed to see his face. 'Dad, you have to tell her. You can't keep this to yourself.'

'I know,' he said. 'It's eating me. What's more, Gillian called yesterday afternoon, after you guys left. I'd asked her, very quietly, to let me know the results of the post-mortem. She spoke to Dr Tracey for me. She said that Daniel had been self-harming for some time, at least a year. And that there were some fresh cuts, on his forearms. Probably made in the last couple of weeks.' He looked defeated. 'I'll have to tell Ella. But I have no idea how.' He met my eyes again, his own full of appeal. 'How in Christ's name am I going to tell her?'

'I don't know, Dad,' I said. 'But you must, and soon. It could be the start.' I reached over to him, took his hands in mine again.

'Of what?' he looked suddenly fearful.

'Of finding out why.' I didn't need to say any more. My father had always taught us that there is nothing more powerful than knowledge. 'And Ella would want to know – just as you want to, just as you *need* to know.' I was suddenly filled with fear for my own children; filled with terror as to what their secret lives might be concealing from me. I needed to get home straight away.

229

'Yes,' he said. 'Yes, you're right. We need to know.'

He looked suddenly more like himself as he spoke. His face reminded me of the time all those years ago after my mother died. That night, Eugene's insistence on therapy had given my father a new and urgent sense of purpose. It was the beginning of his recovery.

'You're right,' he said again. 'I'll do it, once the funeral is over. I'll wait until Ella is a little more rested. But I'll tell her.'

I believed him. We spoke of the funeral on the coming Thursday, of the days after that. Of the need for some oasis of normality from time to time.

'We're drifting,' he said. 'I have to put a bit of structure back.'

I was shocked. What did you expect? I wanted to say. But of course I didn't. I realized that that response was absolutely in keeping with my father, with his rigorous, scientific view of the world and how it worked. By the time I left, he was calmer. 'Will you sleep?' I asked as I was leaving.

'Yes,' he said. 'At least for a few hours.'

At the front door, he hugged me. 'Thanks, Rebecca. Goodnight, now. And drive safely.'

I held onto him for a little while longer. I couldn't speak. And anyway, right then, there was really nothing left to say.

As I drove home, back to my family, I was consumed by memories of Daniel. As a sweet child, as a talented musician, as my father's son. And then I imagined him sitting, with a blade in his hand, cutting deep into his own flesh. Hiding, leading a secret life; suffering.

Then I cried. All the way home.

I could not wait to be back with my own children.

Patrick

As soon as Rebecca and I had waved goodbye, I'd crept up the stairs to look in on Ella. She was asleep – if that's what you could call it. She lay in the grip of that still, drugged oblivion that she disliked, but upon which I insisted. The days were already much too long. By mid afternoon, Ella seemed to crumble, as though her allotted span of energy for the day had just run out. To sleep, even for an hour or two, meant that we could sit out the evening together, doing whatever needed to be done, sharing whatever comfort we could.

The mornings were the worst. Each of us, on waking, knew that we had to face yet another day without Daniel. And we still had the funeral to get through.

That afternoon, after Rebecca left – perhaps it was the whiskey, or the heat of the conservatory after I'd closed the curtains, or perhaps the longing for even a brief moment of forgetting: any one of these on their own might have done it. I sat in the armchair and I slept.

But there was no respite. My dreams were filled with my son.

Daniel, knocking at the window, begging me to let him in. But I couldn't. Each time I tried to struggle towards him, he moved further away. My feet were planted in quick-drying cement; I kept faltering, keeling over in my eagerness to get to him. A tapping sound filled the room. It wrenched me back towards wakefulness, my heart pounding.

And then, at last, I opened my eyes.

I stumbled into standing. My whole body was drenched in perspiration. For a moment, I stood there, confused. I knew where I was, but the room looked unfamiliar, the furniture ghostly. Then the tapping came again, but gently, hesitantly. There was nothing insistent about it: it was tentative, like a question. There was somebody at the front door. I moved towards the hallway, as quickly as I could.

I opened the door to find Maryam standing there, her eyes red and raw-looking. Edward was at her side, hunched. His eyes searched the ground, as though he had just lost something.

'Maryam,' I said. I made a huge effort to sound welcoming. I also made a physical effort to shrug off the fog of sleep. Seeing her there, I felt guilty all over again for having shut her out on Sunday night. The poor woman had done nothing wrong. And she'd called yesterday, too. I'd seen her: the way she backed away from the gate, once she saw Frances's and Rebecca's cars. I opened the door wider. 'And Edward. Please, come in, both of you.'

They followed me inside, Maryam's eyes darting everywhere. She was looking for Ella, of course.

'Ella is resting, Maryam. But I'll tell her you called. She will appreciate you both being here.'

Maryam held out her hands to me. The words she spoke were careful, measured. Her simple dignity moved me. 'Patrick, I am so very sorry for your loss,' she said, her voice trembling. 'Rahul and I and all our family give you our deepest sympathies,' and then she couldn't do it any more. She wept without restraint. She bowed her head, but held onto my hand and I drew her towards me, putting one arm around her shoulder.

'Thank you, Maryam. You are both very good to call.' I looked towards Edward. His face was contorted and I felt suddenly, bitterly sorry for him. For all the adult suffering that had suddenly been foisted upon him.

'We loved him,' Maryam sobbed. 'Your boy. Like our own family.'

'I know, I know,' I soothed. 'Please, Maryam, sit down, and Edward, you too. Let me get you both something.'

'Maryam.' Ella stood in the doorway. Pale, haunted-looking, but somehow more composed than she had been yesterday morning when Rebecca had first arrived. Nevertheless, I stood guard, afraid for just a moment of what she might do.

Maryam got up at once and went straight to her. She took Ella in her arms and they stood together, holding onto each other for some time. It reminded me of that June day in our garden, the day of our wedding party; Maryam and Ella had embraced then, too.

But I didn't want to think about that.

Then Ella walked over towards Edward, holding out her hand. I was proud of her. She did not flinch. 'Edward. So good to see you. Let me make us all some tea.'

We sat, the four of us, in an atmosphere that for those moments, at least, had lost some of its rawness. Ella and Maryam made tea, and we drank it together, the biscuits untasted before us. Out of the blue, Edward spoke.

'Daniel was my best friend,' he said.

Oh, God, I thought. I can't bear this. I interrupted him: I needed to temper the steel of this moment or Ella would slip away from me again.

'We know that, Edward. You've always been a wonderful friend. And Daniel knew that, too.' I reached out, patted his shoulder.

'You don't understand,' he said suddenly. His voice was choked. 'There was something wrong, on Sunday—'

I could see Maryam flash him a warning glance, saw Ella catch it in flight.

She put down her cup. 'Tell us, Edward. Patrick and I would like to know what you think was wrong. Please, it would help us. You are safe here – you can say whatever it is you're thinking.'

Edward glanced over at his mother and she nodded.

'I have only started playing football,' he began. 'Just since we went back to school this year. I'm only a sub, but I like it.'

He sounded defensive and I wondered why.

'When Daniel came over to us on Sunday, he'd forgotten that I had an extra practice session. We have a match on Thursday . . . I mean . . .' his voice trailed off. He looked stricken. Two days ago, he'd been preparing for a football match; now he'd a funeral to go to. He struggled for a moment, then he began again. 'But Daniel wanted to do other stuff.' He shifted uncomfortably on the chair.

'What other stuff?' Ella asked, gently, before I could.

'He'd brought his camera. He wanted us to cycle over to the bird sanctuary again, but I couldn't.'

The misery in the boy's face made my heart ache for him. I admired the way he held Ella's gaze, though. He didn't falter.

'He was angry with me. When I wouldn't go, he just ran off. I tried to text him later, but he didn't answer.' Edward slumped forward.

Maryam watched her son. The room filled with a tense, expectant silence. I felt it necessary to break it. 'You did well to tell us, Edward,' I said.

Ella leaned forward. 'Edward. Look at me.'

He did, his eyes filled to overflowing.

'This is not your fault. Nothing Daniel did is your fault. I want you to hear that.'

He started to sob, loud, choking sounds that were startlingly male, as though he had aged from boy to man since he came through the front door. 'But he wouldn't talk. He just slammed down the stairs and out the—'

Ella reached across and took his hand. 'This is not your fault, Edward. You are very brave to come here. You are not responsible for this. What I would like is for you to tell us, his dad and me, everything that you can about the past three weeks since you went back to school. Can you do that?'

I sat back in amazement and watched my wife. Somehow, I felt the faintest, most fragile stirrings of hope in the way she spoke to Edward. Gently, so gently, that the boy finally allowed himself to be comforted.

'He was fine,' Edward concluded. 'Really. Everything was fine. This year, the Jays pretty much left us alone. It was way easier than first year.'

'The Jays?' Ella asked quickly. 'Who are they?'

Edward looked uncomfortable. 'They're just three guys, sometimes four. Last year, they pushed us around a bit, but this year there's been nothin'.'

'What do you mean, "pushed you around"? How did they do that?' I asked. This was dangerous territory for me. I could feel my anger rising already.

Edward shrugged. 'One of them stuck a compass in Daniel once; they broke his violin. And they used to call us names.'

I began to feel fear settling around my heart. How much did this boy know? How much was he about to reveal to Ella, before I could prepare her? I sat forward on my chair. There was nothing I could do except wait.

'What sort of names?' Ella was watching him intently.

'They called me Paki, or darkie. Sometimes nigger.'

I saw Maryam look away.

'And Daniel?' Ella's voice was soft.

Edward looked distressed.

'It's okay, Edward,' I said. 'We'll have heard them all before. Don't worry. Just say them.'

'Gay boy. Queer. Steamer. Things like that. But not this year,' he added quickly. 'There's been nothin' this year, I swear.'

Ella caught my eye. I sat back again, said nothing. 'These boys,' she said quietly. 'Do you know them well?'

Edward hung his head. For a moment, he didn't speak. 'A bit,' he said. 'Just this term, since we went back, like.' He raised his head and looked across at us. 'They're on the football team.'

I felt as though I had been slapped. Something, some knowledge hung in the air around us; I had the sense of things beginning to shift into place. I could see Daniel as he must have been on Sunday. His disappointment; his best friend playing football with the enemy. His sense of betrayal. But that wasn't enough, surely, to drive him to do what he did.

There was something else, there had to be. A bleak memory of the hotel room in Madrid suddenly made it harder to breathe.

'What are their names?' Ella asked. Seeing Edward's troubled face, she added, quickly, 'It's just for us to know, Edward. We would never involve you in anything.'

He nodded. 'There are three of them, well, four really, but Leo's kind of on the outside.'

We waited.

'Jeremy Toolin, he's in third year, and then James McNamara and Jason MacManus. They're second years. And Leo Byrne, he kind of hung around with them.'

I saw Ella stiffen.

'Jason was the worst, though. He always started it.'

Some memory began to stir, somewhere at the back of my head. Something that had to do with that name. Jason. It felt important, whatever it was. I cursed my growing forgetfulness. I'd learned recently that if I stopped trying to force it, the memory would come back eventually, sometimes in the most bizarre way. It would be dragged to the surface of that murky pond of forgetting by the most unexpected of hooks.

'Thank you, Edward. You've really helped us. Thank you.' Ella squeezed his hand.

Maryam stood. 'We should go. You both need to rest. Is there anything we can do for you? Anything at all?' I could hear the entreaty in her voice.

Ella tried to smile. 'Thank you, Maryam. I think that you and Edward have already done it. We're very grateful.'

Maryam bent and kissed her. Edward shook our hands, awkwardly. He was anxious to be gone, and I couldn't blame him. I saw them both to the front door.

When I came back, Ella was writing something.

'What is it?' I asked.

'The names,' she said. 'They could be important.'

I nodded. What could I say? That it wouldn't matter who they were, that bullying was a fact of life, that nothing we could ever do would change that fact? I was angry. And I didn't want to be angry with her. Pete Mackey's taunting face loomed up in front of me, his features reappearing after some sixty years. I felt the satisfaction of breaking his jaw all over again.

'Edward said that Jason was the worst,' Ella said.

Then I remembered her reaction when Jason's name had been mentioned. 'Do you know him?' I was puzzled.

She looked at me. 'His family emigrated when he was about nine. To the States. They only came back last year, during the summer. Don't you remember?'

I shook my head, frustrated with myself.

'It's Jason MacManus,' Ella said softly.

But I hardly heard her. Something important had finally

struggled to the surface, getting in the way. 'T-shirt Boy,' I said suddenly. 'That's who it was. When Daniel was the T-shirt Boy.' I was exultant. I had remembered.

It was Ella's turn to be puzzled.

'Don't you remember? When Daniel rescued some poor little scrap in the playground who was being bullied? Oh, it's years ago. Daniel must have been about eight. I can't remember the child's name, but I remember the bully.'

She nodded, slowly. 'Jason MacManus.'

'Yes,' I said, 'that's the name.'

She looked at me. 'Jason MacManus. Jason MacManus is Fintan MacManus's son.'

For a moment, I didn't understand. When I did, I felt my legs give way, my eyes cloud over. I have never, ever, experienced such a rush of pure rage in all my adult life. 'Jesus Christ,' I said.

'We have to find out more, Patrick. We have to find out everything. It's the only way we are going to survive this.'

I nodded. 'Yes.'

Ella was looking at me, her eyes full of appeal. But there was something else. She was present again, present in a way she had hardly been since Sunday.

Now was the time. I had to try. I couldn't keep it from her any longer.

'I have something to tell you, Ella. I don't want to, but I can't hold onto it any longer.'

She looked at me, her gaze not wavering. 'I've been waiting. I know you've been keeping something from me,' she said. 'I'm ready. Nothing can be worse than what I've been imagining.'

I reached over, took both her hands in mine.

I told her. About the train to Toulouse, about the Prado, about the hotel room in Madrid. Gillian's phone call. All of it.

And then I waited.

Daniel

AT FIRST, it feels like nothing is really happening, nothing at all. Then all at once, tiny dark beads appear, unstoppable and shiny and red. Carmine, Miss O'Connor would probably call it. Or maybe even crimson – depending on the light. Sylvia was disgusted when Miss O'Connor talked about how artists used to boil dried insects in water to extract the carminic acid. She hated that sort of stuff. I loved it. And the names of all the colours, and their history. Art class was definitely the best. Sometimes English, but always art.

I like Sylvia. She's not like most of the others. She's softer. Edward asked me did I fancy her and I said yeah. But it's hard to know what to do about it when we only sit beside each other in art class. We sit together at break, though, and most lunch-times. Edward comes to our table as well, when he's not doing extra athletics. But I think I'll have to stop because the Jays never stop whistling and whispering dirty things to Sylvia on their way past. It's not fair. It's me they hate, not her, but she's getting some of it as well.

Once the blade stops, the red blood rushes out and the beads just disappear, running together, like they are hurrying one after the other to merge into one long line. And then, but only then, the feeling starts. At the end of first year, when things weren't as bad as they are now, it was like a great big sigh of relief every time I did it. Like holding your breath for ages and finally letting go. Now, though, it feels like more of a shout. Something builds and builds inside, fighting to get to the outside and the only way to let it out is to cut.

When I do, I feel happy. Light and free and as though nothing can ever touch me again. But it does touch me again. It always comes back. I know when it is starting, building up like layers, one on top of the other. A bit like strata in the sedimentary rocks that we learned about in geography, the ones formed from the remains of living things. That's how it feels: all that heaviness, pressing down on even more heaviness, making it hard to breathe.

I know it's wrong to keep doing it. I mean, my head knows it's wrong. Mum almost caught me once, but I got away with it. I didn't hear her come into my room. But I was able to fob her off. She wouldn't understand, and it would really upset her. And Edward nearly saw it once, too. He came into the second-year boys' cloakroom, just as I'd finished. That's only a week or so ago. That kind of frightened me. I really don't want him to know. I think he'd tell.

I'd never done it at school before that – and it was just that one day. What happened was, I'd forgotten to take Granddad's Swiss Army knife out of my jacket pocket the night before. It's just as well nobody saw me – there would have been murder if I was caught bringing a knife to school. When I felt it, lying there under my fingers at hometime, just waiting for me, it was as though I couldn't put off the cutting any longer, although I hadn't been thinking about it until right that minute.

That was one of the really bad days. I don't mind the physical stuff as much as the messages. I think I'd prefer all the pushing and shoving I got last year to the messages. I'd ask to swap them if I could. There were ten texts waiting when school finished, and then more came every few seconds. The phone didn't stop vibrating for ages. Edward doesn't know about them either. I'd never tell him. He sees what happens sometimes in school and that's okay, well, not okay exactly, but the name-calling happens to both of us because we're the same because we're different. But I don't think he gets all the phone and message stuff. If he does, he doesn't tell me. And he has to share the one computer with his dad and his brothers so even if he did, he probably wouldn't see them as much as I see mine.

Once I got home that day – it was a Wednesday, our half day – the messages kept coming every couple of seconds after I logged on. One of them was the same, over and over again, and I couldn't help it. I followed the link. It was www.welovedaniel.com and it was the same sort of stuff, but even worse than what they sent me when I was in Spain with Dad. The day we didn't go into the Prado. I could see how puzzled he was, but the pictures on my phone had made me sick. Pictures of me doing it with a dog. With another boy. With an old man. And videos – I don't know how Jason made them.

I almost told Dad that day. But I couldn't do it. When I was just about to, he took a hanky out of his pocket and wiped his forehead. He was really sweating. He kind of sank into a chair in the shady outside bit of the café and tried to smile at me. But his face had sort of collapsed and there were lines suddenly everywhere around his eyes and his mouth.

'Are you okay, Dad?' I was glad that Mum was coming tomorrow. Right then, he looked really old.

'Mighty,' he said. 'Just a bit tired.' He tried to smile, and it was better this time, but it still wasn't his usual one. 'I'm glad we're not staying long in Madrid. Be nice to get back to the sea.'

Then he had a beer and I had a Coke and he started to look a bit happier. Back at the hotel, I asked if I could use his laptop. He only uses it for emails to Mum and to buy tickets and stuff like that. He'd never guess, so I didn't mind being in the same room as him.

There were dozens of photos. My head put on bodies that weren't mine. Naked bodies, some of them. Gross. Messages on Facebook telling me how much everyone hated me. Tweets saying the same things. Things I don't even want to remember. And then, some emails from Edward and from Sylvia asking me why I had sent them such nasty messages. But I hadn't; I never would.

I emailed back, from my Dad's account. Then, just in case Sylvia wasn't at her computer, I texted her. I told her what had happened, that it wasn't me saying all that stuff, that someone had hacked my email account. That was the worst. Someone else pretending to be me and sending out stuff I'd never written, the sort of stuff I'd never write.

Sylvia said okay fine, and I think she believed me. I know Edward believed me. Sylvia said she was pretty sure it wasn't me, but it had upset her anyway, the things they said. Then we gmail chatted for a bit on Dad's laptop and she was really nice about it. At the end, I got a bit brave and said that I was really looking forward to seeing her again, although I wasn't looking forward to going back to school. But I didn't tell her that last bit. And then she said that she was, too. So that made me happier.

I know it's the Jays. James is a bit of a thick, Jeremy is the biggest, he's the one who pushes people around, but Jason is really clever. He can do all that sort of password stuff, no problem. He's always boasting about how far ahead California is in technology. He knows a lot, and he can't stop showing off. He showed off from the minute he came to secondary school. His mum and dad brought them back to Ireland after four years away. Jason thinks he knows everything. Mr Kelly in English asked him to tell us about his time in California, about what was different about living there. Jason gave this big talk about Silicon Valley where his dad worked and about the weather and the freedom and then about why they'd all come home. He said that Ireland had so many more opportunities now, except he said 'opportooonities' in that real American accent he has, but sometimes he lets it slip. He loves being the centre of attention. I remember him from primary school, and all the stuff he got up to. And he remembers me.

The others just go along with him, I think. They are all happy for him to be the boss. And this year, his gang just gets bigger and bigger. There's loads of second years in it. It even has some third years now, and that new guy from our tutorial class, well not so new any more, called Leo. They're just – they're everywhere. I've tried not looking at my phone but I can't. I need to know what they're saying. I just can't switch it all off. It keeps going around and around inside my head, building up into another shout.

I'm glad Edward is around. Most days, we just do our own thing in school, I mean separately. We're not in the same stream for most subjects, apart from English. He hates the Jays as much as I do. They were always after us last year. But Edward thinks this year is easier, because they don't wait for us at the bicycle shed any more, and they don't trip us up in the corridors. That's why I say nothing about the messages. For me it's worse, way worse than last year. And Sylvia is nice to me. I'd never tell her anything about how bad it is, though – when I'm with her I just laugh it off.

But at least the weekends are good. I don't switch on the computer when Edward's here. And we don't in his house, either. Some Sunday soon we'll cycle over to the bird sanctuary again. I'll bring the camera. It's good that Edward doesn't know, it really is. It means I can forget about the messages for a bit. We just use the 3dx or something. And we'll probably go sailing again with Dad before the end of the season.

At least on Saturdays and Sundays I can kind of forget about — all of it. About all of them. At least I have that.

Patrick and Ella

ELLA HAS LISTENED TO ME, filled with an extraordinary calmness.

'He was self-harming,' she says. 'And I had no idea. No idea at all.' She leans forward into the armchair, raising both hands to cover her face. 'Jesus Christ, how could I not have known.'

It is not a question. I hold her hands, urgently, lower them so that I can see her face, her eyes, properly. I remember how she comforted Edward. 'It's not your fault—' I begin.

But she cuts me off. 'I'm a fucking counsellor, Patrick. A *therapist* – I'm supposed to know this stuff. I'm supposed to see it in others – including my own son. Especially my own son.'

She struggles to her feet, kicking at her dressing gown as its folds seemed to entangle her. 'Of course it's my fault.'

She paces, angrily, dragging her hands through her hair. She feels coiled, tight like a spring.

I stand up and pull her to me. 'Then it's my fault, too. I didn't even know what I was seeing that day in Madrid. I had no real idea of what I was looking at.'

'Neither did I,' she says.

Tears begin to stream down her face. She starts to struggle in my embrace and suddenly stops, becomes limp. 'But I do now, and it isn't even three weeks ago.' She covers her eyes with her hands and weeps.

I am lost. I don't know what she's saying. I watch my wife's face darken as she remembers.

Daniel

I WISH THAT somebody would make them stop.

Now they're sending around one of Jason's made-up photos where I'm kissing another boy. You can't see who the other boy is, but you can see me. Everybody has it on their phones. Everybody's grinning as they go past me in the corridor. Even people I don't know think it's funny.

In the queue for the canteen the other day, some big guy from transition year nudged me and told me to lighten up.

We're not even back three weeks yet. It feels like forever.

During the summer, I could forget. At least until they sent all that stuff while I was in Madrid with Dad. That brought it all back.

It really started to get bad at the end of first year. I remember one day in art, sitting beside Sylvia. We'd to do a picture based on the theme 'Flight'. I liked sitting with her. She was nice. That was one of the really bad days, until I started to draw. Then I was able to let it all out onto the page, and it was a good feeling. Plus it was a Friday, last class, so I knew I could escape.

Me and Edward were going out with Dad on the *Aurora* on Saturday. Out in the middle of the lake, nothing could get me. The signal always failed around Casey's boatyard, and Edward just had an ordinary Nokia, one where Mrs Maryam would text him if he had to go home.

It feels like they are closing in on me this year. The Jays.

Even Leo. He hasn't done anything since we went back, but I always feel like he's waiting for their signal. He just stands there, ready to pounce.

That picture was one of my best, I think. I know that Sylvia was curious, I caught her looking at it when she thought I couldn't see her. I almost told her that day, but I didn't. I couldn't. Even though I had done nothing wrong I felt ashamed.

Some days, I can hardly breathe. Some days, I want to cry, to tell Mum what's going on. To ask Dad's advice.

But I can't. They'd be so upset. They'd go to the parents and the school and everything would just be one big mess.

I have to try and sort it on my own. I have to. And some things are still good. Like sailing. Like drawing. Like chilling out with Edward in the TV room.

It'll be okay.

It will. It will be okay.

Ella

IT IS A FEW DAYS into the new term. Daniel has cycled home from school and left his bike in the garage, as usual. Ella smiles at her son as he enters the kitchen. He drops his rucksack just inside the door and heads straight for the fridge.

'Hi there,' she says. 'Have a good day?'

He shrugs, staring at the shelves full of food. But he doesn't choose anything. He stands there, just looking. Ella comes and stands behind him. She puts one hand lightly on his shoulder. To her surprise, he flinches and moves out from under from her touch. She is about to say something, but he walks away.

'Daniel?' she says. 'There are some wraps left over from lunch, if you want.'

'Nah, it's all right. Not really hungry.' He walks back to the kitchen door and grabs his rucksack, slinging it over his right shoulder.

'Okay,' she says, easily. 'I have a client at five, so we'll eat about seven. If you change your mind, you know where everything is.'

'Yeah,' he says. 'Thanks. See you later.'

She watches him leave, puzzled. She'll have to choose her time, probe a little deeper. Something is not right. Something must have happened at school. Ella sighs. Ever since school started again, there is a reticence, a secrecy to Daniel that makes her feel uneasy.

She and Maryam have already spoken of it. And Patrick. 'Rahul says that Edward is becoming a man, that I must step back,' Maryam says. She shrugs as she says this, raising her palms in the air to show her lack of comprehension. 'He says that it is normal to make a distance with your parents when you are their age.' Which is pretty much what she and Patrick have already discussed, too.

But still – there is something here, something about her own son that Ella cannot quite put her finger on, something new that makes her feel as though a vital link between them has suddenly weakened, or gone missing.

The Daniel she met up with in Madrid, less than two months ago, has nothing in common with the Daniel who has just walked out of the kitchen.

Some hours later, Ella stands at the bottom of the stairs and calls out to her son. Patrick is in the kitchen, serving food. 'Daniel? Dinner's ready, love.' But there is no answer. She calls him again. Silence. Exasperated, she begins to climb the stairs. She knocks on his bedroom door. Nothing. So she knocks once more, and pushes the door open at the same time. She calls his name again.

Daniel is sitting on his bed, his back to her. She can see the white of the earphones, the curve of his navy sweater as he bends over something, absorbed. 'Daniel?' she says, and takes a tentative step towards him. She's afraid of startling him. Suddenly, he jerks around towards her, tugging at the slender cable of his earphones. One by one, they fall to his shoulders. He stands up, pulling at the cuffs of his school shirt. He looks distracted, his face flushed.

'Are you okay?' she asks.

'Yeah,' he says. 'I didn't hear you come in. Just listening to

Bob Dylan. Ian was right. He really is deadly.' And he grins his old grin.

Ella feels an inexplicable jolt of relief. Its intensity puzzles her. What exactly has she been she afraid of? There is nothing wrong here, after all. Her son has just smiled at her. 'Dinner's ready,' she says. 'I've been calling you.'

He nods. 'Cool. Down in a sec. Just need to use the bathroom.' And he pushes past her.

Now she remembers the smears of what she'd thought to be red paint on the sleeves of his school shirt. Smears that he'd *told* her were red paint, no more than two weeks ago. 'Sorry, Mum,' he said, 'didn't see the stuff on the desk. But it's not oil. It's poster paint – it'll wash out fine.'

And it had. Daniel had filled the washing machine himself – one of his usual Saturday chores. On Sunday night, as normal, he'd ironed his school shirts for the week. It was a token independence, but Patrick had insisted that he learn these things.

'Learn them early,' he'd said to Daniel. 'It's no fun not being able to look after yourself.'

Daniel had grumbled a bit at first; but more, Ella believed, because he felt he had to. Afterwards, he never complained.

'See?' Daniel had lifted the shirts for her inspection on that Sunday night. 'All the paint's washed out.'

Ella stares at Patrick now, finally understanding the gnawing sensation that she'd felt, listening to her son's casual explanation. She pulls away from him, searching his eyes. And the horror grows as she sees Daniel again, smiling, standing at the ironing-board. 'How bad?' she asks Patrick. 'How bad was the self-harming?'

Patrick moves closer to her. 'Bad. Gillian said there are new scars as well as old.'

'Where?'

'Where we'd never be likely to see them. Tops of his thighs; abdomen; shoulders. The newest ones are on his forearms.'

'Jesus.' She covers her face with her hands for a moment. 'What are we going to do? What are we going to do with all of this?' She gestures around her, her face, her hands: helpless.

'We're going to find out what happened,' Patrick says. He takes her in his arms. 'And, once tomorrow is over, we're going to go back to Edward, to the school, to everyone we can think of. We'll find out, I promise you.'

Patrick

I DON'T WANT TO SPEAK too much about the funeral, Daniel's funeral. When Thursday morning dawned, we were both already awake, Ella and I. I had been for hours. Without a word, we turned to each other and held on tight. Last night's conversation had given both of us a new impetus. Everything was out in the open: no more secrets. Now, at last there was, perhaps, something we could do for our son.

'We'll get through it,' I whispered. 'Somehow. We'll get through it together. I love you so much.'

'Don't let go of me today,' she said. 'Not even for an instant. I need to feel us holding onto each other.'

'I promise.'

We came downstairs that morning to the heady scent of lilies and roses. The whole world had brought or sent flowers. The house was filled with them. Frances had arranged them everywhere. Every day since Monday, she and Sophie brought with them vases and bowls and blocks of green oasis that shed small dry pellets of itself everywhere.

I know they tried their best to bring solace where they could. Each of my three daughters did. They seemed to be everywhere, no matter where I looked. And yet they moved almost silently around us. The three of them: woven together into a tight tapestry of loss. I caught them weeping together in the kitchen on so many occasions. Their grief for Daniel touched me, but

I had to ask them eventually to take the flowers away. Their beauty made Ella ache.

'I can't look at them any more,' she said, when the funeral was over. 'Give them away to someone – anyone. I can't bear to watch them die.'

On the day of the funeral, once again, Ella and I had to endure that strangely comforting pain of other people's kindness. Even now, I remember every minute of it. It was an extraordinary day. Its very existence was unspeakable, and yet the comfort it brought us both was immeasurable.

Every hour of it was filled with family; with men and women who had once been colleagues of mine and of Ella's; with neighbours who came from miles around; with friends. It was as though the whole world stood guard over us. I can still see George Casey's crumpled face, feel the almost painful grip of his handshake. Distress was carved into every one of his elderly features. 'A grand boy, a grand boy,' he kept saying, over and over, as though everything he could ever want to say was contained in those few words. He trembled as he spoke.

Daniel's schoolmates – all of the second-year students, both boys and girls – arranged themselves into a guard of honour and accompanied him to the altar on that last morning. The youngsters' school uniforms were pristine, their shirts a blare of white against the sea of navy. Some wept, some looked straight ahead. Others had that blank, nervous stare of those who are terrified of doing something inappropriate – like laughing, or letting flowers fall, or stumbling against the coffin.

It was, of course, a day of exquisite beauty, the sort of Indian summer that an Irish September can bring. Blue sky, fragrant air, and temperatures of a kind not experienced since early spring.

But I was filled with suspicion as I watched all these young people and their adult, stately progress down the church. I felt as though I had been filled with sand and gravel, something hard and gritty that would cement itself against my insides, making speech or movement impossible. I had to force myself not to give way. I made certain instead that my grip on Ella was sure and strong, just as I had promised.

Instead of tenderness, I felt rage as I watched their young faces. I saw another kind of familiarity – a familiarity that brought me back almost sixty years to the cold halls of boarding school. Knowing what Edward had told us, and Gillian, and the pieces that Ella and I had put together for ourselves the night before, the teenagers' features now became suddenly sharper, their eyes unkinder. A whole hierarchy was revealed in the solemn line that made its way down the aisle of the church. Half-remembered incidents returned to taunt me. Faces from almost six decades earlier began to trouble me again; they became indistinguishable from the faces of those I'd believed to be Daniel's friends.

Watching the young people in the church that day, I was consumed with questions. Was it you? I asked myself. Or you, who tormented my boy? I searched all the faces before me for the nine-year-old Jason, the one who'd been a bully even then. Rage filled me, taking the place of grief.

A young girl called Louise sang 'The Lord is my Shepherd'. She was a soprano, a natural, with a voice of soaring beauty. I listened, bitterly, to the words. Ella had been right after all. There was no God, or at least none that listened to us. Daniel's nieces and nephews – Rebecca's, Frances's and Sophie's children, boys and girls alike – hefted his coffin onto their shoulders and made their way down the aisle. At that moment, I had to gather Ella to me, lift her bodily from the kneeling-board onto which she had crumpled.

Enough.

The day ended eventually. All days do. It ended in a blur of daughters and grandchildren, of food uneaten, of drinks untasted. I know that when we got home, Ella and I sat in the dark, unmoving, unspeaking, holding each other through the night. When the sun rose, we went upstairs and lay on the bed.

It seemed right, somehow, that the old order be broken, or at least challenged. What was night had become day; what was day had become night. We slept a little, I remember. When we woke, Ella's grief terrified me all over again.

But this time, she let me comfort her. She willed herself back towards me, towards calmness. 'We'll find out what happened, won't we, Patrick?'

'Yes,' I replied, with the certainty that now fuelled every waking moment. 'We will.'

'It's the only way I can even begin to bear it,' she said. 'I have to understand whatever it was that we didn't see.'

I pulled her even closer, kissed the top of her head. 'We're going to find out. I won't rest until we do.'

Edward

It happened last Sunday exactly a week ago and I can't stop thinking about Daniel. There are a few different things that I just can't forget.

Like there was this day at the start of second year only a couple of weeks back. I found Daniel in the cloakroom after going-home time. He didn't come down to the bike shed and I was fed up waiting for him. Then I saw the Jays hanging around the boiler house smoking with some of the third year girls. They the girls I mean had already hitched up their skirts the way they do as soon as school's over. There were three of them hanging around James and Jeremy. Jason had two girls of his own. He's way taller this year than last and he was in California for three weeks early in the summer so he's brown. All the girls are falling all over him since we went back. Even the older ones.

There's a spot just behind the boiler shed that can't be seen from the school and it's where everyone smokes during break. But Miss O'Connor has copped it I know because I saw her nab two third years while she was on break duty the other day. There's no need to smoke there after four o'clock because everyone's gone home even most of the teachers but the Jays do it anyway. It's like the school is their kingdom and maybe if they go outside it they'll lose some of their power.

There still wasn't any sign of Daniel so I went back inside.

I didn't want the Jays to see me waiting. I was afraid of what would happen next if they did. The bike shed was where they always hung around at home time, waiting to do stuff. Like that time in first year when they broke Daniel's violin. Hey Paki, they said when we went to get our bikes. And the Lady Daniel as well – that was Jason saying that. The three of them surrounded us and took our jackets and our rucksacks and Daniel's violin. But that time we fought them. Daniel got really mad and landed one on Jason's jaw. It was more of a lucky punch and not all that hard but I think Jason was really shocked instead of hurt. Daniel had never done that before. So Jason just lifted the violin case and whacked it on the ground. Jeremy gave me a bloody nose but I got in a good punch or two and the same with James. Then the caretaker Mr Green appeared and shouted at us. The Jays ran. Me and Daniel cycled home.

I didn't want to go through all that again this year. They have been leaving us alone but. There's been nothin this year although I keep waitin for it to happen. But I got lucky at the football tryouts and that shut them up too. Maybe they've moved onto someone else younger like the new first years. I don't know but I'm just glad that they are leaving me and Daniel alone. So that day a couple of weeks back when I found Daniel I'd sneaked back into the blue corridor and run around to the green. And nobody saw me. Daniel was just sitting there in the cloakroom hunched over like he had a pain somewhere. There was a smell of feet in the cloakroom like there always is but there was a smell of something else as well that I didn't know what it was not then I found out later. What's up I said aren't you comin home. He got a fright he hadn't heard me come in. When he looked up his face was all dirty and his eyes looked really blue like he'd been crying and I think he had. He wiped his nose with his sleeve something he never did and there was a trail like a snail makes of all snot and tears.

I remember everything he said but it didn't make a lot of sense to me not then. He kept saying he was different and he didn't fit in he'd never fit in. Then he said that he was like an alien the mothership had left behind. I laughed out loud but he was dead serious. I sat beside him and there was that smell again only a bit stronger like sweat that has gone all warm and coppery. He wiped his nose in his sleeve again and I saw it. Blood was on the inside of his wrist not like from a cut but kind of like someone's painted it on with a smeary paintbrush.

What's that I said what happened nothin he said I just cut myself by accident. Then he stood up and said let's go. I thought maybe he'd had a fight with Sylvia. He really liked her and I think she liked him too. She used to go to another school before ours. She said she had to improve her English before they'd let her into ordinary school. That was when she changed her name from Sylwia to Sylvia. Because people kept saying it wrong. But I didn't ask Daniel if he'd been fighting with her not then. I didn't ask him anything that day. He took his rucksack and swung it up onto his back he pulled his sleeves down hard and jammed his baseball cap on his head. Usually he waits for me but that day he cycled ahead so fast I couldn't keep up. See ya I called at his gate but he didn't answer so I just went on home.

We'd had English last class that day and Mr Kelly had brought in this story from a magazine about someone called Matisse. He said it was arts journalism at its best and could we see where the writer was been subjective and where he was been objective. We had to read it and underline what bits we thought were one thing and what bits the other and then he asked did anyone know who Matisse was and Daniel said yes without thinking. I know it was without thinking because he went red and then white and kinda sank into his seat. But the whispers had already started and Daniel knew it. Mr Kelly was good at knowing where they were coming from and he stopped them right away. He has a sharp tongue himself so he does. But Daniel wouldn't say any more. So Mr Kelly did instead and he went on and on about collage and stuff and I could see that Daniel had that look again like he was in pain and it would never go away.

Daniel didn't say anything else for the rest of the class and Mr Kelly didn't ask him and he got me to leave the afternoon roll book down to the office quickly because he'd forgotten. I ran all the way but the bell went and when I got back everyone was gone Daniel as well. I took my rucksack and went to the bike shed I had no coat because September was warmer than summer had been. That's when I waited for Daniel and he didn't turn up which is why I went back to look for him in the cloakroom.

I wish I'd said something. I don't know who to maybe Mr Kelly or Miss O'Connor they're both kind or Mr Byrne the woodwork teacher he's sound. Now I don't know what to do I feel sick all the time. I thought it would be better after the funeral but it's not it's worse. But at least the Jays are quiet everyone is.

Sylvia hasn't stopped crying. A lot of the girls haven't. But Sylvia's the one who knew him best. I'd like to talk to her but I can't. I still can't feel anything I keep expecting to see him around the corner. I don't think I can say anything because how much am I to blame for last Sunday when he came over and then left without hardly saying anything. I don't know what else I could of done and I wish I did it feels like something heavy is hanging out of my neck that I have to carry everywhere even at night when I'm asleep. And Mum's starting to ask me if I know anything that might be helpful and I keep saying no.

Besides, Fathersir says that other people's battles are their own and people like us should keep ourselves to ourselves and our own counsel and our powder dry he says.

Part Three: Aftermath

Sylvia

I KNEW NOTHING AT ALL until I came to school last Monday. We live too far away for any news to reach us quickly. What I remember is how quiet the school was that morning. Nobody was outside when I got there.

I was late, almost twenty minutes late. I couldn't find my phone. I looked everywhere. Finally, I found it behind the cushions on the sofa, but by then, Dad was shouting at me that I was going to be late for school. Oscar must have hidden it. He's always doing things like that, just to annoy me. It was out of charge so I just left it there and ran. I hoped I might be able to sneak in through the senior mall once the first class was over. I'd done it once before and I'd got away with it.

When I got to school, I hurried to put my bike in the shed. I couldn't find the key to the lock either and finally I just dumped it there. I felt really angry then: everything was going wrong. I didn't care about the bike. It was old anyway, so probably nobody would want it.

Miss O'Connor was waiting at the door to the junior corridor. I just thought, great. No way of slipping in past her this time. Now I'll get detention as well. It wasn't the first time I'd been late since school began. And she had warned me twice this term already. But this morning she just looked blotchy, as though she had been crying. I thought it was funny that she didn't look cross – I mean, strange, not really funny.

'Good morning, Miss,' I said. But she didn't answer. She just held out her hand to me and touched my arm.

'Sylvia,' she said. 'Come with me.'

I was puzzled. But still I thought that I was the one in trouble. She brought me into her office and patted the back of a chair that stood in front of her desk. 'Sit down, Sylvia,' she said. But she didn't sit behind her desk. Instead, she took the chair beside me.

I sat. And then I waited. I knew that something really strange was going on. I knew that class would have started ages ago and the corridors would be quiet anyway, but this was a different sort of quiet. Miss O'Connor seemed to have difficulty speaking and I began to feel afraid right then. 'Is there something wrong, Miss?' I asked. I mean, I knew I'd get into trouble, but I didn't think it would be this bad.

'Sylvia, I have some bad news.'

Bad news? At first, I was confused. So this wasn't about being late for school, after all. So what was it, then? My thoughts started to get a bit wild. I'd just left Dad so it couldn't be him. Had something happened to Mum on her way to the hospital for the early shift? Or to my little brothers? I think Miss O'Connor must have seen what I was thinking because then she began to speak all in a rush.

'I am so sorry to tell you that there has been a terrible tragedy involving one of our second-year students,' she said. 'One of your own classmates.'

What was she talking about? I could feel that I was beginning to take something in, whatever it was, but she was only feeding me bites of information little by little. 'Who?' I said. I felt stupid then. I didn't even know whether that was the right question to ask.

'Daniel Grant,' she said.

'What's happened to Daniel?' I could feel my heart begin to thump. It was almost painful, the way it suddenly started knocking loudly against my ribs.

Then she reached across and took my hands in hers. 'There is no easy way to tell you this,' and she paused for a minute. Now I was really frightened. 'Daniel died yesterday,' she said quietly. 'I know how close you both were. I am so, so sorry.'

At first I didn't believe her. 'No,' I said. 'We had art together on Friday.' You were there, I wanted to tell her. You taught us, you silly cow. I began to get angry. 'No,' I said again. 'It's a mistake. What are you saying?' And I wrenched myself away from her.

She put her hands on my shoulders and made me look at her eyes. 'I am so desperately sorry, Sylvia, but there is no mistake. Daniel is dead. He died yesterday afternoon.'

At first I said nothing. I just kept looking at her, waiting for her to change her mind. Waiting for the story to be different. And then I wailed. Her eyes were so clear and so honest that I had to believe her. I don't remember the next bit very well. I know that she gave me a glass of water, that she sat close to me, that she stayed with me until I stopped crying, at least for a while.

I had to ask. 'How?' I said. I had to ask her this question, although I was suddenly terrified inside that I already knew the answer.

'He committed suicide, Sylvia. I'm sorry, there is no easy way to tell you that either.'

'Does everyone know?' I don't know why I asked her that, but it seemed important at the time.

She nodded. 'Yes. Mr Murray and Father Kelly and Reverend Lane are with all of the second years now, in assembly. I'll take you there in a few minutes, as soon as you feel ready.'

'I couldn't find my phone,' I blurted. 'My little brother hid it behind the sofa cushions and then it was out of charge this morning. And then I lost the key to my bike.' I was wailing again, but it wasn't about the phone or the key or the bike, not really. Everything made me sad all over again. Everything made me see Daniel's face in front of my eyes.

She squeezed my hands. 'I know. It's okay. We waited for a little while, but we had to start without you.'

I saw our class list on her desk. My name was highlighted in yellow along with a few others. But the others all had ticks beside them, and mine didn't.

'I'm sorry,' I whispered. 'I'm sorry I was late.'

'Sylvia, that doesn't matter. What matters now is that you are with your friends. Are you ready to come with me, or would you like a few more minutes here?'

Suddenly, I wanted to be with Aoife, Niamh and Clare. My friends. 'No, I'm ready to go now,' I said.

She stood up. 'Your friends will show you where you can leave a message of condolence for Daniel's parents,' she said. 'That's if you'd like to. And there are no classes for second years this morning.'

She handed me the box of tissues off her desk. I'd started crying again, every time I thought of his face.

'Mr Nolan and Miss Burke will spend the whole day with you. You can talk to them on your own or with a group of others, whatever you decide. And there will be other counsellors coming too, later on this morning.'

I think I nodded my head. I'm not sure. I don't think that I even said thank you.

'And, Sylvia, I know that you and Daniel had a special friendship. Two of my most talented artists.' And she tried to smile. 'You can also come and talk to me, or to any of the teachers, at any time. Is that okay?'

I know I nodded this time. Then I followed her out of her office and down the corridor to assembly.

*

I spent all that Monday with Niamh and Aoife and Clare. I didn't want to see anybody else. We texted you, they said. We tried to call, loads of times. I told them what happened. They brought me to a table in the mall where somebody – Mr Murray or Miss O'Connor, maybe – had put a framed photograph of Daniel along with some flowers and candles. There was a beautiful white cloth on it, with loads of lace around the edges. It was the kind of lace that Grandma makes. That made me cry so hard I thought I was going to be sick. Then there was a wall – a real wall, I mean, not a Facebook wall – where we could post messages about Daniel. There were some drawings there already, and some poems and then lots of short messages. And there was a Facebook wall later too, but I didn't want to go there. Not after all the things that had happened. Later, Miss O'Connor told us that everything – I mean the real messages – would be put into a beautiful bound book and given to Mr and Mrs Grant.

I wrote them a long letter, but I didn't put it on the wall. Instead, I cycled over to Daniel's house and gave it to his parents myself. I didn't want other people reading it. They were really nice to me, and made me a cup of tea.

I still don't believe it. I can't. I don't want to.

I told Miss O'Connor afterwards about the day in May when we had the substitute teacher. The day when Daniel painted his 'Flight' picture. I told her what I saw.

And I told his parents, too. About that, and about the nasty emails from Daniel, except they weren't, and about the text messages from Spain. I told them everything.

I had to.

Ella

WHEN ELLA WAKES that morning, she does so completely.

The need to know has been weighing on her like water. It has flooded her dreams. It is impossible to resist its pull, impossible not to swim up to the surface. Patrick lies very still beside her. She leans towards her husband, sees that his face is lined and shadowed even now. He stirs, as though he senses her presence. But she will not disturb him, not this morning.

In the past week, ever since that awful Sunday, Ella has slept three, maybe four hours a night at most. She has grown used to waking suddenly, her heart pounding, her eyes seeing shadows flicker above the bed. Or she has watched her dreams flee towards the darkened corners of the room: always just beyond her reach. As she glances over at Patrick now, something sad and tender clutches at her. His face betrays every one of his seventy years. Before he comes to, Ella slips out of bed, her bare feet silent on the wooden floor.

She makes her way to Daniel's bedroom. She stands at the open door, looking in. Everything is in its place. The single bed, the chest of drawers beside it. The squat wardrobe that has been part of this house for as long as she has lived here. And the blue chair, standing silent in the corner. Her breath catches as she remembers.

'See, Mum?' Daniel is looking at her eagerly. He twirls the

old chair around on one of its legs, an apprentice magician about to perform some sleight of hand. Ella has gone in search of him one evening to the garage: he's done his usual trick of going missing just as dinner is ready. 'I've fixed it. All it needed was a couple of new dowels. I asked Mr Byrne about it and he showed me how to do it today. What do you think?'

And Ella looks at the wooden chair, listing sadly again to one side: its white paint cracked and flaking. She falters. 'It doesn't seem very different,' she begins.

'No, but look.' Daniel puts it right-side up and sticks the toe of his trainer under the one leg that is still shorter than all the others. Immediately, Ella can see the transformation. The solid, undulating seat looks steady once more. The broken spindle at the back has been replaced. Finally, it looks like a chair again. Up until then, it has simply been one of her father's belongings, something hiding in the garage because she can't bear to throw it out. Her father had thrown nothing out: he'd believed that everything could be mended.

'The only thing I have to do is strip off all the old paint, glue a new piece to the front leg, and then sand everything back. Mr Byrne says one coat of primer, two undercoat an' one top-coat an' it'll be like new.'

Ella laughs. 'You are more like Granddad than you know! Well done.'

'Can I have it for my bedroom, then?'

Ella nods. 'Of course. It's yours.'

Daniel stands back at once, making a pretend lens with his hands, squinting through the rectangle formed by his fingers. 'Blue, I think,' he said. 'A really old-fashioned chair with a really modern colour. What do you reckon?'

'I reckon that's just fine,' she says, taking her son firmly by the elbow. 'Although the chair might die of fright: it hasn't been painted in about thirty years.'

'Deadly!' He loops one arm around her waist and they walk back to the kitchen together.

Ella swallows now as the memory engulfs her. Just one short year ago: a happy boy, starting secondary school. Filled with enthusiasms new and old: art, woodwork, drama workshops. She has not been able to touch that chair since Daniel died. All she has been able to do in the days that followed, is to stumble to his bed and inhale her son. She breathes in the sour note of his sweat, undercut with the sharp, metallic scent of the violent-blue shower gel that he liked.

But this morning, she is finally ready. Something in here is waiting to be found. It feels urgent: she just doesn't know what it is yet. It came to her last night as the sleeping tablet was beginning its work. In that drowsy, heady stage of oblivion, Ella had a sudden, blinding vision of her son's bedroom. The walls with their posters and photographs. The furnishings that have remained resolutely closed to her since his death. It was as though her unconscious self had been getting ready to see it all again, but this time from a different angle.

As she struggled against sleep, something began to insinuate its way to the surface. She tried to swim towards it – a bright corner of alertness – but her limbs refused to cooperate. Then sleep had overcome her; or what passed for sleep these days. A thin, restless covering that wavered over and around her for a few hours and then disappeared, leaving her hot-eyed and exhausted. But she supposed that Gillian and Patrick were right: that it was better than nothing.

She should probably wait until Patrick wakes before she does this. He might be upset that she has come here without him again. But, right now, she is too impatient. She steps across the threshold into her son's room. If there is something to be found here in this space, then she will find it.

Even in the midst of her grief during those searing first days,

Ella had worried about Daniel's mobile phone. She and Patrick had searched everywhere for it. They'd wanted above all to make sure to switch it off, to avoid its ghost startling them with one of Daniel's many alarms and reminders.

'We have to find it,' Ella said. 'I can't bear the thought of hearing it ring. And there have to be names, numbers, messages that he kept private. They have to tell us *something*.'

But they hadn't found it in his rucksack, his jacket, or beside his computer: all the places where it normally lived. Last night and this morning the memory of that absence has begun to return with renewed insistence, a loose thread among so many others. Ella moves over to the bed and slowly, carefully, lowers herself onto it.

She glances at the wall to her right, the one behind the headboard. This space between the window and the corner is almost completely covered with one enormous collage: Daniel's prize-winning photographic essay, from Christmas of first year. She can still remember the October evening when she and Patrick watched as Daniel had manhandled a large piece of plywood from the garage into the conservatory. His body was still slight, still compact. He hadn't grown the coltish legs and arms that Ella had observed on other teenagers. He hadn't yet acquired their awkwardness either.

'Can I use the table here?' he'd asked, breathless. 'It's wider than Granddad's bench in the garage.'

'Of course,' Ella said, swiftly moving one of her mother's pieces of porcelain out of the way. A shepherdess with sheep grazing forever at her feet. She'd never liked it: the coy smile, the knowing eyes, the colours that now seemed garish. For a moment, she regretted salvaging it. 'What are you making?'

'A collage. I'm going to use all the old photographs you said I could have.'

'Any particular reason?' Patrick asked.

Daniel had grinned. 'For a competition at school. Someone has made an anonymous donation of a prize – it's five hundred euro.'

'For what?' Ella was intrigued.

'For an essay. It's to be a narrative about the events and the people that have influenced your life.' Daniel scrubbed at the plywood, smoothing and cleaning it with a damp cloth. 'I'm going to sand this and paint the background white.'

'A narrative?' Patrick sounded puzzled.

'Yeah.' Daniel's eyes had lit up. 'A narrative. Loads of people are talkin' about what they're going to write.' He paused. 'But no one said it had to be written.' He looked from one of his parents to the other. 'You can have a visual essay, right? A visual narrative?'

Ella remembers nodding. Patrick didn't look convinced.

'Well, the prize is "to foster creativity", according to Miss O'Connor. So I'm gettin' creative. It's to be finished by the end of November. Loads of time.' His smile had been broad by then. 'I can buy a deadly new camera for five hundred euro.'

'Go for it!' Ella said. 'What a great prize!'

'Do you need anything else from the garage?' Patrick had asked. Ella remembers being taken aback at his response. He'd looked tentative, almost apprehensive. She asked him about it later.

Patrick shook his head. 'Don't worry about it. It's probably nothing. I'm sure it's me, not him.'

'How do you mean?' Ella was curious. Patrick looked suddenly uncomfortable.

He half laughed. 'Well, where I went to school, if you raised your head above the parapet like that, your life wouldn't be worth living.'

'You mean they'd make fun of you?'

'Worse.' His expression was grim. 'Fun has nothing to do

with it. It'd be hell. But,' and here he paused, looking at Ella, 'I guess times have changed.'

'I guess they have.' Ella remembers that conversation vividly now. She remembers how she'd turned and looked at Daniel, his head bent over the table, the photographs spread out all around him. She'd had a sharp stab of misgiving. But what were they to do? Curb their son's enthusiasm? Dumb him down so that he wouldn't stand out from everyone else? Her spirit rebelled at the notion. Nonetheless, she remembers the worry – remembers it all the more acutely now, this morning, in Daniel's silent, empty bedroom.

She has deliberately avoided looking at that same collage until this morning. Now she examines it steadily. She does not avert her eyes. Instead, she searches it, looking for something, anything that might illuminate her son's last days, weeks, months. She wonders if Jason MacManus appears in any of the photographs. She wonders if she'd recognize him: whether he looks like his father.

There are dozens and dozens of images making up the collage – each one carefully cut from larger photographs, all arranged into the jigsaw of Daniel's young life. Most of them had once been part of Patrick's photographs – innumerable boxes of black-and-white images that he had collected over the years. Ella concentrates on the pictures before her, wondering if she will be able to bear seeing them with different eyes.

There is the bridge over the stream where Daniel had taken his first steps. There are the bird tables in winter, as she and Daniel's younger self leave out bread, hang up small nets of nuts. They are wearing wellington boots; there is a thin covering of snow on the ground. Daniel had considered each photo very carefully before cropping it; had taken hours to choose its final position on the board.

Other pictures were taken by Daniel himself: photographs of

the bird sanctuary; of the *Aurora*, with Edward grinning at the tiller; of a young girl, with blonde hair that almost reaches to her waist. Ella looks closer. The girl is smiling into the camera, a direct, unselfconscious gaze. Ella has no idea who she is. She has no memory of this photograph. In fact, she is sure she has never seen it before. As she runs her finger over the edges, it seems that this photo was added later. It does not sit as smoothly as the others.

The image gives Ella pause. Who is this young girl? Although the photo is in black and white, Ella recognizes the girl's uniform as belonging to Daniel's school. They have to visit, she remembers suddenly, she and Patrick. They must go, and soon. There is Daniel's locker to be cleared out, teachers to be spoken to, questions to be asked. Perhaps they can even get to speak to this young girl, whoever she is. She might have something important to tell them. Ella examines the other images before her, one by one.

Right in the centre – the fulcrum from which all the other images radiate – is the interior of her father's garage. Daniel has photographed it as though it were an Aladdin's cave. The garage with its tools and all its dark corners and boxes and jars full of bits of oddly shaped metal: it suddenly looks mysterious, alluring, full of treasures. If she looks closely, she can see a tiny image of her father and herself – the photograph taken on his eighty-fifth birthday party. Ella remembers the day Daniel borrowed it, the way he'd hugged it to him as he disappeared into the garage along with his camera. She remembers, too, how he'd replaced the photograph carefully in the conservatory afterwards. His young face had been alight with the excitement of this new project.

Ella stands up. She can't bear any more of this. She will come back later. If she stays, she will feel all the strands of herself unravelling again. Besides, it has told her enough for this morning. Right now, she has to do something practical, useful; she needs to keep moving.

'Where is your phone, Daniel? Where did you hide it?' She moves towards the wardrobe, puts one hand on the handle and stops for a moment. Then, almost briskly, she pulls both doors open together and stands, foursquare, in front of the open shelves. One of the wooden doors creaks faintly at first, pulling away from her a little. Then it stops, suspended.

She reaches in and pulls out the tumble of clothes that crowd the bottom shelf. Sweaters, sweatshirts, single socks, tracksuit bottoms. She begins to fold each one, smoothing it against her as she does so. She has all of the shelves emptied, and part of the hanging-space, when she becomes aware of Patrick's presence.

She turns to see him watching her. She starts and feels immediately guilty when she sees his face. If anything, he looks worse than ever this morning: gaunt, haunted. It's as though he's kept going right up until the funeral was over, standing guard over her, over all his family. Now, he seems to have faded, to have fallen in on himself. He is looking at the piles of neatly folded clothes on Daniel's bed. She can see by his expression that he is shocked, as though she has transgressed in some way.

'What are you doing?'

Ella goes to him at once and takes his hand. 'I'm searching, Patrick. There has to be something here that will help us understand what happened to Daniel.' She gestures around her with her free hand. 'We never found his phone. We haven't even looked at his computer.' She shrugs. 'Maybe there are notebooks, or emails or *something* that will give us some sort of a clue. And there are so many photos that we need to look at more closely.' Her husband's face is impassive. 'But it's the phone above all. He loved that iPhone, sweetheart. Don't you think it's strange that we haven't found it?'

Patrick sighs, and Ella thinks for a moment that his knees are about to crumple under his weight. 'I need to sit down.' She hurriedly pushes two towers of sweaters out of the way and Patrick sits, heavily, onto the single bed. 'Don't you think it's too soon to be clearing out his room?'

'I'm not clearing out his— Patrick, what is it? What do you mean? ' Ella is shocked. She is able to hear the fear in her own voice.

Patrick turns to face her. His eyes are two deep pools of grief. His unshaven face is suddenly white, vulnerable. Old. 'We didn't see what was going on under our noses. We are guilty of not seeing things, of not intervening, of just being plain fucking *useless*. Both of us.' He begins to cry. Great, gulping sobs. Ella kneels on the floor in front of him, places her arms around his waist and rests her head against his chest.

'Don't, Patrick. Please don't. We can't go down that road, not yet. We owe it to Daniel. All I know is I need to find out. I need to look for the truth.' Her voice breaks and Patrick's hand is instantly at her face, cupping her chin. He looks into her eyes.

'Are you sure?'

'Yes.' She holds his gaze. 'And you're right. I *am* afraid of what we're going to find out. But I'm even more afraid of *not* finding out. We need to know, Patrick, and we need to start looking now.'

He nods. 'Yes.' And 'Yes' again. He sounds resigned.

She kisses him. 'Why don't you sleep, or just rest a little more? I'll finish in here and maybe later, we could take a look at his computer?'

'I can't rest,' he says. 'And I can't sleep. Let's just do this, bit by bit. And let's do it together.'

Ella watches as his eye roves around the room. His gaze alights on Daniel's computer. 'Have you switched it on yet?' he asks.

Ella shakes her head. 'No. I couldn't bear to. I wanted us both to do it together, when we felt ready.'

'Do you feel ready now?'

'Yes. I do.'

Patrick takes her by the hand and sits on Daniel's swivel chair. Ella pulls over the blue chair, hesitates, and finally lowers herself onto the wooden seat. She glances to her right. Patrick is composed again; there is something of his old purposefulness struggling to the surface.

'Okay,' he says. 'We are going to try every combination of names and numbers that we can think of, to see if we can unlock the password. Have you any idea what it might be?'

Ella shakes her head. 'He told me once that my password was too weak. That I should have numbers as well as letters. I can only assume that his will be strong.'

'There are ways of doing this, you know, even if we can't.' He looks at her. 'I've already spoken to Sophie. She says there are all sorts of specialized software packages that can unlock passwords. She's promised to help if we can't do it ourselves.'

Ella's face lights up. 'Sophie! Of course! I never even thought of her, but, yes, of course!' She feels suddenly filled with all the optimism of possibility.

'Do you still want to have a go?' Patrick is watching her. 'Or will we just get Sophie to come over tonight?'

'I don't want to wait,' she says. 'I want to try. It's important. We can always call Sophie later on if we aren't getting anywhere.'

Three hours later, they have given up. Patrick sits back in the chair and admits defeat. 'That's everything I can think of,' he says.

'It doesn't matter,' Ella says, 'now that we know Sophie can help. Call her, Patrick. Call her now. Let her know what we need.'

There is the sudden, unexpected peal of the doorbell. Patrick stands up. 'I'll go,' he says. At least he's fully dressed. Ella pulls her dressing gown more tightly around her.

'I'd better change,' she says. She hurries towards their bedroom.

When Patrick opens the door, there is a young girl standing there, about Daniel's age, dressed in a school uniform. She is small, slight, with the bluest eyes he has ever seen. Her white-blonde hair is roped into two severe plaits that hang almost to her waist. Her expression is grave, her cheeks flushed with embarrassment.

'Mr Grant?'

'Yes,' Patrick says. He makes sure his tone is gentle. 'Can I help you?'

She holds out one hand, awkwardly. He shakes it, surprised at this old-fashioned formality.

'I am Sylvia. A good friend of Daniel's.'

Patrick stands back, opens the door wider. 'Sylvia. You are very welcome. Please, come in.'

Sylvia

I WASN'T SURE where to start, and I probably babbled on too much, but I told Mr and Mrs Grant everything I could. I must have jumped about a bit because his dad looked puzzled and asked me a question from time to time. I thought it was important to tell them first that Daniel was really good at art. That Miss O'Connor loved him; we could all see that. I was sometimes a tiny bit jealous of him. In my old school, before we ever came here, I was the best of everyone at art. I won the prize every Christmas. But even I could see that my pictures were only pretty. Daniel's were different – always dark, always full of movement. 'Dynamic, powerful': these were only some of the teacher's words. She would write her comments on the back of all our pages and Daniel was always eager to read what she had said about his. I did not even need to peer over his shoulder to see her praise: he would always show me. He was proud, but in a nice way. I had to get used to being second best.

Then I told them about how I got to know Daniel, when we were still in first year. She – Miss O'Connor – arranged us all in random groups for our project. I ended up sitting beside Daniel for that, and even when the project finished, we kept on sitting together. Miss O'Connor never minded if we chatted, as long as we got on with our work. And we always did: Daniel was serious like that. And so was I. I also liked the way he helped me sometimes. He would tell me something if he thought

I was stuck. And often, when Miss O'Connor got into one of her abstract moods, I *was* stuck.

I liked the still lifes or the playing with colour best. I even liked the drawing with charcoal – I did some really good portraits of Lisa in charcoal. Daniel grinned when he saw what I had done. I'd made Lisa's nose even longer than it is, and made her ears stick out more. Just a little, so that it looked like I was at fault because of my drawing. I was careful not to 'stray into caricature' – we'd all been warned about that. But I don't really like Lisa, and she does look down her nose at me. So I thought it was the right bit of her face to emphasize.

'She looks *so* snobby,' Daniel said, almost under his breath. I was startled – I hadn't realized he was looking. I think I blushed. Either way, my face felt warm and I looked away.

'It's great,' he said. ''Cos she *is* snobby.' He nudged me with his elbow, forcing me to turn and look at him. And then we both grinned. We were good friends after that.

The day I remember most was sometime last May, just before we broke up for the summer. Miss O'Connor was at some teachers' meeting, and we had a substitute, Miss Clarke. She was useless. Totally useless. It took her ages to get the class under control. 'No more talking', she kept shouting, over and over. She was the one making all the noise. What is wrong with talking when you are working? I have never understood that.

In the end, she only managed to control us because Miss O'Connor had left us work to do, and it had to be collected once the double period was over. Most of us groaned when we heard what it was. Another one of Miss O'Connor's 'concepts' – I never knew what to do with these random words that she used to write on the board. Things like 'Wild' or 'Serenity' or 'Progress' – stuff like that. They were words that always made me feel helpless, but Daniel loved them.

When she finally got us quiet, Miss Clarke wrote just one

word on the board: 'Flight'. That was easier than most, I thought. I was relieved – at least I'd be able to produce *something* before the class ended. I looked over at Daniel. He was very quiet, but he often was when he was thinking something out.

'You okay?' I whispered. Miss Clarke glared in my direction, but I ignored her. She'd disappear after class anyway, and we'd probably never see her again. Lots of teachers came and went in our school. Students, I think. They were hardly ever any good.

'Yeah.' He nodded, but he really didn't look at me. Instead, his head was bent and he started work immediately. I thought maybe I'd done something on him, but then he looked up and smiled and I knew it was okay. He looked very pale, though, and his freckles stood out a lot. I never got to ask if there was something wrong. I tried to catch a glimpse of what he was drawing, but Daniel could be very secretive until he had finished whatever it was he was doing. It kind of annoyed me that day. It's not like primary school, is it, where people curl their arms around their copy-books in case someone else tries to steal their answers? You can't really copy someone else's art homework, can you?

Anyway, I'd seen pictures of an albatross on the telly, just a few nights beforehand. Dad loves watching National Geographic and sometimes I sit with him. 'The greatest wingspan in the world,' he said, pointing at the TV screen. I have to admit it was impressive, especially when you saw a person standing beside the bird in a colony somewhere in New Zealand. It was *huge*. My idea was to fill the page with the wings of the albatross: just that, as though I was looking down on the bird from above. That way, the picture would say that the albatross was flying, but so was the artist. I'd have to be in flight too, wouldn't I, to capture the bird from above? I was pleased with that. It seemed to fit the 'concept' that Miss O'Connor was always going on about.

By the time I got started, Daniel was really into it. He used to get that way sometimes. His face would become one whole focus, like a lens directed towards the page. His mind must have gone away somewhere else, too, because he never even looked up when I asked him to pass me the pencils.

We started packing up around ten past three, our usual ten minutes before class ended. Miss O'Connor was always very fussy about things being put back in their proper place, pencils in their boxes, or brushes cleaned if we were using them, paper tidied away. When Daniel left to put the A2 sheets on the shelf, I sneaked a look at his page.

For a moment, I couldn't move or think any sort of a thought that made sense. Daniel's page – all of it – was filled with the most dramatic picture I'd ever seen him do. This was way beyond Miss O'Connor's 'dynamic' or 'powerful'. It frightened me. It was like a vision from hell. I saw what Daniel had done: he'd taken 'Flight' to mean 'Escape'. My first, almost jealous thought was that Miss O'Connor would be well pleased with him. This was a concept, all right – and I bet he was the only one to twist it around like that, in a good way, a real artist's way.

There was a figure in the top left, fleeing from whatever was pursuing it. The figure was just like what Daniel had done lots of times before, only better. With a few bold, black strokes, the figure shimmered. It seemed to move across the page, hands outstretched, running for its life. In pursuit were three – what can I call them: hounds? Again, just a few strokes to create strange creatures, with fangs and eyes that were wild and staring. And then there was a fourth figure, in the lower left-hand corner. This figure wasn't chasing; it was crouching instead, looking ready to pounce at any minute. There was something familiar about all four of them. Something that made the back of my neck prickle. While Daniel's back was turned, I pulled the sheet of paper closer to me, while pretending to be busy packing away the pencils.

As I looked, each of the creatures' faces began to settle into something that I recognized. But I still didn't know what it was that I recognized. It was something that disturbed me, and I could not get it out of my head.

Miss Clarke came along then, telling us all to hurry up, the bell was about to go and nobody was going anywhere until the room was left as it should be, blah blah blah. Once the bell went we ignored her, of course, all spilling out into the corridor at the same time.

I never got the chance to ask Daniel about it. And by the time Miss O'Connor would have seen it, it was too late. The summer holidays had already begun: and maybe she never meant to see that day's work, anyway. Maybe it was just a way to keep us quiet for Miss Clarke.

It was around ten that night. I'd finished my homework and Oscar and Philip were already in bed. Mum was getting ready for the night shift at the hospital, and Dad was on the sofa. I'd known that things were bad from the moment I came in from school. Dad hates doing nothing. Hates it even more when he sees Mum going out to work. It's not her fault. And of course it's not his fault either. I feel sorry for her, for both of them. That's not why we came here: we could have had it this bad in Poland, without ever leaving home.

It was when I heard the front door close that I realized it.

The creatures in Daniel's drawing had faces, real human faces. Recognizable faces, and I know that sounds mad. Because when I looked first, all I saw were fangs and eyes. So the shock when I understood it made me feel breathless for a moment. The hounds had the faces of the Jays – Jason, James and Jeremy.

The crouching figure, that one that looked like a lion, that was Leo. Which meant that the fleeing figure had to be Daniel. I didn't know what to do with that knowledge.

I wish I had known. I wish that I'd done something anyway, even if it didn't make any difference.

I wish I'd had somebody to tell.

Patrick

IT MUST HAVE BEEN early in the week following Daniel's funeral. Things get a bit hazy, they slip from my memory from time to time, so I that can no longer be certain of exact days or dates, but I don't struggle any more if they evade me. Such exactitude is not so important now, anyway, three and a half years later. What is important is our first meeting with Sylvia. I remember opening the door and being surprised by this diminutive presence standing between two pots of hydrangeas. She looked both terrified and determined.

I had no idea who she was back then, or why she had come. Of course, I knew that she had to be a student at Daniel's school. Her navy uniform told me that. She introduced herself and I invited her in. I don't remember exactly what I said to her, but I know that I did my best to make her feel welcome.

I remember, too, that I suddenly had no idea what to do with her. Do you offer tea to an unknown teenager? Should she even be in my company while on her own? What laws of political correctness was I breaking?

To my relief, Ella appeared in the hallway almost at once. Sylvia held out her hand to her. 'Mrs Grant,' she said in that grave way she had, 'my name is Sylvia. I am a friend of Daniel's.'

I am a friend. That use of the present tense.

I saw Ella look at her intently, as though she already knew her. She held onto the girl's hand in both of hers. But she didn't know her, did she? Did we? If we did, then I had forgotten.

'Sylvia, how nice to meet you. I was just looking at your photograph upstairs. I was admiring your lovely hair.'

I was startled. What had I missed out on? Or, more likely, what was I forgetting?

The girl's lip trembled. 'Daniel kept a photo of me?'

'Yes,' said Ella, gently. 'In the collage he did of his life. He only included those people who were significant to him. You were one of them.'

She bowed her head. I was afraid she might cry, or flee from us.

'How about I make us all some tea?' I said. The Irish solution to all crises, national or domestic – but what else could I do?

'Yes, please,' the girl said. I was surprised at how she had suddenly composed herself. She turned to Ella. 'I hope it is all right to come here today. My parents said yes and Miss O'Connor has given me permission.'

'Of course it's all right,' said Ella. 'We are very glad to meet you. Come and sit down, Sylvia.' Ella led her into the conservatory, I busied myself with the tea things. When I followed them in, Sylvia had an envelope in her hands. I couldn't help feeling intensely curious about its contents and about her visit.

'I came to give you this,' she said. 'It is my letter to Daniel. There are others in the school, but I wanted this one to be private.' She handed the envelope to me.

I was nonplussed. What was expected of me?

'I wanted to tell you some things, also,' she said. 'My father has said that they could be very important.'

Ella leaned towards her. 'We would be very happy indeed to hear anything you could tell us. Anything at all that might help us understand what made Daniel so unhappy.'

She nodded. 'I'll tell you,' she said. 'I will tell you everything I know.'

Sylvia

AND THEN I TOLD them that I liked Daniel.

He was not the same as the other boys. He never called me Polack or signed rude things with his fingers or made fun of the way I speak.

Daniel told me about going sailing and birdwatching and how he wished he had a brother, but he didn't, and Edward was almost as good. I knew that the Jays had been horrible to him and Edward at first. I knew that they had broken his violin and pushed him over in the corridor and things like that. I thought to myself that they would probably stop over the summer holidays.

I went home to Poland for June and July to stay with my grandmother and grandfather. Anyway, I started getting messages from Daniel at the end of July on my email. They were horrible. They said things that weren't true. And there were some photographs. Of me, with no top on – but they weren't of me at all, just my face. I cried and cried. Then I emailed Daniel and told him to stop and why was he being so horrible to me. He wrote back at once and said he was in Spain with his dad. He said that his dad's email account was safe and I could answer him there. Someone had got into his address book he said. He promised he had not said any of those bad things.

I believed him. We talked some more on gmail chat and then we texted each other. He said he knew it was the Jays.

Mostly Jason, though – the others were too thick. He said they had a website of him with dirty pictures and that they were sending nasty messages to everyone they could. He said it never stopped and that he would prefer them to beat him up. At least they can only beat you up in school, he said, but with the messages they can beat you up all the time even at night and even when you are in your own bed.

When we went back to school this September he was very quiet, but Daniel was often quiet so I didn't mind. But then the Jays started whistling every time they saw us together at break-time or lunchtime, and James kept on making rude sounds. I don't think I have ever heard James speak, not proper words. He just grunts, like an animal. Daniel said to ignore them and they would go away. But they didn't go away.

When this happened to Daniel last week, I remembered the picture that he had done just before we broke up for the summer holidays.

The one where the Jays are chasing him and Leo is waiting to jump.

I told Miss O'Connor about it yesterday and she promised to go and find it just as soon as she could. She told me not to say anything to anybody yet because this could be very important evidence. But I had to tell you and I had to give you this letter because I can't stop thinking about him and I can't stop crying.

I miss him and I don't know what else to do.

Patrick

I KNOW THAT ELLA and I sat in stunned silence for several minutes. Sylvia wept so hard that I could feel my own tears begin to well up in response. The poor child was broken-hearted. We had sat, riveted, throughout this young girl's story. She was articulate, thoughtful and emotional by turns. At one point, she seemed unbearably vulnerable. At another, she unspooled her narrative with a degree of sophistication and awareness that astonished us both. We discussed her endlessly afterwards.

Ella stroked her hands. 'Thank you for telling us, Sylvia. We have an appointment with Mr Murray tomorrow morning. It's really useful for us to know all of this before we meet him.'

Sylvia sobbed and sobbed, and Ella tried to comfort her. But my thoughts were racing ahead of myself. I could hardly keep up with them. Would there be a record somewhere of Daniel and Sylvia's conversations? Of their texts? Could these be evidence against whoever these obnoxious – dangerous – Jays were? Would we be able to gather enough to go to the Guards? I was impatient to phone Sophie. I wanted her here, today, tonight, so that we could follow this trail and see where it led us.

I felt my thinking become clearer, faster. It was as though new neurons were firing, that new pathways were being carved – pathways that would lead us out of this maze of uncertainty and take us towards resolution. I had not felt so alert, so consumed with a sense of purpose in a long time. I remember another strange realization, too. I remember feeling that I had suddenly entered another world, one in which events were spinning around me, chaotic, disparate, puzzling. It was similar to what I had felt on the day we returned home to find Daniel in his bedroom. On that occasion, I felt that the world had suddenly spun out of control, that my own life eluded my reach and my grasp. But this time, I felt that there were things I could control, things I could structure, things I could organize towards knowledge. It was, finally, a good feeling.

But now I had to ask this young girl something. I'd be as gentle as I could. 'Sylvia,' I began. 'We both know how very difficult this must be for you.'

She looked at me, her eyes bluer than ever.

'You came to us because you want to acknowledge your special friendship with Daniel, and because you'd like to help, isn't that right?'

She nodded. I took a deep breath.

'We need to start gathering evidence of everything that was happening to Daniel. Do you by any chance have the texts and the emails that Daniel sent you? Could we see them?' My fists were clenched in my trouser pockets. I couldn't bear it if her reply were to crush the first tentative stirrings of hope. I could see Ella watching me: I knew that she was thinking the same things I was.

Sylvia motioned towards the envelope. 'They're in there along with my letter. Dad said they might be important. We printed them off last night and he took photos of the texts for you – but they're still on my phone as well. I didn't delete them. You can borrow it if you want.' Her face was earnest, tear-stained innocence.

I was swamped with an intensity of relief that left me breathless. 'Thank you and your dad very much for this, Sylvia. I can't tell you how grateful we are.'

We sat and Ella talked to her. I couldn't. My mind was working the way it should be at last, stripping away the inessentials, planning the outline of my response, winkling out every bit of information that might serve our cause. With a jolt, I remembered something that Sylvia had just said, had just reminded me of: that Daniel had used my laptop in Madrid on that fateful afternoon. My email account, rather than his own. I remembered that distinctly. I didn't even need Sophie to find that bit of evidence – I could do it for myself.

I was impatient now for Sylvia to be gone. I know that that was an ignoble way to feel, but that is the plain truth of it. There were so many things I needed to do.

She left, finally, thanking us shyly for the tea. She refused a lift back to school, said that her bike was just outside. Ella took her phone number, gave her ours, told her to call at any time, that she would always be welcome. She got the girl's permission to ring her father, to thank him.

I think Sylvia was proud of what she had done. When she left, her eyes were brighter and there was no longer any sign of embarrassment in her gaze. We promised we'd be in touch soon. Then we waited until she was safely on the road to school, waved, and closed the door behind her.

Ella looked at me, her eyes full of anguished hope. 'Patrick – tell me that that's all really useful. I mean, now we can begin to grapple with what happened to Daniel, can't we? What sort of monsters are these three boys?' And her voice cracked on the final word. I held her hand, gripped her firmly.

'Yes,' I said. 'Yes, we can get a proper handle on it. Thank Christ for Sylvia and her father.' My tone was as grimly determined as I felt. I reached out for Sylvia's envelope.

'Come on – let's go and find out what Daniel left on my laptop while we were in Madrid.'

Edward

ASSEMBLY WAS REAL quiet on that first Monday. We were all
told to go there instead of to our classrooms and Mr Murray
the principal and Miss O'Connor the deputy principal were
waiting for us. I looked everywhere for Sylvia but she must of
been late because I didn't see her until much later and I knew
to look at her that she had been crying. Edward, she said, and
then couldn't say any more. I put my arms around her and she
sobbed and sobbed. Everybody was hugging everybody else and
nobody said a word. Nobody was messing like other days either.
It was like as though everybody knew how to behave even
though nothing like this had ever happened before. I looked
out for the Jays and they were there but you wouldn't know
by them that they had anything to feel bad about. They were
standing beside Leo Byrne the guy who only arrived when we
were halfway through first year. He came from the city so he
didn't really have any friends at least not in the old crowd.
I didn't really know him just that he sometimes hung around
with the Jays. He looked sicker than any of the others that
morning and I wondered if there was something he knew.
Mr Murray was asking us to speak to the counsellors if we had
anything to say even if it didn't seem important or significant.
We had our own counsellors that we knew and there were
another two we had never seen before, plus another chaplain.

It's okay I said and patted Sylvia on the back but it wasn't okay. I had to stop her from going over to the Jays, but. She said something about a picture and how they'd been chasing Daniel but I didn't really understand her she was crying too hard. All the counsellors were saying how important it was to tell everything we knew that might have hurt Daniel. They said it over and over again, except in all different ways. Miss Burke was nice to me once and I just decided there and then to put my name onto a slip of paper and have a confidential meeting on my own. She waited until Miss O'Connor called everyone into the cafeteria for tea and biscuits. Sylvia had gone over to her friends. That way nobody would notice me gone, not with all the moving around that was going on.

I followed her into her office and she was kind. Once I started talking to her I wasn't able to stop. I cried when I remembered what first year had been like for me and Daniel and I told her everything. I told her that mostly I got called Paki and darkie but once nigger and one of the teachers was standing behind us so Jason got into a shitload of trouble. I told her the way they used to pick on us most days especially Jason but I think that sometimes Jeremy was worse. He was bigger and a year older and he was the one who pushed into us in the corridor and Daniel fell and banged his head against the wall he didn't cry but I could see that he wanted to and Miss O'Connor came running down the corridor. Sorry Miss Jeremy said I didn't see him. But she just looked at him and said outside my office now. And I told her as well that Daniel said later that Miss O'Connor made it worse even though she was trying to make it better.

Fathersir always told me to say if I got racist stuff like that but I never told him not once what was the point. Things only got worse when Daniel played the violin at the Christmas concert but he wouldn't give in I kind of admired him for that but the Jays told us we'd better enjoy that Christmas because it was going to be our last.

Patrick

ALL THREE OF MY DAUGHTERS arrived together that evening.

I mention them here because I have become increasingly aware as I write – and indeed, I was also aware even at the time – that, despite my best efforts, I had again begun to take the support of each of them for granted. It brought back painful memories of life after Cecilia's sudden death, and I confessed as much to them.

'It's nothing like that time, Dad,' Frances said. She shook her head at me. 'You are a different man, and this is a very different loss.'

We were in the kitchen together, just she and I, making coffee. The others were in the conservatory.

'I want you to know that I appreciate – that Ella and I both appreciate – all that the three of you have done. I don't believe we'd have got through that first week without you.' I meant it. Their presence had been an inexpressible comfort to me. I had felt profoundly sorry for Ella in her isolation: no brothers, no sisters, no family. No children.

Frances kissed me. 'We're here for you, all of us. You only have to ask. And,' here she looked at me, 'you might take some small solace from the fact that Rebecca deeply regrets the breach between you. She really wants to make it right.' Frances paused. 'I'm sorry, I've probably spoken out of turn. I should let her tell you yourself. Daniel's death has truly devastated her.'

It was a solace: a small, surprising one, but something nonetheless. It made me want to be generous towards my eldest daughter. Life is much too short.

Sophie was already working on my laptop when we carried the coffee into the conservatory. Ella was at one shoulder, Rebecca at the other.

'You're right, Dad, it is all here,' Sophie said. 'Nothing has been deleted, as far as I can see. His email to Sylvia, hers to him, and the entire content of their gmail chat. I've managed to print it out, just for ease of access for you.'

Rebecca's face was a white mask of fury. 'Who are these poisonous little bastards?' she said, her words exploding around her.

I think we were all taken aback. We stopped whatever we were doing and looked at her. I suppose Ella and I had had our initial shocks in small stages. We had begun to expect the worst: indeed, we were dedicated to finding it. But this was the first time any of my daughters had had to face this . . . this evil. It is not a word I use lightly. Nor was it, I believe, too strong a word in the circumstances.

'They are known as the Jays,' I said, calmly. 'Three boys, Jason, Jeremy and James with someone called Leo on the sidelines. They attend Daniel's school. We're going there tomorrow to empty Daniel's locker. We'll meet the principal, and at least start a conversation about all of this. But we can't really move on it until we have more evidence.'

Rebecca was livid. 'I've heard of this, of course,' she said. 'This cyber-bullying. But I didn't realize how vicious it could be.' She was shaking. 'What can we do with the information we have?'

The 'we' touched me.

'Gather all of it,' said Ella, at once. 'Go to the school, gather more. Then go to the police, once we've gathered everything we can.' As she spoke, she was putting Sophie's pages into a folder, along with what Sylvia had given us earlier. We'd kept the girl's letter separate, though. It was a careful, youthful outpouring, and its innocent tenderness had moved us both beyond words.

Sophie nodded. 'We can't access the website that they created, the one that Sylvia mentions here. I suspect because they closed it down – either because they'd already had their fun with it, or because they suddenly got scared. I can't get to it, not without more sophisticated methods.'

'Is it possible to retrieve it?' Ella asked.

'Most things are possible,' Sophie said. 'I have a friend who works in the forensics lab. He's brilliant. His name is Kieran and I'm meeting him tomorrow. I'll know better then what the lie of the land is.'

We had told them all about Sylvia, of course. About her visit that morning, her shy, earnest presence. I had found it particularly painful, looking at Daniel's first potential girlfriend. But Ella took great comfort from her being with us. It might sound an odd thing to say, but I had the sense even then that she and Sylvia would become close. I was right. They still are. We both, but Ella in particular, have been supporters of Sylvia over the last few years. She will go to university, as will Edward. All of these things bring with them mixed emotions. I think my wife is better at dealing with all of them than I am.

Later that night, Ella brought my three daughters upstairs to Daniel's room to see Sylvia's photograph on the collage. When they had left the conservatory, I remember that the air seemed to settle into an extraordinary stillness. I had a long moment of peace, of utter tranquillity – probably the first such moment since my son's death.

Right then, I felt him close to me. His presence was all around me. I saw him again as he was on that memorable day when we had gone fishing together. When we'd come home, I'd given him – we both had – some precious bits and pieces that had once belonged to Dan. A hand-carved wooden box filled with the bright, jewel-like spinners that the old man had once made by hand. A calligraphy pen and some bottles of ink: we knew that this would appeal to the artist in Daniel. And the old man's Swiss Army knife. Never to be taken from the house, we'd warned. Only to be used under supervision.

I can still see my son's bright smile. His eagerness to try out the calligraphy set, to paint the brightly coloured spinners. His solemn promise that he would never take, or use, the Swiss Army knife without permission.

I remembered that then, and I remember it again now. Did we trust him too much? Were we not vigilant enough as parents? What kind of world was this that our only son could no longer live in it?

We were on the threshold of finding some, if not all, of the answers.

The following morning, Ella stopped, just as she was about to get into the car. She seemed to stumble and I reached out instinctively to place one hand under her elbow. She turned to me and smiled the palest ghost of a smile.

'Poor Patrick,' she said. 'You're spending your life on high alert. I'm okay. Let's just get this over with.'

It had been a tense morning, ever since we woke. The visit to the school loomed over us – a huge, threatening mushroom cloud. Both of us were emotional, in a way I hadn't expected. I was learning all over again the ways in which grief fools you. The occasional moment of calm in which anything feels possible, even recovery, suddenly recedes; it leaves you beached, unprepared for yet another onslaught, the wave which has been gathering strength on the horizon while you looked the other way. That is the sort of morning this was.

I squeezed her arm. I could not trust myself to speak. I felt like a fish trapped in a net. I could still swim back and forth, there was the illusion of space, of freedom – sometimes even of open water. But, this morning, it felt as though things were closing in on me. It felt merely a matter of time before I found myself flapping, flailing, discarded carelessly on some cold quay wall, like the trout that Daniel and I had once caught together.

I'd been stung to hear Ella refer to me as 'poor Patrick' – as though I had merely some ancillary, supporting role to play in all of this. As though I wasn't as consumed with grief and bewilderment as she was. *I* needed somebody's hand under my elbow, too, from time to time . . .

And then, just as soon as the feeling had formed, I was awash with shame. This was becoming the pattern. I was learning to recognize it, learning a whole new language: an immersion course in chaos that threatened to unravel me, little by little.

'You're very pale,' Ella said to me now, sitting into the passenger seat. 'Did you sleep at all?'

I turned the key in the ignition. 'A little.' I smiled at her. At least she was *with* me this morning, present in her eyes, in her whole expression, in a way that she often wasn't. I'd been keeping a diary, making notes of everything that happened between us. I felt an urgent need to *remember*.

Ella sighed, clicking the seat belt in place. 'Mr Murray said to come straight to his office. If we get there before nine-forty, the kids will all be in their classrooms. The corridors will be empty.'

Her voice broke on the last sentence. I reached out to her, stopped the car before we reached the road. 'We can do it another day,' I said. 'If it's too much today, just tell me. It will wait.'

But she shook her head, and I saw again how her determination suddenly ignited: the determination I had seen so many times over the last days.

There were still a few, navy-uniformed stragglers making their way across the schoolyard as we arrived. They were surrounded by an air of weary indifference – that 'too cool to care' attitude that Daniel had never affected. Looking at them now, I was jolted into an awareness of how different our son must have seemed. I glanced across at Ella, wondering if she had seen what I just had, but her gaze was focused on the school door.

'Ella?'

She turned to look at me, her whole face a blank.

'Do you feel ready?'

She nodded. 'Do you?'

I didn't mean to, but I know I shrugged. 'It has to be done. I guess we're as ready as we'll ever be.' I stepped out of the car and made my way around to the passenger door. Ella took the hand I offered her. 'Hold on tight,' I said. 'Remember, this too will pass.'

She didn't answer.

We gave our name at reception and I could hear the hush that descended behind the glass hatch. Voices were suddenly quenched. It felt that everything around us – air, bodies, furniture – became immersed in stillness.

'Please,' the woman said, 'take a seat. Mr Murray will be with you in just a moment.'

Almost at once, a door opened behind us and the principal stepped into the corridor. He approached us, buttoning his jacket. He held out his hand to each of us. 'Mr and Mrs Grant, please, come this way.' We followed him into his office. He indicated the two chairs in front of his desk, but neither of us sat. 'Can I offer you something?'

We shook our head. 'No, thank you.'

'Please allow me to express again . . .' He tried to continue, but Ella cut him short.

Graciously, politely, but nonetheless, she cut him short. 'Thank you, Mr Murray. We appreciate everything you and your staff have done. More than we can say.'

I could see that she was struggling. Mr Murray glanced at her, his face alight with compassion. I could see in his expression the helplessness that had become all too familiar to me in the last couple of weeks.

'Mr Murray,' I stepped in. 'Daniel's phone is missing. That, and some other personal things. We're here in case there is anything in his desk, or his locker, or a cloakroom – anywhere where kids might leave things.'

He nodded. 'I understand. I took the liberty of summoning the caretaker when I knew you were coming in. If you don't have a key, we'll need to cut the lock in order to access Daniel's things. We didn't want to do anything without your permission.'

'Thank you.' Ella had found her voice again. 'And, no, we don't have the key.'

'As for anywhere else – we've searched all the public areas, the cloakrooms, bathrooms and so forth. Even the woodwork and metalwork rooms, and the art room. We have some pictures for you, but nothing else, I'm afraid. My deputy principal, Miss O'Connor, would particularly like to speak to you. If not today, then she is very happy to visit you at home, if that would be more helpful.'

I suddenly needed to swallow. I could see the big black portfolio behind Mr Murray's desk, one white paper corner peering out the top. It was creased, smeared with paint and its unexpected vulnerability made me want to weep. I imagined Daniel's thumbprint there, could see him, vividly bent over his task, absorbed in that complete way he always had. Alert, attentive, focused on the moment. Was this, maybe, the picture that Sylvia had described to us? Had it been found?

'Thank you,' Ella repeated. 'I think we'll call Miss O'Connor and make an appointment for later. But perhaps we could open the locker now, before the change of class?'

I knew that Ella was terrified of meeting any of the children. For myself, I would not have been responsible for my actions if I thought I recognized even one of the Jays. I wanted to have the locker opened and emptied and be done with this place.

Mr Murray stood. To be fair to him – but I didn't want to be fair to him, not on that morning: I felt suddenly enraged – he looked sad, distressed, his anxious face almost as crumpled as his linen suit. I decided there and then that today was not the day to discuss the Jays. They would have to wait until I had learned what to do with this abrupt surge of anger, with this wholly unexpected and overwhelming need to blame.

'Of course,' he said, quietly, 'please follow me.'

Ella gripped my hand and we followed him down the corridor. I heard the muted sounds of learning all around me: a suddenly raised teacher's voice, the murmur of readers, and, in the distance, the dull *thunk* of hammer on metal. It made the hairs stand up on the back of my neck.

A tall, rangy man was standing by a bank of lockers, a metal cutter poised over locker number four hundred and forty-nine. I could feel Ella begin to breathe deeply. The caretaker, a Mr Green, stepped forward and shook hands with both of us. I was taken aback. I don't know why, but I had not expected such a courtesy from a school caretaker. For a moment, I was very ashamed of myself.

'A lovely lad,' he said quietly. 'My deepest sympathy.'

'Thank you,' Ella's voice was an ache.

Mr Green handed us a sturdy supermarket plastic bag. 'I'm sorry,' he said, 'I couldn't find anything more suitable. For Daniel's things.'

'That's very kind of you,' I managed. I was kicking myself for my lack of forethought. I should have brought his ruck-sack—

There was the sharp, metallic sound of the lock being snipped. Mr Green stood back at once. 'Take your time,' he said, softly. He glanced at the principal. Both men turned and walked several steps away from the bank of lockers and Ella pulled open the small door.

Neither of us looked as she tumbled the contents into the plastic bag, which I held up at the mouth of the locker. Both of us had been seized by a need for secrecy – something beyond privacy – as we gathered our son's belongings to us. They were all we had left of him.

Ella folded over the top of the plastic bag while I made one more sweep of the locker floor with the palm of my hand. Nothing. She nodded.

'May I offer you anything – some tea . . . ?' Frank Murray's voice trailed off.

'I think we'll be on our way, thank you,' I said. I was aware of time slipping by. I wanted us to be well out of there before curious, raucous bodies tumbled out into the corridor at the change of class. I did not think that we would be able to bear such energy, such life.

'Of course, of course.' The principal held out his hand to each of us, and we shook. 'Please remember that we are here, to help in any way we can. In any way at all that you might feel appropriate in the coming months.' He looked me right in the eye as he said this.

I was startled. Did he know? And if so, how? Had others already learned what we'd been forced to find out? I glanced at Ella, but she was speaking to Mr Green. 'Thank you,' I said. 'I will be in touch. I appreciate your support.'

Ella was smiling at Mr Green. She took a step towards him. 'Thank you so much for your help. You came to Daniel's rescue once, when he had a puncture. He spoke about you. Thank you for helping him.'

'You're welcome,' he said. I shook his hand again, too, although I could not wait to get out of there. I turned to Ella. 'I think it's time we went home. Classes will be changing soon. If you'll wait for me in the car, I'll go and collect Daniel's portfolio.'

Mr Murray spoke at once. 'Please, Mr Grant, allow me. If you would accompany your wife to the car, I'll get the portfolio for you. I'll be with you in just a moment.'

We walked down towards the double doors that led out onto the car park. As we did so, I could hear a noise growing in the background – a sort of preparatory noise, a subterranean rumble that precedes bodies spewing out onto corridors. I remembered it all too well. Shades of boarding school.

I put one hand firmly under Ella's elbow and we fled.

As we drove home that morning, I was consumed, all over again, by memories of my own schooldays. If there was one thing I'd have willingly given my own life for, it would have been to save my son from the suffering I endured at school. In those days, cold dormitories were matched only by the coldness – and the brute strength – of those who were supposed to watch over us. I spent my life cowering. Not even my parents would listen to my pleas. I wanted to come home. I wanted to go to the local school, to be the same as my neighbours, to leave my house every morning and come home again every evening. But that was not to be tolerated.

My father's advice, gruffly given, but with affection none-theless, was to 'toughen up'. He knew the world better than I did, he told me. I should listen to him. I tried, but with limited success. Taunted beyond endurance on the rugby pitch one day – I was an indifferent player at the best of times, and an unenthusiastic one – I punched one of my tormenters in the face. I remember I was stunned by what I had done. Even I knew that this was not 'like me': in the words of one of the teachers. But I remember being unrecognizable that day, even to myself. I'd broken under the unseen assaults of the bullies, felt the pieces of myself loosen and crumble as, once again, in the scrum, someone reached across and squeezed my balls until the pain blinded me. I lashed out, far harder than I knew, breaking Pete Mackey's jaw. And then all hell broke loose.

I was punished severely, of course. My parents were sum-moned. My father said what was expected of him in the presence of Father O'Carroll. Afterwards, he put one hand on my arm, wordlessly. My ever-prim mother, her gloved hands and stylish hat so very much out of place in those grey surroundings, murmured that I had certainly deserved my punishment. 'Try to behave, dear,' she said, sighing, as she fixed the brim of her hat with one hand, taking my father's arm with the other. I watched them walk away, down the long polished corridor. We never spoke of it again.

My schooldays were, most emphatically, not the happiest days of my life. After the fracas on the rugby pitch, I earned a modicum of grudging respect from some of my peers. The others left me alone. I had quiet friendships with one or two of the more bookish boys, but nothing significant. I shook the dust of that place off my feet at eighteen years of age and I never looked back. Not once, not even in my imagination, have I ever willingly returned there.

But I believed that things had changed in the intervening half-century. I believed, perhaps because I wanted to believe, that the light and air and openness of my son's school meant that the cruelty that had driven me to violence would no longer be possible, no longer be acceptable.

On that day, my own past resurrected itself, refusing to be buried.

When we got home, we sat at the table in the conservatory and Ella placed carefully between us everything from Mr Green's plastic bag. A geography book, a metal pencil-case, a ring binder that had seen better days. 'There is nothing here,' she said now, looking at the pitiful array in front of us.

'Is that everything?' I asked. I could hear my own disappointment even as I asked the question.

'Yes.' Ella rested her forehead in her hands, propping her elbows on the table. She looked defeated.

I reached across the table and took her hands. 'Can you bear to look at the portfolio?'

She glanced towards where I had stood it against the sideboard, then she looked back at me.

'You?'

'The best way I can put it is to say I can't bear not to.'

She nodded. 'Okay. After this morning, how bad can it be?' Her mouth trembled. 'All those kids, just going on, life as normal. Bells ringing, teachers teaching, lunches prepared and eaten. What am I going to do without him, Patrick, what am I going to do.'

It wasn't a question. I remember thinking that even if it were, I was the last person to be able to answer it.

We sat huddled at the table, our son's geography book between us, his metal pencil case, and the ring binder that had seen better days.

And then the wave passed. We were calm again. I reached for Ella's hands, filled with an overwhelming tenderness. She sat across from me, her head bent and I could see the threads of grey that were suddenly visible in her hair, shown up by the streaming morning sunshine. I was shocked. So soon?

As though she had read my thoughts, she suddenly said: 'God, Patrick. I feel so old this morning. Old and wasted.'

I didn't reply immediately, I remember. Perhaps because I had also felt 'old and wasted' myself. But as my wife was so much younger than I, I felt in some absurd way that my position had been usurped.

I stood up. 'Let's take a look at this portfolio.'

I brought it to the table and pulled open the sturdy elastic ties that kept the two sides together. There were perhaps a dozen sheets, filled with Daniel's recognizable style. Some were formal studies: still lifes of fruit and vases and jugs, that kind of thing. A couple of portraits of classmates sitting on chairs. And there was one other – a much smaller portrait, taking up the lower corner of one of the A2 sheets.

It was a sketch, I suppose, more than a portrait – it looked more hurried than the larger ones. But it was of Sylvia, in profile. Of that there was no doubt. She was concentrating hard, her eyes focused on something in the distance. Whatever it was, she seemed completely unaware that Daniel was drawing her. Her hair was loose this time, flowing over her shoulders. A tiny earring was just visible in the lobe of one ear. I thought it was perfect. A simple, intimate moment. We framed it later, in a miniature Victorian frame, and gave it to Sylvia. She still has it.

And then I pulled out the picture that she had described for us. She was right: it was vivid, dramatic, terrifying. Ella could not tear her eyes away from the fleeing figure in the top corner. 'Jesus, Patrick. He must have been absolutely terrified. What an appalling thing to do to anyone.' She ran her hand over the drawing.

'Yes,' I said. 'I just don't understand it. Never did.'

She looked over at me. 'I am so angry, Patrick. So angry that I could kill someone with my bare hands.' She stopped. 'These boys must be punished. This cannot happen again to anyone else's child. Ever.'

I had no answer. I feared that it would. But I also knew that, at that moment, Ella's grief began to be channelled in another direction. From then on, her instinct – a strong one – was to try to forge something different from her loss of Daniel: something other than rage and loss and bitterness. It did not mean that her sadness was any less – far from it – but her emotional intelligence led her to begin to transform her searing sense of loss into something that would eventually aid her in her recovery.

I have never quite managed such a transition. But perhaps what lies ahead in the coming weeks or months might enable me, some day, to meet that altruistic transformation at least part of the way.

I remember on that morning, too, the urgent need to do something ordinary. I felt as though the walls of the house had begun to close in on me. I needed air and light and outside space.

'How about,' I said, 'just for an hour or so, a drive to the coast? Some fresh air and a walk along the beach?'

Ella brightened. 'Yes,' she said. 'Why not?'

But we didn't get there, at least not that day. Events began to speed up. The ordinary had to be postponed.

For now, the extraordinary continued to demand our attention.

Ella

But as Ella goes to collect her coat for that ordinary drive to the coast, she spots a shadowy figure in the porch. A large, bulky figure that is stepping from side to side – into view and out of it again. It seems to her to be indecision made flesh.

Curious, she goes to open the door. 'Mr Nugent,' she says in surprise.

The figure turns fully and looks at her. 'Miss Ella,' he says. He touches the peak of his none-too-clean cap. She doesn't know what to say. Peter Nugent, a neighbour. The youngest of the three brothers who farmed less than two kilometres away. Her father had been particularly fond of David and Robert, the older boys – men – now both dead. Peter was the youngest by some fifteen years.

Apart from Daniel's funeral, when the man had come and stood beside her, wordlessly wringing her hand, Ella has not spoken to him in some time. There has always been the polite salute along the road, the friendly wave, the courteous doffing of his cloth cap as she passed in the car. Ella wonders what has brought him here, what neighbourly duty he now feels compelled to complete.

'Why don't you come in?' she says, breaking the silence. She stands back and opens the door, conscious of the ludicrous contrast between the vibrant pink of the hydrangeas and Peter Nugent's muddy boots.

'No, no, Miss, not at all. It's just that I have something that I think might be yours.' And still he seems to be undecided.

Patrick comes into the hallway then, looking for her. 'Ella? Is everything okay?'

She watches as Peter Nugent's face floods with relief. 'Mr Grant,' he says, 'how are you?'

'I'm well, Peter. And yourself?'

They shake hands. Ella waits while this interminable choreography of politeness plays itself out. 'I think Peter has found something, something that might be ours,' she says, unable to be patient any longer.

Patrick looks at him questioningly. And then: 'Come in, man, for God's sake. We don't keep our guests standing in the porch. Never mind the boots – it doesn't matter a curse.'

Peter Nugent steps inside, Ella takes his coat and Patrick leads the way into the conservatory.

'I'll make us some tea,' she says.

When she takes the tray into the conservatory, she knows that words have already been spoken, man to man. Patrick stands up. 'You sit down, Ella. I'll look after the tea. Peter has something he'd like you to see.'

'I didn't . . . I thought . . . if you were on your own . . .'

'It's fine, Peter. Ella understands that you wouldn't have wanted to come here if she'd been on her own. That you didn't want to upset her. We appreciate your kindness.'

Ella sits. She's puzzled at the man's arrival, but Patrick has explained enough. So she waits. She knows that Peter Nugent will get to the point in his own time. She notices how calloused and scratched the man's hands are, how black and broken the fingernails. When he opens both hands, he displays a phone that fits easily into one of his palms. Ella cries out. 'The phone! It's Daniel's iPhone!' She looks from him to Patrick and back again, her eyes suddenly alight. 'Where did you get it?'

'You're sure?' Patrick asks her. 'You're sure this is Daniel's?' But she knows by his tone that he is sure, too.

'Absolutely. Look.' She reaches forward and takes the phone in both hands, hardly noticing that she is already crying. She sees discomfort written all across Peter Nugent's face and she hastily pulls herself back together. She wipes her face, tries to smile and looks at him again. She turns the phone over and points to where Daniel had inscribed his initials in silver paint.

'I'm so sorry – but you have no idea what this means to us. We've been looking for it ever since . . .'

'I understand,' he says. His voice is full of quiet compassion. 'I am very glad I have found both of you here today.'

'Please,' Ella begs him. 'Please tell us where you got this.'

And he begins, hesitantly at first. He tells them of a journey by car, a journey that took place on the same morning that Daniel fled from Edward's house and cycled towards home like a demon.

'I passed him on the road, when I was on my way home from my sister's,' he says. 'He was fairly flyin' so he was. I overtook him just at Duffy's yard, and gave him a little beep as I passed. He didn't wave back, and I was surprised, so I was. Always very polite, your Daniel.' He pauses. 'When I reached my own home place, just mebbe fifteen or twenty seconds later, he was still keepin' up with me, pretty much. Then, just as I got to my own gate, he waved. At least I thought he did. His arm went up into the air, like this,' Peter demonstrates a vigorous movement, 'and I waved back from the car.'

Ella can barely hear him over the buzzing in her ears, the sound of her own blood surging in her veins. 'What happened?' She keeps her voice as quiet as she can. She has never heard Peter Nugent talk so much.

'I didn't think any more about it until . . . until I realized what had happened to your boy. It puzzled me then. And yesterday, it just came to me. That arm movement,' he demonstrates again, 'that was no wave. That was him throwin' somethin' over the hedge. So I took myself down to the lower field and I started to look. I had a good idea where somethin' might land. I'll make a long story short, and say that I've just found it, not an hour ago. I figured it must be his.'

Peter Nugent sits back, takes a long draught of the cup of tea that Patrick has handed him.

Ella finds her own voice at last. 'We can't thank you enough. Truly. This is a really important find.' She stops. 'When you saw Daniel last Sunday, did he look upset?'

Peter Nugent looks first at Patrick, as though for permission, then at her. Slowly, he says, 'The boy was in a great hurry, Miss Ella. That's all I can tell you.' He looks down at his hands. 'And for some reason, he threw away his phone. Mebbe someone was callin' him, annoyin' him, like. Who knows?'

Ella feels her heart race. Little does he know, she thinks. Little does he know.

They talk, the three of them, for a few minutes more. Ella can't wait for him to go, but she cannot bring herself to be impolite. Finally, with minutes courteously managed to their optimum, Peter Nugent stands up.

'I had best be goin',' he says. 'A lot still to do.'

They see him to the door, where he once more affixes his cap to his head, getting the position of the peak just right. 'My sympathies again to you both,' he says, gravely. 'A grand young lad, your Daniel. Very like his grandfather.'

'Thank you, Peter. For everything.' Ella tries to smile at him.

'Yes, indeed. Much appreciated.' Patrick shakes his hand vigorously once again.

Peter Nugent walks down the driveway, towards the road. His feet scrunch the gravel. Ella waits until he reaches his battered little silver car and then she closes the front door. But

Patrick's face does not share the relief she is feeling. 'Patrick? What is it?'

He places both hands on her shoulders. 'I don't want us to get our hopes up,' he says.

'You mean me. You don't want *me* to get my hopes up.' Ella feels anger flare. 'Why? What's wrong? Why shouldn't I?'

'Because,' and his tone is gentle, 'this phone has now been lying in Nugent's field for over a week. In dew, in rain, in cold enough temperatures at night. I have no idea whether we'll be able to get any information off it.'

He sees her face fall. He puts both arms around her, draws her to him. 'I'll call Sophie. She'll know. It's just so cruel to feel so close to getting somewhere, and then to have to pull back. I wish I wasn't so ignorant about this stuff. All of it.' He pulls her closer, kisses her forehead. 'One way or the other, it's wonderful it's been found. Let's just hold onto that.'

Soon after Peter Nugent's visit, events began to accelerate all over again. It was strange the way time changed its contours once more. All around us, the air felt charged with electricity: a force that seemed to make things happen of their own accord. Within an hour of my call to Sophie, she rang back, jubilant. 'Good news, Dad. The information on the phone is safe: it doesn't even matter if the handset is damaged, everything is still there. They've even got stuff off iPhones that have been lying outside for three months or more.'

I was so relieved I found it hard to reply. I'd been haunted by the image of Daniel cycling home that Sunday around midday, tormented by yet another text, or a call, perhaps, already fleeing from what he saw as the betrayal of his best friend.

My diary tells me that later that day – although my memory has fixed it on the following one, but it no longer matters –

Miss O'Connor arrived at the house. She'd asked to see us after school.

'Of course,' I said.

Her visit reinforced that extraordinary sense in those days of something always about to happen, and of both of us, Ella and I, waiting, always waiting. We lived within that strange co-existence of opposites.

Ella greeted her at the door. 'Miss O'Connor,' she said. 'We've met before. Daniel was extremely fond of you. Please, come in.'

She shook hands with both of us. 'It's Helen, please,' she said. 'Daniel was a wonderful boy. I am so sorry for your loss.'

I liked her at once. I liked the directness of her sincerity. She made both of us feel at ease. And she did not keep us waiting.

'I know that you have already collected Daniel's portfolio,' she said. 'I have also photocopied that picture that Sylvia described to us. Without her coming to me, I would never have known of its existence. It took a while before I could track it down.'

I nodded. 'We are very grateful to Sylvia,' I said. 'She has already been to see us.'

Helen O'Connor nodded. 'She's a really good kid,' she said. 'And so are most of the others. However,' and she looked at both of us, 'we have a few bad apples, as I think you know.'

'What's going to happen to them?' asked Ella, quietly. 'We really need to take this further. We can't let it go.'

Helen nodded vigorously. 'We're doing everything we can to progress that,' she said. 'We want you to know that we have begun our own investigation, and it is very heartening, the number of students who have come forward with information since Daniel died.'

I glanced at Ella. 'What sort of information?' I asked, quickly. 'Is it to do with the Jays?'

'Yes,' she said. 'I can't be too specific just at the moment, but I will tell you that we are in the process of gathering evidence about a systematic campaign of bullying against Daniel, and a couple of other young students. We won't rest until we have what we need.'

'Will the police be involved?' Ella asked.

'I believe that is entirely likely,' Helen said. 'We think there will need to be a criminal investigation.'

Ella and I talked about nothing else after Helen O'Connor left.

'It will be difficult,' Ella said. 'This is a very small community, and we are really going to rock the boat. Fintan's family is very well connected. I don't know the others all that well – and, of course, I've no idea who Leo is.'

I looked at her in surprise. I hadn't even thought of our rocking the boat, as she put it. But then, I hadn't been born in this place. I was far more accustomed to the anonymity of the urban. I always will be, no matter how long I live here. 'Does that upset you?'

She shook her head. 'Not at all. I'm just saying that we can prepare ourselves for some resistance.'

I felt angry again. It was an emotion that lived very close to the surface in those days. 'I don't care,' I said. 'Let them do their worst. We're going all the way with this.'

In the meantime, other events were occurring: events that brought us hope and help from a source we could never have imagined.

Edward

THERE IS LOTS OF TALK about Daniel. The teachers mention him almost every class and the counsellors still drop in to see us second years, maybe once a day now, now that things are back to normal. They always say the same sort of stuff. About how information will be dealt with in private. About how certain things are 'implicated' in Daniel's death. About how important it is to find out what happened so that we can stop it ever happening again.

Sylvia reminded me of the emails from Spain. She told me about the website and the pictures and I hadn't known about those. I felt bad that he hadn't told me. We sat beside each other at lunch and break sometimes and the Jays left us alone. There was no more whistling or whispering at least that. They've been very quiet the past few days. Jeremy doesn't come to the second-year mall like he used to. He sticks to the third-year end and good riddance to him. Jason and James are still around though.

Jason came up to me yesterday. I ignored him. Edward he said. Then I looked up. He had his hands in his pockets. His face was still brown from the summer, his hair nearly white from the sun. I don't know why but that made me madder than I already felt. Oh you mean Paki don't you I said. I must of shouted although I didn't think I did. I want to ask you something he said. Then the bell rang. Fuck off I said. Why don't you. Just fuck off.

He waited for me at the bicycle shed at home time. I just stood there looking at him. We didn't move. He was on his own and that's the first time ever that's happened. I want to know what you told them he said and he walked towards me. But I stayed where I was. Held my ground as Fathersir would say. Why what are you afraid of I asked. Just tell me what you said. To the counsellors.

I stuck my face into his. I told them you were a shit I said. You and James and Jeremy. The three of you together. Just a bunch of little shits. Now get out of my way.

He looked different so he did without the other two around him. But he clenched his fists then and started back into me. I pushed him and he stumbled and then he fell. Right then, I couldn't believe my luck. It made me braver. Remember what I told you this morning I said. You fuck off and don't ever come near me again.

I got up on my bike and cycled home. Then I cried for only the second time since he died. Pushing Jason wasn't much but at least it was something I'd done for Daniel.

At least it was something.

Ella

When Christopher's call came, Ella felt as though time had suddenly stilled.

'I've had this approach,' he said, 'and I hardly know what to say to you.'

Now her heart began to speed up. Whatever it was, it had to do with Daniel. Everything had to do with Daniel. 'Go on,' she said, 'tell me.'

'Well, it has to do with the parents of some young lad at Daniel's school. His name is Leo Byrne. I don't know him or them; apparently they're pretty new to the area. I mean, they're not natives.'

Ella heard the sound of papers being rustled, could see Christopher at his desk, his glasses perched high up on his bald head. 'The family have taken over some relative's farm, I understand. My local GP approached me on Sunday morning: they asked him to make contact with a counsellor, and he thought of me.' Christopher paused for a moment. 'The boy's parents went to see Dr Keane on Saturday. Apparently, they're beside themselves with worry. Their son is in a very bad way emotionally. I know nothing other than that.'

Leo, Ella thought. It had to be him: it had to be *that* Leo. It could hardly be any other. She gripped the phone tighter, afraid to let it go, to let anything go. 'What does he want – what do they want?'

'A discreet approach to you, apparently. They want the boy to see you, to talk to you. That's all they would say. They wouldn't come direct, in case you wouldn't speak to them. And that's all I know.' He paused. 'I suggested that he could talk to me, that you might not be in a position to see anybody right now. But they were insistent. They wanted to ask for you first.'

'I'll see him,' Ella said quickly. 'I'll see him immediately.'

Christopher sounded surprised. 'Are you sure?'

'Positive. I'll explain another time, Chris. I need to see this boy.'

'Okay, then. But let's talk immediately afterwards.'

Patrick has counselled caution. He is not sure he likes this. 'I'll be right outside,' he says. 'All you'll have to do is call. I think I'd prefer this Leo to say whatever it is he has to say to the police.'

'Let me meet him, Patrick. Please. I need to speak to him – to listen to him.'

She kept seeing Leo, the crouching animal at the corner of her son's picture. The one who had not yet pounced. She needed to hear his story.

And now she opens the front door to a tall, gangly figure with his hands in his pockets. 'Leo?'

He nods, wordlessly.

'Come this way.' She walks in front of him down the corridor, steeling herself to face him once they reach her consulting room. She is conscious of Patrick's unseen presence behind the door of the kitchen. It comforts her. When she reaches the office, she stands back, and allows Leo to walk in before her. 'Here we are,' she says.

When Leo enters the room, Ella feels the air displace around him. He ploughs his way in, takes a sharp turn to the left, dives into the armchair that she is just about to indicate. He flings himself forward, his legs splayed. He bristles, his energy radiating towards her in angry waves.

'Make yourself comfortable, Leo,' she says. 'My name is Ella.'

He doesn't answer. One knee bounces up and down as he keeps the ball of his foot slammed into the wooden floor, his heel in mid-air. 'I don't want to be here. My parents made me come.'

Ella sits and waits for a moment. 'You're angry,' she says.

His leg continues to jerk, up and down, up and down, even more furiously than before. Ella notices his right hand, clenched around the arm of the chair. The index and middle fingers are stained a rusty brown. A smoker. And the nails are bitten to the quick.

She waits for a moment, to let him settle. The rage is a shield, she's sure of it. She looks at him now, curious. Right this minute, he doesn't look anything like a crouching animal. He looks much more like a terrified and guilty child. She breathes deeply, quietly. He is not leaving this room until she knows whatever it is that he is hiding.

'You have a choice,' she says, after a moment. She makes sure that she is sitting well back in the chair, her hands resting lightly on the arms. Her tone is neutral, careful. 'You can walk out of that door any time you like. No one is forcing you to stay.'

He glares at her. The eyes are unblinking. 'I said I would,' he said. 'It was the only way they would leave me alone.'

'They?'

'My parents. They keep at me an' at me.'

'And have you any idea why?'

He shrugs. 'Just stuff.' He shoves at something with the toe of his trainer, concentrating very hard on the floor.

Ella wants to make eye contact again, however briefly. More than that, she wants him to start talking. She is finding it increasingly difficult to sit and face one of Daniel's tormentors. 'Well,' she says, 'as long as you're here, why don't we just use the time to have a conversation? If we don't like each other, you can go and talk to someone else. Either way, you'll have done what your parents asked, and they might give you a break.'

She says this with a small smile. Leo looks up, catches it. Just for a moment, his leg stops jerking up and down. Then it resumes, even more quickly than before. 'This is all bullshit,' he explodes.

She gestures towards the door. 'Then leave. You can tell your parents you tried. But that it's all bullshit.' She prays, silently, that she is making the right call.

Now he meets her gaze, flinches at the challenge he sees there.

'I can't,' he says. 'I agreed. They made me promise.' The admission seems to deflate him. His leg stills and he has sagged forward, as though the force of his anger is all that has kept him upright.

'Okay, then.' Ella nods. 'We can spend the time in silence, or we can talk. It's up to you.'

He just stares at her. His eyes give nothing away.

'There is something troubling you, Leo, and you obviously can't talk to your parents about it. My job is to be objective, not to judge you on whatever it is I hear. You can say what you want. And I won't be shocked.'

'How do you know?' He seems to shoot the question at her.

'How do I know what?'

'How do you know you won't be shocked?'

'That's a good question. Maybe because I'm trained not to be shocked. I've been doing this job for over thirty years, so I've probably heard about problems a lot more than most people.

The thing is, you don't need to be afraid of what you think, or feel – you are free to say it here.'

'I'm not afraid,' he says, too quickly. Ella notices that his tone is no longer so aggressive.

'Okay, then. So, where would you like to begin? How about explaining the promise you made at home? How did that come about?'

He shrugs, looking at the ground again. 'They think I'm depressed.'

'And what do you think?'

He squirms, his fingers plucking at something on the arms of the chair. 'How would I know? Everyone just keeps gettin' at me. It's pissin' me off.'

Ella waits until he looks up – not quite at her, but somewhere in her direction. 'Let's take a step back, Leo. Why don't you tell me a bit about yourself first, about your family, your school – whatever comes to mind.'

Suddenly, he's wary again. He glances towards the door. Ella raises both hands, a gesture of surrender. 'The door's open, Leo. You are still free to go.'

He runs his tongue over his lips which suddenly look cracked and dry. 'Would you like a glass of water?'

He nods. 'Yeah.'

She pours them both a glass of water. And then she waits.

Leo talks, at last, his long body leaning back into the armchair, the restless movement of his foot finally stilled. Ella learns that he's the middle of three boys, that he lives on a farm some thirty kilometres away, that he wants to be a footballer. And that his family moved from the city ten months ago, his father inheriting land from an uncle.

'And how do you like country living?' Ella asks, smiling. She doesn't know how long she can keep this going, this even, bland, counsellor talk. Part of her wants to leap to her feet and grab this young man by the throat. She wants to shake the truth out of him.

'I hate it,' he says. 'I hate the smells an' the shit an' the way that I have to get a lift everywhere. It's like bein' a prisoner. I don't know why we had to come here.' His face is suddenly contorted with anger.

She decided to shift things up a gear. 'What about school?' she asks. 'Has it been easy enough to settle?'

Leo glares at her. His foot starts its restless jerking again. 'I don't want to talk about school,' he says. She notices that his hostility has returned, redoubled. It's like a cloud around him, red and ragged at the edges.

'Okay, that's fine, Leo. We can come back to it, when you feel like it. *If* you feel like it,' she adds, seeing his expression. His rage is so close to the surface again that she knows he will not be able to contain it for too much longer.

She leans forward in her seat now, looks him directly in the eye. 'Why don't you tell me what's happened, Leo? Why don't you tell me what has brought you here?'

And suddenly, everything changes.

The boy looks at her, his face a ghastly white, shading abruptly to green. She thinks he is going to be sick. 'Breathe,' she says. 'Take five deep breaths, one after the other, slowly, slowly. And don't try to talk. It's okay, Leo, you're safe.'

She doesn't move from her chair. She waits, watches as the boy struggles with something: watches as, finally, he breaks.

'It's not okay,' he sobs. 'It'll never be okay.' He takes three rasping breaths, hiccups, coughs. Ella hands him the box of tissues. Still she says nothing. Finally, he quietens. She pours him another glass of water and one for herself.

'What is so wrong that it can never be okay, Leo? Why don't you tell me?'

He looks at her, two spots of livid colour are high on his cheekbones now. 'I didn't know what to do,' he says, balling up the damp tissues in his hands. 'I didn't know what to do.' He begins to shred the flimsy white paper, pushing the tiny pieces back again into the sodden mass that lies between his palms.

'You didn't know what to do about what?' Ella waits, wanting him to explain, wanting to hear aloud whatever words have been choking him since he crashed into the room.

'I didn't know what to do about Daniel.' He will not look at her as he says this. His voice wavers on the last two words. But once they are spoken, he seems to sag back in the seat. His feet in their new and pristine trainers look suddenly vulnerable, as though they have grown too large for him too quickly, making him loose and ungainly, ill at ease in his own body.

'I saw everything that happened,' he says, suddenly. 'And I didn't stop it. I wasn't able to stop any of it.' He's gripping the arms of the chair again. He's agitated, his foot beginning to pound the floor; the knuckles of both hands are white, small pyramids of bone that look as though they might break through the taut surface at any moment.

'My parents said I have to tell you.' His eyes fill and he begins to shake, trembling all over. Ella takes her wrap from behind her chair where she'd hung it earlier. She crosses the room and places it gently around Leo's shoulders. The movement releases something inside her.

'It's all right, Leo,' she says. 'I know you were not to blame. I'm listening. Tell me what you know.'

He falters at first, and then the words come tumbling. She has to stop him from time to time, to ask him to explain, to clarify, to sort out the tangle of names and places that fall from him, giddy with release. It is as though these words have filled him, fuelled his restless leg, kept him perched as though he would fly out of the room at any moment, darting past her in a single black blur. Without the words, he is now calmer, his face washed of the fear that has clouded it.

She hears about Jason, about James, about Jeremy. She hears, over and over, what she already knows, what she and Patrick have already learned. She listens as Leo describes the escalation of the assaults over the summer, Jason's technological expertise, his hatred of Daniel.

'I didn't like the website,' Leo told her. 'The pictures and all that sort of stuff. They made me feel weird. I told Jason I didn't like it, that it was going too far, but he just told me to fuck off, that I was a wimp.'

'Did he continue?'

'Yeah. All through the summer. He said it was fun and, besides, he had nothin' else to do. Him and James. But James just did whatever Jason told him.'

Ella says nothing.

Leo rummages in his pocket. He pulls out a small, black memory stick. 'I took a copy of it, of the website. Before Jason closed it down. I don't know why.' He shrugs. 'I just didn't like it.' He hands her the memory stick. 'It's all true, I swear it.'

Ella is careful with her reply. She clutches the memory stick, feels the shock of its potent presence in her hand. 'I believe you, Leo,' she says. 'Now, I'm going to have to ask you to listen to what I've understood. If I get something wrong, correct me. Otherwise, just listen.'

He nods, looking exhausted now. 'Okay.'

Ella chooses her words carefully, professionally, masking the turmoil that is suddenly boiling and spilling inside her. It is as much as she can do to sit in the chair, to rest her hands lightly on the arms. She is having difficulty coming to terms with the casual, unthinking cruelty that has led to her son's death. The only way she can continue is to focus on the words that give shape and structure to Leo's narrative.

When she finishes, Leo nods. 'Yeah,' he says. 'That's what I saw. An' what I heard. It's all true.'

She leans forward. 'This is very serious stuff, Leo. And I think you know that. It's been clear for some time that the police will have to be involved. Are you prepared to tell the Guards what you have just told me?'

He nods. 'Yeah. My parents say I have to. And I think it's right. I mean, right to tell. It wasn't fair, what they did to him.'

'Thank you, Leo.'

When she lets him out, a woman probably her own age, is standing by the door of her car. She nods at Ella, and opens the passenger door for her son. She does not say anything, not that night.

Ella goes back inside and Patrick is waiting.

'Well?' he says.

She nods. 'Everything,' she says. 'Everything we suspected is true. And he'll tell the Guards all that he's just told me.' She holds up the memory stick. 'Leo copied the website – the one that Daniel saw when you were in Spain. The one that upset him so much. It's all here.'

'Jesus,' Patrick says. He holds out his hand. 'Let me see that.'

But Ella holds onto it. 'We'll look at it together. I need to see this, too.'

Patrick shakes his head in disbelief. 'Why?' he says. 'I mean, why was this kid involved? Why was he even on the outskirts of it all? And what did Daniel ever do to him?'

Ella sighs. 'Nothing,' she says. 'It's not about anything Daniel did. It's about what he was. Different. Gentle. Sensitive. Leo's not a bad kid – he just wanted what they all want. To belong. To be one of the gang.'

Patrick pulls her to him. 'You're exhausted,' he says. 'You have to rest.'

Ella sobs. 'It's over. I think it's finally over. We have enough.'

She puts her arms around Patrick and they stand there, in the hallway, while the night gathers in around them.

Part Four

Thursday 21st March, 2013

Sylvia

IT WAS NIAMH who told me first. She had seen the comings and goings around Mr Murray's office that morning. She'd heard all the commotion, too, except that she couldn't make out what the people inside were saying. Then, just as she was collecting the photocopying from the school secretary for Mr Kelly, Jason came out of the principal's office, on his own, and waited in the corridor.

She knew who he was, of course. Everybody knew who Jason was. So she delayed a little, pretending to count the pages, to collate them – the way you do. Then the door behind her slammed open and she jumped, suddenly dropping the pages for real. They all slithered away from her and she had to bend down and start picking them up.

'Come on, Jason,' she heard a man's voice say. 'We don't have to stay and listen to this. I'm taking you home.' She watched, she said, as Mr MacManus frogmarched Jason down the corridor and out of the front door. Almost immediately, Mr Murray followed them into the corridor. But they had already turned the corner at that stage.

For a minute, he looked as though he was going to hurry after them. But then he turned on Niamh instead. 'Niamh Bolger,' he said, 'what on earth are you doing?'

Niamh said she'd never heard him so angry, not like that. Annoyed, yes, irritated by misbehaving first years, but never angry. She was flustered, she said. Embarrassed. Terrified that he'd think she was eavesdropping which, of course, she was.

'I'm sorry, Mr Murray, I dropped Mr Kelly's photocopying. I'll just be a minute.'

Then he turned on his heel and went back into his office. Niamh gathered up all the pages as quickly as she could and ran.

By eleven o'clock break, the news was all over the school. I remember it very clearly. It may be more than three years ago, and I may have been a very young fourteen, but I knew exactly what Jason's departure meant. All of second year did.

Aoife filled me in on the next bit. Some guy in her class had got a text from Jason at lunchtime, saying he was grounded. He wouldn't be back to school, he said, until he'd been cleared of all the 'unjust accusations' against him. Even at the time, the language didn't sound like Jason, not at all. It didn't fit the Jason we all knew and loathed.

In the way that these things happen, it was impossible to keep any news about Jason from spreading like a forest fire. It was Clare who had the next bit. She cycled all the way out to my house to tell me, one Thursday evening. It was much too complicated and exciting to deliver by text and, after all that had happened, she was terrified to go on gmail.

A friend of her mum's called Sharon cleaned for Jason's mum in those days, and she was there, in the house, when the squad car arrived. There were a lot of details embroidered onto this description, some of them in very lurid colour. There would have to be, with Clare telling the story, so I'll be brief. The upshot was that the Guards came into the house, put everything into tamper-proof bags and took it away with them. I knew that they'd done the same with Daniel's stuff a couple of days earlier, but Mr and Mrs Grant asked me not to say anything. They took computers, laptops, phones. When they left her house that day, Mrs MacManus was standing weeping in the hallway.

The buzz around second year the following day was unbearable. So much so, that Mr Murray and Miss O'Connor held an assembly at twelve o'clock. This was most unusual. They were open and straightforward in what they had to say and then they sent us to the canteen for a longer lunch than usual.

They tried to keep a lid on things. Mr Murray talked to all of us about an 'ongoing police investigation' and that students would only be questioned with their parents' permission. He spoke about the law 'having to take its course' and that everybody was entitled to a 'presumption of innocence'. But no matter what language he used, everyone understood. It was strange, that. Even the dumber kids were in no doubt as to exactly what he meant. Jason was in deep trouble and we should tell our parents, and the Guards, anything we knew. End of.

There was a lot of talk over the following weeks – some informed, some dreadfully misinformed – about IP addresses and embedded data and forensic software. About how easy it was for the police to track the senders of messages, and photographs, the makers and uploaders of videos. There was a lot of nervousness around in those days.

I never saw Jason again. I heard that he'd been sent to some other school, a boarding school, but I have no idea whether any of that is true. Jeremy left after he'd finished third year. He's still knocking around, somewhere. Leo stayed, and settled into second year along with the rest of us. What was left of it, once all the upheaval died down. Leo was okay. Nobody gave him a hard time.

That only leaves James, the grunter. His parents took him out, too, and he went to another school about thirty kilometres north of here. I used to see him around at Christmas and Easter, never in the summer, though. And I haven't seen him this year at all, not anywhere.

In one way, what happened to Daniel feels a very long time ago. In another, it's still way too recent. Mr and Mrs Grant gave me a tiny portrait that Daniel had done of me, during one art class when I wasn't looking. I had a copy of it made, a smaller one, and I wear it around my neck in the locket that Grandma left me when she died last year.

Edward and I are still friends. We still go to see Mr and Mrs Grant often – sometimes together, if it suits, but most of the time on our own. I guess we knew different Daniels.

Tonight, though, we are both going to Mr Grant's birthday party. We've to be there at seven. When we spoke, Mr Grant told us it was a very important evening – and not just because it was his birthday. He said he had an announcement to make. Maybe it's about his memoirs – Mrs Grant told me he was writing them. Edward and I have bought him a beautiful fountain pen.

I'm sure it will be a lovely evening. Sometimes I worry that Edward and I will remind the Grants too much of all that happened; that our presence reminds them of Daniel's absence. But they keep inviting us; they keep including us in all sorts of things. My mother says it comforts them.

Every time I see his parents, I have to wonder what sort of a person Daniel would be now. It still comes as a shock, each time I remember that he's dead. But I won't say that, of course. I'll wish Mr Grant a happy birthday and we'll just remember the better times.

Like when Daniel was still here, still with us, just as he is in that gorgeous photo hanging above the piano. He's standing on his dad's boat, a fishing rod in his hand. His hair is standing up every which way and he's grinning from ear to ear. Behind him is the shadow of Casey's boatyard. And just to the left of the boat, there are two swans – exactly like the ones that Daniel used to draw.

Silent. Serene. Their beaks almost touching each other.

The white, elegant curve of their necks; their whole bodies almost like question marks.

Frances

DAD IS SEVENTY-FOUR TODAY. We haven't gathered on his birthday in some time – not since the year before Daniel died, in fact. On that occasion, my Tom gave him a home-made birthday card, one that he had put together with great care.

Tonight, or rather this evening, we'll all be together again to help him celebrate yet another year of survival. I worry about my father. Since Daniel's death, he has faded greatly. He has never lost the stoop that he seemed to acquire overnight. His robustness has all but vanished. In its place, there is a fragility that I see all too clearly – but a fragility that is nevertheless still fierce in its protectiveness of Ella. And another thing: my father has become kinder. He sees people in a way that he didn't before. He anticipates, rather than reacts. He is altogether gentler.

I see Ella watching him from time to time. On the last occasion, I had to turn away from the intimacy of that glance: a look full of love, of sorrow, but also imbued with a stubborn facing towards tomorrow.

In many ways, I fear that that is what my father has lost above everything: a sense of purpose for the future.

But we will go and we will celebrate and we will wait to hear whatever announcement it is that he wishes to make. The years since Daniel's death have been difficult ones. We have stopped asking about the legal process. After such apparently heady progress in the early months and years, it seems that everything has slowed to a crawl.

Rebecca kept up the pressure, though. Of all of us, she took that particular ball and ran with it. She has helped Dad negotiate his way through the minefield of paperwork, of witness statements and affidavits and police procedure. She never once got frustrated. Instead, the two of them became more dogged, more determined as time passed. It was good to see that something was being mended between them after all those years.

Rebecca doesn't travel as much, now. In fact, she's hardly ever away from home. About a year after Daniel died, she set up her own private mediation service. The state one was too slow, she told me, for people who wanted to end their marriages with a modicum of dignity – and efficiency. Things are going well. And it's good that she's home. As Sophie and I predicted, Aisling has become a real little madam. Rebecca has her work cut out there.

I think that the three of us – Rebecca, Sophie and I – have all become a lot closer in the last few years. In the more distant past, it was often difficult for the three of us to get together. Sophie and I had two full-time jobs and five full-time kids between us, plus school committees and fundraisers and social lives. It was never easy to carve out sister-time. And Rebecca was hardly ever available. But Sophie and I kept trying to meet: even the attempt to do so was important to both of us, I think.

Sometimes back then – rarely – Rebecca would join us; far less frequently than she does now. The problem was, I think, that once Adam walked out of her life, our still intact families put Rebecca on the defensive. Any mention of husbands and fathers made her go all stiff and silent. I think she regarded both of us as insufferably smug. Or maybe that's just how I interpreted her silences. I think I felt it more than Sophie. Sophie tends to keep her own counsel: she is often surprised by my interpretation of things.

Once, she told me to stop being such a fixer. The thing is, I knew exactly how she meant it, and instead of being hurt or annoyed, I laughed. The three of us are easier together now, although Sophie and I still occasionally meet – just the two of us. Some habits are hard to break. We don't tell Rebecca, though. I suppose, overall as sisters go, things are good between all of us.

I worry about the future, too. About my sons, about all our children. Sometimes, when I remember Daniel on the night of his thirteenth birthday, the night he played the violin with such haunting presence, I feel something clutch at my heart. I cannot believe that such a life force has been snuffed out so brutally.

It makes me hover around Tom and Jack, and I know it drives them nuts. But what can I do?

Tonight, I'll also see Sylvia and Edward again. That is always something to look forward to. Such a lovely girl. And Dad and Ella continue to be so kind to both of them.

That's what I mean about Dad. About his becoming a kinder person. He once claimed he didn't believe in altruism. But when Edward began studying for his Leaving Cert, he had a really tough time. His younger brothers drove him to distraction. There was no peace from them, no escape, no quiet places. So he came to Dad and Ella's instead. He didn't stay, but he did take over one of the spare bedrooms at their invitation and made it into his study. Edward is a scrupulous student. Serious, hardworking. Dad took him under his wing, quietly, unobtrusively, saying he needed a bit of help now and again in the garden. It gave everyone a dignified solution. Edward hopes to study structural engineering at university – and this delights Dad.

A fine young man, my father says. The brother Daniel never had.

Ella

ELLA IS READY.

She has watched the slow creep of the legal process over the last three and a half long years, the obstacles put in its way. Although she has never told Patrick this, Ella knows that there have been murmurings locally, flashes of dissension, the occasional declaration that 'boys will be boys'. It hurts: the manner in which some have intimated that perhaps Daniel had somehow contributed to his own death. That his nature had made him culpable in some obscure way.

Ella has kept all of this secret from her husband; he has been purposeful again and she does not want to cloud his determination with rage. Instead, she has watched as Rebecca and Patrick together have become a force to be reckoned with. The delays, the false steps, the obstructions: all have been grist to their united and passionate mill.

She remembers the day when the Guards came to remove the computers from their house. They arrived late, by arrangement, just a woman and a man, in a discreet, unmarked car.

'My name is April,' the woman said to her, holding out her hand. 'I'll be your liaison officer. I'll keep you up to date with everything that's happening.'

Ella accompanied April and her colleague, Mark, to Daniel's

bedroom. She watched as first they bagged his computer, his iPhone, then her and Patrick's laptops. She felt choked all that night, unable to breathe or speak. Somehow, the clinical nature of tamper-proof bags, and their removal from her home, told her beyond doubt that Daniel was not coming back.

Ella knew that other houses had been visited in a similar way and their technology removed: the whole town knew that, the news spreading instantly, insistently. During those days, Ella and Patrick stayed close to home. Maryam came and went constantly, bringing meals, shopping, the occasional news update.

Some days later, April called again. She sat at the table, at Ella's invitation. Patrick made tea.

'I have something you may wish to hear, or not. It's up to you.'

Ella remembers the way that she and Patrick stared at her.

April touched a folder in front of her. 'There are several text messages for Daniel on his phone, sent to him after he died.' Her tone was gentle, ready for their questions. For a moment, the silence in the conservatory was absolute.

Ella looked at her, not understanding. 'What do you mean?'

April took some pages out of the green folder. 'Teenagers do this. It's as if they don't understand the finality of death. They do the same with Facebook pages – send messages as though people who are no longer alive can still receive them.'

Ella's stomach shifted. The base of her throat felt sour. 'What do they say?' She could see Patrick about to move in her direction, ready to stop whatever might be coming next.

'They are all benign,' April said at once. 'All very loving. I'm sorry – I should have said that at the outset. They are from Daniel's friends: none of the phone numbers of origin matches those of the bullies. I thought you might like to have them.' She stopped for a moment. 'Shall I leave them with you, or would you prefer me to take them away?'

Ella looked over at Patrick. His eyes had filled. There was no question of not having them. 'Leave them, please. Thank you.'

They read them together after April left. Ella sometimes wonders whether that was a mistake. The way they broke her husband that day still haunts her.

But now it is Patrick's birthday and everyone is waiting. Ella has been happily occupied all day. The children have kept her company, wrapping small gifts and hiding them for the ritual treasure hunt that has always been part of Granddad's party. She does not want to think about the advancing years, not this evening.

Patrick will make his announcement tonight. He and she will face the coming weeks together. She will be by his side, always.

There is nowhere else she wants to be, ever.

Patrick and Ella

I WILL BE BRIEF.

Today is here at last. I know that our guests are expectant, and I will not keep them in suspense. I will not disappoint them. I think, that no matter what happens over the coming weeks, my story has reached its conclusion. Ella agrees.

Less than a month ago, we received the communication for which we have been waiting for so long. The ups and downs of this exhausting, interminably distressing legal process no longer matter. What does matter is that the director of public prosecutions has finally decided that there is a case to answer. Starting next week, Ella and I will face our son's tormentors in court.

Jason MacManus, Jeremy Toolin and James McNamara. Leo Byrne is one of our witnesses. Such ordinary-sounding names. Such innocent vowels and consonants. We want to spare Sylvia and Edward if we can, but they have made it clear that they are ready if needed. I think they both want to do this one last thing for Daniel.

The sheer weight of evidence against Jason is significant. We have, I believe, a good case. The others I am not so concerned about: it is the mastermind I want to see punished. The one who did what he did simply because he could.

And Ella was right. She said we would meet with some resistance, here in this community. She has told me of the silence of Leo's mother, for example, when she collected her son that first evening. The evening when Leo confessed. Ella remembers that there was something in the way the woman looked at her that made her feel her unspoken support. Later, Mrs Byrne sought Ella out, but quietly, discreetly.

'Mrs Grant,' she said, 'we're not from here, and I've been told that we don't understand how things are done.' She looked at Ella, steadily. Her voice never wavered. 'I want you to know that we've come under some pressure not to speak out, but my son knows right from wrong. I want you to know that.'

And then she disappeared just as quickly as she'd arrived. We mulled it over afterwards, Ella and I. We never found out exactly what she meant – and by then it no longer mattered anyway – but we suspected Fintan MacManus's hand in whatever Mrs Byrne and Leo had suffered. We weren't surprised – which is not to say that we weren't extremely grateful to her. It's hard to put your head above the parapet: in a family, in a school, in a community. I have a fair idea of what that courage must have cost her.

And so, next month, we'll go to court. I am ready to hear what I know I must hear, all over again. In recent months, my strength has all but failed me. My courage, too. But Rebecca has kept me going. And Ella, of course. Always Ella.

As I suspected, Ella has channelled all her energies in a new direction, ever since we lost Daniel. She visits schools, talks to students, trains teachers in the art of discernment. I have seen the way they listen to her: she tells stories that might be of Daniel, or that might not, but all of them illustrate the need to seek out the bully, to stop the torment before it exercises its murderous grip. Her helper in all of this is Maryam. A quiet presence; a woman made of conviction. She has even won over her husband to her new role. I am filled, again, with admiration for all of them.

341

Although I feel profoundly tired today, I also feel the distinct creep of new steel into my spine. Getting dressed for this party downstairs, I have just now stood up straighter. I have settled my jacket more firmly around me. I feel my old sense of purpose stalking me, somewhere in this room. I feel that we will meet again, sometime in the coming days. I am ready.

I fix the cuffs of my shirt one last time.

The door to the bedroom opens. Ella stands on the landing, smiling. She has already dressed, has already been busy downstairs with champagne and finger food and the surprise parcels that the children like to hide.

'Ready?' she says. 'Everyone's here.'

I nod. 'Ready indeed.' And I stride towards her, upright, confident, determined.

'You look very nice, Mr Grant,' she says. She kisses me.

I hold out my arm to her. I bow. 'Madam,' I say. 'Allow me.' And I escort her down the stairs.

Ella holds onto his arm as they descend the stairs to the hallway. She is filled with all the resonances of the evening. A beginning, an ending. Her heart is full.

Earlier that afternoon, she watched the birds get ready to fly south. They were later than usual – maybe the last of the stragglers. Their presence in the garden reminded her all over again of her father, and her son. She remembers, in particular, Daniel's return from one of his many visits to the bird sanctuary.

'He's very knowledgeable,' Patrick had said when they joined her in the kitchen. He laid one proud hand on his son's shoulder. 'I've promised to take him to Mazamet in the South of France next year, if he's still keen.'

'I'll be keen, Dad,' Daniel had said eagerly. 'I'll always be keen. And look, Mum – the notebook you gave me is almost full already.' He opened the laminated cover of the notebook she had given him for his birthday, showed her the tidy lines of writing, all done in a neat and steady hand. Beside his notes, he'd drawn sketches of the birds he'd seen: quick, darting black lines that seemed to catch each bird in flight.

That evening, over dinner, she told him all the collective names for birds that she could remember: the same ones her father had taught her, all those years ago. An exaltation of larks. A flight of swallows. A murder of crows.

An unkindness of ravens.

She holds tight onto her husband's hand now and enters the waiting conservatory. Everything is ready.

Patrick squeezes her hand and draws her with him into that bright circle where their family is waiting.

Missing Julia

By Catherine Dunne

We all make choices.

Some will haunt us forever.

A powerful and compelling story which explores one of the most difficult decisions we might ever have to make.

One morning in October, William Harris is confronted by the shocking disappearance of the woman he loves.

Julia Seymour has vanished without trace – from his life, from her daughter's and from her own. Her sudden departure seems to be both deliberate and final.

But William is determined to find her. In the days that follow, he tries to piece together what might have driven her away. His search takes him to London, to India – and to Julia's life before he met her.

In the process, William discovers secrets about Julia's past that challenge and disturb his view of all they shared together. Secrets that illuminate the present in ways he could never have expected.

ISBN 978-0-330-50757-8

Set in Stone

By Catherine Dunne

Every family has its secrets.

Most are best left alone . . .

Lynda Graham has been fortunate in life. She is happily married, with two wonderful children, Ciarán and Katie. She has a beautiful home and garden in one of the most affluent suburbs of Dublin. Her world feels safe and uncomplicated, one thing she now takes for granted. That is until Jon, a friend of Ciarán's from university – handsome, charming and clever – inveigles his way into their lives.

There's something about Jon that Lynda finds unnerving – he is almost too perfect. And her instinct is right: Jon's arrival sets in motion a spiral of events that contributes to the gradual disintegration of all she holds dear.

When Jon leaves, his disappearance is even more destructive than his presence. Lynda's quest to track him down reveals unpalatable truths about his past and the reason for his existence in their lives. Lynda knows that Jon is out there somewhere – watching, waiting, malevolent.

And she also knows that she must do whatever it takes to protect the most precious thing she has – her family.

ISBN 978-0-330-50754-7

extracts reading groups
competitions books new
discounts extracts
competitions
books
new
events books
extracts
new reading groups
interviews
events extracts
discounts
new books events
events new
discounts extracts discounts
www.panmacmillan.com
extracts events reading groups
competitions books extracts new